THE BIVOUAC

To
His Excellency, Constantine Henry
Earl Mulgrave,
Lord Lieutenant and Governor General of Ireland
Grand Master of the most illustrious order of Saint Patrick,
K. H., F .R. S., etc., etc.

With his gracious permission, this work is inscribed,
by an admirer of refined taste and literary talents,
the author of *Stories of Waterloo*.

THE BIVOUAC

OR, STORIES OF THE PENINSULAR WAR

W. H. Maxwell

NONSUCH

First published 1837
Copyright © in this edition Nonsuch Publishing, 2008

Nonsuch Publishing
Cirencester Road, Chalford, Stroud, Gloucestershire, GL6 8PE
www.thehistorypress.co.uk

Nonsuch Publishing is an imprint of The History Press Limited

British Library Cataloguing in Publication Data:
A catalogue record for this book is available from the British Library

ISBN 978 1 84588 361 4

Typesetting and origination by The History Press
Printed in Great Britain

CONTENTS

INTRODUCTION TO THE
MODERN EDITION

IN THE AUTUMN OF 1807, Napoleon of France moved more than 100,000 troops through Spain in order to begin an attack on Portugal. But he unwisely created a new enemy in Spain by deposing the existing Spanish monarch in April 1808 in order to place Joseph—his brother—on the throne. The Spanish uprising that followed was enough to persuade Britain to send an expeditionary force to the Iberian Peninsula, and thus began the six-year-long Peninsular War (1808–1814).

In August 1808 the British forces arrived at the mouth of the Mondego river in Portugal under the command of Lieutenant-General Sir Arthur Wellesley. Their position was attacked from the east by General Jean-Androche Junot on 21 August in what has become known as the Battle of Vimeiro. Napoleon's offensive tactics ultimately failed against the British infantry line and Junot was defeated. The British victory was sufficient to force the French troops to evacuate Portugal as part of a highly controversial agreement known as the Convention of Sintra.

Wellesley was called back to Britain to discuss the contentious Convention and was replaced temporarily by Sir John Moore, who now came to lead the 30,000-strong British army in Portugal. The scale of the war in the Peninsula escalated with Napoleon's arrival in Spain at the head of 200,000 veteran troops. Moore was successful in his attempts to draw French forces away from southern Spain, but was then forced to retreat westwards himself. His army evacuated the

Peninsula by sea in January 1809 and Moore lost his life later the same month. Napoleon, meanwhile, had transferred command to Marshal Nicolas Soult and had himself withdrawn to Paris.

In April 1809 Wellesley returned to Portugal and immediately assumed command of all British and Portuguese forces. He furthermore implemented three tactical innovations in the organisation of his army: firstly, the infantry were to be divided into autonomous divisions; secondly, each infantry brigade was provided with a minimum of one company of riflemen; and lastly, one battalion of Portuguese infantry was to be placed in each of five British brigades.

May 1809 saw Wellesley's troops cross the border into Spain and join forces with the Spanish general Gregorio García de la Cuesta. The new strength of the British-Portuguese-Spanish alliance ensured success at the Battle of Talavera in July, but the victory had nonetheless been costly, and the troops were once again forced to retreat.

By September 1810, French troops had reassembled under the leadership of André Masséna and marched decisively through Ciudad Rodrigo and Almeida in a fresh attempt to retake Portugal. Wellesley—now Viscount Wellington of Talavera—was compelled to take refuge behind the Lines of Torres Vedras and a stand-off ensued, until a lack of supplies and the imminent arrival of British reinforcements in the spring of 1811 led Masséna to fall back. His failure to retake Portugal subsequently led to his replacement by Auguste Marmont.

A further battle took place at Albuera on 16 May 1811 as Marshal Soult was intercepted by the combined British-Portuguese-Spanish force under William, Viscount Beresford. During this battle, the French made their single largest infantry attack of the Peninsular War, but Soult was nevertheless forced to retreat.

Wellington suffered a further costly assault at Badajoz in April 1812, but morale was again raised in July after his crushing victory at the Battle of Salamanca. At the same time, Napoleon's invasion of Russia in June had been disastrous and, with Prussia re-entering the war against France in March 1813, Napoleon had no fresh troops for the Peninsula. Furthermore, reinforcements continued to be fed into

Wellington's army. As a result, the French armies became increasingly pinned down by allied and guerrilla forces.

These events culminated on 21 June 1813 in the Battle of Vittoria—the battle that is said to have categorically sealed Napoleon's fate. In October, Wellington crossed the Bidassoa into France and by November the French defences along the line of the Nivelle were broken. In February 1814 Wellington attacked and defeated the French marshal at Orthez. Despite Napoleon's vigorous defence of France, the allies entered Paris on 31 March. The last battle of the Peninsular War was fought on 10 April and two days later Wellington had received news of Napoleon's abdication. The Peninsular War was over.

The impact of the war was undoubtedly immense. It affected all involved, both directly and indirectly, as the death count rose to well over 20,000. In addition, the French lost 7,000 men as prisoners and the number of casualties suffered by allied and French forces alike was enormous. It remains an intensely interesting period in European history as we are drawn by a combination of fascination and repulsion to delve into the details of combat almost exactly two hundred years after Napoleon's fatal usurpation of the Spanish throne in 1808.

Accounts of the battles of the Peninsular War have featured prominently in the literature of the period in both fictional and non-fictional genres. This perhaps reflects a desperate attempt on the part of authors to come to terms with the horrible realities of war. It may also be an attempt to preserve in memory the lives of those who fought so valiantly for their country in the face of such fearful opposition. But above all, these books have kept alive the very essence of war, the dreadful sense of foreboding on the one hand, but the wonderful sense of hope and glory on the other. W. H. Maxwell's *The Bivouac*—first published in three volumes in 1837—is one such example.

Maxwell (1792–1850) is widely acknowledged as the originator of the military novel. Although his claim to have been at Waterloo, or even in the army, is unfounded, Maxwell's unwavering interest in the Napoleonic Wars is certain. In addition to *The Bivouac* he wrote, amongst other works, *Stories of Waterloo and Other Tales* (1829) and a *Life of Field-Marshall His Grace the Duke of Wellington* (1841). He also edited *Peninsular Sketches by Actors on the Scene* in 1845.

The Bivouac's sensitive blend of fact and fiction brings to life the horror of the battlefield while preserving the dignity of all involved. Its careful and detailed narration allows the reader accurately to trace the soldiers' movements throughout the Peninsular War as seen through the eyes of the soldiers themselves. Maxwell clearly felt the necessity of preserving, through literature, a pivotal moment in history, and one which he, fortunately, was able to live through, in order to pass on to future generations a sense of its enormous impact upon Britain and its people.

VOLUME I

I

THE VILLAGE—THE GIPSY—
AND THE ROUTE

How often have I paused on every charm,
The shelter'd cot, the cultivated farm,
The never-failing brook, the busy mill,
The decent church that topp'd the neighb'ring hill.

GOLDSMITH

"SWEET VILLAGE! I MUST LEAVE thee soon"—exclaimed a tall military personage, as he laid aside the newspaper, in which the immediate embarkation of reinforcements for the Peninsula was announced. "I must exchange thy quietude for fields of blood. Well—'tis for the better—a longer stay would but endanger my own happiness, and peril that of another already far too dear. Would that the parting words were spoken, and the broad sea rolled once more between us!"

He sighed heavily as he approached the window, and looked out upon the village street. It was, indeed, a peaceful and a lovely scene. The neat and snow-white cottages, trellised with jasmine and roses, peeped from the shading of the full-grown sycamores that overspread their roofs; while the pointed steeple of the church, overtopping the foliage of the trees, displayed its ancient weathercock. Under the open casement of the Greyhound some rustics were regaling. Further off, a small, but sparkling rivulet glided under the dark grey arch that spanned its flood, and in the distance flung its waters over a limestone ledge upon a mill-wheel, which was now revolving merrily.

But on none of these were the soldier's eyes turned. Through a vista in the trees the tall and shafted chimneys of the parsonage-house appeared, while the building, imbosomed among flowering chestnuts, was scarcely visible. There, the fixed and melancholy look of the stranger was directed, as abstractedly he thus gave utterance to his thoughts:

"Yes, Mary; we might have been happy had fate permitted it. I would have sacrificed the field of glory for the home of love. Hand in hand, we would have passed through life together; and the tranquil enjoyment of domestic felicity would have amply compensated the wild excitement that attends a martial career. Pshaw! this is dreaming; rouse thyself—here comes the harbinger of war!"

As he spoke, a light dragoon rode forward at a brisk trot, and pulling up at the door of the Greyhound, held a brief colloquy with the orderly in attendance, to whom he surrendered his bridle. The clattering of a steel scab bard on the brick pavement of the corridor announced his approach to the chamber of the commandant; next moment he was in the presence, and delivered a sealed despatch, marked "Private."

Its contents were brief and important; an intimation that the detached companies of the ——th might expect an immediate rout for Portsmouth, to join the battalions in Spain, and the peaceful village of Ashfield would be exchanged for cantonments on the Douro.

"Ay, it is what I anticipated," said the tall soldier, after he dismissed the dragoon, and gave the despatch a hurried perusal. "But a few hours more, and thou and I, Mary, will be as if we never met!" For a minute he paced the apartment in deep thought, then seizing his forage-cap and cane, issued from the Greyhound, and directed his steps to a shaded avenue leading to the church yard, which formed the customary lounge for the idlers of the little garrison.

The arrival of a private despatch had quickly transpired, and of course occasioned some military speculation. Divers were the conjectures touching the contents of this official epistle. Major O'Connor alone could solve the mystery and before he had taken a second turn in the church avenue, two personages approached and joined him.

The taller, and elder of the twain, was a man remarkable for his personal advantages. His features were strikingly handsome, and regular almost to effeminacy; his figure slight and graceful, with that air of nameless elegance, which is rarely found but in the foremost ranks of fashion. Nothing could surpass the polish of his manner, the insinuation of his address; and a cursory observation would tell why Captain Phillips had been reputed an object of envy with one sex, and a dangerous acquaintance for the other.

His companion was a mere boy, who had scarcely numbered sixteen summers, and appeared far too young and inexperienced to encounter the vicissitudes of the dangerous profession he had selected. He had lately quitted a peaceful home to join the detachment at Ashfield; and full of boyish hope, little suspected the trying ordeal that was so soon awaiting him in another land.

"You have had a despatch," said the handsome captain.

The major bowed his assent.

"We are all dying to know what its contents were," continued the inquirer.

"I regret it exceedingly, as I fear your curiosity must for some time remain ungratified. But do not permit suspense to prove fatal. Possibly the next post may solve the mystery."

"Then it was a private communication?"

"Strictly so, or I should have freely disclosed it," replied Major O'Connor.

"I trust that we shall not be moved," said the captain; "I am half reconciled to my present banishment, and a change of quarters might devote us to some unknown hamlet, even less endurable than Ashfield."

"I think, without breach of duty, I may relieve you from the horrors of a move," replied the commander, with a smile.

"If we do change quarters," said the young ensign, "I hope it may be for service. Summer is coming, and a campaign will be delightful. How pleasant, after a long march, to sleep on the flowery banks of a mountain river, or beneath the rich blossoms of the orange-tree; and when the battle's ended, bivouac in a vineyard, or be cantoned among rosy monks, and dark-eyed nuns!"

The elder soldier regarded his youthful comrade with a melancholy smile. "Such, then," he said, "are thy notions of campaigning! I remember when mine were as vivid, and about as accurate, as yours. Dream on, boy! A short time will show how like to reality is the picture your fancy has sketched of war."

They had approached within a few paces of the churchyard, when a female unclosed the wicket that opened on the shaded avenue, and suddenly confronted them.

"It is that cursed gipsy!" exclaimed Captain Phillips, evidently annoyed at her proximity. "I hate to meet the jade. I but brushed her lightly with my cane, to free myself from her impertinence in the forest, and ever since she regards me when I pass her, as a surly mastiff scowls at a ragged beggarman."

"I am ignorant," returned the major, "of the mode by which I conciliated her favour; but my 'good morrow' is acknowledged with a smile, and, when we part I am rewarded with a hearty benison. She is a strange person, after all. In the only colloquy I had the honour of holding with her on the common, from some loose hints she carelessly threw out, she seemed to possess a knowledge of private transactions that to me appeared utterly incomprehensible."

"Pshaw!" said Phillips, "they are all rogues and impostors. Were the predictions of these vagabonds examined, they would all prove rank mummery."

"Yet," said the boy, "I should like to know my fortune."

"Would you?" replied the major. "If so, now is the time. The gipsy for a few shillings will unclose the book of fate—tell you what the stars ordain—inform you of the colour of your true love's eyes—and prognosticate the very day on which you shall be gazetted a major-general."

As he spoke they approached the woman, who had advanced a step or two to meet them. Her appearance was very remarkable. Just at the noon of life, and with a tendency to become corpulent, her face retained its freshness, and her figure its accurate proportions. Handsome as the females of that singular community are generally reputed, Ellen—for so she named herself—must, a few years before, have been pre-eminently so. The lustrous darkness of her eyes, the marked intelligence of her countenance, united to the sweetest smile imaginable, had once made her beauty irresistible. She accosted O'Connor with kindness; carelessly addressed his young companion; then turning a searching glance at Phillips, measured him from head to foot with a look in which hatred and scorn were combined.

"Ellen," said the major, addressing her, "we would have our fortunes told. I presume that I must lead the way"—and taking some silver loosely from his pocket, he presented his offering to the gipsy.

She received the largess graciously.

"Ay," she said, "bold and generous as a soldier should be—a stout heart and open hand. But stop: the fated hour of your fortune is not yet come—another day will rule your destiny."

"Another day! Ellen. Is the time so near?" And the soldier smiled incredulously.

"Yes; and another hour may bring with it strange and momentous tidings."

"Now, on my soul!" exclaimed Phillips, as he burst into a scornful laugh, "this is most barefaced foolery. The woman saw the dragoon ride in, and, as we all have done, concluded him the 'avant courier' of a military change, which probably the arrival of the post will promulgate."

The gipsy answered him with a deadly glance.

"'Tis false as himself, major. All morning I have been absent from the village, and, until this moment, knew not that an express had been received." Then, turning to Captain Phillips, she continued, "You call me an impostor, and laugh my art to scorn. Will you have the future told? The past, I know, you dare not listen to."

"Dare not! woman."

"Ay, *dare not!* Well—let that bide. Now for the future. Your hand."

Phillips hesitated. The gipsy's request was annoying, and yet he was ashamed to refuse it. He saw that O'Connor's curiosity was raised, and that his young companion was laughing at his embarrassment. With a forced effort he took a piece of money from his purse, and presented his oblation to the sibyl. She took it suspiciously, held it for a moment at a distance, and then flung it scornfully on the ground.

"I would not keep it," she exclaimed, "were it the reddest ore on which a king's image was ever stamped! Evil luck attends the gift of him predestined to evil fortune. Give me your hand, and remember what I tell you. You shall know the worst, but the knowledge shall not avert the mischief."

His companions looked on with mingled curiosity and surprise; but Phillips became pale as ashes, while the flashing eyes and heightened colour of the gipsy bespoke, on her part, an unusual excitement.

"'Tis all plain palmistry," she continued. "The lines so strongly marked, that even a child might read them. Bright, but momentary success—speedy and permanent misfortune. Disappointment when hopes are highest, and the colour of the life dark, hurried, and dishonourable. Let me see the end. Mark ye that red line?" and she pointed to one far more strongly defined than those which intersected it.

"And what may that one bode?" inquired Captain Phillips, under evident agitation.

"Death!" she replied, in a low, hollow voice, a sudden and a bloody end!"

"Well, after all," said the young subaltern, "it is but the soldier's fate."

"No!" replied the gipsy, sharply, as she suddenly caught the boy's hand in hers. "See there! That is the symbol of death upon a battle-field. Poor youth I must not look again; I would not damp thy spirit. Alas! ere winter strips the trees, a manly breast will mourn in silence, and a mother's wail be heard for her dead boy!"

There was a pause. Phillips, with assumed indifference, broke it by inquiring, "What was the fate she predicted him?"

Casting his hand away, the gipsy looked him steadily in the face, and in a deep tone replied, "A felon's!"

"A felon's!" he shouted. "Now, by Heaven, were you not a woman this whip should repay your impertinence."

"Then would the prophecy be the more quickly fulfilled," she replied, thrusting her hand within her cloak, and producing a short poniard. "Farewell, gentlemen. Every tittle I have told shall be accomplished. You and I, Major O'Connor, shall meet ere long." Then turning to Phillips—"Mark my words, and remember them in your parting agony. For the mischief you are doomed to work—quick, deep, and deadly, shall be the retribution."

She waved her hand, flung the wicket to as if she wished to tear it from the hinges, turned down a cross walk leading to the forest, and was speedily out of view.

All were surprised, but Phillips for a while was speechless with rage.

"This insult," he at last exclaimed, "is not to be endured. By Heaven! I would give ten pounds to him who would drag her through a horsepond. I wonder, major, that you should patronise a foul-mouthed vagrant like yon harpy. Come, Tom." He took his companion's arm, and, piqued at the coldness of his commanding officer, turned down the avenue, leaving O'Connor to enjoy a solitary walk if he desired it.

The major's stroll, however, was quickly terminated. The winding of a horn was heard, and the postman's horse clattered over the gravelled causeway. The hour was come when the truth of a portion of the gipsy's prophecy would be tested; and O'Connor directed his steps to the domicile of Miss Burnett, who discharged the double duty of furnishing the villagers of Ashfield with the latest news and newest fashions.

The shop of a smart milliner has always been the favourite lounge of gentlemen of the sword, when abiding in country quarters; and Miss Burnett was pretty and *piquante*. She was busily engaged with a fair customer, when the mail arrived. The contents of the bag were quickly spread beside the riband-box; and the particulars of the village correspondence might be easily collected from the passing observations of the handsome postmistress.

"One, two, three. Bless me! only seven letters—one for the vicar, another for the apothecary, three for Major O'Connor, and two for

Captain Phillips. I positively believe that wicked captain receives none but *billets-doux*. See, these are written on perfumed paper, with French mottos on their seals. I have never remarked any coming to Major O'Connor. Is it not a strange thing, Miss Jones? But here he comes, and a noble-looking fellow he is: were I a lady, I should prefer him to Captain Phillips, handsome as he certainly is."

The object of Miss Burnett's admiration walked slowly down the street, and no wonder that he had found favour in her sight. Considerably above the middle height, O'Connor's figure combined strength with symmetry, while a firm step, assured look, and easy carriage, became one well who bore the reputation of being a stout soldier. His features were far from regular; and his face, darkened by exposure to a tropic sun, was scarred deeply by a sword-cut, which traversed half the forehead;—but his teeth and eyes would have redeemed a plainer face, for both were beautiful. His voice was full-toned, and sweetly modulated, with an accent just sufficiently marked, to intimate that the Emerald Isle was the place of his nativity.

A hasty glance at the envelope of the official letter presented to him by the fair milliner informed the gallant major that the route was come, with an order to march for Portsmouth on the third morning. Having despatched the important packet to the acting adjutant, O'Connor proceeded to examine the remainder of his epistles; but before he had perused his first letter, Phillips and the young soldier entered Miss Burnett's shop.

"The news, major?" was the captain's hurried inquiry, as he directed a careless glance at the seals upon his billets.

"Is briefly told"—was the reply: "I have despatched *the route* to the adjutant."

"Good God! Where for—and when?" and the captain's agitation was quite apparent.

"We march on Thursday—our destination Portsmouth"—returned the major calmly.

"Then we are for the Peninsula?"

"Assuredly we are," responded the commanding officer.

"How unfortunate!" ejaculated the captain.

"Unfortunate we should have been, had we been over-looked"—replied Major O'Connor.

"You and this silly boy may think so; but, 'pon my life I have no fancy for trudging over the wide world in what old people called a marching regiment."

"Then why, my dear fellow, did you join one?"

"Simply," returned Captain Phillips, "because I had no particular desire to broil a dozen years in the East. What else would tempt any man to leave the light dragoons? I must try for an exchange. Time is short—but will you let me run up to town, and try my interest at the Horse Guards?"

"Can you be serious, Phillips? Leave a detachment under order for the Peninsula! What will the world say? Do consider well, before you take a step that must for ever compromise your honour as a soldier."

The handsome captain listened impatiently to the friendly remonstrance of his companion—his features betrayed vexation—and it was evident that there was a mental struggle which was extremely painful for the time. It was, however, short—as with a passionate exclamation he said, "No, no—it is utterly impossible! I would not leave England at this moment to win a marshal's baton. Have I your leave, O'Connor? I shall be back tomorrow evening."

The commanding officer bowed a cold affirmative; and, mortified at the conduct of his companion, turned to the door, and broke the seal of a letter that still remained unopened. "Surely, it cannot be cowardice!" he muttered. "No, no; it must be madness. His reputation will be ruined for ever! By Heaven! if I know myself, there is no earthly consideration but one that could induce me to hold back from embarkation, or do the act that Phillips seems determined on!"

The *marchande de modes* and young ensign had listened in silence to the brief colloquy. Phillips, although wounded at the major's remonstrance, which imputed much more than the words exactly conveyed, assumed that simulated indifference with which men of the world often mask from observation feelings which they wish to conceal, and busied himself in selecting gloves from a parcel.

O'Connor calmly read the first sentences of his letter, when suddenly his brow reddened—his eyes flashed—and without the customary ceremony of bidding Miss Burnett a "good morning," he started from the shop, and turned his footsteps towards the forest.

"Alas!" said the fair milliner, "I fear the dear major's letter conveyed bad news, and now that I recollect it, the seal was a black one."

"Pshaw!" replied Captain Phillips, as he curled up his lip sarcastically, "these Irish are blessed with an interminable relationship; and the fatal despatch merely announces the demise of some fiftieth cousin. Has Mary Howard been in town this morning?"

"Oh, no, poor girl! she little suspects how soon she shall lose the major and yourself," returned Miss Burnett.

"O'Connor seems touched in that quarter. Don't you think so, pretty one?" inquired the captain, carelessly.

"Yes," she replied. "Few look on Miss Howard with impunity. There are others beside the major who may leave their hearts behind," and she looked archly at the lady-killer.

"Ah, the girl's passable. Well enough for a country beauty, certainly. Come, Tom, you must do some little matters for me in my absence, as our 'séjour' is rather limited. *Addio, mia bella*—till tomorrow, I kiss your hands."

Passing his arm through that of his youthful companion, he gracefully saluted the *marchande de modes*, and headed towards the Greyhound, to order post-horses for the metropolis.

The pretty milliner looked after him as he walked down the village street.

"He is more than handsome," she muttered; "and yet one honest smile from that dashing major were worth all his heartless homage. I marked them both. How differently was a summons for the field received! One eye brightened, while the other quailed. O'Connor, one whisper of regard from thee would win my heart, even if I loved yon spiritless puppy. He that wears a soldier's uniform, and courts disgraceful inactivity, could never estimate a woman's love!"

The milliner was right.

II

THE FOREST AND
THE FORTUNE TELLER

Pacing the forest,
Chewing the food of sweet and bitter fancy.

SHAKESPEARE

Down in the valley come meet me tonight,
And I'll tell you your fortune truly.

MOORE

EDWARD O'CONNOR WAS AN ORPHAN from the cradle. His father was killed early in the revolutionary war, and his mother survived her husband but a twelvemonth. Thrown upon the world helpless and unprotected, the infant was abandoned by every relation but a maiden aunt. She nursed him tenderly, and he grew up a stout and manly boy. In compliment to his father's memory, he was presented with an ensigncy at fifteen. Fortune smiled upon him, for his daring spirit placed him in her path. Years rolled on, and O'Connor returned to his fatherland with a majority.

From the neglect of his relations, the young soldier held intercourse with none of them, save her who had proved his protector. His boyhood had passed away unnoticed, and his existence was only ascertained by his name being continued in the army-list. But when that name was honourably mentioned in the affair of Lugo; when after being wounded at Talavera and Busaco, his fortune carried him safely through the breach of Badajoz, the leader of a forlorn hope, and his gallantry was rewarded with promotion; then did these cold-hearted relatives, who had deserted him when an infant, offer their congratulations which he as proudly rejected. The grave covered the only one of his kindred whom he had ever loved; and when his aunt died, O'Connor endeavoured to forget that any of his lineage existed. What then must have been his astonishment when various accidents, in six short months, removed all that stood between him and a fortune!

Such was indeed the case, and the letter he had opened in Miss Burnett's shop announced that an inheritance of two thousand pounds a year was his.

When O'Connor cleared the village, he struck into one of the numerous paths that intersected the low brushwood, with which the forest was overgrown. A fine spring evening was closing in, and the silence of the hour was only broken by the twittering of birds, and the more distant tinkle of the sheep-bells. It was a place and time fitted for a lover's meditations; and as the soldier pursued his solitary walk—no object disturbed the eye, no sound dispelled his musing—deeper and deeper he involved himself among the tangled underwood, until the baying of a dog roughly dispelled his reveries, and a light stream of curling smoke, eddying over the foliage of the copse, intimated to the wanderer, that "something living" was in his immediate vicinity.

The path had gradually narrowed until the hazel-boughs united with each other, and almost barred a further progress. Voices were more distinctly heard, and the dog's bark became louder and more impatient. O'Connor pushed the branches aside, and emerged suddenly from the thicket. A forest glade lay before him; and on its green and level sward he discovered a group of gipsies preparing their evening meal.

A sweeter spot could not have been selected than that on which they were encamped. Belted by a close and almost impervious thicket, the gipsy bivouac was difficult of approach, while the high copse afforded it both shelter and concealment. The whole scene was wild and picturesque. Several rudely-constructed tents encircled a brilliant wood-fire, over which a huge camp-kettle was suspended. The party consisted of some forty; and in that number every age of human life was embraced. The old were seated on panniers in the tents—the children were sprawling round the fire—donkeys of every size were left to graze at large, while a large gaunt mastiff, whose barking had already apprised his owners of O'Connor's approach, advanced boldly to the opening of the thicket, as if determined to withstand the entrance of a stranger.

A low and peculiar whistle at once recalled the dog, and a dark and keen-looking man civilly requested the soldier to "come forward to the fire." The invitation was accepted. A girl of uncommon beauty instantly arranged a turf seat; the soldier joined the group, and found himself in the centre of the wild community, an object of curiosity to all.

"It grows duskish," said the old man. "Probably you have strayed from the forest road?"

"Indeed I have," replied the soldier, "and I must require some assistance from you, to enable me to recover my way."

"You walk late, sir," said the gipsy.

"Yes—I was wandering in the woods, and accident conducted me to your bivouac—a lovelier glade to encamp on those could not desire, 'under the greenwood tree who love to lie.' Is this your favourite retreat?"

"No—we are sometimes here; but we have other haunts as sheltered and remote as this one."

"Yours is a pleasant and a careless life," pursued the soldier.

"Ay," said the old man, "when leaves are green, and birds are singing, the copse and hedgerow are merrier than the town. Seasons will change, and boughs grow bare; and you, who have never known an unsheltered head at midnight, would then own the comfort of a roof, no matter how low the walls were which it covered."

While the old man was speaking, a female issued from one of the tents, and strode forward to the place where O'Connor was seated. The elder gipsies regarded her with deference, while the younger ceased their play, and scattered from before the fire, to enable her to pass them. One glance satisfied the soldier that she was known to him—and Ellen, from whom he had lately parted at the churchyard gate, now stood beside him in the gipsy bivouac.

"And has he never known a wet sward and starry sky?" she exclaimed, in answer to the old man's observation. "Fool!" she continued; "often has the night-wind moaned over him as he lay upon the ground, where none could tell the living from the dead."

O'Connor started and looked up, while the gipsy scrutinised his features. "Yes," she continued, "all is written there—the past, the present, and the future. Speak—shall I tell of battle-fields—or turn from war to love, and name a name far dearer to your ear than ever was the maddening cry of victory?"

"You know me then?" said the soldier. The gipsy bowed her head slightly.

"What you told me in the churchyard avenue has happened; a strange and unexpected turn of fortune has befallen me."

"Yes; I could not be mistaken. I know the past—I see the present—and I can foretell what the future must be. Come, sir, I would speak with you apart—follow me—for I have that to say which requires a private hearing."

She lifted a billet from the fire, while O'Connor rose from the turf, and accompanied her to the extremity of the glade, where a projecting clump of copsewood concealed them from the observation of the gipsy bivouac. His dark companion took the soldier's hand, and by the flickering light of the firebrand examined its lines attentively.

"Enough," she said. "Two hours since I told you the time had not arrived. I warned you of a sudden and unforeseen event. Has the prediction not been fulfilled?"

"It has, indeed."

She looked again at the soldier's hand "Ay," she muttered rapidly, "the tale is clear, although the web is tangled. Fame and wealth—danger and disappointment—all mingled in the same fortune—the career brief and glorious—the end—but let the future rest. Will you listen to the past, ere I unfold what yet lies in the womb of time?"

"If you please, Ellen," returned the soldier, struck with the imposing solemnity of the gipsy's manner, while once more he submitted his hand to her inspection.

"All is distinct and legible—the beginning and the end alike—a red cradle and a red grave—one parent weltering on a bloody field—the other filling an early tomb" She turned her sparkling eyes upon the listener, and asked him, "was it so?"

"You are indeed right, Ellen," replied the major; "but this disclosure is no proof of second sight—my orphanage, and its attendant circumstances, are generally known.

The gipsy proceeded without noticing his observation.

"Nursed by a fair woman, the child became a boy—and the boy would be a soldier. He crossed the ocean wave—and before the down blackened on his cheek, heard the roar of battle beneath the burning skies of Egypt. Years passed, and the boy ripened into manhood. Again I see him on the field of death—no longer with the advancing step of victory, but struggling on a brokers bridge, among the last combatants of a retreating army. The scene has changed anew—on a green hill, encircled by vineyards and cork-trees, two hosts are striving for the heights. Where is the soldier now? Bleeding on the ground, while a woman hangs over him like a mother, and recalls him back to life!"

O'Connor started—"Surely," he exclaimed, "there is no imposture here!—Tell me, I adjure you—"

"Hush!" replied the gipsy; "be patient, and listen for a minute. View but another scene, and then say, if the picture of a past life be truly painted." She made a momentary pause, and then continued—"The sun set upon a proud city, and a beleaguing host; the storm of artillery, which through the day had raged, was ended; darkness and silence had succeeded; and, wearied with noise and blood, the contending foes had sunk to rest. Rest! Ay, such as that unearthly calm which precedes a tropic hurricane! Hush!—'Tis the measured tramp of massive columns, moving silently towards yon broken wall. They approach the breach unnoticed and unassailed; not a bugle sounds; not a musket betrays the midnight advance. Another minute of harrowing silence—and the volcano bursts! Rockets and blue lights flare across the murky sky—cannons roar—shells hiss—and cheers, and yells, and curses, add their infernal accompaniment. The forlorn hope are struggling through the ditch—a shower of death reigns round them, and the breach is choked with corpses. Again, and again, the assailants mount the ruins, mown down in hundreds by the withering fire of a hidden enemy, or empaled upon the bayonets of their comrades. Where is the soldier now?—Mark yon remote rampart which a daring band has carried by escalade! There—pressing on the retiring French; there—cheering on his desperate followers; *there*—is the soldier—while the wild cheers of his companions, rising above the hellish din of battle, proclaim the fall of Badajoz! Is the tale true?"

"True!" exclaimed the soldier, as his kindling eye and outstretched arm showed the excitement which the gipsy's vivid painting had aroused. "True! it is witchery—every event from childhood—my whole career displayed as in a mirror—my parents' death—the fight of Alexandria—the pass of Lugo—the plains of Talavera—the heights of Busaco—the storm of Badajoz. Woman—whence is this knowledge—how tell the story of a life, so little marked as mine?—you, to whom but a few days back, I was an utter stranger!"

"Indeed!" said the gipsy, with a smile; "I am forgotten—you are not. I have loosely sketched some passing scenes—there is one which must be more plainly pictured.—Attend to me.

"It was during the disastrous retreat from Astorga—imagine a pressing enemy—roads, almost impassable from tempestuous weather, and the multitudes that broke up their surface—rain, and snow, and storm—no fire to warm—no roof to shelter—and say, would not these united miseries overcome the endurance of the boldest soldier? Then fancy a deserted woman, cumbered with a sickly child, and loaded with booty for which she had periled the dangers of the battlefield, and which she now wanted resolution to abandon—what would be the chances of escape? The winter blast was howling mournfully, and night set in—the British, harassed by a long march, were halted for the night on a bare hillside, that afforded but little shelter from the piercing east wind. The last of the retiring soldiery had crossed a wooden bridge, which a young officer and part of the rear-guard were directed to cut down, to place the flooded river between the retreating troops and their pursuers. The work of destruction was rapid—the last planks were tearing from the beam that supported them, when a wretched follower of the camp, urged on a weary and over-laden mule. The French light troops were already pressing down the hill—and, in another minute, she must have been exposed to plunder, and probably some nameless insult. She reached the river banks—she called, by his own hopes of mercy, for pity from the soldier—but he laboured on. Another blow or two, and the plank would have fallen—another minute, and the enemy be up. Desperately that helpless and devoted wretch prayed in her child's name for succour. It was hopeless, and death appeared inevitable; but it was otherwise decreed. Her cry was heard, and he who commanded the party rushed back to her deliverance. He stayed the pioneer's axe, seized the bridle of the mule, goaded him with his sword across the tottering bridge, and assisted the poor wretch to follow—while the enemy were seen through the gloom. 'We shall be taken!' exclaimed the soldier, with an oath, as he flung away the hatchet. The young officer caught it up. 'Fear nothing!' he said, 'The act was mine, and on me be the consequences. Fall back, men!' They obeyed, and found shelter behind a copse, from the spattering of the French advance—all were safe except the gallant youth who had saved the deserted woman. He stood alone, and his blows fell quick as lightning on the fragment of the woodwork. 'Run,' cried a soldier; 'run, sir, or you are a prisoner!' But next moment a splash in the water told that the destruction of the bridge was completed; and unhurt, the bold commander of the rear guard effected his escape, amid the cheering of his comrades.—Is there any passage of your life that in aught resembles this scene?"

The soldier had listened with deep interest.

"Yes," he replied, "I remember a similar occurrence.—Pshaw! after all it was a trifle; and who; for the chances of a random shot or two, would abandon a woman who had asked assistance?"

"You knew her, of course?" said the gipsy.

"No—I never saw her before, and never met her afterwards."

"Indeed!—Methinks that gratitude should have obliged that woman to have sought her deliverer.—Listen. War continued; and under another and more fortunate leader, the young soldier was again engaged. From the heights of Busaco, he viewed a sight that would almost gladden a coward's heart. It was the evening before the battle. Far as the eye could range, the French divisions were extended over an expanse of country—and from every rising ground, lance-blades and bayonets were flashing. Gradually these masses were condensed—they neared the bottom of the Sierra—and when night fell, bivouacked beneath the same heights on which the English had taken their position.

"Morning came—and a lovelier never dawned than that of Busaco. The roll of cannon, the rattle of musketry, ushered it gallantly in. Smoke-wreaths obscured the base of the hill, and rolling slowly upwards, announced to its defenders, that the storm of war was coming. The broken surface of the mountain became the scene of numerous combats; but though outnumbered far, the British kept their vantage-ground, and repulsed the attempts upon their left. On the right, an accidental success led to a bloodier encounter. Covered by the smoke, the French light troops swarmed over the face of the Sierra, and gained the summit of the ridge; while a mass of infantry, following the voltigeurs in close column, struggled up the heights, and nearly reached the table-land. This was the crisis of the day. An English brigade, couched behind the hill for shelter from the cannonade, suddenly sprang up and met them. One close and shattering volley arrested the French advance. Vainly their leaders rushed to the front, waved their schakos above their heads, and shouted "Forward!" Just then a rush was heard—a wild hurrah rose above the thunder of the cannonade. The smoke parted—and glancing in the bright sunshine, the British line were seen advancing to the charge. The French delivered a feeble volley, recoiled, wavered, broke, and ran down the hill, leaving the Sierra in the possession of the conquerors. Where was the soldier then? Extended on the ground, faint and bleeding—a woman's arm supported his drooping head—a woman's hand moistened his parched lips—and though the face of the heights was ploughed by shot and shells, she never left him for a moment, until a fatigue party of his own regiment carried him, to the rear."

"Now, by Heaven!" exclaimed O'Connor passionately, "I would almost give my right hand to prove my gratitude to that female—I recollect the moment well—as we pressed forward with the bayonet a ball struck me, and I went down. I lay for some time insensible, and when I recovered a woman hung over me, holding a canteen to my lips. Never shall I forget the brilliancy of that dark eye, which was bent in pity upon mine!"

"And have you never seen that countenance save on the hill of Busaco?"

"Never!" said the soldier.

"Was she your countrywoman?" inquired the gipsy.

"Even that I cannot tell. I should say not. Her cheek was swarthy—her hair black as the raven's wing—her air and look foreign."

"Surely you have often met features that would recall her memory?"

"I may," replied the soldier; "but I did not particularly remark them."

"And would you still wish to meet that dark woman?" she inquired sharply.

"I should, indeed."

"Look then on *me!* she whom you saved at Lugo is before you—and the same hand that on the mountain-ridge of Busaco held the wine-flask to your lips now grasps yours!"

"Heavens! am I dreaming?" exclaimed the soldier. "It is the same dark eye—it is the same brown cheek!"

"Attend to me," said the gipsy "it is now past sunset, and three hours hence the village will be quiet. When the clock strikes ten, meet me under the lime-tree in the centre of the churchyard. There we shall be safe from interruption.—Has Major O'Connor any objection to the place and hour?"

The soldier smiled.

"Death and I," he said, "are, as you know, old acquaintances; and I shall not be reckoned an intruder on his domain.—At ten, Ellen, I shall be waiting at the lime-tree."

"Enough; we part now—Rosa!"

At her summons, the pretty gipsy whom the major had already noticed came forward.

"Conduct this gentle into the forest, and point out the shortest path to Ashfield. Farewell! and remember that we meet again," she said, and turning away, rejoined the party at the fire.

The girl entered the thicket, and O'Connor followed her in silence. For a moment the sparkle of the blazing wood scintillated through the openings in the coppice. Presently the light vanished—the hum of voices died away—nothing indicated the proximity of the gipsy cantonment; and apparently, the only wanderers on the forest were the soldier and his handsome guide.

III

THE REJECTION

Alas, poor Romeo, he is already dead!
Stabbed with a white wench's black eye.

SHAKESPEARE

My hand met here with trembling touch;
'Twas the first time I dared so much,
And yet she chid not.

MOORE

FOR A QUARTER OF AN hour O'Connor accompanied the young gipsy through a succession of glades and thickets, which, in the gloom of evening, would have been impracticable to a stranger. To Rosa, however, the difficulties of the forest appeared familiar, and she led the way at a quick pace, until the last clump of underwood was cleared, and the sparkling lattices of the village were seen at the distance of a mile. Receiving the soldier's gratuity with a courtesy, his pretty guide bade him a kind good night, entered the copse again, and left O'Connor to pursue his way in solitude.

His late interview with the strange female whom he had so unexpectedly encountered had left a deep impression. How any person could have been so intimately acquainted with every incident of a military life, passed chiefly in a foreign land, was unaccountable; and that that person was a woman, enhanced the mystery. At present the thing was inexplicable, and he determined to control his curiosity until the hour of meeting came. The effort was successful; and, in a short time, the gentle object that had occupied his bosom when he entered the forest again engrossed his thoughts.

"Fate has removed the only barrier between us," he muttered, as he hurried towards the village. "I now may choose the walk of life I please, and Mary's want of fortune presents no obstacle. Yet it is a deep sacrifice. I, who have already won a name, to quit the path of honour, and, in the very noon of manhood, sink into an inglorious obscurity—and for what?—a woman's love! Love! Am I certain that Mary Howard has a heart to give? That question must be speedily determined. I can no longer bear suspense, and endure the torment of uncertainty. This hour should end it. Should? *It shall.* The trial must be made—and on Mary's decision my future course shall hinge."

Without entering the village street, O'Connor turned into a green lane that led directly to the parsonage. The moon was just rising—and as she topped the dark foliage of the lofty chestnuts flung a silvery light upon the white building they overhung. He paused, and, leaning against a close-cut hedge, which separated the flower knot from the paddock, silently examined the dwelling of his mistress. All around bespoke an humble but happy home—all around was peaceful, calm, and tranquillising. The lofty poplars flung their lengthened shadows across the turf, while many a shrub and creeper exhaled, in the dew of evening, a fresh and grateful perfume. A glare, redder than the moonbeams, flashed from an open lattice on the green parterre. In that lighted room the lady of his love was sitting. O'Connor sprang over the enclosure—a few steps more—and Mary Howard was before him!

Concealed by a full-grown myrtle, the soldier gazed in silence on her whose fiat was presently to decide the character of his after life. She was the sole occupant of the apartment, and, unconscious that she was observed, seemed wrapped in deep and painful meditation. One glance at her intelligent eyes betrayed mental inquietude, and more than once a deep sigh escaped her. O'Connor gazed upon the beautiful girl with pleasure mingled with apprehension. A few minutes, and the secret of his heart would be confessed! He wished the essay made—the trial ended. Yet there he stood, rooted to the spot, timid and irresolute; one who had been foremost where all were desperate, could not now muster *hardiesse* to urge the pleadings of an honest passion; and he

> Who all unmoved had led
> Over the dying and the dead,

quailed before the look of love which beamed from the downcast eyes of village beauty!

A rustling noise from the leaves of the myrtle, which an involuntary movement of the soldier occasioned, seemed to dispel Mary's reverie. She turned over the leaves of an open music-book, took up a guitar that was lying on the table, and striking a few chords, sang, in a voice that thrilled through the listener's heart, a ballad that was not unknown to him.

THE HIGHLAND SOLDIER TO HIS MISTRESS

I

Give one this valley for my home,
  The heather for my nightly pillow,
And I will ask no more to roam,
  Or brave the field, or dare the billow.
Yes, love, for thee I'll all forego,
  With war's red honours cloy'd and weary;
What bliss can Donald's bosom know
  Like thy sweet smiles, my artless Mary?

2

For me the bugle sounds no more,
  Nor drum shall beat its loud alarm;
Again I seek my native shore,
  To shield thee, love, from scaith and harm.

He who has roam'd the world as long,
    Will own his wanderings sad and dreary;
For, oh! among the tinsell'd throng,
    He'll find no heart like thine, sweet Mary!

Before the last sounds of the symphony had died upon the strings, O'Connor stood before the startled musician. A deep blush overspread her countenance, as, with mingled feelings of pleasure and surprise, she took his hand and bade him a warm welcome. For some minutes both laboured under evident embarrassment; but the major's self-possession speedily returned, and he placed himself upon the sofa beside the timid girl.

"Well, Miss Howard, is not this profession of arms a sad one? Just when friendships have been formed, and we have learned to esteem our friends, an arbitrary command removes us unceremoniously from the objects we regard. You have heard, no doubt, that we are under orders for the Peninsula!"

"Alas yes," she replied, while her eyes filled with tears; "but a short time since I learned that we are to lose you in a day or two: indeed, Major O'Connor, your removal will cause deep regret to my father and myself."

"It is the fate of war," said O'Connor, with a forced smile.

"Alas!" returned the fair girl with a sigh, "what a long period may probably elapse before you revisit England."

"Ay, my dear Miss Howard, and the odds are pretty heavy, that many of us shall never return."

"It is a fearful thought;" and her pallid cheek and broken voice betrayed her feelings. "This sudden order must have surprised you, major?"

"Not particularly, Miss Howard; I have been frequently moved from quarters before now, even with slighter ceremony.

"Miss Burnett, who was lately here, mentioned that your letters appeared to be of more than ordinary interest."

The major smiled: "And did the pretty milliner observe the interest they excited?"

"She did, and feared, from your abrupt departure, that some evil tidings had been communicated."

The soldier sighed: " Alas! Miss Howard, it proves how little the expression of the countenance may be taken as a faithful index of the heart. That letter would be reckoned by most men the harbinger of joy, for it announced that one who stood between me and a fortune was gone."

"Indeed, major."

"Such indeed was the intelligence that made me oblivious of my parting good-morrow to the pretty post mistress."

"Thank Heaven! I rejoice that our apprehensions were unfounded. When do you expect to move?" and she sighed heavily.

"In two days hence."

"And you will embark—"

"Almost immediately. The drafts of the respective regiments are already at Portsmouth and ours, I fancy, is the last."

There was a long and embarrassing pause—the soldier broke it—"'Tis late, Miss Howard; I have stolen upon you unannounced; am I an intruder?"

"Oh, no; I was so lonely when you came in. My father was obliged to visit a sick friend, and his residence being distant, it will be late before he can be home. But for your visit, major, I should have had a long and solitary evening to contend with. How much my father will regret his absence—you are such a favourite."

"Am I, indeed?"

"Indeed you are. I had an only brother. He died before I can remember the event—my father still loves to speak of him; and from some fancied similarity between you, he imagines that, had his boy lived, he would have been such another as yourself."

The soldier smiled, and Miss Howard continued:

"Pray, when is Captain Phillip expected to return?"

"You are aware, I presume, that we are about to lose him?"

"No—yes"—and she coloured slightly, "in fact, Miss Burnett told me something of it."

"I regret it on his own account, it is a rash and dangerous experiment."

"Might not circumstances however, justify the step?" she inquired with considerable animation.

"None could, Miss Howard. Phillips has already declined the call of duty, and given up a regiment rather than leave the kingdom. This second refusal to go on service will lower him sadly in military estimation."

"You are not a fair judge, major, for you are a professional enthusiast." She blushed deeply. "Pardon this boldness—this impertinence—and let me question even your own wisdom, in leaving a land of peace, for scenes of violence and human suffering. Have you not made a name? Have you not already distinguished yourself? and now, when fortune unexpectedly heaps her favours on your head, why not seek and secure that tranquil happiness and quiet, which I have heard you say that, in earlier life, you so much longed after?"

While she spoke, a deeper blush overspread her cheeks, and her soft and beaming eyes fell timidly before the ardent glances of her companion.

"Miss Howard," said the soldier, "you have unconsciously touched a chord that awakens the softest—or it would probably be juster to term them the weakest—feelings of a heart not much accustomed to indulge in sentiment. It is true that, hitherto, mine has been a wild career of danger and excitement, and that a fortune more than sufficient to realise every reasonable want or wish lies suddenly devolved upon me; yet there exists but one consideration that could induce me to abandon a profession which in boyhood was the object of my pride, and in manhood the hope of my ambition—Listen to me, Mary!"

It was the first time that name had ever passed his lips. Miss Howard was deeply effected, and O'Connor's faltering tones betrayed emotions too powerful to be concealed. He took her hand, and thus continued:

"Mary I have been from infancy an orphan, and never known the ties of love and kindred, save for one, who now sleeps in the grave.

I have been a wanderer on the world. I have had no home whereto
I might turn my weary steps—no heart rejoiced for my successes;
and no eye would have wept for me had I fallen. What have I, then,
to do with the gentler felicities of life?—I, who have never known
what is conceded to the humblest peasant—the happiness of loving
and being loved!"

He stopped: his hand was burning—his voice became inarticulate
while Miss Howard's tears told how much the soldier's warmth had
touched her.

"Yet, Mary, it is not that I could not love—that mine has been a
cold and reckless existence. There is one for whom my heart beats—
there is one whose form is ever before me; one for whom even glory
itself would be resigned!" He made a long pause. "Mary! canst thou
not read the secret of my heart? Mary—*thou art that one* whom I so
love and idolise!"

As O'Connor proceeded, Miss Howard's flushing countenance
became more deeply crimsoned. But when he named her name—
when he declared her to be the object of his adoration—the roses as
rapidly died away, and an unearthly paleness succeeded them.

"Oh God!" she exclaimed, "what a trial is this! Let me collect
myself: my thoughts wander—my brain is burning! This is indeed so
unexpected!"

He had placed his arm round her, and Mary Howard suffered it
to remain.

"O'Connor" she said faintly "if there be on earth one whom I
regard with sisterly affection, you are the man. Were I to name him
with whom my happiness would be secure it should be you. Yet, much
as I admire—much as I respect you—much as I esteem a declaration
of a affection, of which the proudest might be vain—beyond the
bond of friendship no other tie can bind us."

The soldier by turns grew pale and red.—"Mary, do I hear you
right? I asked you for your heart, and—"

"Alas! I have none to give you—mine is already gone—my hand
is plighted to another"

"Another?"

"Yes, O'Connor. Oh, that we had met earlier or never met!"

"Say on, Mary."

"I cannot. Spare me till tomorrow, and not a secret of my heart shall be hidden from you."

"Tomorrow, Mary?"

"Yes; but in Pity leave me now. Alas! that I should ever speak a word to pain the man whom I regard so dearly."

The soldier had sprung from the sofa, and stood with folded arms, and eyes fixed on his lost love. Miss Howard rose, and offered him her hand.

"O'Connor, will you love me as a brother?"

"As a brother?"

He gazed on her for a few moments with a melancholy look—caught her to his breast, and madly pressed her lips with his. "Mary, may you be happy as I am wretched!" he said—rushed from the apartment, and bounding across the hedge, Mary Howard was left to weep alone.

IV

THE CHURCHYARD MEETING

I cannot prate in puling strain,
Of lady-love and beauty's chain:
If changing cheek and scorching vein,
Lips taught to writhe, but not complain;
If bursting heart, and madd'ning brain,
And daring deed, and vengeful steel,
And all that I have felt and feel
Betoken love—that love was mine.

The Giaour

IT MIGHT SEEM SURPRISING THAT one whose character was firm almost to sternness, should feel a rejected suit so deeply as Major O'Connor appeared to do, when he rushed wildly from the parsonage, and again turned his steps towards the outskirts of the forest. It was indeed a moment of exquisite suffering—his fairy fabric overthrown—his cherished hopes blasted in their very infancy. But a few hours since, to part from Mary Howard might have caused him inward pain, but certainly he would have exhibited his customary resolution. Every thing, then, prohibited him from loving. He was poor—the member of a dangerous profession—his inheritance a sword—his road to fortune perilous and doubtful. Now he had become wealthy, only to be wretched—and when every apparent obstacle was removed, he had to learn that the only woman he ever loved had already bestowed her affections upon another.

Had he not met Mary Howard, O'Connor would most probably have passed through life with an unscathed heart. He had been taught to consider the marriage of a soldier to be an act bordering upon insanity. A thirst for military glory rendered his adoration of the sex a light pursuit—a wayward fancy. The bustle of active service left him no leisure to cultivate the tenderer impressions. His passion was fugitive regard, and the whole aim and object of his love,

> "To sport an hour with beauty's chain,
> Then throw it idly by."

But when in the tranquil solitude of Ashfield, the fair and unsophisticated girl became the frequent companion of his forest walks—when in the quiet of a happy home the place where woman's gentler virtues are best discovered, he witnessed the artless qualities of her mind apparent in all the nameless attentions that a devoted child bestows upon a beloved parent—the soldier saw realised a being whom before his fancy had but sketched. Gradually his heart felt the softening influence of a first passion; and before he suspected danger, O'Connor's peace of mind was lost!

Yielding to the tempest of his feelings, he marked not the flight of time. Night fell—the moon poured a flood of pale light over the surrounding forest, and the chimes of the village clock smote his ear with sounds melancholy as if they knelled the ruin of his hopes. He counted the quarters—the hour of his appointed meeting with the gipsy was near. Collecting his wandering thoughts, he hastened to the Greyhound, gave some necessary orders to his servant, wrapped a cloak about him, took his sabre in his hand, and as the last stroke of ten was beating from the tower, crossed the stile of the churchyard, and walked slowly towards the well-known rendezvous.

All around him was silent; the vibrations of the bell gradually died on the night and the loneliness of the dwelling of the dead was disturbed by no living thing but himself. Beneath the shade of the lime-tree, a figure was indistinctly seen: it was motionless as the effigies of the departed; and until he had approached within a pace or two, the soldier doubted whether the object on which he looked was breathing clay or inanimate marble.

"You are true to your tryst," said a low and well-remembered voice, as the gipsy glided into the moonlight.

"I fancied that I should have been first at the appointed place," was the soldier's reply.

"Anxious, no doubt, to learn your destiny from one who knows it well."

"You are wrong;" and a bitter smile passed over his face; "I have already put my fortune to the test, and for the knowledge of what remains I would not give one farthing."

"Indeed, major!"

"Ay, had there been aught to tell, our meeting should have been somewhat earlier."

"Would that it had!" returned the gipsy; "then would you have been spared the humiliation of a rejection."

O'Connor started back as he passionately exclaimed, "Woman! how comes it that my life, past and present, is open to your view? Scarcely an hour has elapsed, and yet you tell me what occurred when, save myself, there was but another present."

"Yes, major, other eyes were looking on, for I was standing in the orchard. I saw Mary Howard in your arms; I saw you rush madly to the forest; I saw the girl sink on the floor in an agony of tears. What did all this tell? That he whose heart had beaten calmly in the battlefield knew for the first time the withering pang of unrequited love; and she, when she refused your hand, felt an ominous conviction that, by that act, she was entailing misery on herself."

"I do not understand you; surely, if she loved another, she was right to refuse her hand, when she had no heart to accompany it."

"She was," she continued mournfully. "Alas, poor girl! she has lavished her love upon a villain—a deep and dangerous villain—and his falsehood will wring her heart.—Did she name him to you?"

"No; she promised to tell me everything tomorrow."

"Tomorrow!" said the gipsy. "Have you then no suspicion who your rival is?"

"Not the most distant."

"Did you ever remark Captain Phillips in her company?"

O'Connor started as if an adder had stung him.—"Ha! Phillips?—Impossible!"

"How blind a lover is!" replied the gipsy. "None else could see them together five minutes and not detect the secret of her heart."

"Pshaw!—I repeat it—it is impossible! "the soldier passionately exclaimed. "Not three days since, I heard Phillips, after dinner, speak so lightly of her, that I felt some difficulty in restraining my indignation. He talked of woman with profligate levity; swore that wealth was the only excuse for matrimony; and declared that nothing besides should ever tempt him to become a husband."

"He swore truly for once," said the gipsy.

"If so, why should he pursue Miss Howard? He would not make her a wife—he dare not dream of her as a mistress."

"*Dare not!*" exclaimed the gipsy. "What will not a libertine dare? At this moment he has marked her for destruction."

"Oh, it is too monstrous for belief!" replied the soldier., "None would be wretch enough to contemplate such villainy—the destruction of that artless and confiding girl—one so innocent, so beautiful!"

"Ay! the more glorious the creature, the prouder is the boast of humbling its beauties to the dust."

O'Connor's face flushed with rage. "By Heaven! if even in thought he wronged her, his blood should answer it. Hear me," he continued in a low and broken voice, "though to speak it pains me. I loved her, madly loved her, almost before I knew it; poverty placed a barrier between us, and I strove and half succeeded in forgetting. Within the last few hours, wealth became suddenly mine—I flew to Mary Howard, and offered her my hand. She heard me with deep emotion, and told me she had bestowed her affections on another. You saw our parting; I swore to love her as a brother, although I little dreamed how soon she would need protection. If, then, there be an earthly object I adore, she is that one—and if a villain harmed her—"

"You would no doubt avenge it," said the gipsy.

"Avenge it!" he exclaimed, in a voice hoarse with passion—"an altar should not shield the villain!"

"Then beware of Phillips, or Mary Howard's ruin is decreed."

With a sudden movement that made the gipsy start, O'Connor suddenly unsheathed the sabre he had been leaning on; the steel flashed in the moonlight, as he continued in deep and passionate tones,—

"Here, in the face of Heaven! here, surrounded by the dead—him who injures thee, Mary, I denounce; where he goes, my vengeance shall follow; and, were it to the verge of hell, I would pursue him, until the stain upon thy honour is washed out in his heart's blood!" He pressed the blade to his lips, withdrew it slowly, and again replaced it in the scabbard. A long pause ensued—the soldier broke it.

"You told me, when parting in the forest, that you had something to communicate—"

"Which your precipitation has rendered of no avail. I suspected your attachment for Miss Howard, and intended to apprise you that a successful rival had already won her love."

"It was kindly meant; but are you certain that Phillips is the person for whom I have been rejected?

"I am," replied the gipsy; "I saw them meet in the forest, and watched the interview; a thicket concealed me, while all that passed between them was under my observation. I heard his tale of love; all that he uttered was believed; and, in turn, she owned a mutual attachment. I saw his arms around her—I saw their lips meet"

"Stop, stop!" exclaimed the soldier: "this is torture—but it is convincing. Would that the hour was come when I should leave thee for ever, Mary!"

"Will you, then, be ruled by me? Have I not proved that every incident in a life of varied fortune is known to me?"

"Say on," replied the soldier, mournfully.

"Avoid Miss Howard, and forget her."

"Oh! that I could—and yet how contemptible is this weakness. Had I but seen the meeting of which you spake, that would have wrought a cure."

"You doubt me, then?" said the gipsy.

"Oh, no! Alas no room for doubt is left me. God knows how sincerely I loved: why marvel, then, how unwillingly I tear the object from my heart?"

"I have much to speak of. Will you meet me at six tomorrow evening—the place where Rosa left you."

"I shall be punctual," said the soldier.

"Farewell—your path lies there;" and the gipsy pointed to the stile. "Good night!" and, turning into a walk that swept round an angle of the building, she disappeared before he could return the salutation.

O'Connor remained for a short time in the churchyard; the chimes roused him from his musing, and he hastened to the village inn. The gipsy's advice was not unheeded; a powerful exertion was required, and he determined to make the effort. With assumed indifference he joined the supper party, who had for some time been expecting him; and no indications of "blighted love" betrayed his recent disappointment.

The night wore on. At an early hour the major left the joyous group, and strove to sleep, and forget the lost one; but ominous visions broke his rest, and objects of love and hate were constantly before him. One while, Phillips was at his feet, and the imaginary exertion of withdrawing his sword from the body of his prostrate enemy awoke him. He dreamed again—it was of Mary Howard. O God! that vision was revolting—and with a deep execration he sprang from the bed, and flung the casement open. The first light of morning had feebly broken, and the village was still buried in deep repose. Gradually the soldier recovered his composure—again he sought his pillow, and once more strove to forget his disappointment. This effort was successful, and he slept until the drum-boy's *reveillée* aroused the little garrison of Ashfield.

V

THE RIVAL SUITORS

And she was lost—and yet I breathed,
  But not the breath of human life:
A serpent round my heart was wreathed,
  And stung my every thought to strife.

The Giaour

If thou wert honourable,
Thou wouldst have told this tale for virtue, not
For such an end thou seek'st.

Cymbeline

THE MORNING TÊTE-À-TÊTE BETWEEN MAJOR O'Connor and Miss Howard was, as it may be imagined, anything but agreeable. The soldier's firmness was often severely tasked, to enable him without emotion to hear from the woman whom he loved a confession of attachment for another; while to her the declaration was embarrassing in the extreme. To the relief of both, the approach of Mr Howard through the orchard ended this painful interview. Soon after, the major took his leave; and Mary retired to weep in her own apartment unobserved.

In declining O'Connor's addresses, there was a presentiment on Mary's mind almost amounting to conviction, that she was then endangering her future peace, and doing an act that would cause her the bitterest regret. The noble qualities of her rejected suitor were justly appreciated; and her better judgment was assured, that in the keeping of the high-spirited soldier, a woman's happiness was safe.

Yet it would have been surprising, if one so artless as the parson's daughter had not been dazzled by the more attractive accomplishments and personal beauty of Captain Phillips. Ignorant of mankind, and educated in the strictest occlusion, she had reached her eighteenth year, and never been a dozen miles beyond her native village. Deprived at an early age of maternal protection, her undivided affections centred in her surviving parent; and though possessed of a warm heart, and ardent imagination, until lately, Mary Howard knew what love was but by name. The remoteness of her father's dwelling precluded her from seeing any of the other sex, except the homely youths who inhabited the adjacent farm-houses. To all around her, Mary was a superior being. With brilliant talents, and a cultivated understanding, her natural disposition was ardent and romantic. Nevertheless, she had hitherto passed through existence "fancy free;" and until, in an evil hour, so rural disturbances occasioned a detachment of the Rifles to be cantoned in the village of Ashfield, Mary had never met an object on whom she could bestow her love.

From the seclusion of the hamlet, the only persons with whom the military held intercourse were the vicar and physician. Mr Howard was friendly and hospitable; and Mary's beauty induced the officers of the little garrison to be frequent visitors at the parsonage. From the earliest period of their acquaintance, O'Connor was taken with the sweet and artless manner of the handsome villager; while she, who "had read of battles," viewed with girlish admiration one whose name had been proudly mentioned "where all were brave;" and marvelled to find the lion-hearted soldier mild and unassuming as a school boy. A closer intimacy must have ended in permanent attachment; but O'Connor's marriage was impracticable; and his high and chivalrous honour obliged him to repress every indication of regard, when prudence forbade him to offer her his hand. Had the slightest indication of affection been offered by the soldier, Mary Howard would have loved him devotedly. A few days more, and fortune would have removed the barrier; but, in the interim,

Phillips unfortunately rejoined the detachment—and his arrival sealed the misery of two persons who otherwise might have been truly happy.

From the moment he was presented to the village beauty, Phillips marked her for destruction. Before, he had never met a being so artless and so fascinating. Her charms inflamed his passions, and her simplicity led him to expect success. Phillips was a heartless scoundrel—a selfish and cowardly wretch;—and the very circumstance which would have deterred any but a villain—that Mary's only relative was a timid and helpless churchman, from whose vengeance a seducer had nothing to apprehend—confirmed him in his unholy designs upon his unsuspicious victim.

He knew his powers well—and hackneyed in those nameless arts which rarely fail to win a woman's heart, Mary was assailed with all the apparent warmth of faithful passion. To see, and hear, and not to love, was impossible. Phillips pursued his advantage with the tact of past experience—in the solitude of the forest, his perjured vows were credited—and Mary Howard, with downcast eyes and blushing cheeks, owned that he had not wooed in vain.

And who was Phillips? That question were difficult to solve—for a strange mystery was connected with his parentage. His reputed father had held a small appointment in the Treasury—and his mother was a woman of uncommon beauty, and but indifferent reputation. It was known that the treasury clerk at his death had been in embarrassed circumstances, yet his widow resided in the western suburbs of the metropolis, the mistress of a splendid house and handsome establishment. Phillips had been educated at a fashionable school, and at an early age was placed in a dragoon regiment. He lived expensively, but seemed always in easy circumstances. That he had interest at the Horse Guards was apparent, from his quick promotion to a troop, as well as the facility with which he effected changes from regiments he disliked, and the extended leaves of absence he obtained whenever it was his pleasure to require them. All this was rife with mystery—and it was generally believed that Phillips and his mother were under some powerful protection; and it was whispered that to a noble duke the captain owed his birth, and the lady her establishment.

The day wore on heavily. The major, in the duties that devolved on him as commanding officer, had much to occupy his attention; and the detachment were busy preparing for the march. To regulate his private affairs—a task of some difficulty, occasioned by his recent acquisition of property—O'Connor sedulously applied himself. Before evening parade he had accomplished his arrangements; and, for the first time, written a testamentary document, which he confided to an old companion, with directions for its being produced, in the event of his falling in the Peninsula.

His friend had just quitted the apartment, when a chaise and four drove to the inn, and, rapidly as it passed the window, O'Connor recognised the traveller to be Phillips. In a few minutes a knock at the door was heard, and the gallant captain was admitted to the presence of his commanding officer.

That two persons so opposite in character and feeling could ever have been on any terms beyond the external civilities of military companionship would be unnatural. O'Connor despised Phillips for his effeminacy; and with the Irish pride attendant on an honourable descent, looked with contempt on the doubtful history of his parentage, and the more disgraceful patronage from which be derived his influence at the Horse Guards. Phillips, on the other hand, viewed the bold major with mixed sentiments of fear and envy. The high reputation this "founder of his own fortune" had acquired, placed him in that position in society which Phillips could never hope to reach; and, had he wanted an additional stimulus to confirm him in his designs upon the village beauty, a suspicion that she was an object of regard with his distinguished comrade would have been a sufficient inducement to press his suit, and thus wound the rival soldier in the only point in which he was, by any possibility, assailable.

Phillips appeared in high spirits. "I have succeeded," he said, addressing the commandant. "I reached town at a most favourable moment—nicked the opportunity, and am happy to acquaint you that I shall be appointed to a troop in the —— Dragoon Guards, in the next Gazette."

"Indeed!" returned O'Connor, coldly.

"Fact, 'pon honour. Had I been an hour later, the chance was lost. Was I not lucky?"

"I think not. Had I a brother similarly circumstanced, I should have been delighted to hear that his carriage had broken down; and had his neck been accidentally dislocated, I fancy I might have outlived the calamity."

"And," returned Phillips, reddening with vexation, "is the interchange of a company of foot for a troop of cavalry nothing in the estimation of Major O'Connor? For my part, I congratulate myself on the event."

"I wish I could do the same," replied the soldier.

"Major O'Connor," returned Phillips, with some haughtiness, "I came here to announce the event, and not to seek your congratulations."

"You did wisely," was the reply, "in not asking what I could not have obliged you with."

There was an embarrassing pause. Phillips was burning with suppressed rage—O'Connor provokingly cold and sarcastic. In a few moments the former resumed the conversation.

"Major O'Connor, you are welcome to estimate my reasons for exchanging as you please; I can best appreciate the motives that obliged it; and it is perfectly unnecessary for me to enter into the private considerations which may have induced me to remain in England."

"Captain Phillips, your motives in taking a step that can only affect yourself, I have neither a right nor a wish to inquire into—doubtless they are important ones."

"There are more reasons," returned the captain, in a sarcastic tone of voice, "than Major O'Connor can at this moment imagine, but which, possibly he may find out hereafter."

"And which he might make a shrewd guess at even now, if he pleased," replied the commandant.

"Oh I perceive it; you have had another peep at the planets— another interview with the gipsy," said Phillips with a sneer.

"I have not *avoided her*, Captain Phillips. There is nothing in the future that *I fear*; nothing in *the past* that I am ashamed to hear repeated."

The major's sarcasm appeared to wound the captain deeply. He continued:

"But there is no mystery in the matter; your approaching marriage is no secret."

"Marriage!" exclaimed the captain, with a laugh; "and with whom?"

"Surely it would be unnecessary to name the lady, to whom, but a few mornings since, Captain Phillips plighted his vows upon the common?"

"Damnation!" exclaimed the captain, reddening with vexation. "I am under espionage, it would seem."

"*I* am no spy upon your actions, sir," returned the major, warmly.

"Well, it is rather hard, you must admit, that a man cannot amuse himself a little in the forest, without having his flirtations chronicled over the country."

"I do not precisely understand the terms you use," said O'Connor, coldly; "nor comprehend how a serious suit like yours to Miss Howard can be so indifferently described."

"Upon my life, Major O'Connor, it would appear that all my actions are to be submitted to a rigorous inquisition. It is rather a novelty in military life, for a man to be censured for his *affaires du cœur* and undergo a jobation from his commander, for kissing a rustic beauty in a clump of trees, with the lady's own consent."

"Captain Phillips," returned the major, with increasing sternness, "I must object to the levity of the language you employ, when alluding to your addresses to Miss Howard."

"And," said the captain, hotly, "*I* must protest against any interference on your part, in an affair essentially my own, and with which you are totally unconnected."

"I *have* a deep interest in Miss Howard's happiness," replied the commander, "and I demand—"

"Nothing, if you please, from me, major. Miss Howard has a father, and I am quite prepared to give him an explanation, whenever he chooses to require one."

He took his hat, and moved towards the door; but O'Connor, with a tone and manner that would not be gainsaid, waved his hand, and signalled that he should remain.

"A few words before we separate, Captain Phillips—and they are the last, except officially, which shall ever pass between us."

"Just as you please," returned Phillips, with a formal bow.

"I have no sister," continued the major, "no female relative that is dear to me. Had I one, and any living man dared tamper with her affections, or think of her with disrespect, what, think you, would be my conduct?"

"Upon my soul," replied the captain, with a puppyish drawl, "I cannot pretend to guess."

"I would exact from him speedy satisfaction, and teach him such a lesson, as should make him tremble for the future, before he trifled with a woman's love."

"Indeed, major!" said the captain sarcastically; while O'Connor continued with increasing warmth,—

"But if the injury were deeper—if, profiting by absence of suspicion, he abused her confidence, and wrought her shame and ruin—what would be my conduct then?"

The captain bowed, and shrugged his shoulders.

"I would follow him to the ends of the earth; I would tear him from a sanctuary; I would hang like a ban-dog on his steps; night and day would I follow him, and never relax my pursuit, until, in the heart's blood of the treacherous villain, I had cleansed the stain upon the lost one's honour, Phillips!"—and he pressed his hand heavily on the captain's shoulder, while his brows grew dark, and his voice became tremulous and hollow—"Phillips! Mary Howard is my adopted sister; wrong her, and an altar shall not save you! Farewell—we understand each other."

He pointed to the door. The captain, with lips pale with rage and craven apprehension, hurried from the apartment—and the major was left alone.

VI

JEALOUSY

Iago.	Pray be content.
Othello.	Oh!—blood, Iago, blood!
Iago.	Patience, I say; your mind, perchance, may change.
Othello.	Never, Iago.

SHAKESPEARE

FROM THE INCONVENIENT HOUR THE gipsy had named for their interview, O'Connor ordered dinner in his own chamber, and declined joining the mess-party. He was anxious to converse with Ellen again; for his recent tête-à-tête with Phillips proved that her suspicions were well founded, and convinced him that the captain's pursuit of Mary Howard was not intended to have an honourable close. But to watch over that still beloved girl was denied, and his departure for the Peninsula would remove Phillips from his *surveillance*. Mr Howard, from the simplicity of his character and ignorance of the world, was but a poor protector. All O'Connor could do, he had done; "Fears for themselves mean villains have;" and personal apprehension might deter Phillips from attempting a seduction which, whether successful or disconcerted, must draw down on him the certain vengeance of a determined enemy. It was only left to him to warn Mary of her danger, and guard the unsuspecting girl against the specious sophistry of an accomplished scoundrel.

By a circuitous route and unperceived, he left the village, and directed his course towards the gipsy's trysting place. A lane enclosed at either side by lofty quickset hedges, just now bursting into life, led round the hamlet gardens to the common. It was an unfrequented path, and from its retirement had been the favourite walk of Mary Howard. The soldier traversed it rapidly, and was emerging from its enclosures, when, at a little distance, he remarked a man climb the paling of the parson's orchard, and a second look assured him it was his rival. Phillips was evidently seeking a private interview with his mistress, and the precautions he took to elude observation showed that he intended his visit should be a secret one.

O'Connor's blood boiled with fury. What was to be done? His first impulse was to confront Phillips at the moment—apprise Mr Howard of all he knew, and all he suspected—and require a distinct avowal of his rival's intentions touching the "old man's daughter." But this was impossible; for at their parting interview Mary had requested him to keep her attachment secret, and exacted a promise that he would not pain her father by letting him discover that he had offered her his hand, and the offer had been rejected. After a minute's reflection, he decided on keeping his appointment in the forest, confiding the whole to Ellen, and taking counsel from her.

He hurried across the common—and, with a heart bursting with jealous rage, reached the rendezvous in the coppice, and found the gipsy already there. Her keen glance rested for an instant on the soldier's countenance, and she perceived at once the storm of passion that was raging in his tortured bosom.

"You are ill at ease, major," she said sharply. "What unusual occurrence has disturbed you thus?"

"Occurrence, Ellen! I shall go mad. Hell is raging in my breast, and I could cut anybody's throat who crossed me!"

"This excitement is indeed singular in one that has buffeted the world as you have, and borne the rubs of fortune gallantly."

"Alas! Ellen," said the soldier in a subdued voice, "till now the breast was never writhed, nor had to learn the agony that awaits a love so warm and hopeless as mine—and that too with the maddening thought, that my happiness has been blasted by a villain, but for whose damning influence, the only heart I ever sought or coveted would have been all mine own!"

"You have seen Phillips?" said the gipsy.

"Ay, and unmasked him, Ellen. Your words were indeed prophetic. She whom I love so devotedly—for whom this breast is bleeding—he regards but as a plaything, to be easily courted, and as easily thrown aside. You spoke truly, Ellen; and Phillips seeks that artless being's ruin."

"And will effect it," replied the gipsy, "unless Heaven has otherwise decreed it."

"Never!" exclaimed the soldier passionately. "I will warn her of his villainy and her danger."

"It will not avail."

"Then, by my hopes of heaven, I'll cut his throat i' the church."

"Will that," said the gipsy, "restore the blighted dower, after his touch has withered it?"

"I will anticipate his villainy," continued the soldier, storming with fury. "He shall fight me before an hour. I'll insult him in the street—I'll strike him in the mess-room!"

"And what will that avail?" said the gipsy, calmly. "The coward can always evade a battle. The act you meditate will only give notoriety to your disappointment, and apprise the world that your suit has been unfortunate, and another's more successful. No, no, O'Connor.—Patience! I will watch over Mary Howard as a mother; and if human means can avert her ruin, I will save her!"

The soldier remained silent for a moment, as if struggling to repress his rage; suddenly he caught the gipsy's hand.

"Ellen," he said, in hollow tones—"Ellen, till lately I never knew what it was to love—and till now I never knew what it was to hate! Is it not distracting to think, that at this moment, Mary may be in my rival's arms, listening to his hollow professions, and answering his false suit with the fond confessions of artless love? Oh, I could strike the villain dead!"

"O'Connor," replied the gipsy, reproachfully, "is this weakness in-keeping with your character? Is it fitting, because a simple girl has fooled away her heart, and bestowed her regard upon a scoundrel, that the soldier should turn driveller—the hero a whimpering schoolboy! Rouse yourself! Sit down upon this bank. You may remember, before we parted last night, I promised, to tell you something of my history."

"Yes," cried the major, eagerly; "do let me hear it, Ellen," and he sighed heavily. "I will try and listen with composure, and—if I can—forget Mary Howard."

The gipsy cast her eyes across the forest, as if to ascertain that the soldier and herself were safe from interruption. Far as her glance ranged, no living thing was visible. She placed herself beside him on the turf, and then commenced her wild and eventful narrative.

VII

THE GIPSY'S STORY

But who was she?
Was she as those who love their lords, or they
Who love the lords of others? Such have been,
Even in the olden time, Rome's annals say.
Was she a matron of Cornelia's mien,
Or the light air of Egypt's graceful queen,
Profuse of joy, or 'gainst it did she war,
Inveterate in virtue?

Childe Harold

How changed since her last speaking eye
Glanced gladness round the glittering room,
Where high-born men were proud to wait,
Where beauty watched to imitate
Her gentle voice—her lovely mien.

Parasina

THE FIRST RECOLLECTIONS OF INFANCY lie in a gipsy encampment. I remember my mother, but of my father have no distinct idea. I have, however confused notions of our wandering life—sometimes reposing in a barn—sometimes bivouacked beneath a hedge—while in our journeyings, I was carried in the pannier of a donkey with a load of tinker's implements deposited in the opposite basket, to form an equipoise.

The next era that I remember in my history, was when residing with a nobleman's park-keeper. The earl's lady was childless; and having accidentally seen me in my mother's arms, was struck with my beauty, and determined to adopt me. I remember that I could scarcely reconcile myself to the quiet and regular household of the comfortable yeoman; I sighed after the erratic life to which I had been accustomed from my childhood, and increased indulgence alone overcame my antipathy to a settled residence. According to the countess's arrangement with my mother, she was permitted to see me twice in the year; and it required all the gipsy's influence to persuade me to remain behind, when she left me after these stipulated visits, and rejoined the wild community to which she was attached.

In three years more I was transferred from the gate-house to the hall, and placed under the house-keeeper's charge. I had risen rapidly in the estimation of my protectors, and become the constant companion of the countess's walks, and an especial favourite with the earl. They were a singular couple; and quarrelled with all their relations, and led a lonely and unjoyous life. I was now in my tenth year; pains had been bestowed upon my education—I was quick, and learned rapidly. Before six months wore away I was removed to the drawing-room; and every effort used to cultivate precocious talents, and bestow upon a gipsy girl accomplishments far better suited for the daughter of a peer.

Three years passed. I grew apace; and the few who were admitted to the hall spoke in raptures of my beauty, while in private they censured the partiality of my noble protectors; and marvelled that they should cast aside those of their own lineage, to lavish their kindness on the offspring of a vagabond.

Time still moved on, and I entered on my fifteenth summer. My talents were sedulously cultivated, and every wish I expressed promptly complied with. The blandishments of my patrons, and the flattery of their guests, were profusely lavished on me, and yet— strange confession! the formalities of polished society were irksome and oppressive; and there were moments when I sighed for the wild freedom that my mother enjoyed, and which was denied to me.

Yet, notwithstanding the marked regard of the earl and his lady, their influence was not sufficient to obtain for their *élevée* a cordial reception in the houses of those with whom they visited. Many of the surrounding gentry took part with the family connections from whom they had estranged themselves. At a contested election, the candidate supported by the earl was defeated, and himself made the subject of several bitter lampoons. His adopting me was the general cause of these attacks; and, as his lordship was a men of rough and inelegant exterior, his opponents took advantage of the circumstance, and caricatured him and me under the designation of "Beauty and the Beast."

In family differences there is commonly great asperity of feeling; and from recent annoyances the earl became more virulent against his relatives, and I was more caressed than ever. But a strange occurrence at this time wrought an important change in his plans, and my destiny. It is briefly told.

His only brother, with whom the earl was at feud, had a younger son who bore but an indifferent character. He was said to be dissolute and extravagant, attached to gallantry and play—and in the fullest acceptation of the word, a *roué*.

He was no favourite with his father; and, holding a commission in the Guards, proved an expensive drain upon the purse of a younger brother who was not over opulent. Yet his parent had been liberal to the utmost extent of his means, relieved him from many pecuniary embarrassments, more than once saved his commission from being sold; and until his son's circumstances became desperate, strained every nerve to prevent his child from being disgraced.

But nothing could reclaim the prodigal. Remarkable for personal advantages, he had, although young, acquired a profligate celebrity; and a mania for play rendered his reformation almost hopeless. In a discreditable gambling transaction, to use the fashionable phrase, he had "broken down." The loss of his commission resulted. His father refused to see him; and the discarded son was the inmate of a neighbouring alehouse, when chance apprized the earl that his ruined nephew was so near, and that his father had disowned him.

The earl was weak, and the earl was vindictive. To succour his brother's discarded son, and replace him in that position in society from which his own imprudence had expelled him, appeared a fitting opportunity to mark his personal feelings, and display his wealth and power. Accordingly, an invitation was despatched to his nephew—of course it was thankfully embraced—and that evening Henry Loftus, the discarded son, was formally presented by the countess to her gipsy *protégée*.

I have already mentioned that our residence was secluded; that the visitings of its inmates were limited; and that, owing to the circumstances attendant on my birth and adoption, an extended intimacy with the neighbouring gentry was denied. Those who resorted to the hall were, with a few exceptions, persons of advanced age; and the younger men of ordinary manner, and indifferent exteriors. Imagine my delight, when a military personage of prepossessing appearance and very elegant address was presented to me. He seemed a being of another caste—something I had read of; but never seen. At first sight Henry Loftus caught my fancy, and with a girlish passion—the strongest while it endures—I loved the handsome stranger.

I need not dwell upon the story of a first attachment. Henry Loftus engrossed my whole thoughts, and while the brief delusion lasted, the world held nothing worth possessing but his love. A month rolled on: while he resided with us, the hall appeared an earthly paradise; but, alas he was already weary of its retirement, and sighed to return to the scenes of dissipation from which his misconduct had exiled him.

Nor was the opportunity wanted long. The earl having been apprized how deeply his brother was annoyed, at his having espoused the quarrel of a child who had so shamefully abused the generosity of a too indulgent parent, executed a will, barring the rest of the family from inheriting some large estates, which he had the power of devising as he pleased, and naming the discarded son his successor. This strange act, however, his lordship kept a secret, although he exhibited unequivocal marks of his partiality. Having ascertained the amount of his embarrassments, he gave his nephew a check for their liquidation; lodged a further sum to enable him to repurchase a commission; and, to his own astonishment and that of all the world, the *roué* was directed to return to the metropolis, pay off his debts of honour; and, if he had grace to profit by past experience, enter upon life anew.

But with Henry Loftus profligacy was too deeply rooted to be eradicated, and his vicious habits were irreclaimable. He was now possessor of a sum of money that seemed inexhaustible, and delighted at the prospect of revisiting London. He came to my dressing-room to say farewell; I was unprepared for a sudden separation—the thought of his leaving me was distracting—and, in the madness of the moment, I owned my love, and confessed that life without him was insupportable. Loftus perceived the wildness of my passion; and, to worthily repay the earl's bounty, and *éclater* his own return to town, he determined that I should accompany him. Deep were his declarations of attachment: brilliantly he pictured the elysium that London alone could realise—and ended in urging an elopement. My vanity was excited—my imagination dazzled—and, in a rash hour, I consented to his request. His servant managed to convey away my clothes and jewels among his master's baggage. At midnight, through a drawing-room window, I stepped out upon the lawn—reached a private outlet from the park—found my lover waiting for me—entered the carriage—and flung myself, in tears, upon his breast! The horses went off at speed—and I left the hall for ever.

We arrived in town, drove to a fashionable lodging, and the re-appearance of Henry Loftus soon caused an unusual sensation. A month before, he had fled from the metropolis, a ruined blackleg; then, "every tongue his follies named"—but now he had returned with a full purse; and, prouder boast, had repaid his benefactor's munificence, by robbing him of his favourite *protégée*.

Brief and brilliant was our guilty career. I figured at the opera, and I was followed in the park. The vanity of Loftus made him desirous of exhibiting his beautiful victim, and I was accordingly brought to every haunt of fashion, where persons like I could gain admission.

But the days of his prosperity were numbered. The demon of play led him to the gaming table again; sharpers abler than himself plundered him without mercy: and, in one month from our arrival, my destroyer was once more a beggar. A few minutes after he had despatched his servant, with a check, to draw his last fifty from the banker, the morning paper was brought in; there the earl's death was noticed, and judge what the *roué's* feelings were, when he read the particulars connected with the event, as set forth in a lengthened paragraph. Enraged at the base ingratitude of his nephew, the earl never recovered the shock attendant on the seduction of his *élevée*. Feeling himself indisposed, he tore the will that had left Loftus his heir, and me thirty thousand pounds, and executed a new one, bequeathing his immense estates to his proper successors. Loftus's name, however, was duly mentioned in a codicil—there was a bequest for his use—a shilling to provide himself a halter! The earl died before he could quarrel with his relatives again. Henry's father had now a title, and a noble fortune to support it; and the profligate, his son, was once more a ruined man—a broken blackguard.

So quickly did the story of this downfall travel, that, in a few hours afterwards, Loftus was arrested; he contrived, however, by parting with his watch and rings, to effect his liberation, and kept close within doors, to evade other creditors, who were seeking him. Late in the evening he sent me to Richmond, with a letter to a friend, who, as he informed me, was heavily his debtor. I sought him at the Star and Garter in vain, and reached home long after midnight from an unsuccessful embassy. I found my lodgings in confusion; Loftus was gone, and my maid, a French woman, along with him. He had stolen my jewels, and she carried off my clothes. Though hurried, he kindly left a note for me; it was short and explicit—telling me that he had left England for ever, and to shift for myself as I best could in a short postscript, he said, that a scoundrel of his acquaintance, whose name and address he mentioned, would take me into keeping, and hinted that to secure this desirable arrangement I should be speedy in making application to "his friend."

I shall despatch the rest of his history in a few words: he went to Paris—haunted the Palais Royal—played, and was cleaned out; cheated, and was kicked by an Irish officer. He was abandoned by his companion, my maid; and one morning found in the Morgue, having been picked out of the Seine, with his throat cut; whether the act was his own, or an assassin's, nobody inquired—for no one cared.

I had been kept in such a whirlwind of pleasure, novelty, and dissipation, that for a time I could not believe myself deserted, and looked at passing events as nothing but illusions. Gradually the truth broke upon me; I became alive to the wretchedness of my situation, and the falsehood of man burst upon me with withering violence. The warmth of my natural temper, an utter ignorance of the world, the suddenness with which the veil was rent asunder, and the being whom I had invested with super human qualities, denuded of his fascinations, and presented to my view in all the nakedness of exposed and acknowledged villainy, was too much—and a brain fever resulted. Youth bore me through. With returning reason, I found myself stretched on a mattress, in the ward of a fever-hospital, surrounded by a score of sufferers, as forlorn and deserted as myself.

I recovered; but where was I to turn to? There was not a being on earth, I thought, that had not some resting-place but me. From the Hall I was totally shut out. The countess would not hear my name mentioned: she had become a Methodist; and one of her fancies was, that her former regard for me had been a delusion of the enemy of man to endanger her salvation. Where was my natural protector, the gipsy? God only knew. Her I determined to seek—for where would the wild bird direct her weary wing but to the nest from which she first stretched her untamed pinion? To find my mother was a difficult undertaking—the migrations of her tribe were chiefly regulated by the seasons, and this was some clue to a discovery. I made the attempt; and, after a world of adventure, reached the bivouac of the wanderers.

I endeavoured to forget what I once had, and what I might now have been, and accommodated my dress to my present destitution. As I neared the gipsy haunts, my spirit appeared to revive. My beauty occasioned me much annoyance, but I evaded or repulsed the impertinences I received; and, with feelings of unspeakable delight found myself, on the tenth evening, beneath the canvass roof that had sheltered my infant cradle.

For two years I led a roving life, wild in the extreme, but not without its pleasures; and, while my parent lived, I never regretted the singular vicissitudes of fortune, that had annihilated my affluence and splendour, and again made me a mendicant and a vagabond.

It was now the end of autumn, and our tribe had formed an encampment upon this very common. My mother, who had been for some days indisposed, rapidly became worse, and the disease was ascertained to be a malignant fever. The weather changed; wind and rain rendered our bivouac cold and humid; and to remove my sick parent to some place where she would at least be certain of shelter from the inclement season, was the only hope that remained of her recovery. But where was that asylum to be found? Few would receive a gipsy when in health beneath their roof-tree; and who would admit the wanderer, afflicted with a dangerous malady? Instantly the poor sufferer grew worse; and, as a last resource, I hastened to the village, to try if there could be found one with sufficient charity to succour a dying outcast. From every house I was harshly repulsed—the name of a contagious disorder brought horror with it to all who heard my story—every shelter was refused—and I was shunned by all, as if the plague spot was on my forehead. Every dwelling was closed against me, and I left the hamlet in despair, to rejoin the dying wanderer in our damp and cheerless hovel, and receive her parting sigh upon a bed of litter, from which a pampered hound would turn.

I had already passed the vicarage, when I perceived Mr Howard standing in the porch of the building, with a sweet little girl in his arms. Both were habited in mourning, for he had lost his lady but recently. A sudden impulse induced me to turn back. I did so; and told him of my mother's misery. He listened with a look of gentle sympathy. "And is she so very ill?" he inquired, in a tone of commiseration, so different from the harsh accents with which the villagers had rejected my suit! "She is dying," I replied. "Dying!

and in the forest. Poor girl, I will go with you." He called the nurse, placed his daughter in her arms, and instantly accompanied me to our wretched bivouac.

The sight of so much misery appeared to shock him. My mother was delirious. Mr Howard bent over and felt her pulse. "It is fever," he muttered, "and of the worst type. She must be removed instantly. It would be a crying sin to desert a human being in the forest, and leave her to perish like a masterless dog. Carry her to my home, and I will go on before and prepare a place to receive her." It was done: the dying woman was borne to the good man's dwelling. She was tenderly nursed; the village doctor attended her; the parson visited her constantly, and was seen praying beside the bed of fever, which the lowest menial of his household could not be persuaded to approach.

But why dwell upon the event, and repine that she was taken from me? It was her hour, and destiny had willed it so. She died: her remains were decently inhumed; and I was left in the world—alone!

A few mornings after the gipsy's funeral, Mr Howard sent for me, and I attended him in his study. He presented me with a purse that contained some guineas and a quantity of silver coins which, after her decease, had been found concealed upon my mother's person. The good man looked at me with deep compassion, as he murmured in an under tone, "She is too young and handsome to escape temptation, and avoid the snares which are ever laid for the unsuspecting. What is your name?" I answered him "Ellen." He said, "I tremble for you. If you attach yourself to those wandering people who left the forest when their companion, your mother, was on her dying bed, you will be assailed by temptations which, at your years, mostly prove irresistible, I cannot see you on the very brink of destruction without an attempt to save you. Here you would be secure. Had my lamented wife been spared, she would have been a more suitable protector. But remain here, and while I live, this roof shall shelter you."

I burst into tears, and accepted gratefully the good man's invitation. I was indeed weary of the world such as it had been to me. I had been the child of strange destinies; a very shuttlecock of fortune; born in beggary and nursed in opulence; courted, admired, and followed;

ruined, plundered, and deserted. Here, in this peaceful and secluded dwelling, I could wear away my appointed days, removed alike from those maddening moments of pleasure and attendant misery, to which the denizens of earth are subjected by the laws of being.

Alas! I little knew myself, when I supposed that one with the wild blood that circulated in my veins would remain long the contented member of a regulated and comfortable household. When spring came, and birds sung, and trees blossomed, I began to recall the many hours I passed in childhood "under the greenwood tree." I thought the forest blither than the town; and, like an imprisoned hawk, longed in secret for one wild flight over scenes endeared to me by a thousand recollections. Yet, there were two objects that bound me to the parsonage, and checked my desire for wandering—the memory of the dead, and love of the living bound me to the place. My mother's grave was in the village cemetery, and I had conceived a deep attachment for the lovely orphan, who had been principally entrusted to my charge. I think these gentler ties might have subdued my wandering inclinations, had not unexpected temptation rendered the impulse I was combating too powerful for resistance.

There was an annual fair holding in a neighbouring hamlet, and the servants of the parsonage had obtained Mr Howard's permission to visit it. They invited me to accompany them; but I had some misgivings that made me decline going. Renewed entreaties, and a promise of gay ribands from my admirers—for I had made some rustic conquests—at last induced me to consent, and we set out for the scene of merriment and love-making.

The first sight of the tents—the distant sound of music—waving pennons and painted show-boxes exhibiting toys and trinkets—and all the display of holyday finery, so tempting to the fancy of the rustic maid, all raised anew my gipsy propensities, and my heart beat with delight in looking at a scene associated with my first ideas of pleasure. I mixed in the merry throng, and had roamed for some time through the crowded fair before I discovered that I had strayed from my companions. I turned instantly to seek them, when a hand touched mine, and a voice, too familiar to be mistaken, whispered, "Ellen!"

It was an ancient female of our tribe: she beckoned me to follow: I obeyed, and we left the throng unobserved.

It is unnecessary to state more of our interview, than that the gipsy urged me to join the community again; that eventually I consented and it was arranged that she should come at midnight to the parsonage, and I should abandon my peaceful home, and once more become a wanderer.

I hurried from the scene of gaiety to one of a very opposite description—the village cemetery; and, sitting down upon my mother's grave, wept bitterly. The evening was closing before I could bring myself to quit the turf that covered her ashes; and with a heavy heart I returned to Mr Howard's residence, to make the necessary preparations for my journey.

As the hour drew near my resolution failed, and I regretted that I had promised to meet the gipsy. I hung over my lovely and innocent charge, as she lay calmly sleeping, and while my tears fell fast, invoked blessings on the child, and covered her smiling face with kisses. Except my mother, I had never loved another half so dearly, and to tear myself away required more firmness than I could command. I was still at the infant's bed when midnight knelled from the old tower. Presently some particles of gravel struck lightly against the casement. I looked out—the gipsy was below. Again and again I kissed the gentle child—flung my bundle to my companion—silently descended from the window—took a farewell look at the parsonage—the forest was before me—I was now homeless and unprotected—and, at nineteen, alone upon the world. But why complain? It was predestined so.

For a time a wandering life passed pleasantly enough. My beauty rendered me an object of consideration as a daughter of the tribe; and among the swarthy community I had more than one suitor. Michael, as the leader was named, honoured me with his addresses. He was a bold and dexterous fellow, acute and daring, with a superior intelligence, that under other circumstances might have earned a name, and placed him high in worldly estimation. But there were countervailing qualities in the gipsy chief. He was violent and suspicious—jealous and vindictive. I disliked him. His suit was urged with that confidence of success which marks an overweening vanity; and when it was haughtily rejected, his rage was boundless. In vain he changed his tone, and tried both flattery and threats—in vain he pleaded that by the wild ordinance of the tribe I had been assigned him as his companion. Flattery failed—and to the gipsy regulations I refused obedience. This infraction of arbitrary laws was of course resented, and Michael's claim upon me as a wife supported by the whole community. It was idle to resist what all had determined; and no alternative remained but submission to an arbitrary decree, or an immediate elopement—and, of course, I chose the latter.

It required, however, considerable caution to effect an escape without risking a discovery, as that event would draw down the vengeance of the tribe, and expose me to the mildest penalty of disobedience—an instant union with the chief. But mine was a determined spirit—and I exerted all my ingenuity to mask my design, and not excite suspicion. As if influenced by the general decision, I gave a reluctant consent. Michael was overjoyed; the gang delighted at an approaching scene of revelry; and the third evening was appointed to witness the performance of that rude ceremony, which constitutes a gipsy marriage.

For two days, I found no opportunity of quitting the encampment unperceived, but on the third I was more successful. I managed to escape, and directed my course towards Canterbury, from which city our bivouac was not very distant.

As I was afterwards informed, my flight was quickly known, and it caused a direful commotion among the wanderers. Instant pursuit was given—the tribe scattered themselves over the country—and from their cunning and celerity it was never doubted that the fugitive would be promptly recovered—and all resolved, that as entreaty failed, force should be employed, if necessary, to make me the consort of their chief.

Michael's rage was awful—his pride was wounded that a gipsy should decline his alliance—and that one so artful and suspicious as himself should be outwitted by a simple girl. His pursuit, of course, was vigorous—he outstripped his companions far—and learning from a beggar the route I had taken, with amazing speed and certain accuracy he followed my flying steps; like a bloodhound on his quest.

Canterbury was in sight, when exhausted by rapid exertions to escape I was obliged to rest, and turning into a small plantation, seated myself upon a fallen tree. I breathed freely—I had succeeded—the city of refuge was before me, and there I should be secure against any attempts which the gipsy tribe should make to repossess their errant daughter. What future course should I pursue? Should I return and claim Mr Howard's protection, or seek fresh fortunes as a wanderer. I smiled, when fancying the confusion my escape would cause, and the fury and disappointment of the fiery bridegroom, when it was discovered that the lady of his choice had played him truant, and left her ardent lover without a parting farewell. "Yes," I said, "it was well planned, and boldly executed; Michael, thou must seek another mistress; I have no desire to become a gipsy queen. How will he storm," I continued, "when evening comes, and the bride is wanting; the fugitive escaped pursuit; and the bridal festival turned into an angry brawl!"—I laughed—"Oh that I could see him for a moment, and whisper in his swarthy ear, that a girl's wit was keener than a chieftain's cunning."

"You shall be gratified," returned a voice that made my blood run cold: I threw back a hasty glance, and over my shoulder peered the vindictive eyes of my exasperated and deserted suitor.

"So, ho!" he said, in a low deep voice—"Is the wild bird so suddenly reclaimed? and did a novice like thee trifle with my love, and fancy she could evade it? Well, you have cost me a ten miles race; but surely a smart breathing was purchased cheaply, by winning a bride like thee, girl? Up, Ellen, thy husband waits for thee."

"Thy husband!" I repeated passionately.

"Ay, thine!—no earthly power shall sever us"—and he gave a fiendish laugh. "Come let us be friends; kiss me, Nell—I forgive thy flight for this time, wench!"

"Kiss thee!" I exclaimed as I sprang up, and waved him from me. "No, Michael, force only could make me yours."

"Indeed!" he muttered, while with a deep imprecation he added, "Then force shall;" and he seized my arm roughly, while I screamed loudly for help. The words were scarcely spoken, when a noise was heard, as if somebody was crushing through the brushwood. The gipsy dropped my arm, and searched his bosom for a weapon. Next moment a man vaulted lightly over the paling, and haughtily demanded the occasion of the outcry.

The stranger was young and handsome; rather above the middle size, with a person that indicated more activity than strength. There was that assured character in his bearing which bespeaks a fearless heart. He was dressed as sportsmen generally are, and bore no weapon, except a walking-stick. Notwithstanding the plainness of his shooting-dress, the air and manner of the stranger were too decided to allow his profession to be doubted for a moment.

Michael glared upon him, with a mixed look of fear and hatred, as he impudently demanded "What brought him there?" The stranger's lip curled scornfully, while he measured the gipsy chief from head to foot.

"Brought me here!" he replied, in a high tone. "Scoundrel! repeat your insolence, and I promise you a broken head." Then turning to me, he continued in a gentler voice, "Has this ruffian alarmed you, my poor girl? Fear nothing; come with me, and I will protect you."

Michael advanced a step—"She is my wife," he said; "beware how you lay hand on what is mine."

"Yours!" I exclaimed. "'Tis false. Yours I am not. Yours I never will be."

The gipsy made a forward movement, as if he intended to seize me again, and I implored the soldier's protection.

"Hallo! fellow," he shouted—"hands off; if you value whole bones. Come, pretty one, I will see you safe to Canterbury"

Michael's looks became darker and more ferocious. Placing himself between me and the gate of the plant he suddenly unsheathed a long and peculiar clasp-knife which he always carried on his person, and swore a deep oath, that if the stranger did not leave us, he would bury the weapon in his heart.

But the soldier was in no wise daunted. He returned his menace with a look of bold defiance and raised his stick, as if preparing to parry the gipsy's thrust. Suddenly, and without any apparent effort, except a slight movement of the wrist, he smote Michael's hand so sharply that the knife flew from his grasp, and fell ten yards' distance into the thick copsewood. The gipsy made an attempt to recover his lost weapon, but the soldier stepped between him and the spot where it fell.

"Halt!" he shouted, in a voice that obliged the ruffian to obey the order. "Fellow, I have given thee a bruised hand, and another step insures thee a broken head. Off! I say or by St Patrick I'll crack that skull of thine as I would a walnut-shell, and leave as many marks upon thy swarthy hide as will cause you to remember the touch of an Irish sapling; ay, to the latest hour of your life."

He said—and taking my hand led me to the gate, without any attempt on Michael's part to bar our egress from the wood. We were now upon the high road, and, of course, in comparative safety. The gipsy lifted his fallen knife and returned it to his bosom, while he looked after us with a demoniac glance, in which hate, jealousy and disappointment united.

"You and I shall meet again, and your best blood pay the forfeit of your interference!" he muttered as he clenched his fist, and grinned like an angry mastiff at the soldier. The person threatened coolly waved his hand.

"Off, you dusky vagabond!" he exclaimed: "I see some of my people approaching; and if my memory holds good, there is a horsepond at no great distance."

The gipsy looked in the direction to which the soldier's eyes had turned, and observed several men in uniforms moving slowly towards the wood.

"Farewell," he said "farewell, Ellen; at least for a time. Many a bitter hour this morning's slight shall cost thee; ay—when thou art mine, and no hand is near to succour."

"*Yours!* Never, Michael!"

He gave a parting look of deadly meaning, tossed his thin arm above his head, and continued, in a tone convulsive from the violence of his passion—"Mine! yes, mine. Men and fiends shall never move Michael's resolution, Ellen," and he dropped his voice—"*mine* you shall be, though I hang for it!"

These were his last words; for, bounding into the coppice, he vanished in the thick plantation.

My deliverer looked for a short space at the place where the gipsy disappeared. "Upon my life," he said, "a pleasant sort of gentleman! a suitor who will not be refused, it seems. How came one so pretty as you, Ellen, to fall into that fellow's company? It was fortunate that I was netting rabbits in the wood, or that bronzed ruffian would have done you some serious mischief."

In reply to his questions, I told him a portion of my story, and mentioned my orphanage, and the varied circumstances that obliged me to fly from the gipsy encampment. During the brief recital he listened with deep attention. "And are both parents dead?" he asked me.

"They are, sir."

"Have you no other relative alive?"

"I have none, except the members of the wild tribe I left this morning."

"Poor soul!" he said: "few are so forlorn as you appear to be. Where do you propose to go?"

"I cannot tell."

"Have you not some acquaintance?"

"None who could serve me."

He looked at me. "I never saw one so beautiful and so desolate. Good heaven! have you considered the risk that one so attractive as yourself must be exposed to in a world where men are nowise scrupulous, and matter not the means by which the end is accomplished?"

I sighed heavily; and the past flashed painfully to my recollection.

The stranger was silent for a moment. "I am but a sorry counsellor;" he said. "Come, you must have me for lack of better; and between danger and yourself I can only interpose the honour of my country. Let me think.—My sergeant's wife will take care of you at present, and we will then try and find out if a better home can be obtained"

He looked at me attentively. "It is wondrous beauty for a wanderer!" and continued in a low tone, "A strange adventure altogether! *I* with the lightest reputation in a dissipated corps—*I* selected to be mentor of a being so lovely as thou, Ellen. Well, no matter—all are not safely judged by look; and in me, notwithstanding all my levity, you may obtain an honester protection than from men of graver exterior. Will you trust me, Ellen; and confide in one who never yet failed friend or foe?"

My eyes turned upon his. I read his countenance with gipsy caution. The handsome outlines had kindled into nobleness; his cheek was flushing; while the honest expansion of the brow told that in his words not a particle of treachery was lurking. What should I do? What but cling to him as a heaven-sent friend, and throw myself fearlessly upon his generosity? I did so, and had no reason to regret it, although my hopes rested on the mercurial fancy of a hair-brained Irishman.

George Harley was four-and-twenty; his father dead; his patrimony wasted; and his sole dependence a company of foot. In all things his was an anomalous character. His habits were simple and luxurious, he was shrewd and witty, weak and improvident; while the warmth of an unbridled temper,

"Mild with the gentle—with the froward, stern,"

led him into eternal scrapes, from which an excellent natural understanding, had it been cultivated and developed, scarcely managed to extricate him. He was perfectly single-hearted, and his purse and person alike ready at a call. Honour with him was a sort of phantom, an undefined idea of a feeling that should direct a gentleman's career. He was humane. To witness the corporal punishment of an irreclaimable delinquent pained him to the soul; although, that same

morning, and for an imaginary offence, he had dangerously wounded
an old companion. His virtues were noble; his failings pardonable;
the whole was a union of opposites, which rendered George Harley
an object of regard and fear—envied by some, detested by others:
in short, a man in different times, and different tempers, pitied and
admired, courted and avoided.

The soldier's wife, to whose care I was consigned, procured me a
lodging beside her own, in a neat cottage in the suburbs of the town;
and, from her kindness and attention, it was evident that Harley's
charges had been strict. Her husband was the captain's pay-sergeant,
she acted as his laundress, and to my young protector both appeared
strongly attached. But Harley was just the man to be a regimental
favourite. His humanity had procured him the title of "the soldier's
friend," while for all his faults there was a ready apology, and the
out-breakings of his temper were reckoned only as the ebullitions
of a martial spirit. No matter how long the march, how heavy the
roads, Harley was always at the head of the light company, while his
gig was laden with children and knapsacks, and his horse mounted by
some soldier who had fallen lame. Haughty and punctilious towards
his superiors, to his men he was affable and kind. He was indeed well
suited for a leader; and those he commanded looked to him with
confidence and regard. In the licence permitted the soldier when
marching, the officer was not too proud to share; and in the hour of
danger, when others would have said "Go on," Harley would have
shouted "Follow!"

There was a studied delicacy observed in my preserver's conduct
towards me, which certainly the circumstances under which we met
would scarcely warrant. Until the second day he left me to myself, nor
did he visit me then, until he had ascertained from Mrs Owen that I
was desirous to speak to him.

When Harley came to my assistance in the wood, he found a gipsy-
girl in the wild costume of her tribe; but when he visited me at the
sergeant's lodging, I was becomingly attired in the neat and simple
dress that I had worn when in Mr Howard's residence. The alteration

in my appearance was striking, if I might judge from Harley's surprise. Nor was he less changed; for the light infantry uniform he was dressed in was well calculated to show to its best advantage a figure light, elegant, and athletic.

Our interview was long. I found his manners extremely prepossessing; for without the tinsel assurance of high life, there was an openness, a manly honesty in all that Harley said, that won me more than a courtlier address, where the polish is quite apparent, but the sincerity doubtful. We parted with an engagement to meet on the morrow, and a promise on my part to acquaint him with the particulars of a history so varied in all its fortunes as mine.

He came next day, and listened with deep interest to a detail of my earlier life. But when I reached the period in my story when Loftus was introduced to the Hall—when I mentioned my elopement and subsequent abandonment, he leaped from his chair.

"The double-damned villain!" he exclaimed, while his eyes lightened with rage. "Alas poor Ellen; and were you, too, that scoundrel's victim? Is it not a strange coincidence in our fates that the same smooth-tongued traitor should have ruined both?"

I expressed astonishment, and he thus continued:

"The tale of folly is soon told. We were schoolfellows, and Loftus my favourite companion. He was weak and timid, and I fought his battles. His allowance was small, mine was liberal—and we had a common purse.

"We separated at fifteen—he to go to Oxford, and I to join a regiment in India, to which I had been gazetted.

"Six years passed. My father died, and I came home and succeeded to my inheritance. It was unfortunately money in the funds, and I had a discretionary power to use it as I pleased. I came to London to purchase my company; and there I found my once-loved schoolfellow, who had left the university, and was now a lieutenant in the Coldstream. Of course, our intimacy was renewed on my part with unchanged affection, on his, with a fixed determination to avail himself of my confidence, and plunder me of any last guinea.

"It is not necessary to follow the scoundrel through all the sinuous plans with which his object was achieved. I was a blind and ready dupe. I had not a suspicion of him, while all besides knew that my false friend was plucking me to the very pen-feather.

"For some months I was absent in Ireland with my regiment, and the vicissitudes of Loftus's fortunes reached me but imperfectly—one paper stated he was ruined; another, that his uncle had adopted him. Again I read a strange story of his carrying off the earl's ward; that he was disinherited, and again a castaway and broken man. All this confliction of statements was puzzling—it was incomprehensible that of one man's doings so many versions should be given and I obtained leave of absence, to find, if possible, where the truth lay.

"I reached London safely, and my first visit was to my friend; but he was invisible. I entered an adjoining coffee-room, and read there a paragraph, in an evening print, that left the ruin of Loftus no longer a matter of report.

"The morning, however, brought with it a full exposé of his villainy; yet, such was my fatuity, that with irrefragable proof before my eyes, I could scarce bring myself to credit it. One by one his deep-laid plans were developed; and it was plain that I had been coolly and unmercifully plundered. Boiling with rage, I determined on immediate pursuit, and drove to my bankers; but there Loftus had anticipated me, and three days before, by a forged check, drawn out my last guinea.

"Nothing but vengeance was left, and I determined to hunt the black-hearted traitor to the death. For a time all trace of him was lost, and two or three attempts which I made to discover him failed. At last, I heard that he had been recently seen in Paris, and thither I proceeded. For several days I haunted the gaming-houses, but Loftus was not there, although until the last week he had been a regular attendant.

"I found him, Ellen!—where?—Where such a villain should be found—in the Morgue! I never saw anything so diabolical as the dead man's countenance! His throat from ear to ear was severed. I gazed on the horrid spectacle, if not with pleasure, certainly without pity. I had been saved some trouble; I should have killed the ruffian had we met; but his felon hand, or (and more probably) a murderer's knife, prevented the necessity of my becoming his executioner."

For a week Harley was a constant visitor, and less acuteness than I possessed would have easily discovered, that every hour he became more fascinated with my beauty. This feeling of affection was reciprocated; the bold and careless soldier was now tenderly beloved; he had treated me with tenderness and respect, and that had endeared him doubly.

It is not difficult to conjecture how our intimacy might have terminated, had events progressed in their common course; but an unexpected occurrence hurried matters to a close.—I had more than once rambled in the evening through the streets, and breathed the fresh air, which, to one like me, was indispensable. Closely muffled, I had, hitherto, escaped observation; and Michael's threats had made me confine my walks to the streets and suburbs. On the preceding evening, a man had followed me. He was troublesome, and to escape impertinence I hurried to my lodgings; and so lightly did I think of the affair, that next day the occurrence was forgotten.

Harley was an early visitor. I was scarcely seated, when a child belonging to the house brought up a sealed billet, which, he said, had been given to him by a fine gentleman, with a request that it should be safely delivered.

Harley appeared astounded; his face flushed; the handwriting was well known to him, and in a flurried voice he addressed me. "You have been but a short time in Canterbury, Ellen, and yet you have made a brilliant conquest."

"I have achieved it unconsciously," I replied in a calm voice.

"Indeed! Know you not, then, the writer of this effusion?"

"I am ignorant of his very existence. Can you tell me his name?"

"It is no doubt detailed fully here"—and he handed me the letter.

"Then pray let me know who my correspondent is?" and I returned the billet.

He broke the seal, and I observed his eyes kindle as he read the note. He closed it again. "Last night, you secured a very ardent admirer. Did any person address you in the street?"

"Yes—my walk was interrupted by a tall man who crossed me repeatedly. He spoke to me without obtaining reply, and obliged me to seek shelter in my lodgings, and followed me to the door."

"Indeed! It were hard that exercise was debarred you by such impertinence, and it shall be looked to. Farewell, Ellen—I shall call early tomorrow. May I keep this billet? and have you no curiosity to know its contents?"

"Retain it, certainly," I replied; "for so little does it interest me, that were it returned, it should be consigned unopened to the fire."

"Once more, farewell, Ellen!" He took my hand in his, kissed me affectionately—and I was left alone.

The evening fell; it was rainy and boisterous. I had some presentiment of evil—the gloomy weather probably induced it, and to divert my melancholy thoughts, I invited the sergeant's wife to tea. Later than usual, Owen came to conduct her home, and I fancied that he appeared thoughtful and dispirited. I concluded that some regimental affair had vexed him, and I regretted it, for the honest Welshman had been kind to me as a father.

Morning came, and morning passed without Harley's customary visit. This unusual absence alarmed me; and my apprehensions were increased, by observing that the sergeant and his wife were visibly dejected, although it was evident that they endeavoured to conceal their uneasiness from me. My inquiries after Harley were evaded, and his absence, when I pressed to know the cause, was excused by saying that he was on duty. But when evening arrived, and my protector came not, my distress became intolerable; and I concluded that some dreadful calamity had befallen my only friend.

I was alone, and weeping bitterly. The time when I might expect a visit had long since passed, and another night of agonising suspense must be endured. I heard the street-door opened, and hoped it might be Mrs Owen with some intelligence; I dared anticipate nothing but evil tidings; yet surely anything was to be preferred to the torturous uncertainty which Harley's unaccountable absence had occasioned.

A step ascended the stairs softly; I dreaded to look up—no doubt the doomed moment had arrived—I should know the worst—and leaning my head upon the table, I burst into a flood of tears. The late visitor entered, and a man's shadow darkened the opposite wall. I sprang wildly from the chair—it was Harley himself! But, my God, how altered! When last he parted from me, he looked a fortunate and reckless soldier; one who would boldly hew his road through difficulties; and the harder the storm fell, the more buoyant would the spirit rise that should control it. Now, his cheek was wan, his eye rayless, he seemed the ruin of himself; one, on whom fortune had exhausted her angry phial—one, from whose bosom hope had fled.

"Ellen," he said, in hollow and unearthly tones, "you have surely heard of my madness! Why ask the question? Evil tidings are quickly carried."

"I have heard nothing, Captain Harley."

"Then poor Owen has been true," he muttered.

"Your absence," I replied, "has made me very wretched; I feared that I had forfeited your regard; had unwittingly offended you, and thus had incurred the misfortune of losing my only protector."

"Protector!" he said, with a laugh that made me shudder. "Ellen, a fool like me cannot protect himself. I am a ruined man!—worse far—a disgraced soldier."

"Ruined and disgraced!" I repeated in horror. "No, no! ruin may overtake the wisest, but disgrace can never rest upon the name of Harley!"

I fancied a smile lighted his wan countenance, as he continued,—

"Alas, Ellen! and you have yet to learn my folly? See—look at this dress! I no longer wear a uniform! From the profession I once prided in, I am expelled. I shall be brought to a court-martial, and my name removed with ignominy from the list that records the brave! I am now alone upon the earth—who will pity one so fallen?"

"Stop, Captain Harley," I exclaimed—"surely you wrong yourself! Probably you have been rash and imprudent; but I would be sworn the taint of dishonour will never rest upon your name. What has happened? What have you done?"

"Ellen before I answer, listen to me, and consider well before you reply. I have told you that I am a ruined man; and fallen as your own fortunes are, mine are still more shattered. Will you with such truth admitted—will you unite your destiny with mine—and all desperate as my future prospects are, will you, Ellen, cling to me through good and evil, and bind your fate to mine?"

Ere he had finished his passionate appeal, I flung myself upon his breast. He swore that for life he would protect me; and in return I plighted him my faith.

"And was the plight kept faithfully?" said O'Connor, interrupting her.

The gipsy's eye flashed fire—"Faithfully!" she exclaimed—"Ay! with a fidelity that the court dame could only dream of. It was the compact of the heart, and not the mouth. Think you, that the shorn priest, when he unites the hands, can interchange the affections? or that the gold wire which glitters on the finger of the bride can charm the heart that haply sighs in secret for another—ay, even at the moment when kneeling at the altar, and when she calls on Heaven to attest her truth? Have I not seen beauty in its very bud consigned to a dotard's arms? Have I not seen the wrinkled matron purchase the false homage of a beardless boy? *Faithfully*, Harley, for five years I followed you in weal and woe; you slept within these arms; and your parting sigh escaped upon this breast. Not even in death did I forget you! for these hands consigned you to the earth, while the fallen brave that lay around were abandoned to the fox and the eagle. In the calm of rustic quietude, in the tempest of war, I never left you. Was this true faith—was this woman's constancy? Yes; though ring, and priest, and all the parade of wedlock were forgotten, the gipsy's love was fixed as the lights of heaven, and ended where it should do—in the grave of him to whom she had devoted it!"

O'Connor gazed on his singular companion with pity and admiration. The question he had inadvertently asked implied doubt, and recalled the latent ardour of her love. The eye kindled with uncommon brilliancy, as she sprang from the turf she had been resting on; and while repelling a suspicion of her constancy, her whole appearance was noble, commanding, and dramatic. But the allusion to the dead excited softer feelings; gradually she melted into tears, and, through deep emotion, her voice became nearly indistinct. It was, however, but a momentary weakness; her firmness returned, and, dashing the tear from her cheek, she muttered—"Pshaw! this is mere drivelling;" and next minute, resuming her place beside the soldier, she thus continued:

But Harley's mishap, though bad enough, was not so ruinous in its consequences as was at first apprehended. I was the unhappy cause. The person who followed me in the street, and sent the billet to my residence, was the senior major of the regiment; and, unfortunately, after he had left me, Harley remonstrated with his superior officer, in a tone that produced an irritating answer. The altercation waxed warmer—became violent—ended in my protector losing all self-command, and laying his cane upon the shoulders of the major.

At first, this flagrant breach of military subordination, it was believed, could only end in a court. In that case, Harley must have been inevitably cashiered. Subsequent inquiry, however, proved that his opponent's conduct had been culpable and his language warm and unguarded; and the affair terminated in both withdrawing from the corps, and both disposing of their commissions.

After the first bitterness that parting from a regiment and profession naturally occasioned, Harley appeared to disregard his loss. He was ardently attached to me: he seemed determined to forget the world—he succeeded—and we retired to beautiful cottage and farm, which the wreck of his patrimony, and the sale of his commission, had secured us.

It was a wild and lovely home. Situated in the remotest of a northern county, we had all the varied scene that makes retirement desirable—bold hills, a sparkling lake, heath and copsewood, while the sweetest rivulet wandered round the cottage, in which ever an angler threw a line, or the village maid performed her ablutions.

The roses mingled with the thatch, and honeysuckle festooned the green veranda. Even winter did not rob the surrounding scenery of its interest; the heights, far as the eye could range, were covered with snow, and sparkled in the sunshine, while the waters of the lake, in summer so bright and glassy, contrasted with the white mountains, and looked dark as a witch's caldron.

A year passed, and what a year of happiness it was! If there be an era that memory dwells on with delight, it is the time when I possessed an humble cottage and the man I loved. Harley was equally contented; he appeared to have forgotten what he had been. In rural pursuits his leisure was occupied, while his active habits found ample occupation in rambling over the hills, or angling in the many waters that were contiguous to our dwelling. Evening saw him return to his happy home, while I watched for his appearance on the heights, and hurried forth to welcome him. Never did two hearts unite more tenderly. Another and a dearer tie had bound us to each other—a child was born. Oh God! when I think of that it maddens me; remembrance traces again that blissful period. In fancy I see Harley regard his offspring with the first love of a father, while I rapturously leaned over the infant's cot, and as I gazed upon my beauteous boy, little dreamed how bitterly that child would wring my heart.

I was sitting on a rustic bench before the cottage, with my infant on my knee. It was a sweet autumnal evening, and all around was lovely and endearing. Harley was fishing in the lake, and, from time to time, my eyes turned from my laughing boy to seek the other object of my love, his father. There was a calm and holy quiet in the scene and hour, and I thought my heart felt an unusual lightness. I kissed my baby's lips—and then blessed Heaven that I was parted from the world. The world! what was it to us? Here was a home with all the joys that love and health and competence could give, and not one harassing care to interrupt its sunshine. I heard the wicket open—the terrier lying at my feet sprang forward with an angry growl. I raised my eyes—and Michael's detested face was glaring in hatred and astonishment on mine!

I was horror-stricken—and, in speechless surprise, stole a side glance at my old admirer. His appearance was sadly altered, he was gaunt and haggard, dressed in the tattered clothing of a sailor, with a small bundle across his shoulder, and a murderous bludgeon in his hand. For some moments we both were silent—but at last Michael addressed me.

"So—we have met once more. I have sought you over England in vain—and many a weary mile the search has cost me. No matter; I am more than repaid for all. And have I found the slippery dame again? Ha! ha! A mother too! Is the child like his father?" And he gave a fiendish laugh, and made a step nearer the bench I was resting on. I screamed loudly, and sprang up, and, in my terror, clasped my baby more closely to my bosom. The ruffian continued with a sneer—"A neat cottage, and a full barn-yard, faith! Few gipsy-girls have found so snug a home. Come—let me see the brat. Why! the squire's heir is not tricked out in gayer finery than the banding of a vagabond! Wilt thou not ask me in, Nell? Methinks this welcome to an old acquaintance is but a sorry one. Wilt thou not offer me a mug of ale? I have walked a weary way to visit you."

I was dreadfully alarmed. There was no one in the cottage; for our domestics, a lad and a woman, were milking in a paddock at some distance from the house. I assumed the appearance of indifference; but, no doubt, an ashy face belied my pretended courage.

"How dare you venture here, Michael? A call from me will bring assistance—and—"

"It will be a loud one," he said, with a fiendish expression of triumphant malice:—"No, no, Ellen—I have lain since noon in yonder copse, and watched your keeper to the lake, and your servants to the paddock."

"See ye a man beside the water's edge? Beware of him, Michael: a second meeting may cost you dearer than the first. You cannot have forgotten him."

"No," said the ruffian coldly; "the man who crosses me, never ceases to be remembered until the injury is avenged. Harley despised and wronged me. He rescued you from my power, for Heaven made him stronger. He spurned me like a reptile—he scorned me like a dog—and, worse offending far, robbed me of your love. The hour of vengeance is at hand—the time of bitter retribution is nigh."

"Villain!—you dare not harm us!"

"That," he returned calmly, "a brief period will discover; I have no time to dally now; I want money, Nell; come, despatch."

I flung him my purse.

"There—for God's sake leave me!"

He lifted the money from the ground, and slowly reckoned it. "Three gold pieces and some silver; the supply was wanted. Farewell, Ellen, for the present. Your friend, I perceive, is turning his footsteps home. Home! Ha ha! How long will that home be left him? Your servants, too, are approaching. 'Tis but a hasty visit, Nell, but we will meet ere long.—Adieu!"

Darting a scowl of unextinguishable hatred towards Harley, he turned a parting glance on me. It was the look of a demon—and like a reptile he slipped away among the underwood, and next moment disappeared.

When Harley saw my pale cheeks, he guessed that some untoward event had happened. A short explanation told him the cause of my alarm; and, seizing a loaded gun, he went in pursuit of the gipsy. It was useless to remonstrate with one of his fiery temperament, and I remained in dreadful uncertainty until he returned from a bootless search. Next day, every copse and thicket was examined carefully; but no trace of the ruffian was discovered. A week passed—another succeeded: no doubt Michael, contented with his subsidy, had disappeared, and dreading Harley's vengeance, left the neighbourhood for ever.

The third week ended; an early frost set in; and the first flight of woodcocks were seen on the heaths above the cottage. A day of successful exertion had closed; and Harley retired to his room at an early hour, and was speedily wrapped in the unbroken slumbers which reward the mountain sportsman.

For my part, I felt an unusual reluctance to go to my apartment; I had vague, but fearful apprehensions, and, though I strove to combat what I fancied woman's weakness, Michael haunted my night-dreams, and was seldom absent from my thoughts when waking. I knew him to be a ruthless villain—implacable in hatred—and constant in the purpose of revenge, as the bloodhound to his quarry. He looked, too, like a broken and desperate man, and that would render him doubly dangerous. Still, I endeavoured to banish these forebodings of evil, and rose and looked at the timepiece. The hand pointed to eleven, and commonly an hour before that, our little household were at rest. Indeed, all but myself were so now. I took the candle from the table, and opened the chamber-door softly. Harley lay in that sound and dreamy sleep, which exercise and an easy mind insure. I looked at my baby; there he lay peaceful and happy, for the smile of infancy was curling on his rosy lips. I kissed his forehead gently, lighted the night-lamp on the hearth, and left the apartment again, to ascertain that the doors and casements were fastened, a precaution I had never taken before.

I found all secure, and determined to retire to bed. Once or twice the terrier had growled, and started from his mat; out if anything moved without, the dog alone could hear it. It was foolish to yield the mastery to uneasy thoughts, and tremble at a ruffian's threats, equally vague and boastful, and which he wanted power and courage to redeem. I extinguished the taper, unclosed a casement looking towards the mountains, and in a few moments the bracing effects of the cold restored my usual tranquillity.

It was a sweet and quiet scene. The little garden stretched downwards to the rivulet, whose waters, sparkling in the clear starlight with a murmuring sound, fell over a ledge of rock, and plunged sullenly into a deep basin which their own restless action had worn in the river-bed. On the left, the dark hedge of the orchard shut in the view; while on the right, the farm with its corn stacks and ample pile of fuel for the winter, gave a peculiar character of comfort and plenty to the prospect afforded from the window. I was about to shut the casement, when once more the dog exhibited uneasiness, and uttered an impatient whine. Nothing that might disturb his jealousy was visible in the, garden, and I threw a careless glance towards the farmyard. Was it fancy? to the shadow of the barn thrown by the starlight on the grass, that a human being was united! I sprang back. Should I give an alarm and call up Harley? I stole another look—the figure, whatever it might have been, had disappeared, and nothing met the eye but the dull mass of shading which the outline of the buildings produced. Why then should I break Harley's rest with a tale of idle apprehension? The shadow might be that of a tree—a passing cloud—ay, or the mere coinage of my own heated imagination; and though under my renewed excitement it would be useless to retire to bed, I decided that it would be unkind to deprive my protector of that tranquil rest which my own fears alone prevented me from sharing. Thus resolved, I secured the lattice carefully, and lighted my candle again.

A newspaper—a thing of infrequent occurrence—had reached us late that evening. Harley was sleepy, I engaged with my child, and, in consequence, the cover remained unbroken. I opened it now; reading would while away an hour, and lead me from thoughts that were most harassing. I skimmed over many trifling occurrences lightly, when, suddenly, my whole attention was riveted by a paragraph headed 'Dreadful Murder.' At the first glance my blood curdled, and I seemed under a horrid fascination, until I read over the whole detail. The narrative ran briefly thus:

"Two sailors were journeying from a northern seaport—one, an aged man, just landed from a long voyage, had been paid his arrears of wages, and, with a full purse and large bundle, was proceeding to an inland village to visit his relations there. It would appear that he was not acquainted with the road, for he mentioned in several places where they had stopped for refreshment that the stranger who accompanied him had been hired as a guide. This man was described to be a person of ill-favoured countenance and shabby exterior.

"On the third day of their journey, the guide led the sailor by a pathway into a thick wood, They were seen to enter it together; the stranger to leave it alone; and, in a few hours afterwards the sailor was discovered in a thicket, with his throat frightfully cut and his purse and bundle gone. Suspicion, of course, fell upon the guide, and instant pursuit was given; the ruffian was traced and overtaken, and only by a miracle escaped from his followers, dropping the sailor's bundle, and throwing away the jacket he had taken from his victim. In the pocket the dead man's purse was found.

It was further ascertained that the murderer was a gipsy named Michael Cooper, who had been driven long since from the gang for stabbing a companion in a brawl. Latterly he had led a solitary life, and, as it was believed, one of continued crime. One hundred pounds were now offered for his apprehension, and as he was known to be skulking on the borders of Cumberland, there was little doubt but he would be speedily brought to justice."

Such was the intelligence the newspaper communicated. And had that murderous villain, not six hours since, been within a knife's distance of me and my sweet boy? I shuddered with horror—a new impulse came over me—that tale of blood had given my fears another bent. I would not be absent from Harley and my child—no, not for a single moment. I put the taper out, and hurried to the sleeping-chamber.

There lay the father and the child, wrapt in as careless dreaming as if crime and suffering were banished from the world. The calm deep breathing of infancy, contrasted with the stormier sleep of manhood—for Harley in fancy was on the hills, and in low mutterings cheered his grey-hounds on the deer. His arm was flung naked above the bed coverings, and, with a woman's pride, I gazed upon its light and sinewy proportions, while on his sleeping brow I could read a character of boldness and decision, that half restored my own. His loaded pistols hung above the chimney-piece, his sabre ready for the master's hand. Surely nothing was to be dreaded here. No assassin would venture on the chamber of a brave man, and he prepared to meet him. I flung my fears to the winds, and, in a few minutes was couched at his shoulder, and asleep.

I could not have been more than an hour in bed when frightful dreams disturbed me. Of course, waking or sleeping, Michael was the demon that pursued me. I woke in horrible affright. Harley was slumbering carelessly at my side, and I thought my alarm must have been a fantasy. I strove to sleep again—was it nightmare?—my breathing was impeded, and a sickening weight pressed upon my lungs and stopped their exercise. I tried to recall myself to perfect recollection. It was the deep hour of night, the lamp was waning on the hearth, and yet the chamber was bright as if a flood of moonlight filled it. A strange and crackling noise fell on my ear. What could this be? I sprang from the bed, flung aside the curtains, and, heavens and earth! all was in a blaze! and dwelling and farm-yard, although totally unconnected, were breaking into one red flame, and simultaneously in a dozen places. My first acts were to wake my lover, and catch up my sleeping child; a dense and smothering vapour vollied into the room, and when the door was opened, the outward chamber was nearly filled with smoke. It was strange that Harley was so difficult to awake, and for a time after he hardly comprehended the danger. His recollection returned slowly; but when it did, all his energies burst out. He woke like a person from a trance, dashed aside the fastenings of door and window, and placing me and thy child beneath the temporary shelter of a garden shed, carried out sufficient clothing and bed-coverings to secure us from the cold.

It was a sorry sight—the flames raged with ungovernable violence, and what a few hours before was a sweet and comfortable abode, would shortly be a pile of ashes.

We were, as I told you, in a solitary and remote situation; and though the fire was speedily discovered, a considerable time elapsed before the nearest of our neighbours could succour us. From all parts they flew to assist, and God knows how feelingly they sympathised in our calamity. Vigorously all exerted themselves, and all that was saved was considered a sacred trust. Every house was open, and every rural ark placed at our command; and, had it been accepted, pecuniary relief was ready. From the ruins we saved some valuables and clothing. The cattle, by Harley's desperate efforts were secured; and with two hundred pounds in the banker's and the relics of the fire, we commenced the world anew.

We removed to a small village on the coast; and it was surprising with what resolution Harley bore his misfortunes and submitted to the altered mode of living our reduced means imposed. For six months we exercised the strictest economy; and it was required; for the trifling property saved from the fire was nearly exhausted. It was time that some future mode of obtaining a livelihood was procured, but what course was one like Harley to adopt?—one who from boyhood had enjoyed a competency and been accustomed to the ease and idleness that mark a soldier's life at home. Were he alone, and obliged to seek a new opening into life, the task would be comparatively easy; but unfortunately, his fortunes were linked to mine, and he was burdened with an infant and its mother. Many plans were devised only to be rejected; nothing was yet determined, when fortune did her worst and left us in a moment destitute. The banker in whose hands the remnant of our means was lodged failed, and we were completely beggared.

It is impossible to conceive the misery this unexpected calamity occasioned; and it was rendered still more poignant, by the exertions we both made to conceal from the other the anguish that each suffered in secret. A few weeks dragged heavily on; and I observed that many trifles which I knew Harley prized had gradually disappeared, while the few valuables I possessed were privately disposed of to supply the necessaries of our scanty table. At last all was gone; and it was doubtful where tomorrow's food should be obtained. That night Harley pretended to sleep, although his tortured bosom never owned an interval of forgetfulness; while I felt the exquisite suffering that the destitution of those on whom my very soul centred must naturally cause.

To witness the concealed agony of a brave man is heart rending, and I dared not fix my eyes on his. The morning meal—the last we had the means to procure—was over, and Harley rose to take his customary ramble after breakfast.

"Ellen," he said, as he kissed me with unusual tenderness, "cheer up, all may yet be well. There is a person in the next town from whom I can procure some money, and before evening I shall be back. Promise that in my absence you will not grieve; for to know that *you* are wretched can only make *me* more so."

I tried to smile, and endeavoured to assume the look of happiness, although God knows my heart was well nigh breaking. I was anxious to question him; but, probably to evade what must have been painful explanations, he hastened his departure, and took the road leading to the nearest garrison.

This circumstance partially relieved my apprehensions. There might be some old companion in the regiment quartered in the neighbourhood, and from him Harley would naturally ask a loan. If he succeeded, we might yet escape the dreadful penury that was impending; and as hope is buoyant to the last, I waited confidently for the promised hour of his return.

Evening came, and so did my protector. I flew to him—he caught me to his heart and covered my cheeks with kisses. Pointing to a small basket which he had carried from the town, he desired me to open it. I did so. It contained some excellent provision; and what for many a month had been a stranger to our table—a flask of wine. We sat down to supper. Harley ate little, but drank like a man oppressed with sorrow and striving to forget. I looked at his face—it was pale, dejected, heart-broken. To rouse him I affected an indifference foreign to my heart.

"Come, love," I said, "how well you have succeeded. Surely this should encourage us. Did you find your friend kind? Did he oblige you without hesitation?"

He smiled, poor soul! I never saw anything so ghastly.

"Yes, Ellen; he never demurred one moment. And you shall be the banker; ay, and a more faithful one than the last I trusted."

His unearthly laughter startled me, while he threw some twenty pounds into my lap.

"What a supply! George. Take courage; ere this be gone, you and I will have the means of earning a living honestly."

"Indeed, Ellen!"

"Yes—why should young and devoted hearts despair? The old and cowardly may despond; not you and I, George!"

"Well said. See how soundly our baby sleeps. Was not my supply a welcome one?"

"Oh, yes. But—but—"

"Go on, Ellen."

"Forgive me, Harley. How came it?"

"Honestly; ay, honestly, by Heaven!"

"You borrowed it?"

"No; it is all mine."

"You make me very wretched. Whence came this money?"

He rose and strode across the chamber, pressed his hand across his forehead, and with a gesture of despair, pointed to his hat. I sprang forward and seized it; and a gay cockade, with flaunting ribands, fell upon the floor. The secret was told. Harley had procured food and money by enlisting.

I weary you; details of poverty and distress cannot interest, and I shall rapidly pass over mine. It is enough to say that I followed the fortunes of my protector, and accompanied him to join his regiment. The fear of recognition by any of his former companions annoyed him but by the use of a dye I darkened his features, and altered his appearance so much, that an intimate friend might have passed him in the street. Before summer ended, Harley's military talents were noticed: he became a favourite with his officers, quick promotion succeeded; and in autumn, when our regiment was attached to the expedition of Sir John Moore, the quondam captain of light infantry wore a sergeant's stripes. His military proficiency would have occasioned some suspicion, had he not stated that he had served in the Irish militia—a body from which the smartest soldiers were then supplied to regiments of the line.

In the middle of October we disembarked at Corunna, and after many delays and tedious marches, entered Salamanca. To the disasters of that wretched campaign, you, Major O'Connor, are no stranger. It was indeed a tissue of mistakes—operating with feeble allies—acting on false information—advancing today, retiring tomorrow—with everything to harass, and nothing to excite the soldier—until, at last, the ill-fated and ill-planned expedition terminated in a ruinous retreat.

Harley was attached to the light infantry, and, of course, was generally with the rear guard. Yet I never was from him for a night, and notwithstanding the dreadful weather, with want of food and shelter, my child bore all bravely. By accidents unnecessary to detain you with, I amassed a considerable sum of money; and, as we were retiring towards the sea, I began to hope that on our return to England, an humble competency might again be ours. Alas those whom I loved were never permitted to revisit their fatherland.

After the brilliant cavalry affair at Sahagun, a movement was intended against Soult on the Carrion; but the unwelcome tidings that Napoleon was advancing in person changed the intentions of the English general, and at once determined him to retreat; and on Christmas morning that dreadful scene of misery commenced.

Early next day our sufferings opened with the crossing of the Esla. The river was already rising; and one huge and ill-constructed ferry-boat was the only means by which to pass over a whole division, its baggage, and its camp-followers. The waters were increasing, the rain fell in torrents, the east wind blew with cutting violence, mules kicked, men cursed, and women screamed; all, in short, was noise and disorder. Fortunately a contiguous ford was declared practicable. The infantry, and their equipages passed safely; and before the flood rose so high as to bar their passage, the whole column were safe upon the right bank.

The French pursuit was marked by the fiery character of their emperor. He crossed the Carpentanos regardless of obstacles that would have discouraged the boldest, and in a hurricane of sleet and hail passed his army over the Guadarama, by a route declared impracticable even to a mountain peasant. This bold operation, worthy of the conqueror of Italy, was followed up by an immediate advance. The English hussars were sharply attacked upon the Esla by the cavalry of Lefebvre; but they gallantly repulsed them; and the British, with little molestation, retreated through Astorga, taking the Camino Real; while the enemy, moving by the road of Ponteferrada, arrived on the 1st at Bernbibre. Why repeat to one who witnessed them, scenes in which he shared? Why—but to prove how deeply and indelibly every occurrence of that disastrous campaign is imprinted on my heart.

Regardless of the dreadful inclemency of the weather, I had kept as closely to my protector as the presence of the French advance would permit. The year opened on us bivouacked on a dreary heath, and we spent the night of the 2nd in a miserable hovel. I remarked that, for the first time, Harley appeared dispirited and fatigued. We ate our wretched meal, and crouched into a corner of the hut that was least exposed to the drifting snow, which the crazy edifice everywhere admitted. It was a sorry lodging, and a gloomy night, and the last, too, that Harley and I were fated to pass together in this world!

Morning broke, the column moved, the rear guard followed, and the dreary march was resumed. The French, as usual, were close to us; but as yet they had only worried the patrols with constant alarms, and been contented with picking off any sick men or stragglers who fell behind. The column had just passed Calcabelos, where the two great roads unite, when, encouraged by some appearance of confusion among the piquets, General Colbert suddenly charged with his dragoons, and a sharp affair ensued. The light troops returned to sustain the piquets, and having occupied the vineyards that commanded the roads, opened a shattering fire. The struggle was short but sanguinary, and ended in the repulse of the assailants. Harley, always foremost in a skirmish, involved himself in the hottest combat which took place round the French commander. General Colbert was killed in the *mêlée*, and my protector, shot through the heart, died in the very act of seizing on his prisoner!

They tore me from the body. Never was an humble soldier more beloved and regretted than my protector. Some of his companions assisted me to lay him in a corner of the vineyard; and, to gratify me, they turned a few turfs with their bayonets, and gave him, at least, the semblance of a grave.

I knew not how I got on afterwards for some days. Harley had hitherto supported my fainting courage, and, while he lived, I did not yield to despair. He was gone, and hope and courage seemed buried in his grave. Still my child remained, and nature prompted me to exert myself for him. For his sake, I did endeavour to escape the horrors of being deserted—and I urged forward the weary mule, on which all our chances of deliverance rested.

Three days of horrible fatigue and hunger were endured. On the fourth, a supply of flour was accidentally obtained, and the lives of my baby and myself preserved. A few hours and our fate would be decided. Preparations for a battle were being made, for Sir John Moore had determined to retreat no further.

Notwithstanding the British were suffering from cold, and wet, and hunger, they fell into position with alacrity. The Minho protected their right, and a ravine separated them from the French, who already in force occupied the heights, and were evidently preparing for an immediate and determined effort. It was made and defeated. Though the enemy attacked furiously, the bayonets of the light companies bore back their daring assailants, and they were repelled from the position with slaughter. Darkness came on—a wild and stormy night, a bare hill, no fire, no food, such was the bivouac of Lugo—such the wretched and cheerless situation of the harassed but unconquerable islanders!

As the morning of the 8th dawned, the British formed line, and prepared coolly for the expected encounter; but it passed over, and the enemy made no hostile movement. The troops were ordered to bivouac as they best could, and, in a short time, a number of rude huts were erected to defend them from the inclemency of the coming night.

But it was not intended to remain longer before Lugo. When darkness hid their retreat, the British filed off silently by the rear. Through a frightful storm of hail and wind, their march was bravely executed—and leaving Lugo and Valmela behind them, they halted at Betanzos on the 10th.

Of my own sufferings it is useless to speak. My escapes from captivity were numerous. Of one you will need no information, for the bridge of Cartoza cannot be forgotten. Let me pause a little, ere I hurry to detail the last calamity that to dwell on would distract a brain, even scathed and callous as my own. Ay! well may I execrate that luckless expedition, for endless misery that fatal campaign wrought me!

The halt at Betanzos afforded us a momentary respite from suffering, and hope dawned in many a bosom once more. The hardships of the retreat were almost ended—the sea was near—the fleet were hourly expected. The weather suddenly cleared up, and, as if to omen better things, the sun again shone brilliantly. It was strange to observe the magical effect which all this produced; battalions, yesterday scattered and disheartened, rallied round their colours; the army, during the last days of the retreat, at times frightfully insubordinate and disorganised into a mighty wreck, once more resumed its discipline; and the appearance of the brigades, as they defiled in column along the Corunna road, was worthy of that gallant army, which, full of life, and hope, and bravery, had three months since debarked, little suspecting how brief and disastrous the campaign would be.

The following nights were passed in comparative tranquillity. I slept in the village of Pallavio; and though my accommodations were most wretched, the amended state of the weather and a feeling that I was secure, made me rest soundly as one left alone in the world could hope to do. My boy, whose fading cheek gave silent but certain indications that his feeble strength was unequal to the privations and fatigue he had encountered, appeared to rally unexpectedly; and it was now scarcely doubtful but he would survive and revisit his fatherland. That morning I had obtained food of a better description than we had for some time seen, and I prepared a comfortable meal. When it was ready, I hesitated almost to awake my baby, his sleep seemed so deep and so refreshing. I looked at his sweet countenance as he lay slumbering on his father's cloak. How like the lost one in every lineament! I gazed until my heart softened, and a flood of tears relieved the sullen agony I had hitherto sustained;—love for the living and sorrow for the dead melted my withered spirit, and again I became a woman.

I set out with some other stragglers for Corunna. As usual, I fixed my infant in a pannier on the mule, and the valuables I had saved with such difficulty were deposited in the other basket. A sum of money, in English gold, I had concealed effectually on my person. It was a lovely morning for the season of the year; the sky of summer-blue was cloudless; my heart felt as if it had lost a portion of its weight, and as I urged the mule on, I occupied my thoughts in devising plans for the future settlement of my boy and myself when we should have landed safely in England. I looked into the pannier—the child was sleeping, and in sleep how like his gallant father! The sun beamed on his eyes—I stooped to arrange the coverings of the basket. Suddenly the ground rocked—a dense mass of black ashes rose to the sky from the heights behind, and with a tremendous crash, as if occasioned by the ruin of a world, the air was darkened—the earth shook—more I know not. I was struck down upon my face, and lay where I fell in a state of total insensibility, how long I cannot guess.

I woke as from a dream—it was already twilight—two dead soldiers were stretched at my side, and I could not for a considerable time remember where I was. With restored memory, my first care was to find my child. Where was he?—the mule—the boy? Oh God! gone—gone! lost—irrecoverably lost!

I wandered in a state of madness, but chance directed me to the right path. Day and night I roamed through herds of camp followers—but no tidings of the lost one. On came the French—the fleet entered the bay—the attack ensued, and Moore, like Nelson, fell in victory. Of all these occurrences I know nothing; for while the contest was raging before Corunna, I was rambling like a maniac over the contiguous country, seeking that darling object, before whom the riches of the earth were but as dross.

How I escaped death, captivity, and insult, I cannot even conjecture. I remember fainting on the beach, and when I recovered, found myself with many a widowed female less wretched, crowded in a transport; and the harbour of Corunna fading from my sight in the haze of a winter evening. I learned afterwards that my escape was purely accidental. A drunken comrade of poor Harley recognised me where I lay, and flung me into a boat; and without any exertion of my own, I was saved, while hundreds were abandoned.

Just then, O'Connor's pretty guide entered the copse and the gipsy rose and met her. A few whispered sentences conveyed the intelligence she brought; the girl immediately retired, and Ellen rejoined the soldier.

"We are likely to be interrupted;" she said, "and I fear my wretched memoir must remain, for the present, unfinished. Has it interest enough to tempt you to the churchyard at midnight? You march tomorrow and I should wish to bid you farewell."

O'Connor was deeply attentive while the gipsy told her harrowing adventures. He made a feeble effort at hilarity, and with a forced smile accepted her invitation to another interview.

"Farewell, Ellen. At midnight we meet again."

She pointed out the road to the village, joined the young gipsy who waited for her at a short distance, and gliding into the thicket, left the soldier once more alone.

O'Connor turned his footsteps towards the village, pondering, as he crossed the forest, on the late eventful occurrences in his own life; and marvelling at the strange vicissitudes that had attended the stormy career of his wild and singular acquaintance.

VIII

THE MESS-TABLE

Prince Henry.   We must all to the wars.
First Part, Henry IV

Falstaff.   Now comes in the sweetest morsel of the night.
Ibid.

WHEN O'CONNOR RETURNED TO THE Greyhound he found his companions sitting at their wine. Phillips was not there; his absence was a relief; and though little inclined to share the revelry of the mess-table, still, to prevent his unusual absence from dinner being remarked, and while the tedious hours away that must intervene before his appointed interview in the churchyard, he entered the room, and took his customary place. The senior captain, a countryman of his own, presided; and judging from the joviality of the merry group that surrounded him, O'Brien had circulated the bottle gallantly.

Unlike Phillips, the worthy president was in wild excitement at the certainty of a move to the Peninsula; and the sparkling eyes and cheerful countenances of all around told that there was no heart there that did not beat with a soldier's ardour, hailing the arrival of the moment when they should meet a brave and chivalrous foe. O'Connor, with a leader's pride, remarked this martial enthusiasm. With one or two exceptions, all these had just entered on their military careers, with the buoyancy of hope which warms the young adventurer, when he first bursts upon the world and sees nothing in his path but success. O'Brien was an old and trusty companion of Major O'Connor; and though several years older than his friend, was junior to him in rank, and secondary far in military reputation; for he had neither equal talents, nor, had he possessed them, that opportunity for their display, which had fallen to his more fortunate countryman. But O'Brien was a brave and single-hearted soldier. He had not a particle of envy in his heart; he loved the major with honest affection; he looked at his well-earned fame with national pride and while he despised Phillips in his soul, O'Connor, according to his estimation, was the beau ideal of what a soldier should be. The appearance of the gallant captain was every inch Milesian. He was a tall, muscular, jovial-looking fellow; one, as he expressed it himself, who "took all as the Lord sent it, and did not care a brass button for what the morrow brought." Shrewd, witty, and sarcastic, he seized on the ridiculous at once. Ardent in his likings and antipathies, he was indifferent in expressing his opinions of men and things, so far as regarded consequences. Vain of his country to absurdity, he adopted a phraseology and mannerism so peculiar, as to entirely prohibit any possibility of mistake touching his being a native of the emerald island.

"I am glad to see you," was his address to the major on his entrance. "I feared that you were going to leave us to find our own way to the Douro. We have lost Phillips, I hear. We have lost a nice man certainly, and the dragoons have got one. Well, the Lord's will be done; and if he was twice as valuable, they are welcome to him; for he was only thrown away on us. Fill your glass, Tom, and let's hear of our acquaintances who else has hopped the twig."

The young ensign, it appeared, had been reading the monthly obituary from the last army list, that had been just received, when O'Connor's entrance interrupted him, and he resumed his task.

"Augustus Koffman, King's German Legion—Thomas Jones, 4th Garrison Battalion—Peter Fogarty, half-pay Irish Militia."

The president struck the table with his broad hand, and exclaimed with strong emotion,—

"Holy Saint Patrick! and has honest Peter gone to look after his patients at last?"

"Did you know him, Pat?" inquired Lieutenant Perceval.

"Know him?" responded Captain O'Brien—"Ah! God rest ye, Peter; you were my first counsellor when I left college for my present Christian-like profession. You're gone; and a better cribbage-player never pegged a game, nor fairer drinker stretched calf-skin below mahogany."

"Was he clever in his profession?" inquired the assistant-surgeon, in broad Scotch.

"Clever? Oh, it's he that was. I never knew one of your calling that could hold a candle to Peter Fogarty."

"He made wonderful cures, I suppose?" said Sandy Anderson.

"Cures!" exclaimed Captain O'Brien: "I have known him remove a complicated disease of head, heart, and stomach, without drug or draught, but a teaspoonful of tooth-powder."

"Indeed!" said the major, smiling—"Why Sandy himself could not pretend to match Mr Fogarty."

"Hoot, man, that's not to be believed!"

"It is true, however, Sandy," replied the captain. "George, order a grilled bone, and during the broiling I'll tell you the story. Heigh-ho! how fast time flies. Then was I like a young bear, with troubles all before me. Come, boys, fill to the memory of poor Peter; and though I must necessarily record some portion of my own history and virtues, if modesty does not choke me, I'll give you the detail."

The president was obeyed, a full and solemn bumper was drunk to the honour of the departed doctor, and Captain O'Brien thus proceeded.

IX

THE CAPTAIN'S STORY

If I had a thousand sons, the first human principle I would teach them, should be—to forswear thin potations, and addict themselves to sack.

Second Part, Henry IV

Doctor. The heart is sorely charged.
Gent. I would not have such a heart in my bosom, for the dignity of the whole body.
Doctor. Well—well—well.
Gent. Pray God it be, sir.
Doctor. This disease is beyond my practice.

Macbeth

AH! GOD BE WITH YOU, old Trinity. Green is your memory, and fondly do I recall the merry days and jovial nights I passed within your honoured precincts. You were then a seat of learning fit for a prince, and, take you all in all, a pattern for colleges at large. In many a stiff hurling and heavy drink have I shared with as true Corinthians as ever slept upon the guard-bed of a watch-house, or tossed a bailiff in a blanket. Companions of my youth—where are they now? Stretched beneath the sward of some half-forgotten field, or gone to their account by the certain, though less sudden, maladies, to which the flesh is heir.

My father was true Milesian. He had a long pedigree and a light purse, for hounds and horses were "the spoil" of him. He lived as a gentleman should live; and died after a grand-jury dinner, drinking Baron Botherem to a stand-still, although the worthy justice could carry off his fourth bottle, and sentence a malefactor next morning, as steadily as a Christian judge should do.

Two sons blest my father's bed, of whom the younger was my unworthy self. We were both destined for professions, and Father Prendergast was our preceptor. Tom, as my brother was named, progressed marvellously in learning—while I, alas! was but a sorry disciple, although the honest churchman followed Solomon's directions to the letter; and whatever timber might be wanting at Killbrannagher, upon my conscience, there was no scarcity of birch. Notwithstanding unfavourable reports, my father fancied I had talents, and it was his pleasure to destine me for the bar. The bar, Michael Prendergast opined I would in good time reach, and that, too, by a less expensive road than the one proposed by my sire—concluding his observations with, "Never mind; push him, the devil, into college anyhow. Bigger boobies have cut a figure there before now."

Well! the point was carried; Tom and I entered the university, and we were consigned to the care of Dr Blundell, as dry a professor as ever produced a thesis. Our Gamaliel was a short, stout, bullet-headed dwarf, his face so fat, and cheeks so flaccid, that, *en profile*, no nose was visible; and it was necessary for him to give, at least, "a quarter front," before the organ of smell could be discovered. His figure was in good keeping; the body resembled a porter-butt on a reduced scale, and was mounted on two thick props, whose extreme curvature obtained for the professor the *sobriquet* of "parenthesis." Such was the learned Theban to whom the hopes of the O'Briens were entrusted.

Tom, from the very start, promised to be a genius of the first order; while my career, I lament to say, was rather bustling than brilliant. Indeed, Doctor Blundell declared we were, in every respect, opposite as the antipodes. I never could comprehend the beauty of a "sorites"— mathematics were altogether beyond my reach—astronomy, in my opinion, only fitted for a fortune teller—while as to mechanic powers, the only one I ever meddled with was the screw, or an occasional exercise of the lever on the person of a dun or watchman.

Indeed the honest professor's estimate of character was correct, for no brothers were ever more dissimilar: Tom would lose his rest to prove that crab-apples did not grow upon a cherry-tree, and fret himself into a fever to discover the parallax of a star. No wonder he was a first-class premium-man, and bore college "honours thick upon him." Yet there were people in the world who considered him little better than a fool—forgetting that to be a philosopher a man must be dirty and eccentric. Certainly Tom had been frequently encountered in the streets with a consequential garment missing; and he puzzled a country postmaster by requiring letters after forgetting his own name. As to his meals, they were at times totally forgotten; and in his annual migrations to and from the university, he was usually consigned to the custody of a fellow-traveller, or handed with a half-crown to the guard, and a request that he should be delivered as addressed.

It was fortunate that Tom's virtues and acquirements acted as a set-off against my delinquency. Yet my career was not unnoticed, and I contrived to obtain the marked attention of my superiors. More than once I was admitted to a conference with the board; and on account, I suppose, of the insalubrity of the city, was recommended by those worthy personages country air for a term of six months; and that too so pressingly, that no demurrer on my part would be listened to.

Three years passed over, when one evening, returning from a tavern dinner, a row was kicked up at the gate, and a desperate assault and battery ensued. A stupid citizen knocked his head against a blackthorn stick, and the accident was so awkward as to occasion a fracture of the occiput, and give the coroner the trouble of empanelling a jury, to inquire into the cause of the same. The affair occasioned a sensation, and a score of us unfortunates were summoned before the board. As the defunct was unhappily a common-councilman, the authorities were loud in their denunciations. The newspapers called us Mohawks and murderers: some said we should be hanged, while others more mercifully declared that the punishment should be mitigated to transportation. In this dilemma,

Doctor Blundell, when transmitting the quarter note, apprised my father of the occurrence, "assured him that all hope of my ever doing good was desperate; and, to evade the gallows, which he proved to a demonstration must be my end, he recommended that I should be permitted to follow my own bent, and enter the cut-throat profession, for which it was *a sequitur* that nature had intended me."

Next post a letter from my father was received, he "concurred with the learned professor; affectionately informed me that I was at liberty to go to the devil as I pleased; sent me some money, and intimated that he had applied for a commission in the militia." This was as it should be. His application was successful; and in a few days I was one of the fraternity of the sword, and duly gazetted to the —— regiment.

The corps I was attached to was at that time encamped at Leighlinstown, four or five miles from the capital; and, as in duty bound, I set out next morning to visit my commanding officer in proper form.

My father had an old acquaintance in the corps, to whose protection I was, by letter, regularly committed. Of course it was to him that I applied for an introduction to Colonel Mahony. I was graciously received by my patron, presented in due form to the commander, and until I could obtain accommodations, hospitably invited, *pro tem.*, to take up my quarters in a corner of the hovel, which Peter Fogarty, as my patron was called, had constructed for his abiding-place while remaining in the field.

Peter was a singular personage—a strange, shrewd sort of oddity, and, in his own way, an excellent fellow. He had been bred an apothecary, married a woman who ran away, failed in business, found favour in the colonel's sight, and through his interest, when the militia was embodied, obtained the surgeoncy of the regiment to which I had been just gazetted.

Peter Fogarty's outward man was not remarkably attractive. He was short and corpulent, with a bull-neck and square shoulders, a small and twinkling grey eye, and a nose snubbed and efflorescent, as the nose of a man delighting in whisky punch should be. Peter was fond of a race or cock-fight, would go twenty miles to be present at a duel, loved a rubber of whist dearly; but cribbage was his delight, cribbage was the road to his affections, and I soon discovered it.

I mentioned that my regiment was under canvass when I joined, and formed a part of some six or seven thousand men, who, pending the explosion of "ninety-eight," were encamped in the vicinity of the metropolis. The officers were generally provided with tents, but some of them had erected temporary habitations, and among the number were Colonel Mahony and his medical adviser. Indeed it was absolutely necessary that Peter's domicile should be contiguous to the commander's. From conjugal regard, the lady had accompanied the colonel to the field, although her health was but indifferent; and the extreme delicacy of her constitution rendered the frequent attendance of Doctor Fogarty indispensable.

Peter's habitation was a wooden hut: one end, screened from vulgar gaze by an old blanket, formed his dormitory, while the other corner was curtained off for me. The centre was used for all the purposes of the body politic. There our *déjeûné* was laid; there, if a sick officer applied, the prescription was written; there when dinner ended and we left the mess-tent, on a small deal table the cribbage board was found—and, better still, an abundant supply of the *matériel* for fabricating that pleasant beverage, which Peter averred to be both safe and wholesome, to wit—whisky punch—was duly paraded for our refreshment.

As the world went, Peter Fogarty should have been a happy man. His means were equal to his expenditure, his wife had run away, and his professional cares were trifling. "The villains," as he termed his "charge of foot," were healthy; their principal infirmity being corns— a disease to which they were obnoxious, from a majority of the corps, prior to their enlistment, having considered shoes a superfluity. Yet Peter had his own troubles; for below, as schoolmen declare, there is no happiness without alloy. Woman, that source of evil, was his bane; and, as in the fulness of his heart he would acknowledge after his sixth tumbler—"but for Mrs Mahony, he would be as happy as the day was long."

Mrs Mahony had been for many years a wife, but, unhappily, as yet had never been made a mother. The colonel was anxious for an heir. Hopes were frequently excited, and they were as often deferred, until the heart was sick. Yet why should Mrs Mahony despond! her grandmother had a son at fifty-two; she was but forty-seven, and why should she despair?

All this, however, was ruinous to the peace of Doctor Fogarty. The least alarm in the day, the slightest movement after night, agitated his interesting patient. Ether had often failed; and even a teaspoonful of brandy at times would hardly prove a sedative. These unfortunate attacks generally took place at an advanced period of the evening, and of course Peter was required. Then the ill-starred practitioner was invariably at whist or cribbage—the colonel's bat-man, a foster-brother of the lady, would be despatched to our wooden habitation, and, with nine scored, and the odd trick actually in his hand, the unhappy doctor has been obliged to abandon his own fortunes, for the desperate chance of endeavouring to continue the ancient lineage of the Mahonys.

Had success crowned his efforts, Peter was not the man to repine. In the triumph of his art, his toils and labours would have found their reward. But, alas! matters daily became more unpromising; and, like the wolf-cry, Mrs Mahony's ceased to interest or alarm. Peter Fogarty, though a good Catholic, was nearly driven to desperation—and before he cut his first honour, he usually prayed from the bottom of his soul for Mrs Mahony's repose temporal and eternal, and the sooner her beatitude was completed, he as a Christian man opined would be all the better.

It was for the season a dark and blusterous night. More than one tent-pole had given way—pegs and cords were tried and found wanting; and in the joy of his heart my host congratulated himself and me on the stability of our wooden dwelling. The last batch of whisky was inimitable; and so said the doctor, after submitting the liquor to a fair test of six tumblers. The cards were decidedly in his favour—fortune smiled upon him every cut—and since the night his wife had bolted, he never had been so happy. It was just ten—the deal was mine—but Peter's cards were beautiful. Suddenly a hurried foot approached the door. Peter remarked it.—"It's the lobsters after all—I knew the devil would not fail me." Knock—knock—"Come in." It was not the lobsters, but Murty Currigan, the colonel's bat-man. The doctor looked dark as Erebus,—the bat-man as if he had been running for his life. The former coughed to conceal vexation. "Ha, ha—hum;—anything wrong?"

"Wrong? You may say that—the mistress is dying," responded Murty.

"Dying?—What the devil would make her die?" said the doctor.

"Sorra one o' me knows," returned the bat-man. Now Murty Currigan being deaf, save when Peter Fogarty elevated his voice to an extraordinary pitch, his remarks touching the diagnostics of his mistress's disease were lost upon the deaf bat-man.

"What 's the matter with her now?"

"It's a kind of pain about her heart."

"Pish!" said the doctor testily—"that's a Connaught symptom for a sprained ankle. Anything else?"

"Her head's dizzy; and she's at times astray," replied the lady's foster-brother.

"Humph! so should mine be after a pint of brandy."

"She's as wake as a cat," quoth the envoy. "She can't move without help."

"Seldom people can when they're regularly smothered" said the leech.

"She has a sort of a twisting in her stomach," added the fosterer.

The doctor's patience gave way. "Silence, you idiot! Would you give her as many ailments as would kill a priest? Off with ye, Murty. Tell them to keep her quiet, and come back in half an hour, and tell me how she is." The bat-man vanished. "She'll be fast asleep then, and we'll not be troubled with her capers. Come—I lead. Fifteen two—fifteen four—a pair make six—and a pair make eight;" and on he went with the jargon of the game.

Now, though the honest doctor counted with some confidence on sleep, that "sweet mediciner," abating the complicated diseases with which Mrs Mahony was afflicted, still he had sore misgiving to disturb him, and these could occasionally be detected, from his confused allusions to the patient and the game.

"Stop, Pat; let me cut. I couldn't have made more of that hand, unless we played the double flush. Your father and I always flushed. Jasus! I wonder what's come over the woman! Every night smothered; and then me tattered out, wet or dry. Asy, Pat—you're pegging too fast; let me see what I have got. Lord! if it was once or twice a week— but every night nothing but "Run for Doctor Fogarty!" I wish she was safe in heaven, or in the county Clare, for my heart's fairly broke. Shuffle them, man—I cut. Give me the bottle; devil a drop of spirits I put in my tumbler, that woman, bad luck to her, bothered me so."

All this time I observed that no preparatory steps were taken for the composition of the healing draught, for which the fosterer had been directed to return; and I hinted, that as the hospital tent was at some distance, the sooner Peter started for his "galenicals" the better. My remark appeared to astonish the worthy man, for he laid down his cards, and looked at me with a broad stare.

"The hospital tent! Is it to go a long half-mile, and a storm raging that would blow the buttons off my jacket? Arrah, what a simpleton ye take me for, Pat! And yet, blessed Virgin! if Murty comes again, what am I to do with him? Was there ever a dacent practitioner so teased by an ould besom as myself, Peter Fogarty? If I had but some simple for her. Oh, murder! not a squig of physic in the house, unless you have it."

I shook my head.

"Death an nouns! have ye nothing—salts, senna, cinnamon— rhubarb, scamony, magnesia?"

I nodded a negative.

"Have you no neglected draught; nothing in the shape of powder?"

"Nothing," I replied, "but tooth-powder."

"Phew!" and Peter whistled—"Beautiful! and by the best of luck I have a bottle."

Up he rose, bolted for a moment behind the blanket, and speedily re-appeared with a small phial. In it he deposited a spoonful of my dentifrice, filled it from the kettle, and shook it, as he said, "Secundum artem." The infusion produced a liquid of bright pink, with an aromatic odour; and Peter having submitted the mixture to the double test of taste and smell, was loud in his admiration.

"Beautiful!"—he exclaimed. "I have spent a winter's morning over the mortar, and not produced a more palatable anodyne.—Don't cut yet—I'll just label the bottle, and then for the flats." Accordingly, he inscribed upon a slip of paper, the following directions for the use of his new-invented julep, and affixed them carefully to the potion: *"A teaspoonful of the mixture to be taken every half-hour until the patient is relieved—shaking the bottle.—For Mrs Mahony."*

It was fortunate for Peter that his nostrum was in readiness. Before he had dealt a second hand, a loud tap at the door announced the return of the fosterer—and bad as Murty's first report was, his second bulletin was infinitely more alarming.

"Well—is she better?"

"Better?" repeated the fosterer with a wild stare.

"Ay—better!" returned the physician in a tone of voice that mimicked Murty's like an echo.

"Arrah! she never was bad till now." Said the fosterer. "Ye can't tell a word she says, good or bad, and she wouldn't know her own maid from the black drummer."

"Ah! regularly sewed up. Here," and he handed him the bottle, "mind the directions; can ye read?"

"If I can't, sure Biddy Toole can."

"Away with ye then, every moment you lose may be fatal; bathe her feet and shake the bottle, and be sure ye tell me how she is—early in the morning."

"Anything else, doctor?"

"Nothing—only don't let her get cold, if ye can help it, and now run, ye devil!"

Murty made his salaam and vanished; and soon after, Peter and I retired to our respective cribs.

Betimes next morning, the bothered bat-man reported that his lady was convalescent; and after breakfast, the doctor departed to his hospital, and I to attend a garrison parade.

On my return, as captain of the day, it was necessary for me to call upon my commanding officer, and accordingly I repaired to the wooden erection, in which Colonel Mahony had deposited his household gods. After being paraded through a sort of anteroom, I found the commander inditing an epistle upon a three-legged table, before a port-hole which it was his pleasure to call a window, while divers cloths and coverlets were suspended from a line stretched across the apartment, and excluded from the gaze of vulgar eyes "the lady of his love." The commander having duly apologised for detaining me a few minutes while he concluded his letter, pointed to a camp stool—and I seated myself and took up the *Evening Post*. But the newspaper was unheeded—voices behind the curtain told that there were others in the chamber of state—and in the speakers I easily recognised Peter and his patient, Mrs Mahony, while a feeble piano in a flat key thus continued:

"Yes, doctor, I will ever acknowledge that, under Providence, I owe my life to you. The first spoonful gave relief, and the second acted like a charm."

"Indeed! Ha!—hem! hem! Allow me: pulse full—a *leetle* feverish—must keep very quiet."

"But, dear Mr Fogarty, I must, you say, be very careful to avoid cold. No doubt the medicine I took last night with such happy effect was very powerful?"

"Most powerful, madam," replied the leech with unblushing effrontery. "The arcana of pharmaceutics could not afford a more effective combination."

"God bless me!" ejaculated the lady—"but for it, I should have been dead—"

"As Julius Caesar, madam," responded the doctor, with a solemn cough.

"I have been reflecting on your advice, doctor. These constant alarms are too much for my nervous sensibility. Would you believe it, ether and a dessert-spoonful of brandy had no effect upon me last night?"

"Indeed!—Hem!—hem!"

"Ay—doctor—you may well shake your head. I would not fret the poor dear colonel; but—"

"I know your feelings, and they do honour to your heart, madam."

"Well, as I was saying, doctor, to leave Colonel Mahony—"

"Madam," returned the false physician, "I can appreciate the strength of your attachment; but there are other and important considerations"—and Peter dropped his voice to a half-whisper, that prevented me from hearing anything beyond detached words. "Delicate situation—hopes of an honourable house—colonels partiality for children—native air—happy result—bark and sea-bathing." And before the commander had finished his despatch the villain Peter, under false hopes, had persuaded the colonel's helpmate to bundle off to Clare, "by easy stages." Whether she carried a bottle of the pink tincture in the carriage, I forget; but, I presume, that she would hardly, when there was balm in Gilead, depart without an extensive supply.

Time passed—and four years after I had left the militia, and volunteered to the line, I had occasion to run up to London, and there encountered my old commander in the Strand. He was a friendly little fellow, and expressed great pleasure at our meeting. I remarked that he was habited in deep mourning; and when I inquired for Mrs Mahony, he sighed heavily, shook his head, and informed me that he had buried her a month before in Cheltenham.

"Ah! my dear O'Brien. It was a black day when I was persuaded to leave home. Fogarty was the only man that understood poor dear Mrs Mahony's constitution. You may remember when we lay in Leighlinstown camp, the desperate attack she had. You and Peter were hutted together at the time." I nodded an affirmative. "Just such another fit carried her off at Cheltenham. Had Peter Fogarty been near us, I should not now be a disconsolate widower as I am, for Biddy Mahony would have been alive."

"We dined together at the Blue Posts in Cork Street. "Sorrow is dry," and the commander was in trouble. At twelve I conveyed him to his lodgings in a hackney-coach; and on our way home, as well as I could understand him—for there was "a ripple" in his delivery—he did nothing but lament, in poor dear Mrs Mahony's last attack, the absence of Peter and his "pink tincture."

X

THE GIPSY'S STORY CONTINUED

Hark! to the hurried question of despair?
"Where is my child?"—an echo answers—"Where?"
Bride of Abydos

Macbeth.   Is he despatched?
Murderer.   My lord, his throat is cut, that I did for him.
SHAKESPEARE

THE NIGHT WORE ON; AND in the merry group who occupied the parlour of the Greyhound there was but one heavy heart, and that was the commander's. For him there was no flavour in the wine, no point in the repartee that "set the table in a roar," and he waited impatiently for the hour of meeting in the churchyard, to listen to a narrative of suffering far more congenial to his present mood than the reckless gaiety of the young spirits who surrounded him. Before midnight he stole from his companions unobserved, and reached the trysting unnoticed. Ellen was not yet come; but ere the first quarter chimed, a figure glided round a buttress of the dark building, and the gipsy joined him under the appointed lime-tree.

"True to your engagement, Ellen," said the soldier; "but is not this a dull place to select for midnight assignations?"

"Ay, and for the confession of a deed of blood!" said the gipsy, in a low tone of voice. "To me there is something associated with this lonely cemetery that is sacred. Here, the ashes of the being whom I most loved are reposing—for in a remote corner of this burial-ground my mother was interred—and I take a melancholy pleasure in visiting her grave when the coward fears of the villagers leave the domain of the dead all mine own. Were there aught to fear from the departed, you and I should hesitate to venture on their dwelling, for both of us have blood upon our souls."

"Yes, Ellen; but if blood has been unhappily shed by me, it was spilt in fair and honourable warfare."

"Ay, ay, there lies the fanciful distinction. Your homicides were legalised by the pleasure of some half dozen sanguinary despots. You smote the brave; I only sped the felon. But to my tale; and it shall be a brief one:—

"The remnant of the ill-fated expedition sailed for the shores of Britain. What proportion returned I know not; but were it ascertained how many perished in the field, died of fatigue, or were transferred to a French prison, the casualties of that gallant army must have been enormous. Many an afflicted family sorrowed for that disastrous campaign; many a wife and mother were 'left lamenting'—but where had any been so unmercifully visited as myself? I left my native land, the beloved one of a brave man. My boy—the loveliest that ever gladdened the heart of a doting mother! The brave was sleeping on the field he died on. The boy—oh, God! where was he? My brain burns when I ponder on his unknown fate. Was he dead? and did the child of my heart heave his last sigh on any pillow but his mother's bosom? Was he living—and if alive—what? The thought was horrible—the menial of a foreigner—the drudge of some bloated monk—the serf of a Spanish peasant—a slave!—

'Nay, the bondsman of a slave.'

God! what is death to such miserable uncertainty? What the freedom of a disembodied spirit to the grovelling existence of a bondsman's thrall?

"I landed, a lone and spirit-broken wretch. Whither to direct my steps I knew not—whither I cared not; the world was all before me, and that world had not an object that could interest me now. If ever there was a withered heart, surely it was one like mine—one, on whom misery had wrought its worst—one, to whom pain and pleasure were but names.

"I procured an humble lodging, and there for several days brooded in gloomy solitude over my destitution. Gradually, however, my sorrow calmed down; and when I could think with some composure on my future mode of life, I determined to return to the vicarage, throw myself again upon Mr Howard's pity, and, if he permitted it, wear out my few and evil days under the roof of my excellent protector.

"When I disembarked I had little clothing left beyond the dress I wore, and it was necessary to procure a supply. Accordingly, on the fourth evening, I left my lodgings for the first time to purchase a decent outfit. The streets were crowded with drunken soldiers, who, availing themselves of the temporary licence granted to their recent sufferings, with the proverbial recklessness of men 'escaped from the slaughter,' forgot in coarse debauchery their past hardships and lost companions. I was frequently accosted by these wanderers as I passed along; but having succeeded in providing the articles I required, I turned my footsteps homeward. One person, an old Jew, had crossed me more than once. In the shops that I entered he, too, appeared to have business to transact; and if he did not follow me in, I was certain to find him lounging near the door. Yet this was not very remarkable. Multitudes of Israelites had flocked to Portsmouth, in expectation of buying up the plunder of the campaign; or obtaining, for worthless considerations, from the unwary, the arrears of pay which had been given them on their landing.

"At the door of the lodging-house there was a temporary delay when I knocked. I stood beneath a lamp that was suspended directly above me, and, throwing aside the mantle I had hitherto wrapped closely over my face, looked carelessly around. Immediately before me the Jew was standing. The lane was narrow; he was in shade, I in the full glare of lamplight. More than the mere outline of his figure could not be discerned, while my features were distinctly revealed to his observation. I heard a foot descend the stairs, the door opened, and I turned in. 'It is herself, by Heaven!' ejaculated a low and hollow voice. I stopped, and looked quickly round—the speaker was gone, a shadow on the opposite wall floated past, and the lane was to all appearance without a living being but myself.

"This last occurrence was alarming; it was quite unaccountable why the old Jew should follow, and, to judge from his exclamation, recognise me as he did. I felt a secret misgiving, and determined to hasten my departure. On inquiry, I learned that every conveyance was engaged by sick and wounded officers, hastening to revisit their respective homes. But to stay longer in Portsmouth I considered dangerous; and I resolved to proceed next morning, and beg an asylum from the worthy man whose house I had once so unceremoniously abandoned. I made up my small wardrobe in a bundle, secured my money carefully, bade my hostess farewell, and at sunrise had cleared the streets of Portsmouth and taken the road to the still-loved village that contained the ashes of my mother.

"For two days I journeyed prosperously; nothing of any moment occurred. All day I kept the road; and at night rested in some hamlet or farm-house. I thought it safer to avoid the towns; and although I had nothing whose loss I regarded now, my courage was sunken and my once proud spirit gone. I dreaded some nameless calamity—I feared I could not tell what—life to me was valueless, and yet there was a coward sinking of the heart, that even when rich in worldly happiness I had never felt before. No wonder that in this depressed and nervous temperament I looked suspiciously at objects, which under other feelings I should have passed by without remark; and when on the second evening of my journey, a tax-cart of peculiar colour, driven by a man wrapped closely in a huge riding-coat, passed me as it had done on the preceding evening, I took alarm at the singular precision with which the stranger adapted his movements to mine, and only felt at ease when I reached the termination of my wayfaring, and rested at the village alehouse for the night.

"Two days more and my labours would be ended, and, as I hoped, a quiet asylum gained. I rose early, and resumed my journey with more alacrity than I had hitherto exhibited; miles were accomplished; and though fatigued by unusual exertion, I persevered and still pressed forward. Evening found me on the verge of a large and dreary moor, and I half determined to turn back and rest for the night in the last hamlet I had passed, and not attempt traversing what, in the haze of evening, appeared a boundless wilderness. But to retrograde some distance would only leave more to be achieved tomorrow; and summoning resolution, I resolved, at all hazards, to cross the waste, and rest in the village beyond it. I was alone—the path was wild and solitary—what then? my sex would protect me from all but the most profligate; and in a humble pedestrian like me, the robber would find nothing to excite his cupidity.

"I walked briskly on, and, anxious to reach my resting-place, redoubled exertions which fatigue had before abated. More than a mile of the lonely waste was passed, and nothing had occurred to alarm me; for I had seen but one straggling wood-cutter, and not a human habitation was visible. It was fortunately a bright night, for the moon was nearly full. Still I struggled onward, cheered by the thought that every step brought me nearer to a place of safety.

"The road—if a passage over moorland, marked on the barren sward by the wheel-tracks of the few vehicles that traversed it; could be so termed—was intersected by another. Three paths lay before me, and which of them should I select? There was a shattered finger-post at the union of these roads, but time and weather had so far obliterated its directions, that by the waning moonlight it was quite impossible to glean any information wherewith to remove my uncertainty. After a momentary pause I took the path before me. As I proceeded, it gradually inclined to the left, and the wheel-tracks became fainter and less frequent. Had I wandered from the right road? I stopped and hesitated. What was to be done? I would have given half the gold I possessed to anyone who would have relieved me from this embarrassing perplexity—but there was no alternative. I must proceed; and with a heavy heart I sighed and walked on.

"A sudden descent, caused by a dipping of the surface, shut out the view of the ground I had just traversed, and there appeared to be a path directly across the ravine which foot-passengers pursued, while carriages were obliged to take a leveller but more circuitous direction. Of course I selected the shorter route—descended to the hollow, climbed the opposite ridge, and again emerged upon the heath. Scarcely had I regained the broader path when a noise caused me to look round, and immediately behind I perceived a vehicle advancing rapidly. It approached and I stopped, hoping that I should gain some information from the traveller. Heavens! it was the same tax-cart—the same driver—that for days had hung upon my footsteps, constant as an avenging spirit! I stood like one spell bound—I could not articulate a word. The stranger swept quickly by—murmured a hoarse "Good night," and in another minute disappeared behind a patch of copsewood.

"I remained rooted to the spot—my brain half crazed with terror. Should I retrace my steps? If I did, was it probable that I should recover the right path, and be able in the dull light to disengage myself from the dreary waste on which I was so unfortunately belated? Should I persevere, it was tempting fate, and following the strange person, whose unabated pursuit had already caused such apprehension. I felt myself in a desperate extremity, and that feeling will sometimes call forth a hardihood in thought and action, which nothing beside could elicit. Such was its effect on me; and after a momentary pause I resumed the road courageously.

"I had scarcely proceeded half a mile when a feeble light twinkled faintly across the waste, and told that a human dwelling was not very distant. The water spring, which the date-trees that surround it point to the thirsty traveller in the desert, could not be more rapturously regarded by him, than that feeble gleam by me. I felt as if new vigour strung my limbs. *There* was hope—*there* was safety. That light was the beacon; and better still, the haven it showed was near. On I pressed, and in a few minutes stood before a small dilapidated dwelling, whose decayed sign-board intimated it to have been once the resting-place of travellers.

"Mean and comfortless as it looked, I should have claimed its shelter with delight; but my joy was abated—my feeling of security destroyed—by perceiving the well-remembered vehicle before the door. The horse had been unharnessed, and of course the driver was within.

"There are times when even woman conquers fear. I felt that there was for me but one course left. If I returned I should be pursued; if I passed the house I should be followed and overtaken. I once had—I now have—the nerve and daring of a man; but then sorrow and suffering had damped my energies and subdued my former spirit. There was no alternative. I taxed my courage to the uttermost, and with at least the semblance of boldness, entered the suspicious mansion.

"The room I was introduced to was not ill furnished, and certainly the outward appearance of the house was far more unpromising than the interior justified. It wanted the neatness of an English inn, but it had still the look of plenty; for an abundant supply of dried meats was hanging in the chimney, and a comfortable wood fire, the beacon which directed me across the heath, was blazing on the hearth. The servant, when I lifted the latch, appeared at first astonished at the visit of a stranger; but with an effort at boorish civility she pointed to a seat, and then left the kitchen, as I supposed, to apprise her master that an unexpected guest was come.

"When left alone I glanced suspiciously round, and many circumstances rather increased than diminished the evil impression, which the neglected exterior of the house had first created. A quantity of game was suspended from the ceiling, and two double guns stood in a corner of the chamber. Rabbit nets, gins of various descriptions and other matters employed in poaching, with whose uses I was well acquainted, were partially concealed beneath a chest of drawers. To judge from the appearance of the whole, I should rather pronounce the place to be the habitation of a smuggler, than a house where the traveller would seek for rest and entertainment.

"My observations were speedily interrupted. Another and a very different-looking female entered; and, after surveying me with a keen and impertinent stare, announced herself to be the mistress of the mansion.

"She seemed to be a woman beyond my own age, and no doubt had once been remarkably handsome; but her beauty was sadly impaired—years could not have done it, and I concluded it was more the work of dissipation than time. She was highly rouged, showily dressed, and wore a profusion of jewellery, which from their bad combination told that quantity and not good taste was her fancy. The richness of these ornaments was far too costly for her walk of life; and it was altogether out of character to see the bustling hostess tricked out like a tragic queen. One thing my quick eye discovered—the ornaments were genuine, and this expensive display added considerably to my alarm.

"With a tone intended to be gracious she bade me welcome, and inquired what refreshment I should choose. I eked for supper; she bowed, told me it should be prepared immediately, and, desiring the country girl to bring more billets to the fire, left the room.

"It was quite clear that I had fallen into dangerous company. The game, the fire-arms, the exhibition of jewels so unsuited to the mistress of a country inn, bore fearful evidence that the calling of the inmates of the house was anything but honest. Determined to see more of the mansion, if possible, I requested the attendant to conduct me to a chamber. She hesitated—took a light, told me to wait a little, and left me, as she said, to speak to her mistress. I heard her as the door was ajar. To her question the hostess replied: 'The back room—if it is ready,' and next moment the maid returned, and beckoned me to follow.

"The upper story of the inn was dirty and uncomfortable. I passed several rooms, and the last in the lobby, as it would appear, had been the one selected for my accommodation, but a glance at the door was quite sufficient to determine me against becoming its occupant. The others had nothing remarkable to attract the eye, but mine was provided with two strong bolts, while on the inside, there was no fastening but a common latch. The bed and furniture were not inviting, and I observed that the window was grated closely. Without permitting the attendant to observe any change in my manner, I returned with her to the lower chamber, and presently supper was laid.

"God knows, I had no appetite for the meal; but I ate—drank some ale—and managed to suppress every symptom of distrust. From the maid, who appeared a simple rustic, I found out the direction to the next hamlet, and ascertained that it was but two miles distant, and that the road was easily found. This was all I wanted—the sooner I set out the better—I requested the attendant to bring in my reckoning, and prepared to start on my hazardous expedition.

"Almost immediately the hostess herself appeared: she manifested surprise and disappointment at my unexpected departure, and endeavoured to dissuade me against leaving the house until morning. 'The heath was unsafe after night—the path devious and hard to find—would I but wait till morning, her husband should drive me to the village, as he was obliged to repair thither on business.' All these arguments were urged in vain, and again I asked, 'what I had to pay for my entertainment?'—'To pay! she exclaimed with a scornful stare—'a poor traveller like thee cannot be overburdened with money, and I can afford a supper.' I thanked her for her kindness, lifted my bundle, and bade her 'good night.' She followed to the door, and renewed her entreaties to remain.

"'And will you go?' she said. I replied that I was determined.

"'I wish you safe,' she continued with a sneer: 'stouter travellers have taken the road, and never reached their destination!'

"She turned in, closed the door, and I found myself once more upon the waste.

"During my short sojourn at the inn, the night had changed, and the sky indicated an approaching storm. The breeze, in unsteady gusts, came moaning across the moorland.—the moon was occasionally hidden—and on the edge of the horizon faint lightnings played, followed by the hoarse murmurings of distant thunder. All foretold a coming tempest, and I hurried on to reach some place of shelter before its fury burst upon me.

"Even in this desolate place and trying hour one circumstance prevented my heart from sinking—I had left the mysterious traveller behind; and the vehicle which had caused me such repeated alarms was standing before the alehouse door, if an alehouse that suspicious dwelling was. As yet no serious impediment had appeared; the road was circuitous but easily found out; and though the moon was frequently obscured by floating clouds, I pursued my journey without interruption. The moorland swelled gradually upwards as I advanced, and on the crest of the high-ground in front, there was a patch of dark underwood to the left; while on the right an object was visible, which, from its appearance, I concluded to be a finger-post.

"I pressed onwards—from this height I should probably discover the village lights, and even a distant prospect of human dwellings would cheer me to new exertion. I entered the brake—shrubs and copse skirted the path. Was it the right one? I raised my eyes and looked at the finger-post. Heavens!—it was a gibbet time-worn and decayed—but still a fragment of the murderer was swinging from its shattered arm; and the blanched skull and bare bones rattled in the night wind, as the unsteady gust struck them in its passage.

"I nearly lost my senses. I have crossed a battlefield days after the work of death had ended, when the unburied slain, stripped of all covering, tinged with the blueness of corruption, and swollen to unnatural size, lay thick around; but that fleshless felon was the most horrible spectacle that ever blasted my sight!

"I dared not look a second time, but rushed madly into the copse. The moon shone forth again, and I found myself in a small glade, shut out from that hideous and disgusting memorial of a murder. Almost exhausted, I stopped for a moment to breathe. A man's hand was laid upon my shoulder. I shrieked and sprang forward: the Jew was at my side!

"'Mercy!'—I cried—'Mercy! I have gold; take it freely, but do not murder me.'

"The stranger remained silent; and from beneath the shading of a hood attached to his horseman's cloak, I could remark eyes of uncommon brilliancy fixed on mine.

"'Spare me,' I continued, 'wretched as a lone wanderer may seem to be, I have more gold than those of wealthier appearance.'

"A smothered and sarcastic laugh was the only answer to my appeal.

"'If you do not want money, why follow, why detain me? I never injured—I never knew you.'

"'Both statements are untrue,' he replied, in a suppressed and hollow voice. 'You injured—and you knew me.'

"'Never!—You mistake me for another.'

"'No, no,' he returned coldly; 'objects of my love or hate have never been forgotten.'

"He held me from him at arm's length—flung off his riding-cloak—and, as it fell upon the ground, exclaimed in a voice that made me tremble,—

"'Does Reuben Woolfe the Jew bear any similitude to Michael Cooper the gipsy?'

"'Michael!' I replied with a shudder—'and has justice not yet overtaken the spiller of blood?'

"'Look at me,' was his answer, 'and it will be idle to reply. I am here. No longer the hunted gipsy, but more powerful than any member of the same people has been, since they left their eastern birthplace to wander among the nations of the north.'

"'What want you with me?' I asked firmly. 'I have offered gold and you reject it. Unhand me. I must—I will proceed.'

"'Must and will,' returned the gipsy, 'are gallant words—but here, I suspect, they are idly used. Once you were in my power, and fortune enabled you to leave and scorn me. Miracles are of rare occurrence. The arm that smote me is cold. Were it not, I have means now which then I wanted, to make thy rescuer wail the hour when he roused my vengeance.'

"'He never feared you, Michael—and he is now beyond mortal enmity.'

"'So much the better for both. Ellen, your fate hangs upon a breath. Hear and decide.'

"I listened to the gipsy chief in breathless astonishment. The coldness of his unimpassioned address made me tremble; for a villain's calmness is more to be dreaded than the fury of the brave. He thus continued:

"'Ellen—I may betray some weakness—no matter—there is no one to witness it. I once loved you, and see how that influenced our mutual fortunes. You spurned the gipsy, and preferred becoming the mistress of an adventurer. Ay, the veriest of adventurers—a soldier— one whose fantastic honour refused you the silly bond of matrimony, which even the humblest peasant exacts from her admirer. You were then in affluence, and I in misery. Let that pass. I shall not say what you are now. Hear what my career has been.

"'There are in this country men of action and intelligence—no matter what the world calls them. I joined them in my hour of danger, and passed among them for a Jew: my face required but the addition of a beard, and that was easily effected. Short as my connection with them has been, I am now a leader of the body, and direct a confederacy that spreads itself over half the island, and defies the law and its myrmidons to break it up. Others are the tools, and I the agent. All connected with the body, from the smuggler to the housebreaker, are under my control; and though they never know from whom the order comes, they are obedient to the mandate of those, of whose names and abodes they are in total ignorance. We procure intelligence—we arrange the plans—and it is their business to carry our orders into execution. Enough of what I am. A few years of success will render me wealthier than ever any of our tribe has even dreamed of being. I will then retire to another country. What will not gold do? My gipsy blood may hereafter circulate in the veins of the proudest noble of the land of my adoption. Ellen, you know me. Ambition has chalked the path out—and stern resolution shall not be wanted to sweep aside every obstacle that would bar me in my bold career.'

"I listened in breathless amazement to the soaring projects of the low-born ruffian. The moon shone brightly out. Fired at the picture his fancy sketched of future greatness, his head was thrown proudly back, his eye compressed and animated; while his wild dress, added to a belt in which were pistols and a dagger, gave to his whole appearance the look of a bold and adventurous brigand. In the same low and unimpassioned tone he thus continued:

"'Ellen, your fate is linked to mine—our fortunes must run together. My slighted love has been deeply avenged, and the temporary success of a hated rival repaid by blood and misery. When the lost child was smiling in your arms, as you sat before the cottage door, and I was constrained to beg an alms to save me from starvation—did you then guess what its fate would be? Or, as you turned an eye of womanly pride towards his handsome father from the abject wretch who was then beholden to your bounty, did you dream, that I, despised and wretched as I was, had doomed my enemy to death?'

"The allusion to my child and his brave father roused my spirit, and I found the blood once more flush my cheek.

"'*You* doom him to death!' I exclaimed. 'No, Michael had you crossed his path, Harley would have crushed you like a worm. No; my loved one died on the battle-field, sword in hand, as the brave should only die. While you, like yonder murderer, will blanch upon a gibbet.'

"'And did I not effect his death?' he said, with a bitter sneer. 'Who drove him to the battlefield on which he fell? Listen, and judge. I found you surrounded with plenty—you had a lover and a child—a home and independence. I visited you—in four days the cottage was a ruin—the corn-stacks dispersed in ashes to the winds. Whose hand fired house and barn, Ellen?'—and he grasped mine with painful force—'That hand holds yours!'

"'Execrable ruffian!' I exclaimed. 'Your boast is indeed too true. You drove us into penury, and death and misery came after.'

"'Well,' he replied; 'my vengeance is now complete. I am not implacable, Ellen. I have removed a rival, and deprived you of a protector. Come—you shall have one more powerful. We'll forget the past, return to the house you quitted—for that and twenty more are at my command. I will deck you in the jewels of a countess. Ask aught that money can obtain in Britain, and it is yours. You are the only mate for Michael. I love a spirit free and fearless as my own. Yes; I have willed it so, and this night you shall be my bride.'

"I was mute with terror and astonishment. If apprehension from his hatred had alarmed me, the avowal of his love was infinitely more revolting; and a thrill of horror rushed to my heart, as I plucked my hand from his.

"'Your bride!—the bride of Harley's murderer! Wretch! before the lips that felt his kisses should be contaminated by a monster like thee, I would stab myself!'

"'Ellen,' he answered coolly, 'this is mere girlish trifling, and suited to neither the time nor place. We are waited for. I told them before I left the house, to prepare a better supper than what was offered you. Come—it may spoil. You and I know each other too well to make further fooling necessary.'

"My situation was very desperate. In the power of one so cold and merciless—resolute in purpose, immovable in temper—threats or supplications with such a man were equally unavailing. Even then, in that dreadful extremity, my spirit bore me up; and I resolved to resist the villain—ay, even to the death.

"'Michael,' I said, 'you have a man's strength, and there lies your only superiority; for in determination I am your equal. Let me pass. If there be a spark of manly spirit in your bosom, you will not harm the woman who asks your pity. You cannot bend me to your will. No—by Heaven!—though you should murder me.'

"'And this would be a fitting place for such a deed,' the villain continued, in the same calm tone. 'You marked the gibbet hard by. Had the light allowed, there is a stone beside it that tells the history. There was a weak and obstinate wench—one like thee, Nell. She had a lover—a wild one, too—the liker Michael Cooper. Well, liker us still, the silly girl knew too many of his secrets. He tired of her, they say, and attached himself to another. She urged a meeting with him here: they met; she upbraided, and he retorted. Words grew warmer; and, stung with jealousy and rage, she threatened a discovery. The result was, that next morning the wench was found where the gibbet stands, with a fractured skull. He managed the matter clumsily, and was hanged; and, a few yards off all that remains of him are a few bare bones shivering in the night breeze. Come, Nell, let us be moving.'

"Seizing my arm, he pulled me some yards along the path; but mustering my whole strength, I disengaged myself from his grasp, and rushed wildly towards the direction in which I thought the village lay. But escape was hopeless;—in a moment I was overtaken, and locked closely in the ruffian's arms. A final struggle ensued—he to retain, and I to break away. Just then the sky appeared to open—everything around was revealed distinctly as at noontide—the vivid flash was followed by a crash of thunder, loud and prolonged, as if it announced the ruin of a world.

"'Hold—Michael!' I exclaimed. 'Hold; hear you not the voice of Heaven? Forbear I'

"His reply was too blasphemous to be repeated. It told my doom— death or insult awaited me! In vain I screamed—in vain I supplicated the scoundrel's pity. My voice died away unheard over the dreary waste, my prayers were unregarded, my strength failed, my limbs tottered, my breath was lost.

"'Now comes Michael's triumph!' he muttered, as he grasped me tighter. Another flash lightened the copse—another crash burst over our heads. For a second the poniard in the villain's belt sparkled. I caught at the handle and clutched it—my energies were overcome—I staggered, and struck a wild and random blow. The weapon, keen as a lancet, pierced the murderer's throat—his hold relaxed—he leaped convulsively from the ground, came down heavily, and lay without motion on the ground beside me. Two hollow groans, a gurgling noise like the choking of a sinking swimmer—one long faint sigh and Michael was a dead man.

"I lay beside the departed murderer—the knife was sticking in his throat, his eyes were open, and as flash after flash came vollying from the heavens, I thought he was grinning at me in deadly but impotent rage. Presently I felt a revulsion to the heart, leaped from the ground, and rushed wildly from the scene of slaughter.

"For a long interval I remember nothing. They found me in the morning roaming through the hamlet, and my senses totally fled. A wounded officer fortunately was on leave of absence there. He recognised me, told the story of my sufferings during the retreat, interested the villagers on my behalf, and had me carefully attended to. My ravings, as I was afterwards told, were frightful, but they were attributed to another cause than the true one. Michael's death was involved in deep mystery; some ascribed it to suicide—a belief almost confirmed by the circumstance that the weapon of destruction was his own; others suspected that he had been murdered by his lawless confederates; and their sudden abandonment of the lonely house upon the moor went far to strengthen that conclusion.

"Why prolong the tale? I recovered slowly, and again found myself upon the world. I had known every alternation of human fortune. Nursed in penury, and reared in splendour—seduced, abandoned, protected, and beloved—now gifted with independence—a mother, and, in all save the name, a wife—then the follower of a camp, bereaved of child and lover an outcast, a murderess, and a maniac!

"I could not rest in England; the loss of my boy partially unsettled my reason; and in the fond hope that he still lived, and that accident might yet restore him, I followed Lord Wellington's army, when a British force was sent a second time to the Peninsula.

"I shall not detain you with the adventures of a camp follower; it is, as you well know, only an unvaried record of perils and privation. More than once I fancied that I had gleaned some intelligence of my child. Alas! it was illusory, and fond expectation ended in the bitterest disappointment. My gipsy habits, and an utter contempt of danger—for life so valueless as mine costs not a thought about its preservation—enabled me to accompany a conquering army. I shared largely in the spoil of many a battle-field, and amassed much wealth. At last, weary of scenes of war, and all hope of recovering the lost one over, I returned to my native land, and rejoined the wandering people where you found me. My power over them is boundless; for gold, that controls all, from the court to the cottage, influences the gipsy bivouac as powerfully as it does the camp of kings. Here, in the same rude tent, where the first cry of infancy was heard, my passing sigh shall escape. I was born free as the mountain deer—I will live the life of liberty—and when my mortal course 'is well nigh done,' the tameless spirit shall part among the untamed, and but one command be given—to bear me hither, and lay me in my mother's grave!"

The solemnity of the place and hour, the confession of a tale of blood, struck O'Connor, firm as he was, with a feeling of unusual depression. Both for some time were silent; but the gipsy was the first to break it.

"You march tomorrow; and here we part."

"And that we ever meet in this world is more than doubtful," said the soldier, with a deep sigh.

"*We shall meet*," replied the gipsy solemnly. "Better we did not, for the meeting will be a melancholy one for both."

"Nonsense, Ellen; you yield to delusive fancies. These are but idle fantasies of a heated brain. Surely you cannot believe that you can know aught belonging to futurity?"

"Yes," she replied. "The gipsy reads what other eyes cannot discern. I know your fortune; your fate is open to me; and yet I am blind to my own."

"Say boldly, Ellen, what that fate will be!"

"A short and spirited career,—a sudden and a glorious death!"

"You foretell a brave and noble destiny."

"I tell only what is decreed," she returned. "I never saw a hand on which one peaceful line of happiness could not be traced but yours. Well, O'Connor, you have the gipsy's blessing—we must separate."

"Stay, Ellen: before you leave me, will you reply to some questions?"

"Ask! they shall be answered."

"You seem to love one person as ardently as you detest another. I mean your regard for Mary Howard appears equalled by your hatred of her lover."

"Why should I not love her tenderly? Breathes there a being that should have the same hold upon this withered heart as she? That sweet child, who lay for months upon my bosom, as though I had been her mother—she, whose rosy lips I kissed before I slept—she, whose infant prattle was the first sound I heard for many a month when waking— she—the child of him who succoured my dying parent, and who, when deserted by all the world beside, sheltered and protected me. O'Connor, if a life could secure the happiness, and avert the misfortunes of Mary Howard, I would buy her weal with mine. But, alas! it is fated; the decree has gone forth, and destiny will be fulfilled."

"Nonsense, Ellen. I am no believer in blind predestination. Warn her of danger, and you will avert it."

"No—she would not believe me—for she could not comprehend the extent of man's villainy—and one honeyed word from that accomplished scoundrel would undo even an angel's warning."

"But why do you attach such mischief to his suit? Why is he more dangerous than other profligates? Mary Howard is too exalted in her purity to dread aught from Phillips. He may woo and leave her. He may wring her heart, and trifle with her affections; but beyond this, nothing need be dreaded."

"You ask me why I fear and hate that man? Listen—and then say whether the designs of such a scoundrel are not more formidable than those of ordinary profligates. From the wild and wandering habits of our tribes things are known to us, that would almost appear, when unexplained, rather the work of divination, than simply resulting from the insight into human life, which an eternal change of place and an extended intercourse with the whole family of man afford to the gipsy tribe. Humble as our influence may seem, it reaches where it could not be supposed. To us, the palace is open as the cottage; and strange and wonderful are the mysteries concealed closely from the world, but every day revealed to us. Those whose rank and intellect would never permit them to stoop and parley with a wandering mendicant, pry anxiously into the decrees of fate; and men who proudly lock their secret thoughts and actions from their equals, open them, unreservedly to a vagabond like me! This may appear incredible, but remember that human nature in all cases and circumstances is the same: the life of the wisest is but a chapter of contradictions—and cunning and folly, weakness and determination, mix in and mar the deepest schemes which mortal foresight forms. Now hear a tale of villainy—and, when you have heard it, judge wherefore I tremble for that artless girl.

"It was late in the autumn of last year, and we had been sojourning in the neighbourhood of a garrison town. We were encamped upon a heath, and I was returning to our bivouac from a village in the vicinity of our halting-place, to which some business had brought me. It was evening—the light was fading fast—and when I came to a part of the forest where the path crossed the highway, I was surprised to see a female on the roadside suffering acutely from illness or fatigue. I approached and spoke kindly to her. She seized my hand in hers, and, with a wild grasp, told me she was dying. I strove to cheer her—despatched the girl that attended me for a cart—seated myself beside the poor sufferer, and comforted her with an assurance of immediate succour. The vehicle came promptly—I removed her in it to my tent—laid her on my own bed—and, to be brief, in two hours she gave birth to a dead child.

I saw that she could not outlive her baby long—she was sinking fast—and all I could do was done. Our humble means and skill were exhausted to save her; but it was vain, for life was ebbing. The delicacy of the skin, the softness of the hand, the fine texture of her under garments, required less than gipsy acuteness to ascertain that the poor sufferer had been cradled in the lap of luxury. Finding herself dying, she requested to be left with me alone; a wave of the hand cleared the tent, and I sat down beside her humble pallet.

"She turned her fading eye on mine—once it had been a soft and lustrous hazel one.

"'Thanks,' she said 'my last thanks! Oh, God! that my mother's child should draw her last breath, disgraced, deserted, and even without the comfort of a good man's prayer! Kind gipsy, listen to me—I cannot leave the world without telling you a tale of crime—you can bear evidence to its punishment. Oh! have my dying request attended to. Let me and the fruit of my offending be laid in hallowed ground, and the child of sin and shame sleep in the same earth that covers its guilty mother.

"'I am the daughter of a field officer. I was born in India—my mother died, and I was sent to England an infant. There I remained for many years, carefully and expensively educated: and at eighteen my father returned and claimed me. From school he took me to a fashionable watering—and in the winter visited London, and next season returned to Cheltenham. There, unhappily, he met a lady of great personal attractions, and, though but a year older than myself, he was weak enough to marry her. A man shattered in constitution and above sixty had little chance of happiness from such a union. His wife and daughter were rivals. Both sought, unknown to the other, admiration from the same source; and, as it may be imagined, mutual ruin was the consequence.

"'My strength is sinking,' she said, 'and let me hurry over my guilty story.

"'We went next season to Harrowgate, and there met one whom, even in death, I will not name. May God pardon him as I do! He was introduced to my unhappy father, brought to the house, and, with the unsuspicious confidence of a man who knew nothing of the world, permitted to domesticate himself in our family. He sought every opportunity to win my affections, and told an artful story which lulled every fear to rest; I believed—confided—was fascinated—and undone!

"'Months passed; shame and guilt are consequent on each other— and mine was not to be concealed. I urged that marriage so often and so solemnly promised, and day after day my request was evaded. At last, wearied by my importunities, or unable to dissemble longer, he abruptly quitted the house. I wrote to him—appealed to his better feelings, and stated the desperation of my own. I conjured him, by every holy oath and promise, to rescue me from the shame he had wrought, and retrieve what before had been an unsullied reputation.

By a chain of accidents, the letter fell into my father's hands the morning after his own wife had eloped with my betrayer!

"'What was the result? The abused old man retired to his chamber, and, while reason was overthrown, destroyed himself!

"'For weeks it was necessary to place me under restraint, I grew calmer, and the physician pronounced me convalescent. The first use I made of liberty was to wander forth in search of my undoer. I discovered that he was in the neighbouring town, and thither I directed my course. Fatigued with exertions too great for my weakness, I rested, nearly fainting, on the bank where you found me. A rush of horses caused me to look round—it was an officer and lady, followed by a servant. They passed me at speed. One glance—and it was fatal. It was my seducer—and his wretched victim—my father's wife!'

"Her failing strength could hold out no longer. She fell heavily on my breast—I called for help, and had wine administered. Once or twice she essayed to speak—but the words were unintelligible—and with one long deep sigh—the parting struggle of a broken heart—she drooped her head forward, and expired in my arms."

"Great God! can there be such villainy on earth, and it remain unpunished?" exclaimed the soldier, as Ellen's melancholy narrative ended. "I had heard that, before he joined us, Phillips had been engaged in an affair of gallantry, but the lady's levity was so great, that in a few months she left him for another."

"Ay," replied the gipsy—"that was the worthless wife. Shame closed the lips of the poor sufferer, and she carried her secret to the grave, while her abandoned step-mother gloried in an open exhibition of her infamy. Thus a part only of the villainy of Phillips was known, and that infinitely the more pardonable of his proceedings. It is time to separate; and we must part."

"I am deeply grieved," said the soldier, "to think that poor Mary should be exposed to the artifices of that accomplished scoundrel. Had I remained in England, my threatened vengeance might have restrained him. All that can be hoped is from her high principles, and his dastardly apprehensions."

"Adieu, O'Connor," said the gipsy, with considerable emotion: "Good fortune follow thee! She who has a loved brother in the field will not joy over his fame and safety more ardently than I will over thine!"

"Farewell, Ellen," replied the soldier. "To you I confide Mary Howard. Watch over her as a mother"—and stooping down, he kissed her tenderly.

"Farewell," she muttered—and O'Connor felt her tears upon his cheek. "It is the parting kiss of friendship; and thine are the last lips that shall ever press the gipsy's!—Farewell."

The words were scarcely spoken until she glided from his side. He saw her dark form vanish beneath the shadow of the tower—her footsteps died away in the silence of the night, and the soldier felt himself now the only living thing among the mansions of the dead.

"Strange and eventful is that woman's history," he murmured. "A heart in which daring and tenderness unite—a mind in which madness and intelligence are so blended." He mused for a few minutes on his own wayward fortunes, and then, with a deep sigh, left, as he imagined, the village churchyard for ever.

When he reached the inn he found that all but his own servant had retired to bed, and he delivered a letter to his master. It was an official note from Phillips, stating that he had been unexpectedly called away, and begging that the major would excuse him from marching with the detachment. His absence was a relief to his rival; and O'connor was thus saved the annoyance of holding any further intercourse with a man whom he so thoroughly hated and despised.

XI

DEPARTURE FROM COUNTRY QUARTERS—A PARTING INTERVIEW

King Henry.	On, on, ye noble English—
	For there is none of you so mean and base,
	That hath not noble lustre in your eyes.
	I see you stand like greyhounds in the slip,
	Straining upon the start—the game's afoot:
	Follow your spirit.

King Henry V

Pistol.   Touch her soft mouth and march.

Ibid.

THE MORNING SUN HAD SCARCELY broken on an unclouded sky when the bugle sounded, and the village street showed signs of military preparation. The baggage was already gone, and the men, in full marching order, were falling in before the Greyhound. Being the *elite* companies of a light infantry regiment, their dress and appearance were smart and soldierly. All were in the prime of life, or entering on the world, with the ardour of "hope-fed youth;" while the prospect of a bustling campaign added to the excitement attendant on a change of quarters.

Yet looking down the line, here and there a face might be discovered, on which symptoms of depression could be traced. Rustic *liaisons* had been interrupted by a summons to the field—the raw soldier fancied he was leaving Ashfield with a broken heart—while streaming eyes from many a cottage window told that he had not urged his suit in vain. For these sentimental sufferings, alas there was no sympathy. At the sorrows of his young companion the older soldier laughed, as he favoured him with a long list of sundry demoiselles whom in his time he had loved and left behind him. It is consolatory, to know that others have suffered and survived. Gradually the "pale lover" became resigned to the visitation, and submitted to his fate; and before the detachment halted in the next town, Pat was singing like a blackbird, and poor Phillis already half forgotten.

The moment for departure had come. O'Connor mounted his horse; the advanced guard was thrown out; the word to march was given; the bugles played a quick step, and Ashfield was left.

As the gay detachment passed through the street, hands were kissed and handkerchiefs waved their mute adieus. Of all the village belles, the prettiest and the tenderest of the sufferers was the fair milliner. Unconsciously O'Connor had achieved a conquest there. His graceful farewell was afterwards long remembered; and for many a month Miss Burnett never named "the brave and gentle Irishman," but an involuntary sigh betrayed the deep impression the manly and unpretending soldier had left behind.

Alas! while he kissed his hand to her, he was only thinking of another. The line of march was directly before the windows of the parsonage; and as he approached the dwelling of his lost love, he felt a sinking of the heart as if he was bidding happiness an eternal farewell. Fearing that any eye should remark his visible agitation, he ordered the music, which had ceased, to play again. Phillips, whose taste was excellent, had occasionally directed the bugle practice, and had chosen pieces for their performance. Among others, he had arranged Mary Howard's song; and, as if it were to more pointedly recall the late scene of O'Connor's rejection, it was that tune that the bugle-master selected.

Mr Howard was standing at the entrance of his avenue, and as the detachment passed him, he took leave of his friends individually. O'connor pulled up his horse and dismounted; while the old man, under considerable emotion, bade him a kind farewell.

"'This is to me, major, a very painful moment. I have now looked at many a face that I shall never look on again. I, who in the course of natural events, should be foremost for the grave, am most probably destined to survive many of those who seem to have only touched on the opening of their mortal journey. Mary wishes to speak to you. I would return with you, but the last duties of religion require my attendance," and he pointed to an approaching funeral, that by a singular accident crossed the line of march, and formed a strange and melancholy contrast to the gay procession it encountered.

"That is indeed, a striking picture," he continued. "emblematic of human life! in which brightness and gloom are so intimately blended! Your procession, full of high hope and entering on its brilliant and exciting career, and yon dark train winding to the close of every mortal course—the same goal at which the race of all, the fortunate and the miserable, must terminate the grave—the grave! God bless you, my friend. If an old man's prayers can win prosperity, you have my warmest ones for your happiness.—Farewell. It is unlikely that in this world we shall ever meet again. May we meet in a better one!"

A tear stole down his cheek as he pressed the soldier's hand, and left him to join the funeral train.

To meet Mary Howard again was what O'Connor neither expected nor desired. It was, however, unavoidable. A servant took his horse, and he hurried along the avenue as if anxious to get a painful interview as quickly ended as he could. In the same room in which his suit had been rejected, he found her whom he had loved and lost.

Mary Howard was in tears; and the soldier was deeply affected as he sat down beside her. She was the first to speak.

"And you would have left us, Major O'Connor, without bidding me farewell. Alas! have I so soon forfeited your friendship?"

"Oh, no, Miss Howard; that would be impossible. I shall ever think of you as a beloved sister. I must confess my weakness. I feared a parting would be painful to us both, and therefore thought it would be better avoided."

"Then I have not unintentionally offended you? I have a request to make, and will Major O'Connor grant it?"

The soldier pressed her hand as he replied,—"It is only for Mary Howard to name her wishes, and for me to see them gratified."

"You are leaving England," she continued, in a broken voice; "and God knows how many chances are against our ever meeting. That my feelings for your future happiness are deep and lasting, my own heart can best tell. Is there any impropriety in confessing that regard which a sister may bestow? Such is mine for you, O'Connor. I am affianced to another; my hand is plighted to him—*him* I shall love as a wife loves—*you* as an only brother."

She burst into tears; and the soldier was deeply agitated.

"The request I would make, is that you will send me your picture. When far away I will think of you and pray for you."

The soldier pressed her to his heart. "Oh! Mary, had we met sooner or never, I should have been spared an aching heart. Your wishes shall be obeyed."

"I thank you. Here is a little token of affection. When you look at it, sometimes remember her that gave it."

It was a locket, containing a well-executed miniature and a ringlet of her beautiful hair. The soldier placed it in his bosom, and for some time both continued silent. At last O'Connor rose—

"It is painful, Mary, to say farewell; but the word must he spoken."

"Farewell, my friend—my brother!" and, yielding to feelings that could not be controlled, she laid her head upon his shoulder, and wept without restraint.

The soldier gazed on the lovely being from whom he was about to separate forever, with a look of mute agony that told the bitterness of parting, pressed her wildly to his bosom, kissed her again and again; then, as if he dreaded a deeper exhibition of his feelings, rushed from her presence, sprang upon his horse, and galloped off to overtake the detachment.

Poor Mary! well might she weep. As true a heart as ever beat for woman had been offered and refused; and, fascinated by the artful homage of a traitor, the cup of happiness had been within her grasp— and in a luckless hour she rejected it!

XII

THE MARCH FROM ASHFIELD

Hermione.	Pray you, sit by us,
	And tell's a tale.
Mamilius.	Merry or sad shall't be?
Hermione.	As merry as you will.

Winter's Tale

WHEN O'CONNOR RODE UP TO the detachment he had resumed his customary bearing, although, a sadder heart never throbbed beneath the semblance of indifference. The only woman he had loved was lost to him—he had parted from Mary Howard forever—he should never see her again; for to see her the wife of another would be distracting. He overtook O'Brien, and, two or three mounted officers who were riding in the rear; while, perfectly unconscious of the pain he was inflicting upon his friend, his light-hearted countryman rallied the commander on his temporary desertion.

"So you have been sentimentalising O'Connor! and no doubt bidding the gentle Mary a soft farewell! Did you vow fidelity and swear, 'when the wars ended,' to return to the lady of your love and lay your laurels at her feet? Poor thing! of course she was dolorous at losing us. The villagers would have it that she was on the eve of promotion; and the only point of difference among them seemed to be, whether she should become Mrs Phillips or Mrs O'Connor."

"Nonsense! O'Brien.—Pshaw!—what business have soldiers with wives?"

"True; and it would appear that poor Mary's swains came to this conclusion. The lady-killer has levanted; and, as the song goes, 'you love and you ride away.'

The major forced a sickly smile, while his tormentor continued,—

"Was the parting very pathetic, O'Connor? Was it prudent and platonic—'hand to hand, like holy palmer's kiss,'—or, as ancient Pistol says, did you 'touch her soft mouth and march?' Egad! I fancy I have stumbled on the truth; for, by the goddess of modesty! he blushes!— Ho—ho—we'll no more of this. Well—it has pleased Heaven to make me of colder clay. I could bid Cleopatra good-by like a philosopher; and exclaim, with honest Nym, "I cannot kiss, that is the humour of it; but adieu."

"But, Pat, what was that you were saying about your cousin and the card-case, when the major rode up?" said the younger of the subalterns.

"Why, that a slight mistake in putting another man's tickets in his pocket cost him a fortune."

"A mistake about a card-case cost a fortune?"

"Precisely so," replied the captain. "For sixpenny worth of pasteboard, Hector O'Dogherty was regularly disinherited by his affectionate uncle."

"Why," said the young subaltern, "what an unforgiving monster that uncle must have been!"

"Yes; honest Roderick was not moulded from the softest clay, and his enemies would tell you that at times he was rather short-grained. Lord! I fancy I see him now—his small grey eye flashing like a cat's in the dark, as he grasped his crutch to demolish Captain Coolaghan."

"Come, Pat, let us have the story," said another of the party.

"It is a long one," returned O'Brien.

"It is liker the march then; and it will get over a tedious mile or two of the road."

"Well, I believe it was the last martial passage in Roderick's history; and you must have it."

VOLUME II

I

THE CARD-CASE

Bardolph. Sir John, you are so fretful, you cannot live long.
King Henry IV

Hotspur.   Tell me, tell me,
        How show'd his tasking? Seem'd it in contempt?
Vernon.   No, by my soul; I never in my life,
        Did hear a challenge urged more modestly.
Ibid.

Caius.   Vat be you all, one, two, tree, four, come for?
Host.   To see thee fight.

Page.   Master Shallow, you have yourself been a great fighter.
Merry Wives of Windsor

IT WAS SOON AFTER THE affair of New Ross that I obtained leave of absence from the general of the district, and repaired to the metropolis. I had been wounded by a rebel from a window with a slug; and though it traversed the bone without causing any injury, yet from the eccentric direction it had taken, an experienced practitioner was required to discover and extract it.

Two or three days after the operation had been successfully performed, I found myself able to move about, and set out to visit some of my acquaintances, who happened to be sojourning to the capital. Among others there was a kinsman of my mother; named Roderick O'Dogherty. He resided constantly in town, occupying a small house in Kildare Street, and thither I directed my course.

Roderick was the youngest son of my grand-uncle. He had him educated for a priest, but Roderick preferred the trade of arms. Early in life he entered the Austrian service; and through many ups and downs of fortune, raised himself to the rank of major-general, with the reputation of being a stout soldier. An unexpected succession to the property of a distant relative fortunately enabled the general to retire from a profession, for which wounds and bad health had nearly rendered him unfit; and with the cross of Maria Theresa, a small pension, and a rich crop of laurels—if his own account were true— Roderick quitted Germany for his native land, and established himself comfortably in the capital. Ten years had passed since he had honoured Dublin with his presence; and time, which ameliorates many of the ills of life, had certainly wrought no change for the better in either the health or temper of my mother's kinsman, the worthy commander.

Whether his claims rested upon reputation in arms or on acquired wealth, no man exacted more attention from his relations to the third and fourth generation, than Roderick O'Dogherty. The most constant and punctilious inquiries after his health were indispensable, and the slightest omission was booked in the tablets of his memory against the unhappy offender. To visit him, Heaven knows, was anything but an agreeable duty. If he happened to be gouty or rheumatic, one was doomed to listen patiently to a narrative of his sufferings, and the deepest sympathy expected in return for this condescension on his part, in favouring you with a detail of his afflictions. If there was any abatement of his numerous maladies, the unhappy visitor was martyred with interminable anecdotes of the seven years' war, and the exploits of a Baron Puffenberg, to whom half a century before, the gallant general had been *aide-de-camp*.

Of all Roderick's kindred, I, probably, was the least assiduous in my attentions. Most of them were more closely related than myself, and, therefore, I was not likely to figure in his last will and testament.

In his best humour the commander was a bore, and in his ill-temper a firebrand. I was not obliged, I thought, to listen to long stories, or submit to his irritability, especially as it was more than doubtful that after he had been gathered to his fathers, I should find in the disposition of his effects any consideration for the same.

On hearing that I had been wounded and was in town, Roderick had despatched his valet, Philip Clancy, to inquire for me at my hotel. This civility on the commander's part of course demanded a suitable return—and on the morning in question, the first visit I made was to my distinguished relative.

I knocked at the door, and his man admitted me. One of honest Philip's intelligent looks told me "to prepare for squalls." "The ould gentleman had the divil's night of it!" he whispered as I mounted the stairs. "There was no standing him this morning good or bad. He was as short in the temper as cat's hair, and would fret a saint, let alone a sinner like me." With this pleasant intimation, and the prospect of an agreeable tête-à-tête, I was conducted to the presence.

I found the commander ensconced in an easy chair with his infirm foot resting on a hassock, and a thick-winded pug reposing before the sounder member. I looked at my distinguished relative, and a crosser-looking elderly gentleman a dog never barked at! If, as it was said, the Irish adventurers so frequently found in the ranks of continental princes were as dangerous to the fair as formidable to their enemies, I am persuaded that Roderick was a virtuous exception. He was now a little pursy man, fat enough for a friar, with thin legs and small grey eyes, ready to fire up at the slightest provocation. His nose was short and upturned, and had never been an organ that a statuary would have selected for a cast. Yet, stunted as it was, a Hulan, it appeared, had fancied it for sabre practice, and by a bisecting scar rendered it the more remarkable. The commander was wrapped in a flannel dressing-gown, and wore a purple velvet nightcap. His hair, white as snow, was combed back into a queue, and secured with an ample bow of black riband. As a sort of moral for a soldier's use, there was no weapon visible in the apartment;

while a crutch standing in one corner gave silent intimation that the warrior's career was done.

The pug hated me; and I, when I could manage a sly kick, returned the compliment. He barked at me to the best of his ability until, exhausted by the exertion, he lay down again panting for breath, while his worthy master bade me welcome.

"Down, Beauty—down, I say. You are so seldom here that Beauty takes you for a stranger. Well—so you had that slug extracted. Pish! Nowadays men make a work about nothing. I remember Count Schroeder got a musket-bullet in the hip, at Breda, and he had it out and was on horseback again the second morning. Soldiers were soldiers then! What the devil were you about at Ross? You managed matters prettily."

"I think we did," I replied stoutly.

"Pish! Why did you let the rebels into the town?"

"Why—because we could not keep them out"

"Pshaw!" he growled testily. "I tell you how poor dear Puffenberg and I would have managed matters. We would have lamed them with artillery—guns double-loaded with grape and canister at point-blank distance—charged while the head of the column was broken, and supported the cavalry with—"

"We had no artillery but a few battalion pieces and a couple of old ship-guns"

"Humph!" growled the commander. "Why not try cavalry?"

"Cavalry could not act. The masses were dense, the street filled with pikemen, and the windows crowded with musketeers. What impression could cavalry make against rebels in close column with pikes sixteen feet long?"

"Humph!"

"It was the gallantest affair during the rebellion, and old Johnson fought it nobly."

"Humph! Well, you dine here today at five. You'll meet your cousin Hector."

"I am unfortunately engaged."

"Humph! Always engaged. No matter. I want to talk to you tomorrow. Come to breakfast. Not later than eleven. Mind that."

I assented, and promised to be punctual.

"Hector is not pleasing me. I'm failing fast. He knows it. But if he disobliges me, and thinks I have not resolution enough to cut him off with a shilling—clip him close as a game cock—he don know Roderick O'Dogherty. Well, I see you are in a hurry, so good morning."

I left him, glad of escaping more of the reminiscences of Baron Puffenberg; and as I was being let out, found Hector the hope of the O'Dogherties knocking at the door. He turned with me down the street, and at once commenced a detail of his sufferings, and a diatribe touching his uncle's parsimony. No one was worse calculated to dance attendance on a peevish invalid than Roderick's heir-apparent. He was a wild, headstrong, mercurial character—a union of opposite qualities—a mixture of good and evil, and, unhappily for himself, the latter predominated.

Hector was scarcely twenty, and one of the handsomest lads I ever saw. His education was imperfect and his principles lax. Had he been carefully brought up, and the bad portions of his disposition eradicated while a boy, he might have made a valuable man. But he had been spoiled by a weak mother—his vices had been permitted to run riot—and at the early age of twenty, Hector was a gambler and a duellist.

His means—those of the son of an embarrassed gentleman—were not flourishing; but his credit, based upon the expectancy of succeeding to the property of his uncle the general, kept him afloat. Nevertheless, a desperate love of play placed him in eternal difficulties, and his pugnacious spirit was under a constant excitement. His end was what might be easily anticipated. He quarrelled at a billiard-table with a gambler as fiery and wayward as himself, and, as we say in Connaught, was left next morning "quivering on a daisy."

Hector took my arm.

"Lord—I'm so glad to meet you, Pat! You have been with old square-toes. Did he blow me up?"

"Why, he did hint something about clipping you like a game-cock, and marking his affection by the bequest of a shilling."

"Oh—the cross-grained rogue! Pat, you would pity me, if you knew half what I undergo. Because he allows me a beggarly hundred a year, every quarter's check accompanied by a groan that would lead a stranger to suppose the old curmudgeon was in convulsions and a torrent of abuse that a pickpocket would not stand, I must visit him twice a day, dine with him on mutton chops, dawdle four hours over a rascally pint of sherry, and listen to his d—d yarns about Puffenberg and Schroeder, and the siege of Breda. Does he suspect that I shake the elbow?"

"Of that, Hector, I tell you more after breakfast tomorrow. I am going to him by special appointment to hear a full detail of your delinquencies."

"Do you dine with the old tiger today?"

"I should be devilish sorry to interrupt your tête-à-tête. I told him I was engaged."

"Ah!—if I dare refuse! But one whisper that I handled a cue or threw a main, and my ruin was complete. I am forced to humour the old salamander, though it breaks my heart. Well, you will meet me at Darcy's? We'll have a grilled bone and some sober conversation."

I declined; but Hector was so urgent, that at last I reluctantly consented. The truth was, he had already embroiled me in a quarrel, and introduced me, on one occasion, to a gaming-house, where I had been pretty smartly plucked.

The lieutenant, burst into a loud laugh "Well said—Pat. Hang it, we never gave you the credit you deserve for high morality, and anti-duelling principles into the bargain."

O'Brien coloured, and replied, "Many, Lorimer, have been misunderstood; and such has been my case. Circumstances involved me in some unfortunate affairs, and obtained for me a character which I neither coveted nor deserved. Quarrels that I never courted have been forced upon me, and accident implicated me in disputes from which nothing but a visit to the field could safely exonerate me as a soldier. There are about me now some two or three, *men* by profession, but *boys* in years and experience. Hear me, lads; and listen to my candid advice. Avoid a duellist as a nuisance—a gambler as the devil. The first is bad enough; but he is innocent when compared with the second. True, he may involve you in a quarrel, but chance may extricate you uninjured, or you may escape with a broken bone—but from the other there is no deliverance. Titled or untitled it is all the same. He who will not spare wife, children, kindred, friends—will he show mercy to an acquaintance? Trust me, no honour binds him. The gambler, when he has you in his hand, will fleece you to the last guinea. Hope nothing from his name—nothing from his character. Though his lineage be old as the Conqueror—though his name be one that fortune enrols as foremost in her list—'the man's a man for a' that.' He plays, and is obnoxious to plunder himself; and if he can do it he plunders in return. The duellist is bad enough; but—"

"Why, d—n it, Pat, you have fought four times your self!"

"I have, and I regret it. One unfortunate affair, I lament to add, has left this hand bloody. I have been twice as often in the field as second; and, thank God, no friend whom I accompanied fell. I have, unluckily, when honourable mediation was rejected or impracticable, been necessitated to resort to the last and worst alternative the code of honour sanctions; but, believe me, boys, he who is from necessity party to a duel, will never experience more pleasure than when he brings two brave men from the ground, uninjured in person and reputation."

"This is a new doctrine of O'Brien's," said a young subaltern. "And we are not to fight, it seems?"

O'Brien regarded the speaker sternly.

"Fielding, I have a nephew about your own years, who carries the king's colours of the 52nd. He is the only child of a devoted mother; her first thought, her last prayer, is for the safety of her beloved boy. Were he insulted—mark my words—and did not assert his honour, I would pass him as an outcast—turn from him as a leper. No, boy, the honour of a gentleman should be his first care. The man whose courage is established is very seldom called upon; and the man who will fight will rarely volunteer a quarrel. Hence, the brave pass through life generally unoffending others and unmolested themselves."

"How came it then, Pat, that with those feelings you have been so particularly unfortunate?"

"Simply because I joined a regiment that was miserably divided among themselves. County politics were its cause—patronage was shamefully abused—men of obscure birth and disreputable character obtained commissions; and in the —— militia there were persons who should have worn no epaulet, except a footman's. But why waste good counsel upon idle boys? all is lost upon them; and though speaking for the last five minutes like an oracle, I might just as well have been whistling jigs to a milestone. But to resume my story. Fortunately for myself I was an hour too late in keeping my engagement with my cousin; and when I reached Earl Street, found Darcy's whole establishment in desperate commotion. There were in every direction the eye turned to incontestable symptoms of a general row; and the mortal remains of plates, dishes, and decanters, were strewn about the room, thick as leaves in Vallombrosa. From a waiter, who had been complimented with a black eye, I learned some particulars of the battle. Hector had been there, and ordered supper; sat down in expectation of my arrival, and managed to kill time while waiting for me by quarrelling with a military party in the opposite box. Two or three Connaught gentlemen espoused his cause of course, it being the wrong one, and a desperate onslaught was the consequence. In the *mêlée* Darcy's goods and chattels were demolished—challenges given and accepted—cards interchanged by the pack—the watch called in—and my excellent cousin borne off in triumph, after performing prodigies of valour by maiming divers of the king's subjects. Having secretly returned thanks to Heaven for my lucky escape, I directed my steps to the watch-house to visit my afflicted kinsman.

"I reached the place, and thinking it prudent to reconnoitre before I made my *entrée*, I peeped slyly over the hatch where was Hector, with sundry other malefactors, in 'durance vile.' By a stranger my cousin might have been readily mistaken for the commander of the garrison, he appeared so perfectly at home, and exercised such absolute authority. The constable of the night and Roderick's heir presumptive were seated in close conclave in a corner, and from their position being contiguous to the door, I could overhear the whole colloquy. Dogberry was remonstrating.

"Arrah, Hector darling. Arrah, now it's too bad—the third night this week. Have ye no conscience, man, in tattering that unfortunate tailor out of bed. Upon my sowl, he has a cough that would scar ye. He's a wakely divil; and as his wife said the last night, if ye'll drag him out of his warm bed, ye'll have his life to answer for."

"Pshaw!" ejaculated the prisoner. "He charges for all in the account. I never knock him up for bail but he lays it thick upon the next order. Send for him, Brady; get in as much porter and whisky as will make all drunk, and we'll sit down comfortably at the fire."

"Make way for Mistur O'Dogherty," roared divers of the body-guard. "Get up, you in the corner there. Arrah! get out of the way; the gentleman's a regular customer, and we don't see you above twice in the twelvemonth." The seat of honour was directly vacated by the minor delinquent, and my excellent kinsman ceremoniously inducted thereunto.

From an imperfect view it struck me that Hector's person had not suffered material damage; but his disordered appearance, and clothes torn to ribands, clearly proved that the affair though short had been both sharp and spirited. Perceiving that my interference was unnecessary, I thought it no hour for salutations, and quickly retreated to "mine inn," leaving the task of Hector's deliverance to the worthy artist, who, as it would appear, was my cousin's "standing bail."

Next day I repaired to Kildare Street in due time; and it was lucky that I was so regular, for Phil made a most alarming report. Overnight the gout had seized upon Roderick's better member; he was in considerable pain, and as Clancy said, "the priest himself darn't go near him." To add to the misfortune, several gentlemen had called early in the morning, stated their business to be urgent, and could scarcely be restrained by the valet from invading the sacred precincts of the commander's bedroom. Thus Roderick had been disturbed before his time, was consequently in most abominable temper, and I, alas! should in all likelihood be obliged to bear the first burst of gout and irritability.

I found him in company with his pug—*par nobile*—Ireland could not match them. Roderick was ready for battle; and though it was not five minutes past eleven, he rated me for the delay. Breakfast passed, and the general commenced:

"I had an infernal night of it—gout in the knee first; then moved to the ankle; lame in both legs; no sleep; could have dozed a little in the morning, when three scoundrels, with knocks that I thought would have demolished the door, disturbed me. Well they did not break into my bedroom! Private business forsooth. I'm pestered with fellows of their kind; force their way up under false pretences, all for one purpose—begging—begging. I have found Aladdin's lamp, I suppose. All—priests and parsons—all ring to the same tune—money, money. 'No family—blest with independence,' and other cant to effect one's spoliation! Hish! what a twinge! D—n it, you never had the gout, and have no more feeling for me than if I was a glandered horse!"

I assured him of my deep sympathy; but I suspect the terms I expressed it in were not over ardent.

"Humph!" he growled. "All words—mere words of course! But, regarding Hector—I hear he is dissipated—drinks—brawls—plays. I want you to ascertain the truth, and give me quiet and confidential information of his general proceedings."

I fired at the proposition, and losing all dread of the commander boldly renounced the commission.

"Why, sir, what the devil do you take me for? I turn spy upon my kinsman! By heaven! if a stranger proposed such an employment, he should dearly repent that he offered such an indignity."

The commander felt the rebuke, and began muttering what he intended as a qualification.

"No, Pat—no. D—n it, I did not mean that you should be a spy; but—but—"

"But, sir, yours was a proposition which no gentleman could listen to; and I wish you a good morning."

"Stop, I say—stop!" The hall-bell rang violently.

"Confound it! the hotness of young men's tempers is nowadays intolerable. This is, I suppose, one of these damned visitors; but if I don't despatch him in double quick, my name's not Roderick!"

The commander was right in his supposition. Clancy announced the stranger as one of the sleep-breakers; handed in a card, on which was engraved, "Mr Alleyn, 40th Regiment;" and next moment the gentleman was ushered in.

He was quite a lad, and also a very young soldier; for whether it was the importance of his embassy, or the vinegar aspect of the comrade of Baron Puffenberg that abashed him I know not, but he coloured up to the eyes, and seemed to be in evident confusion. I pointed to a chair—a civility which Roderick had omitted; and the following colloquy ensued:

"You are General O'Dogherty?" said the stranger as he referred to a visiting-ticket in his hand.

"Yes, sir, I have that honour; and you, sir, are Mr Alleyn?" and the surly commander examined the young man's card.

"Yes, sir, my name is Alleyn; and, sir—hem—it has given me pain, to be obliged—hem—to call on you—for—"

"Sir—I understand you—I am a plain man, and hate long speeches. In a word, sir, you might have spared your call; it will procure you nothing from me."

"This is very strange, sir—your character—"

"Pish! sir. I don't care a fig what any man says—and to cut short the interview, you may be off and try some other fool."

"Sir—this is unaccountable! I am not experienced in such matters, and confess I am rather embarrassed."

"No doubt, sir, a common consequence of imprudence. I am busy, sir, and you intrude."

The young man reddened to the ears.

"Sir, this won't do. If you think to bully, you are mistaken. I insist on an immediate explanation."

"Why, zounds! Do you threaten me in my own house? I suppose you intend committing a burglary. Here, Clancy, show him the door."

"You shall hear me, sir! I have claims upon you that must be satisfied before I leave this."

"Why, you audacious scoundrel! Go for a peace officer, Clancy. I'll have you settled."

"Ah! I understand you; and it is time to leave you, sir, when you resort to the police. But let me say, that your conduct is ungentlemanly, and your meanness disgraceful to the profession you dishonour."

Roderick seized upon the nearest weapon of offence, the crutch, while Clancy by bodily force fairly ejected the visitor. He was expelled with great reluctance, and departed from the house vowing vengeance against the commander.

Roderick was nearly suffocated with fat and passion. He growled like a worried bear; while smart twinges of his disorder, accelerated no doubt by recent irritation, came faster and fiercer on.

"I wish I knew where the scoundrel could be found, I would indict him. I would, by everything litigious, for attempting to obtain money by intimidation. Hish!—my toe—my toe! The villain—to fancy that I was to be bullied. Hish!—hish! Another fit brought on."

He continued grumbling and groaning for a quarter of an hour, until the malady abated, and his violent excitement had exhausted itself. Once more I rose to take my departure, when another thundering summons was heard at the hall-door—another card introduced—and immediately after, "Captain Coolaghan of the South Cork" was ushered into the presence of the ex-general. He too, as Phil Clancy mentioned in a whisper, was one of the sleep-breakers.

If the former visitor had evinced some diffidence in the opening of the interview, there was no indication of any tendency to blushing on the part of Captain Coolaghan of the South Cork. I examined his figure hastily—for it was rather remarkable. In age he was above fifty; in height, I should say, approaching to seven feet. His shoulders were broad—his legs thin—while his whole appearance had what the Irish call "a shuck look," and told plainly that the visitor had never considered abstinence and water-drinking necessary for his soul's weal. No man could be better satisfied with himself, or deemed his place in society less equivocal. He entered Roderick's "great chamber" with a smile, nodded graciously to us both, established himself in a chair, produced a silver snuff-box of immense capacity, took a deep pinch, and then protruding his long chin sundry inches beyond his black stock, politely inquired, "which of the gintlemen was the gineral?"

A more infelicitous opening to an interview could not have been conceived. That there could be any doubt of his identity, or that the imprint of his former glory was not stamped upon his exterior, was death to Roderick; and quickly did he remove the stranger's uncertainty.

"*I*, sir!" he exclaimed testily. "*I* am Major-general O'Dogherty."

"Then, sir," responded the visitor, "I am proud of the pleasure of making your acquaintance. Your friend, I presume?" and be bowed graciously to me.

"Yes, sir; and here with me on particular business."

"I comprehend—all right;" and Captain Coolaghan closed his left eye knowingly. "We may proceed to business then at once; and faith, when a man kicks up a dust and gets into scrapes, why the sooner the thing's settled the better."

"Kicks up a dust—gets into scrapes! Why, sir, what the devil do you mean?" exclaimed the friend of Puffenberg, as he looked daggers at his new acquaintance of the South Cork.

"Why then, indeed, general, your treatment of my young friend of the 40th was not the civilest in the world. But come, come—when men grow ould they always get cranky. We ought to make allowances. God knows, neither you, nor I, when we come to his years, will be able to kick up such a rookawn;" and he smiled and nodded at me; while Roderick, who was making himself up for mischief, impatiently exclaimed in a voice almost smothered by passion,—

"Who the devil are you? What do you mean? What do you want?"

"Faith, and I can answer you all. My name, Charles Coolaghan, of the South Cork—my meaning, that you insulted my friend; and my business, a written apology. But come, we won't be too hard—We'll try and plaister it up without burning powder. Say ye were drunk. Do what my young friend asks, and there will be no more about it"

Roderick, who had with great difficulty waited for the close of the ambassador's address, now awfully exploded.

"Captain Coolaghan, sir. There is one thing I regret."

"Arrah, stop, general. It must be on paper—just for the sake of form. We won't publish it. We won't, upon my honour."

"Blood and thunder! Hear me, sir. What I regret is, that I did not knock out the scoundrel's brains; and if your business is in any way connected with him, I beg, sir, you'll oblige me with your absence"

"Well, upon my conscience," returned he of the South Cork, "a more unchristian kind of an ould gintleman I never talked to. You—with one foot in the grave—arrah, for the sake of your poor sowl, you ought to make atonement. Come, give us what we want—write the apology—say you were drunk—and—"

"Why, you infernal scoundrel!" Up jumped the captain—up rose the general—I flung myself between them. Coolaghan had seized his cane—Roderick grasped his crutch—while Phil Clancy, hearing the fresh uproar, rushed into the room, and was directed by his master to exclude the visitor, and that too, if necessary, *vi et armis*. The captain slowly retired, notifying his wrath as he departed.

"Ye ould firebrand—sure gout and a should have taken the divil out of ye before this. Killing waiters—murdering a whole company—and when gintlemen sind for satisfaction, nothing but the grossest abuse! But I'll have ye out. Troth I'll parade ye on the fifteen acres: ay, if you come hopping there upon that wooden prop;—or if ye don't, I'll post ye over Ireland—ye cantankerous—ould—desperate—"

The rest was lost in his descent of the staircase; but the terrific slam of the hall-door told plainly enough that Captain Coolaghan of the South Cork had "exited" in a rage.

"Pat," said the commander, as he endeavoured to recover breath, "bring me my pistols. If any more of these ruffians come, I'll shoot them though I hang for it. Holy Mary!" and he crossed himself devoutly. "What sins have I committed, that a poor, quiet, easy-tempered old man can't, in his last days, his own house, and a land of liberty, remain in his afflictions, without being tortured by a gang of villains, who first beg, then try robbery, and if you don't submit to plunder, coolly propose your assassination?"

A thundering rap interrupted the *jérémiade* of the unfortunate commander. Up ran Phil Clancy pale as a ghost.

"Another of them divils, that was here this morning," quoth the valet.

"Let him up," replied the general, while his brows contracted, and his look bespoke desperate determination—"Let him up. If I miss him with the crutch, do you, Pat, knock him down with the poker." And Puffenberg's confederate prepared for action, and I to witness the termination of a scene, that at present was strange and inexplicable.

The door opened—a very fashionable-looking dragoon presented himself—inquired "if General O'Dogherty was at home?" and on being answered in the affirmative, begged to have "Captain Hay of the Fifteenth" announced as having called. Roderick, with more politeness than I expected after his recent visitations, struck with the superior manner and address of the newcomer, requested him to take a chair, and then intimated that the general was present. The dragoon looked rather sceptically at the commander, and then turned his eyes on me.

"Really, gentlemen," he said, "I feel myself a little puzzled. You, sir," as he addressed me, "seem far too young to have attained that honourable standing in the army. And you, sir," and he turned to Roderick, "much too infirm for the extraordinary exertions which last night's affair at Darcy's must have required."

The commander stared—while a faint and glimmering notion of the business flashed across my mind. Of course I kept my suspicions to myself, and the general testily, but politely, entreated the captain of cavalry to be more explicit.

"May I inquire, in the first place, which is the general?"

The commander, with great dignity, announced himself to be the real Simon Pure.

"There must be a palpable mistake in the whole business," and the light dragoon laughed. "May I ask, without intending the slightest disrespect, if you supped at Darcy's last night?"

"Supped at the devil!" exclaimed the admirer of Baron Puffenberg. "Sir, I beg your pardon. Excuse my being irritable. Bad gout, sir. Saints would swear under half the provocation I have endured since daybreak. You'll forgive me?"

The captain smiled and bowed.

"My dear sir," continued Roderick, "I have not been out of my house these three months."

"Then," said the dragoon, "my conjectures are correct; and it is impossible that you could be the gentleman who knocked down Captain Edwards, blackened Mr Heywood's eye, and broke the waiter's arm with a chair."

My worthy kinsman repeated the charges categorically in a tone of voice so ludicrous, that neither Captain Hay nor I could refrain from laughing; and then added,—

"Really, sir, I am astonished, and at a loss to know why such inquiry should be made of me."

"The simplest reply, sir," returned the dragoon, "will be given in the Hibernian style, by asking another question. Pray, sir, is this card yours?" and he handed one to the friend of Puffenberg.

The general rubbed the glasses of his spectacles, and examined the ticket attentively; and then with a look of unqualified surprise replied,—

"It is mine—mine beyond a question!"

"Someone, then, has used your name and address with great freedom," observed Captain Hay.

"That person, if my suspicions be correct, shall rue his freedom dearly;" and the old man knit his brows, and desired me to ring for Clancy. He came; and the commander asked for his card-case. It was brought, and opened. No ticket of his was to be found; for those within were inscribed with Hector's name and residence. Conviction rested on the general's mind, and Clancy, ignorant of the consequences, sealed my cousin's fate. "Mr Hector," he said, "had been fiddling with the case." Such, indeed, was the fact. The unlucky youth, struck with the similarity between his uncle's and his own, had been examining the cases, put the wrong one in his pocket, and in the confusion of the preceding evening, had flung those of Baron Puffenberg's contemporary to his antagonists, and never discovered the mistake until the blunder had cost him an inheritance.

As to the quarrel at Darcy's—as well as I can now remember the wind up—it terminated in Captain Coolaghan losing a finger and Hector a new hat—while one of the Connaught gentlemen, who had so handsomely volunteered his services on that fatal evening, was duly cased in lead and transmitted to the abbey of Burashool, there to repose in peace with a long and distinguished ancestry.

While these important events were being transacted, Roderick was no idler. For a fortnight he was denied to his acquaintances, and as Phil Clancy whispered, "was writing continually;" for, as it subsequently appeared, he was engaged in altering his will, and cutting off his unlucky nephew with a shilling, which he had the barbarity to have regularly tendered to him by his attorney. But the poor lad did not live to feel the effects of an uncle's wrath, produced by his own imprudence. He quarrelled at a hazard-table with a ruffian; he and his antagonist were men of a similar stamp—both were blacklegs, and both bullies—they adjourned of course to the field—and Hector fell.

I have only to add, that the friend and admirer of Baron Puffenberg, even after death, contrived to keep all his relatives in feuds and litigation. He left a most voluminous and unintelligible will; and in it bequeathed his property to three old maids, two grand-nephews, a cousin, and a priest; with a sum to found a friary, and a large bequest to form a fund for supplying masses for the repose of his soul. Me, he cut off one morning that I had unwittingly displeased him, with a legacy of one thousand pounds—a donation for which he expressly provided, and which, as it turned out, was the only legacy paid. For so confused and contradictory were the remainder, and so ingeniously did one provision nullify the next one, that of course the property was thrown into chancery, and there it continues to this day.

If Roderick's deliverance from purgatory depended on the payment of the mass fund, all I can say is, that there he lies, snug and warm!

II

THE RIVAL ARMIES

By heaven! it is a splendid sight to see,
For one who hath no friend, no brother there,
Their rival scarfs of mixed embroidery,
Their various arms that glitter in the air!

Three hosts combine to offer sacrifice;
Three tongues prefer strange orisons on high;
Three gaudy standards flout the pale blue sky;
The shouts are—France, Spain, Albion, Victory!
Childe Harold

A MONTH HAD PASSED AWAY, and O'Connor was in another land. The embarkation at Portsmouth of a large reinforcement for the several battalions of his regiment, cantoned on the banks of the Douro, was promptly effected. The wind was favourable; and as it blew half a gale from the time they cleared the Channel, the transports anchored in the Tagus on the sixth evening from that on which they had lost sight of the chalk-cliffs of Britain.

A new scene had opened on O'Connor. The bustle of an approaching campaign occupied his thoughts; and, in martial preparation, he strove to forget the disappointment his rejection by Mary Howard had occasioned.

Nothing could equal the enthusiastic ardour with which the British soldiery looked forward to the recommencement of active operations; nothing could surpass their high discipline; and the organisation of the army was complete. During the period they had remained in winter cantonments, every arm of the force had been perfected, and the materiel of the English army was magnificent. Powerful reinforcements, including the Life and Horse Guards, had joined; and Lord Wellington crossed the Douro with nineteen regiments of cavalry, splendidly equipped and mounted. The infantry, recruited from the corps at home and volunteers from the militias, were vigorous and effective: the artillery was powerful and complete in every requisite for the field; while an experienced commissariat and well-regulated means of transport, facilitated the operations of the most perfect and serviceable force with which, since the days of Marlborough, a British general had opened a campaign.

Never did a commander take the field under more glorious auspices. Supported by numerous bodies of native troops, and assisted by the most daring of the guerilla leaders, Wellington broke up from his cantonments with summer before him, and a rich and luxurious country through which to direct his line of march. His troops were flushed with victory—his opponents depressed from constant discomfiture. The opening movements indicated this feeling strongly. The French were already retrograding; the British preparing to advance. No wonder, then, the brilliant hopes of that splendid army were fully realised; and the glorious career of English conquest almost continued without a check, until the fields of France saw its banners float in victory; and the last struggles at Ortez and Toulouse attest the invincibility of Wellington!

While the British were preparing to march, the army of the centre, under Joseph Bonaparte, followed by those of "the South," and " Portugal," retired slowly on the Ebro. As they were not pressed by the British light troops, the French corps moved leisurely along their route, accompanied by an immense train of equipages and baggage. The appearance of the whole army was picturesque and imposing, from the gaiety of its equipment and the variety of its costume. Excepting the infantry of the line and the light battalions, few of the

French regiments were similarly dressed. The horse artillery wore uniforms of light blue, braided with black lace; the heavy cavalry were arrayed in green coats, with brass helmets. The chasseurs and hussars, mounted on slight but active horses, were variously and showily equipped. The gendarmerie à cheval—a picked body, chosen from the cavalry in general—had long blue frocks, with buff belts and cocked hats—while the *elite* of the dragoon regiments, selected for their superior size and height, wore bearskin caps, and presented a fierce and martial appearance.

The regiments of the line had each their grenadier and voltigeur company; and even the light corps were provided with a company of the former. The appearance of the whole force was soldierly and effective—the cavalry was indeed superb—the artillery excellent, their caissons, guns, and harness, in excellent order, and the horses in the highest condition.

Though the rival armies were in discipline and efficiency to all appearance perfect, a practised soldier would remark a striking dissimilarity in the *materiel* of their respective equipment. Everything attached to the British was simple, compact, and limited as far as its being serviceable would admit; while the French corps was encumbered in its march with useless equipages, and burdened with accumulated plunder. That portion of the Spanish noblesse which had acknowledged the usurper now accompanied his retreat—state functionaries in court dresses and embroidery mingled with the troops—calashes with wives and mistresses moved between brigades of guns—while nuns from Castile, and ladies from Andalusia, mounted on horseback and attired *en militaire*, deserted convent and castle, to follow the fortunes of some "bold dragoon." Never was an army, save that of Moscow, so overloaded with spoil and baggage as that of Joseph Bonaparte with which he retired upon Vittoria.

Though the circumstance had neither escaped the observation or animadversion of its officers, the retreating columns, as yet, had experienced but little difficulty in transporting the unwieldy ambulances which contained more spoil than trophies. Looking upon Spain as a hostile country, the means necessary to forward their convoys were unscrupulously seized, and every horse and mule was considered to be the property of the finder. The roads were good—the retreat unmolested. Even on the 16th no enemy had appeared; and to all appearance the allies remained quietly in their cantonments. The apathy of the English general was extraordinary; and many a prisoner was tauntingly asked by his French escort, "Was Lord Wellington asleep?"

Nothing, indeed, could equal the astonishment of the usurper, when informed, on the evening of the 18th, that the allies were in considerable force on the left bank of the Ebro! All the French arrangements were overthrown, and an instant night-march was rendered unavoidable. The drums beat to arms—the baggage was hastily put in motion—and the whole army, which had been collected in Pancorbo, or bivouacked in its immediate vicinity, defiled towards the city of Vittoria.

The point on which the corps of Joseph Bonaparte had concentrated is situated on the great road leading from Burgos to Bayonne. It is defended by a strong fort placed on a commanding eminence, which the French occupied with a regiment. A narrow valley, surrounded by rocky heights and crossed by a mountain torrent, affords barely space for the road which traverses it; and the scenery was singularly contrasted with the rich country the retreating army had just abandoned, for nothing could be more savage, rugged, and uncultivated.

Vittoria, on which the French fell back, is in picturesque situation second to no city in Spain. Placed on a gentle eminence, a level champaign country immediately surrounds it, encircled in the distance by a mountain ridge. On the north-west, the Zadorra is crossed by several bridges; while, on the other side, a bold and commanding chain of heights overhangs the road leading to Pampeluna. Across the valley, which there becomes gradually enlarged, are the villages of Gamarra Major and Abechaca, while the beautiful river ranges over a fine and cultivated scene, giving to the environs of Vittoria a rich yet romantic character.

There, after a harassing march of thirty miles, the army of the South halted on the evening of the 19th. A more confused and crowded place could not be imagined, and it displayed a strange medley of magnificence and discomfort. Earlier in the evening, the court of Joseph, his staff and guards, the headquarters of "the centre," convoys and equipages, cavalry and artillery, occupied the buildings, and crowded the streets; while every hour increased the confusion, as portions of the executive and military departments flocked in and formed an embarrassing addition to an unmanageable mass of soldiers and civilians, already far too numerous to find accommodation in a town unequal to shelter half that number which occupied it now.

But yet a stranger scene was enacting at Vittoria. While the city was brilliantly illuminated in honour of the visit of the king, and a gayer sight could not be fancied than its sparkling interior presented, beyond the walls an army was taking its position, and a multitude of wretched serfs were employed at the point of the bayonet in throwing up field defences, and assisting those who ruled them with an iron hand to place their gulls in battery, and make the other military dispositions to repel the very force that had come for their deliverance.

III

OPENING OF THE CAMPAIGN—AFFAIR OF ST MILAN—THE BIVOUC

Perish the man whose mind is backward now!
King Henry V

No MOVEMENT OF THE PENINSULAR campaign brings to the retired soldier more interesting reminiscences than the rapid advance of the British army, from the time it crossed the Douro on the 1st of June until it halted on the evening of the 19th on the banks of the Bayas.

By the able manoeuvring of Lord Wellington, Joseph Bonaparte had been obliged to abandon his line of communication with the capital, and fall back on Burgos to concentrate. Contrary to the expectation of the French, their retreat was unmolested; and it was considered very doubtful whether the English commander would break up from his cantonments and become assailant.

But they mistook the man when they imagined that Wellington intended to remain inactive. With characteristic celerity, his whole army was put in motion, and the Douro, the Carrion, and the Pisuerga were crossed successively. A demonstration was made on Burgos, and the French were obliged to retire from the place and blow up its defences. Unopposed, the fiery chief reached the valley of the Ebro, and by a route considered by Napoleon's officers impracticable for the movement of an army, pressing forward without delay, he crossed the bridges of the river and established himself on the left bank.

It can hardly be imagined what additional interest this operation, brilliant equally in its execution and results, acquired from the nature of the country across which the line of march passed. The scenery was beautiful and diversified, displaying a singular combination of romantic wildness with exquisite fertility. One while, the columns moved through luxurious valleys intersprinkled with hamlets, vineyards, and flower-gardens; at another, they struggled up mountain ridges, or pressed through alpine passes overhung with toppling cliffs, making it almost difficult to decide whether the rugged chasm which they traversed had been rifted from the hillside by an earthquake, or scarped by the hand of man. If the eye turned downwards, there lay sparkling rivers and sunny dells; above, rose naked rocks and splintered precipices; while moving masses of glittering soldiery, now lost, now seen, amid the windings of the route, gave a panoramic character to the whole, that never will fade from the memory of him who saw it.

Some sharp fighting occurred on the 18th, between the light troops of the rival armies; and two retreating brigades of the enemy were overtaken and brought to action by the Rifles and 52nd. The affair terminated, on the French part, in the loss of much baggage and some three hundred prisoners, although Jourdan, by attacking the British left at Osma, thought to impede the advance of the allies, and afford sufficient time for his own column retiring from Frias to rejoin the main body without loss.

There is nothing more exciting in warfare, than when a small portion of an army operates in the presence of the whole. The feeling that their comrades' eyes are turned on them stimulates the combatants; while an intense anxiety for the success of their brethren in arms animates the coldest of the lookers on. This was strongly experienced during the short but decisive struggle on the heights of Millan. Although the ground was most unfavourable for an assault, nothing could surpass the splendid style in which the light brigade attacked the enemy. The road by which it was necessary to advance was rugged, steep, and narrow, overhung with crags and underwood, while a mountain-stream protected the French front, and some straggling houses increased the difficulty of advancing, by affording cover to the voltigeurs who had formed behind them. After a sharp fusillade the enemy gave ground, and the light brigade was pressing forward, when, suddenly, a fresh column debouched from a ravine, and appeared upon the flank of the assailants. Both rushed on to gain the crest of the hill—and both reached the plateau together. The 52nd, bringing their left flank forward in a run, faced round and charged with the bayonet. The conflict was momentary, the French broke, threw away their knapsacks, and fled for the adjoining high grounds; while a wild cheer from the supporting regiment—near enough to witness but not assist in the defeat—bore a soldier's tribute to the gallantry of their companions.

It was the first time that many of the young men who accompanied O'Connor from England had been "under fire," and seen hostile shots exchanged; and as the casual ties had been trifling, there was no drawback to damp the *éclat* of a successful affair. Never, indeed, did a young soldier commence a campaign, whose "starry influences" were more auspicious. The weather was fine—the country through which the line of march lay rich and picturesque—the troops moved as men move to victory—while a friendly population everywhere hailed the approach of their deliverers. The peasantry received them with "*vivas*"— the Spanish girl met them with her tambourine and castanets—while the nuns, leaving relic and rosary to gaze upon the glittering bands as they defiled in quick succession, showered rose-leaves from the convent grates; or, if the building was too distant from the line of march, waved, with their white veils, a welcome to the conquerors.

The spot where the Rifles bivouacked after the affair of Saint Millan was a wild and romantic valley upon the bank of a bright and rapid stream. The French had occupied it the preceding evening; and, with the variableness of war, the victors established themselves in the same cantonment that but a few hours before had been tenanted by the vanquished. It is marvellous with what celerity soldiers arrange their resting-places. Within an hour from the time the advance halted, the mules were up, the baggage unpacked, fires lighted, and supper in full preparation. No delay impeded these important operations; the whole of the martial community were actively employed—one carried wood—another watched the camp kettle; this man mended his shoe—that one cleaned his musket; all were busy—while the light and careless jest, which occasionally elicited a roar of laughter, might have been expected rather from a peaceful merrymaking, than from men after a sharp encounter, and preparing for a more decisive conflict on tomorrow.

In the ruined shell of a goatherd's hovel, a party of some seven or eight of the Rifles had cantoned themselves for the night. Their beds were laid around the walls, a tablecloth was spread in the centre of the floor, each quickly produced the necessary implements for attacking the contents of the camp kettle; and as all had contributed to the *cuisine*, the mess presented a strange combination of different viands, united in one general *mélange*. Men engaged warmly in the morning with an enemy are not fastidious in gastronomy in the evening; and an olio that would have poisoned an alderman, comprising salt and fresh beef, fowls, rice, vegetables, and a hare, was pronounced exquisite. Each from the grand depot selected the food his heart loved; while a large skin-bottle of country wine, and divers flasks and canteens filled with rum and brandy, indicated that due precautions had been taken to insure a merry night. When the meal ended, the kettle and its contents passed to the uses of the domestics, who had formed a rude bivouac beneath a spreading sycamore.

"Fill, lads—fill a high bumper," said the senior officer of the group who tenanted the ruins of the goatherd's hut. "Here's tufts and short barrels. I never was prouder of my brave lights than today; our success was decisive, and our casualties but few."

"Poor Robinson!—His was a short career. He fell at the very moment that victory was certain."

"Then," said Major O'Connor, "he fell where the brave should. Come, George—thou hast for the first time heard a bullet hiss! What think you of a smart affair like that of Saint Millan?"

"Think!" replied the enthusiastic boy, for the speaker had scarcely reached sixteen—"I think that the only thing on earth worth living for is such a scene as the one I shared in this morning."

"Right, boy," and O'Connor sighed heavily. "What are the tamer occupations of peaceful life, compared with the brave and brief career the soldier runs? That wild hurrah that echoed through the mountain passes, when the French were driven from the heights—what mortal sounds could thrill the heart as they did? Ay, George, let sluggard spirits dream their life away, the brave alone feel that rapturous excitement which makes existence tolerable."

O'Brien stole a side glance at the speaker: the eye was fired—the cup was at his lips—but yet, even in that maddening hour of high excitement after victory, the worm was gnawing a breast that seemed steeled to softer influences.

"How delightful," said another of the neophytes, who had landed but a few days before from England, "is this wild mode of life! Have we not all that man can desire? and a newness and uncertainty that make it doubly agreeable? Here we are cantoned for the night, and Heaven alone can tell where we shall bivouac tomorrow."

"Yes, Aylmer," replied O'Brien—"a summer campaign is not objectionable; but O'Connor could probably inform you that there are times when a bivouac is not so agreeable. Do you remember when we were hutted at Alcanza?"

The major smiled.

"Yes, Denis; our accommodations were not just so comfortable."

"I shall never forget the last night we occupied that infernal outpost. It was the morning after Busaco, when Massena, repulsed in every attempt to force our mountain position, endeavoured to turn it by marching in the direction of the road to Oporto. Of course a correspondent movement on our part was indispensable; and on the 29th of September we retreated upon the lines of Torres Vedras. We reached our entrenchments with little molestation, and there occupied the cantonments, where we were afterwards obliged to winter.

"From the perfect state of the lines, an assault upon them was utterly hopeless; and after a careful *reconnaissance*, Junot abandoned all idea of forcing the defences, and changed his operations to a blockade.

Nothing could exceed the privations which the French soldiers endured in their miserable cantonments. With scarcely any shelter from the inclemency of winter weather—food in scanty supplies, and of the most wretched description imaginable—disease gaining ground—desertions every day more numerous—while the mortality among the horses was tremendous, as from a scarcity of forage the poor animals were obliged to feed on rotten straw and vine-twigs. Our situation was better than that of the enemy, particularly in being tolerably supplied with corn and provisions; but as to the huts, I suspect both parties were pretty nearly on a par. We certainly, as they say in Ireland, 'kept open house,' for the wind and rain entered at every corner.

"Our habitation was constructed of sods, old boards, and branches, and thatched with heather. Straw was too scarce to be obtained; and the heath we substituted for it, when ever the rain fell heavily, was pervious everywhere. The inside of our wigwam, although the dimensions were limited, contained seven officers and a brace of greyhounds; while the beds, comprising stretchers, mattresses, a bear-skin, and two or three trusses of straw, were arranged round the walls, leaving a space in the centre for the rude apology which a shattered door formed for a table. When the night was wet, it was amusing to see the different expedients that each man resorted to, and the ingenious contrivances devised to obtain shelter from the rain. Some extended their blankets upon upright sticks, and stowed themselves beneath it; others put their faith in the tablecloth as a canopy. But these contrivances, however, were generally found wanting; when fully saturated, the cloth brought down the sticks, and the sleeper had the whole collection of water in one plump; and instead of receiving it by the drop, he got it by the gallon. Llewellin, the little Welshman who was killed at Badajos, was the most comical figure upon earth, as he sat on a truss of straw in the corner, under a tattered umbrella—while O'Shaughnessy and Daly, wrapped in their cloaks, remained all night stoutly at the table, discussing brandy punch, and playing 'spoiled five,' from a pack of cards reduced to twenty-seven, and whose backs, from divers stains, were to both just as familiar as their faces were. But the last night topped all. The roof, surcharged with moisture, became too weighty for its frail supports, and down it came upon the unhappy community; and men and dogs—sleepers and card-players—were all involved in one general ruin. Poor Daly—a six-pound shot closed his account at Salamanca—roared lustily for help. O'Shaughnessy in vain struggled to liberate himself from a ton of wet heather. The little Welshman was all but smothered under his own umbrella; while the dogs, believing themselves assaulted, bit the legs of the man next the peg they were secured to. Gradually, however, all got disentangled from the wreck, and obtained a lodging from their comrades, who, like ourselves, were hutted at this execrable outpost."

"Ah!" said O'Connor, "that is not the kind of concern that Edwards would fancy. His bivouac must be a *cottage ornée*, with a murmuring rivulet and a vineyard in full bearing. The casements should be trellised with ever-blowing roses, while grapes and oranges ripened against the wall, and he had merely to open the window to gather a dessert."

There was a laugh at the romantic picture the young soldier had drawn of campaigning—the goatskin bottle was nearly finished—one after another the revellers stretched themselves on their humble resting-places—in half an hour the bivouac was silent as a peaceful hamlet, and its occupants slept calmly, as if no struggle had occurred that day, and no battle was expected on the morrow.

IV

VITTORIA

SOME RAIN HAD FALLEN DURING the night, but a lovelier morning than the 21st of June never broke. The sun rose brilliantly, and the blue sky was cloudless. On either side all was prepared for a conflict—a battle was inevitable—the English commander being resolved to offer, and the French marshal to accept, the combat.

The enemy's position was well chosen, but it was rather too extended—on one side it rested on the heights of La Puebla, and on the other occupied the ridge above Gamarra Major. The French order of battle embraced two lines—the armies of Portugal and the South were in the first, and the cavalry and army of the centre were placed in the second in reserve. The entire, with the exception of a small corps, were drawn out in front of Vittoria, and formed on the left bank of the Zadorra, which sweeping round the whole position rendered it truly formidable.

While the front was defended by the river, the great roads to Bayonne and Pampeluna, in the event of any disaster, offered every facility for retreating. In many respects the French position at Vittoria was excellent; the communications were direct, and not liable to obstruction; the artillery were in battery, and a large proportion covered by a field-work in the weakest point (the centre), near the village of Gomecha; while the plains around Vittoria offered every advantage for the operations of cavalry; and that arm of Joseph's concentrated force was both numerous and well appointed.

The only means of attack upon the centre of the French position was by crossing the bridges of the Zadorra, and they were in every place commanded by the guns, and open to a charge of cavalry. Everything that could cover an enemy's advance had been carefully removed, and few beside British soldiers would have dared to bring on an action, where so many difficulties were to be encountered in the very opening of the contest.

Soon after the action commenced, Joseph placed himself upon a rising ground that overlooked his right and centre. His own guard were formed in his rear, and a numerous and splendid staff surrounded him. Wellington had chosen an eminence commanding the right bank of the Zadorra, and directly in front of the village of Arinez. Dressed in a short grey coat closely buttoned, his Spanish sash and plumed hat alone marked his rank. He remained for a long time on foot; and while the contest on the heights of Puebla continued doubtful, his glass was turned almost exclusively upon that point, as he watched the progress of the contest with the same coolness with which he would have regarded the manoeuvres of a review.

There never was, during the Peninsular campaigns, a battle that required nicer combinations and a more correct calculation in time and movements than that of Vittoria. It was impossible to bring up to the immediate proximity for attack every portion of his numerous army, and hence many of Wellington's brigades had bivouacked at a considerable distance from the Zadorra. Part of the country before Vittoria was difficult and rocky; hamlets, enclosures, and ravines, separating the columns from each other. Some of them were obliged to move by narrow and broken roads, and arrangements, perfect in themselves, were liable to embarrassment from numerous contingencies. But the genius that could plan these extended operations could also remedy fortuitous events, if such occurred.

The attack commenced by Hill's division moving soon after daylight by the Miranda road, and the detaching of Morilla's Spanish corps to carry the heights of La Puebla, and drive in the left flank of the enemy. The task was a difficult one. The ground rose abruptly from the valley, and towering to a considerable height, presented a sheer ascent that at first sight appeared almost impracticable. The Spaniards, with great difficulty, although unopposed, reached the summit; and there among rocks and broken ground became sharply engaged with the French left. Unable, however, to force the enemy from the heights, Sir Rowland detached a British brigade to Morilla's assistance, while, alarmed for the safety of his flank, Jourdan detached troops from his centre to support it. A fierce and protracted combat ensued, and Colonel Cadogan fell at the head of his brigade. Gradually and steadily the British gained ground; and while the eyes of both armies were turned upon the combatants and the possession of the heights seemed doubtful, the eagle glance of Wellington discovered the forward movement of the Highland tartans, and he announced to his staff that La Puebla was his own.

To support the attack upon the heights, O'Callaghan's brigade of the second division crossed the river and assaulted Sabijana de Alava. Notwithstanding a sharp resistance the place was carried most gallantly; but as the village was in advance, the French made repeated efforts to repossess it. The British, however, held it bravely, until the centre and left having closed up enabled the English general to make a decisive movement of the whole line.

Meanwhile the light divisions had left the road, and formed in close columns behind rocks and broken ground at some distance from the river. The hussar brigade remained dismounted on the left;

while the fourth division deployed to the right, and took its position for attack. The heavy cavalry were in reserve to support the centre, should support be required before the third and seventh came up and occupied ground on the left flank. During this time the first and fifth divisions, a Spanish and Portuguese corps, and a strong body of dragoons, were marched from Morgue, to place themselves on the road to Saint Sebastian, and there cut off the enemy's retreat.

While O'Callaghan's brigade was repeatedly attacked in Sabijana de Alava, and some anxiety was caused from the delay of the centre and their exposed position, the opening of Sir Thomas Graham's cannonade announced that the battle had commenced on the left. Presently Lord Dalhousie notified his arrival at Mendonza with the third and seventh divisions, and Lord Wellington ordered a general attack on the whole of the French position.

The light division moved under cover of a thicket and placed itself opposite the enemy right centre, about two hundred paces from the bridge of Villoses. On the arrival of Lord Dalhousie the signal was given to advance; and at the moment a Spaniard announced that one of the bridges had been left undefended. The mistake was quickly seized upon. A brigade, led by the first Rifles, crossed it in a run, and without loss established itself in a deep ravine, where it was protected from the cannonade.

Nothing could be more beautiful than the operations which followed. The light division carried the bridge of Nanclaus, and the fourth that of Tres Puentes—the divisions of Picton and Dalhousie followed, and the battle became general. The passage of the river—the movement of glittering masses from right to left far as the eye could range—the deafening roar of cannon—the sustained fusillade of the infantry—all was grand and imposing—while the English cavalry displayed in glorious sunshine, and formed in line to support the columns, completed a spectacle, that to a military observer would be unequalled.

Although perfect success had attended the combined movements of the different brigades, the village of Arinez resisted every attack, and even the 88th were repulsed in a daring attempt to storm it. This, probably, was the doubtful struggle of the day, and the French fought desperately. Their artillery played at point-blank distance—the village was filled with infantry—the whole place was shrouded in smoke, while the hissing of shot and bursting of shells added to the terrors of the scene.

But this was but a momentary check. Wellington in person directed a fresh assault—the 45th and 74th were led forward, and Arinez carried with the bayonet.

While the battle was raging in the front, the flank movement on Gamarra Major and Abechuco was being executed by the first and fifth divisions. The bridges in front of these villages had been fortified and were obstinately retained; but when the centre was forced at Vittoria, their defenders gave way, and Lord Lynedoch occupied them.

The whole of the enemy's first line were now driven heel—but they retired in perfect order, and re-forming close to Vittoria, presented an imposing front protected by nearly one hundred pieces of artillery. A tremendous fire checked the advance of the left centre, and the storm of the guns on both sides raged with unabated fury for an hour. Vittoria, although so near the combatants, was hidden from view by the dense smoke, while volley after volley from the French infantry, thinned though it could not shake Picton's "fighting third." But it was a desperate and final effort. The allies were advancing in beautiful order, and confusion was visible in the enemy's ranks, as their left attempted to retire by echelons of divisions, a movement badly executed. Presently the cannon were abandoned—and the whole mass of troops commenced retreating by the road to Pampeluna. The sun was setting, and his last rays fell upon a magnificent spectacle—the red masses of infantry were seen advancing steadily across the plain—the horse artillery at a gallop to the front, to open its fire on the fugitives—the hussar brigade were charging by the Camino Real—while the second division, having overcome every obstacle and driven the enemy from its front, was extending over the heights upon the right in line, its arms and appointments flashing gloriously in the fading sunshine of "departing day."

Never had an action been more general, nor the attacks in every part of an extended position more simultaneous and successful. In

the line of operations six bridges over the Zadorra were crossed or
stormed. That on the road to Burgos enabled Lord Hill to pass; the
fourth division crossed that of Nanclaus; the light, at Tres Puentes;
Picton and Dalhousie passed the river lower down; while Lord
Lynedoch carried Abechuco and Gamarra Major, though both were
strongly fortified and both obstinately defended.

From a hillock on the other side of Vittoria, Wellington viewed the
retreating enemy and urged forward his own troops in pursuit. What
a sight to meet a conqueror's eye! Beneath him the valley was covered
for a mile with straggling fugitives—for the French army had totally
lost its formation, and neither attempted to rally even or check the
pursuit of the British. The horse artillery were already posted on an
adjacent height, showering upon the crowd below them a storm of
shot and shells—the light troops and cavalry still pressed forward—
while around, the entire *matériel* of an army was scattered as it had
been left, and the whole of a magnificent park, with the exception
of a few guns, abandoned to the victors. Night alone closed the
pursuit—and favoured by the broken ground the shattered battalions
of the usurper effected their escape. The *déroute* was perfect—and two
leagues from the town, the fiery chief reluctantly ceased to follow, as
darkness and previous fatigue rendered further operations impossible.
The advance bivouacked on the ground where they halted; and
Wellington, returning slowly to Vittoria, entered it at nine at night.

Never had defeat been more decisive than that which the pseudo
king sustained. An army, complete in every arm, was totally dispersed;
and though the prisoners bore but a small proportion to the killed
and wounded, that could be ascribed alone to the rapidity with which
the French retired, abandoning everything that could impede their
flight, and favoured by a rugged surface, broken roads, and seasonable
darkness. Through streets thronged by a victorious soldiery and
choked with captured equipages, the English commander and his
weary staff rode slowly to their quarters; and the same city that, but
two nights since, had illuminated in honour of the King of Spain, was
blazing now to welcome the conqueror of the usurper.

On the morning of the 22nd, the field of battle and the roads for some miles in the rear exhibited an appearance it seldom fails within human power to witness. There lay the wreck of a mighty army; while plunder accumulated during the French successes, and wrung from every part of Spain with unsparing rapacity, was recklessly abandoned to any who chose to seize it. Cannon and caissons, carriages and tumbrels, wagons of every description were overturned or deserted, and a stranger *mélange* could not be imagined, than these enormous convoys presented to the eye. Here was the personal baggage of a king—there the scenery and decorations of a theatre. Munitions of war were mixed with articles of *virtu*; and with scattered arms and packs, silks, embroidery, plate, and jewels, mingled in wild disorder. One wagon was loaded with money—the next with cartridges; and wounded soldiers, deserted women, and children of every age, everywhere implored assistance or protection. Here a lady was overtaken in her carriage—in the next calash, was an actress or *fille-de-chambre* while droves of oxen were roaming over the plain, intermingled with an endless quantity of sheep and goats, mules and horses, asses and milch cows.

That much valuable plunder came into the hands of the soldiery is certain; but the better portion fell to the peasantry and camp followers. Two valuable captures were secured—a full military chest, and the baton of Marshal Jourdan.

Were not the indiscriminating system of spoliation adopted by the French armies recollected, the enormous collection of plunder abandoned at Vittoria would appear incredible. From the highest to the lowest, all were bearing off some valuables from the country they had over-run. Even the king himself had not proved an exception; for, rolled in the imperials of his own carriage, some of the finest pictures from the royal galleries were discovered. To facilitate their transport they had been removed from their frames, and were destined by the usurper to add to the unrivalled collection, that, by similar means, had been abstracted from the Continent to centre in the Louvre. Wellington, however, interrupted the Spanish paintings in their transit, and the formality of a restoration.

V

MOUNTAIN COMBAT— FRENCH BIVOUAC—MILITARY REMINISCENCES

King Richard.	Up with my tent: here will I lie tonight;
	But where tomorrow?—Well, all's one for that.
	SHAKESPEARE

AFTER THE DEFEAT OF JOSEPH Bonaparte, a brilliant continuation of successes attended the British arms. Passages and Paucorbo were taken, Pampeluna strictly blockaded, and the siege of Saint Sebastian commenced. Soult, after his appointment to the command, with a recruited army, endeavoured to succour these fortresses. A series of sanguinary combats in the Pyrenees terminated in his total discomfiture; and, with severe loss on both sides, the French marshal was pursued across the frontier.

No operation could have been more brilliantly executed than the mountain march of the light division in pursuit of Soults rear-guard, after he had been defeated before Pampeluna, and driven back upon the passes of the Bidassoa, which, but a few days before, he had forced in the full confidence of succeeding. The French army suffered heavily in their obstinate and repeated efforts to arrest the advance of the English general. On the 31st of July it continued retreating, while five British divisions pressed the pursuit vigorously by Roncesvalles, Maya, and Donna Maria. Nothing could equal the distress of the enemy—they were completely worn down; and fatigued and disheartened as they were, the only wonder is that multitudes did not perish in the wild and rugged passes through which they were obliged to retire. Although rather in the rear of some of the columns, the British light brigades were ordered forward to overtake the enemy, and, wherever they came up, bring them to immediate action. At midnight the bivouacs were abandoned—the division marched—and after nineteen hours' continued exertions, during which time a distance of nearly forty miles was traversed over Alpine heights and roads rugged and difficult beyond description, the enemy were overtaken and attacked. A short but smart affair ensued. To extricate the tail of the column, and enable the wounded to get away, the French threw a portion of their rear-guard across the river. The Rifles instantly attacked the reinforcement—a general fusillade commenced, and continued until night put an end to the affair, when the enemy retreated over the bridge of Yansi, and the British pickets took possession of it. Both sides lost many men—and a large portion of French baggage fell into the hands of the pursuing force who had moved by St Estevan.

That night the British light troops lay upon the ground; and next morning moved forward at daybreak. Debouching through the pass at Vera, the hill of Santa Barbara was crossed by the second brigade, while the Rifles carried the heights of Echalar, which the French voltigeurs seemed determined to maintain. As the mountain was obscured by a thick fog, the firing had a strange appearance to those who witnessed it from the valley, occasional flashes only being seen, while every shot was repeated by a hundred echoes. At twilight the enemy's light infantry were driven in; but long after darkness fell the report of musketry continued, until, after a few spattering shots, a deathlike silence succeeded, and told that the last of the enemy had followed their companions, and abandoned the heights to their assailants.

The next march was but a short one. The light division had been dreadful for the three preceding days, and it was necessary that time should be allowed for the leading columns to arrive. Fortunately a commissary got up to the front that evening; and better still, some private supplies arrived most seasonably. Soldiers speedily forget their past fatigues; and a very slight addition to their simple comforts dispels the recollection of the privations they have recently endured. Such was the case upon the night of the 4th of August, when the Rifles found themselves in the bivouac that the French rear had just quitted. As this post commanded a bridge and ravine, it had been occupied during Soult's advance and retreat—and with more comfort than such rude halting-places generally exhibit, the interior of the wooden huts bore testimony to the taste and ingenuity of their late inhabitants.

The whole appearance of what had been a French bivouac for a fortnight was perfectly characteristic of that nation. Some clever contrivances for cooking, rude arm-racks, a rough table and benches to sit round it, still remained; while one gentleman had amused himself by drawing likenesses of British officers with a burnt stick, in which face, figure, and costume were most ridiculously caricatured—while another, a votary of the gentle art of poesy, had immortalised the charms of his mistress in doggerel verses scratched upon the boards with the point of a bayonet.

As the party was unusually large, and there was no chance of the baggage being up for a day or two, "a ready-furnished house," as an Irish servant termed the wooden hovel, was indeed a treasure. A fine clear stream was running before the hut; and, never imagining that they should be so unceremoniously ejected from their wooden habitation, the French had collected a quantity of billets for firing, and in their hurry off, left a sheep and hare behind them. From the commissary a supply of brandy and biscuit had been obtained—and, at nightfall, a merrier party than that within the bivouac on the Torra never finished the contents of a canteen.

"Hurrah! my boys!" exclaimed Major O'Shaughnessy, as he turned down a tin measure of brandy-and-water. "Here we are safe and sound—owners of a house fit for the summer residence of a London alderman—a deep drink for the taking—and such a dinner! Isn't Peter Bradly the devil at a stew? What a pity it was that his mother did not bind him to a pastry-cook! Well—it was dacent, after all, in them French fellows to leave us meat, fire, and lodging. They do now and again exhibit some civility."

"Yes, they show a marked distinction in their treatment of us and our good allies," said O'Brien. "It was strongly instanced this morning. While we were forcing the road, a company had scaled the rocks above it to dislodge the tirailleurs who were firing at us from the heights. A poor fellow of mine, whose complexion is uncommonly swarthy, was wounded in the leg and fell. Unfortunately two or three retreating Frenchmen passed accidentally the spot where he was lying, and mistaking him for a Portuguese sharpshooter, stabbed him in several places, and flung him over the precipice; while they raised his comrade from the ground, placed a knapsack under his head, and gave him a drink from a leathern bottle of excellent tinta, which one of them had slung across his shoulder. On coming up we found the sufferer stretched upon the road, and with difficulty he told us how he had been treated. We of course rendered him some assistance; but Sergeant Corrigan's remarks, as he was binding a cloth round his fractured leg, turned our condolence into laughter. "There now," he said, as he propped the wounded man against a rock—"there you are as snug as if you were in the barracks of Kilkenny. Didn't I always tell ye, that yalla face of yours would bring ye into trouble? No wonder the French mistook ye for a Portagee. It's yourself that could travel from Badajos to Giberralthur, and you're so like a native, the devil a dog would bark at you the whole way. If you get better, Barney dear, write for the priest's lines that you were bred and born at Shannon Bridge, and ye can paste it on the back of ye'r knapsack."

"An instance of French confidence occurred yesterday, after we debouched by Vera," observed one of the lieutenants. "I was with a section of the company in the advance of the test, when, on turning a sudden angle of the road, we perceived, not twenty yards off a wounded voltigeur extended on the ground, and a young comrade supporting him. The Frenchman never attempted to retreat, but smiled when we came up as if he had been expecting us. 'Good morning,' he said, 'I have been waiting for you, gentlemen. My poor friend's leg is broken by a shot, and I could not leave him till you arrived, lest some of these Portuguese brigands should murder him. Pierre,' he continued, as he addressed his companion—'here are the brave English, and, you will be taken care of. I will leave you a flask of water, and you will soon be succoured by our noble enemy. Gentlemen, will you honour me by emptying the canteen. You will find it excellent, for I took it from a portly friar two days ago.' There was no need to repeat the invitation. I set the example, the canteen passed from mouth to mouth, and the monk's brandy vanished. The conscript—for he had not joined above a month—replenished the flask with water from a spring just by. He placed it in his comrade's hand, bade him an affectionate farewell, bowed gracefully to us, threw his musket over his shoulder, and trotted off to join his regiment, which he pointed out upon a distant height. He seemed never for a moment to contemplate that possibility of our sending him in durance to the rear; and there were about him such kindness and confidence, that on our part no one ever dreamed of detaining him."

"There never was, and probably never will be," said Captain Mornington, "so powerful an example of the influence of national confidence and courtesy, remaining unimpaired even during the continuance of a ferocious engagement, as that which Talavera exhibits. No fighting could be more desperate than that which marked the meeting of the French and English. Victor, considering the heights occupied by Hill's division the key of the position, concluded that if he could carry them, the remainder of the ground would then become untenable. To effect this, he resorted to a night attack. Lapisse made a feint upon the centre, while Ruffin and Vilatte ascended the heights, and for a short time had them in their possession—but Hill recovered them with the bayonet, and repulsed another furious effort made at midnight. Even though the French by pretending they were Spaniards and deserters, penetrated the British line, they were driven back with frightful slaughter; and so desperately was this night fighting carried on, that the assailants and the assailed frequently were engaged in a *mêlée* so close, that the men fought with clubbed muskets. All morning the battle raged, and the day assault was as unsuccessful as the night attack had proved. Both armies had lain upon the ground, but none had slept—the trooper with his horse's bridle round his arm—the soldier in momentary expectation of a fresh attempt, listened in every noise for the enemy's approach. No wonder, then, that a sultry day in July found both sides overcome with heat and hunger—and by a sort of common consent, long before noon, hostilities ceased, and the French cooked their dinners, while the English had wine and bread served out. Then it was, that a curious scene ensued. A small stream, tributary to the Tagus, flowed through a part of the battle-ground, and separated the combatants. During the pause that the heat of the weather and the weariness of the troops produced, both armies went to the banks of the rivulet for water. The men approached each other fearlessly, threw down their caps and muskets, chatted to each other like old acquaintances; and exchanged their brandy-flasks and wine-skins. All asperity of feeling seemed forgotten. To a stranger they would appear more like an allied force, than men hot from a ferocious conflict, and only gathering strength and energy to recommence it anew. But a still nobler rivalry for the time existed—the interval was employed in carrying off the wounded, who lay intermixed upon the hard-contested field; and, to the honour of both be it told, each endeavoured to extricate the common sufferers, and remove their unfortunate friends and enemies without distinction. Suddenly the bugles sounded the drum's beat to arms—many of the rival soldiery shook hands and parted with expressions of mutual esteem, and in ten minutes after they were again at the bayonet's point."

"How miserably a portion of the Spaniards behaved!"

"Yes," said O'Connor; "only for their cowardice the British would not have suffered so dreadfully as they did. But what could be expected from troops led by such miserable officers, and commanded by an imbecile old man like Cuesta? I saw him the day before the battle commenced. He was mounting his horse to look at some brigades of ours; two grenadiers lifted him bodily to the saddle, while an aide-de-camp passed his legs across the horse's croup, and an orderly fixed his foot within the stirrup! The rosary were better fitted for one of his infirmities than the baton of command. When he was with great difficulty dismounted from his charger's back, they transferred him into a lumbering coach drawn by half a score of mules, and thus he proceeded in state to his headquarters."

"Pray did not the old boy decimate the runaways?" inquired the lieutenant.

"No—Lord Wellington interfered, and saved the greater portion of the scoundrels. The lots were drawn—officers and men prepared for immediate execution—when, at the request of the English commander, the condemned were decimated anew, and thus nine out of every ten escaped, and only five officers and thirty men suffered."

"Do you recollect the circumstances that marked the close of Talavera, O'Connor?"

"Alas! what a terrible accompaniment to the after horrors of a battlefield! From the heat of the weather the fallen leaves were parched like tinder, and the grass was rank and dry. Near the end of the engagement both were ignited by the blaze of some cartridge-papers, and the whole surface of the ground was presently covered with a sheet of fire. Those of the disabled who lay on the outskirts of the field managed to crawl away, or were carried off by their more fortunate companions who had escaped unhurt; but, unhappily, many gallant sufferers, with 'medicable wounds,' perished in the flames before it was possible to extricate them. I walked over the ground next morning, and, as if to exhibit violent death in all its horrifying variety, the writhed and distorted features of the blackened corpses I passed by showed in what intolerable agony they had breathed their last!"

"And how did the battle terminate?" inquired one of the lads.

"Aubrey can best answer you," replied O'Connor; "for he was then in the 48th, and saw the last struggle the French made."

"It was a beautiful movement," said the officer to whom the major had referred. "The enemy had been repulsed and followed. The Guards, carried onwards by victorious excitement, advanced too far, and found themselves in turn assailed by the French reserve, and mowed down by an overwhelming fire. They fell back; but as whole sections were swept away, their ranks became disordered, and nothing but their stubborn gallantry prevented a total *déroute*. Their situation was most critical.

Had the French cavalry charged home, nothing could have saved them. Lord Wellington saw the danger, and speedily despatched support. A brigade of horse were ordered up, and our regiment moved from the height we occupied to assist our hard-pressed comrades. We came on at double quick, and formed in the rear by companies, and through the intervals in our line, the broken ranks of the Guards retreated. A close and well-directed volley from us arrested the progress of the victorious French, while with amazing celerity and coolness the Guards rallied and re-formed, and in a few minutes advanced in turn to support us. As they came on, the men gave a loud huzza. An Irish regiment to the right answered it with a thrilling cheer. It was taken up from regiment to regiment, and passed along the English line; and that wild shout told the advancing enemy that British valour was indomitable. The leading files of the French halted—turned—fell back—and never made another effort. Both armies remained upon the ground; but during the night Victor decamped, and left victory and an undisputed field to his conqueror."

"Gentlemen," said O'Connor, "the night wears fast. Methinks we have had enough of martial reminiscences. Come, fill; and let us change war for a softer theme. I'll give you a toast—'Lovely woman!'—And I propose, as a suitable accompaniment, that O'Shaughnessy shall favour us with the true detail of one of his amatory adventures."

"Bravo—nothing can be more apposite to the toast"—responded Captain O'Brien. "Come, Terence, my jewel; forget your national bashfulness for half an hour, and give us the interesting particulars of the first of one of your numerous attempts at matrimony."

"Why then, faith," replied the gallant major, "my opening effort to become a Benedict was nearly as big a blunder as it well could be. Here, hand me that leathern conveniency"—and he pointed to a wine-skin—"though, upon my conscience, those young scamps have lessened its contents amazingly. Heigh-ho! It was a queer business, and I will make the story as short as I can."

Major O'Shaughnessy' having fortified himself with a stoup of tinta, thus commenced the affecting narrative of his first disappointment in love.

VI

CONFESSIONS OF
A GENTLEMAN WHO WOULD HAVE
MARRIED IF HE COULD
(FIRST CONFESSION)

Come, come with me, and we will make short work;
For, by your leaves, you shall not stay alone,
Till holy church incorporate two in one.

Romeo and Juliet

Duke.   What! are you married?
Mariana.   No, my lord.
Duke.   Are you a maid?
Mariana.   No, my lord.
Duke.   A widow then?
Mariana.   Neither, my lord.
Duke.   Why, thou
          Art nothing then: neither maid, widow, nor wife.

Measure for Measure

YES—HERE I AM, TERENCE O'SHAUGHNESSY, an honest major of
foot, five feet eleven and a half, and forty-one, if I only live till
Michaelmas. Kicked upon the world before the down had blackened
on my chin, fortune and I have been wrestling from the cradle, and yet
I had little to tempt the jade's malevolence. The young of an excellent
gentleman, who, with an ill-paid rental of twelve hundred pounds, kept
his wife in Bath, and his hounds in Tipperary, my patrimony would have

scarcely purchased tools for a highwayman, when in my tenth year my father's sister sent for me to Roundwood; for hearing that I was regularly going to the devil, she had determined to redeem me if she could.

My aunt Honor was the widow of a captain of dragoons, who got his quietus in the Low Countries some years before I saw the light. His relict had in compliment to the memory of her departed lord eschewed matrimony, and, like a Christian woman, devoted her few and evil days to cards and religion. She was a true specimen of an Irish dowager—her means were small, her temper short—she was stiff as a ramrod, and proud as a field-marshal. To her, my education and future settlement in life were entirely confided, as one brief month deprived me of both parents. My mother died in a state of insolvency, greatly regretted by everybody in Bath—to whom she was indebted; and before her disconsolate husband had time to overlook a moiety of the card claims transmitted for his liquidation, he broke his neck in attempting to leap the pound-wall of Oran-more, for a bet of a rump and dozen. Of course he was waked and buried like a gentleman—everything sold by the creditors—my brothers sent to school—and I left to the tender mercy and sole management of the widow of Captain O'Finn.

My aunt's guardianship continued seven years, and at the expiration of that time I was weary of her thrall, and she tired of my tutelage. I was now at an age when some walk of life must be selected and pursued. For any honest avocation I had, as it was universally admitted, neither abilities nor inclination. What was to be done? and how was I to be disposed of? A short deliberation showed that there was but one path for me to follow, and I was handed over to that *refugium peccatorum*, the army, and placed as a volunteer in a regiment just raised, with a promise from the colonel that I should be promoted to the first ensigncy that became vacant.

Great was our mutual joy when Mrs O'Finn and I were about to part company. I took an affectionate leave of all my kindred and acquaintances, and even, in the fulness of my heart, shook hands with the schoolmaster, though in boyhood I had devoted him to the infernal gods for his wanton barbarity. But my tenderest parting was reserved for my next-door neighbour, the belle among the village beauties, and presumptive heiress to the virtues and estates of Quartermaster Maginn.

Biddy Maginn was a year younger than myself; and, to do her justice, a picture of health and comeliness. Lord what an eye she had! and her leg! nothing but the gout would prevent a man from following it to the very end of Oxford Street. Biddy and I were next neighbours—our houses joined—the gardens were only separated by a low hedge—and by standing on an inverted flower-pot one could accomplish a kiss across it easily. There was no harm in the thing—it was merely for the fun of trying an experiment—and when a geranium was damaged, we left the blame upon the cats.

Although there was a visiting acquaintance between the retired quartermaster and the relict of the defunct dragoon, never had any cordiality existed between the houses. My aunt O'Finn was as lofty in all things appertaining to her consequence as if she had been the widow of a common-councilman; and Roger Maginn, having scraped together a good round sum, by the means quartermasters have made money since the days of Julius Caesar, was not inclined to admit any inferiority on his part. Mrs O'Finn could never imagine that any circumstances could remove the barrier in dignity which stood between the non-commissioned officer and the captain. While arguing on the saw, that "a living ass is better than a dead lion," Roger contended that he was as good a man as Captain O'Finn; he, Roger, being alive and merry in the town of Ballinamore, while the departed commander had been laid under a "counterpane of daisies," in some counterscarp in the Low Countries. Biddy and I laughed at the feuds of our superiors; and on the evening of a desperate blow up we met at sunset in the garden—agreed that the old people were fools, and resolved that nothing should interrupt our friendly relations. Of course the treaty was ratified with a kiss, for I recollect that next morning the cats were heavily censured for capsizing a box of mignionette.

No wonder, then, that I parted from Biddy with regret. I sat with her till we heard the quartermaster scrape his feet at the hall-door, on his return from his club—and kissing poor Biddy tenderly, as Roger entered by the front, I levanted by the back door. I fancied myself desperately in love, and was actually dreaming of my dulcinea when my aunt's maid called me, before day, to prepare for the stage-coach that was to convey me to my regiment in Dublin.

In a few weeks an ensigncy dropped in, and I got it. Time slipped insensibly away—months became years—and three passed before I revisited Ballinamore. I heard, at stated periods, from Mrs O'Finn. The letters were generally a detail of bad luck or bad health. For the last quarter she had never marked honours—or for the last week closed an eye with rheumatism and lumbago. Still as these *jérémiades* covered my small allowance, they were welcome as a lover's billet. Of course, in these despatches the neighbours were duly mentioned, and every calamity occurring since her "last" was faithfully chronicled. The Maginns held a conspicuous place in my aunt's quarterly notices. Biddy had got a new gown—or Biddy had got a new piano—but since the dragoons had come to town there was no bearing her. Young Hastings was never out of the house—she hoped it would end well—but everybody knew a light dragoon could have little respect for the daughter of a quartermaster; and Mrs O'Finn ended her observations by hinting, that if Roger went seldomer to his club, and Biddy more frequently to mass, why probably in the end it would be better for both of them.

I re-entered the well-remembered street of Ballinamore late in the evening, after an absence of three years. My aunt was on a visit, and she had taken that as a convenient season for having her domicile newly painted. I halted at the inn, and after dinner strolled over the way to visit my quondam acquaintances, the Maginns.

If I had intended a surprise, my design would have been a failure. The quartermaster's establishment were on the *qui vive*. The fact was, that since the removal of the dragoons, Ballinamore had been dull as ditch-water; the arrival of a stranger in a postchaise, of course, had created a sensation in the place, and before the driver had unharnessed, the return of Lieutenant O'Shaughnessy was regularly gazetted, and the Maginns, in anticipation of a visit, were ready to receive me.

I knocked at the door, and a servant with a beefsteak collar opened it. Had Roger mounted a livery? Ay—faith—there it was, and I began to recollect that my aunt O'Finn had omened badly from the first moment a squadron of the 13th Lights had entered Ballinamore.

I found Roger in the hall. He shook my hand, swore it was an agreeable surprise, ushered me into the dining-room, and called for hot water and tumblers. We sat down. Deeply did he interest himself in all that had befallen me—deeply regret the absence of my honoured aunt—but I must not stay at the inn, I should be his guest; and, to my astonishment, it was announced that the gentleman in the red collar had been already despatched to transport my luggage to the house. Excuses were idle. Roger's domicile was to be headquarters; and when I remembered my old flame Biddy, I concluded that I might, for the short time I had to stay, be in a less agreeable establishment than the honest quartermaster's.

I was mortified to hear that Biddy had been indisposed. It was a bad cold, she had not been out for a month, but she would muffle herself, and meet me in the drawing room. This, too, was unluckily a night of great importance in the club. The new curate was to be balloted for; Roger had proposed him; and, *ergo*, Roger, as a true man, was bound to be present at the ceremony. The thing was readily arranged. We finished a second tumbler, the quartermaster betook himself to the King's Arms, and the lieutenant, meaning myself, to the drawing-room of my old inamorata.

There was a visible change in Roger's domicile. The house was newly papered; and, leaving the livery aside, there was a great increase of gentility throughout the whole establishment. Instead of bounding to the presence by three stairs at a time, as I used to do in lang syne, I was ceremoniously paraded to the lady's chamber by him of the beefsteak collar; and there, reclining languidly on a sofa, and wrapped in a voluminous shawl, Biddy Maginn held out her hand to welcome her old confederate.

"My darling Biddy"—"My dear Terence!"—and the usual preliminaries were got over. I looked at my old flame—she was greatly changed, and three years had wrought a marvellous alteration.

I left her a sprightly girl—she was now a woman—and decidedly a very pretty one; although the rosiness of seventeen was gone, and a delicacy that almost indicated bad health had succeeded; "but," thought I, "it's all owing to the cold."

There was a guarded propriety in Biddy's bearing, that appeared almost unnatural. The warm advances of old friendship were repressed; and one who had mounted a flower-pot to kiss me across a hedge, recoiled from any exhibition of our former tenderness. Well, it was all as it should be. Then I was a boy, and now a man. Young women cannot be too particular, and Biddy Maginn rose higher in my estimation.

Biddy was stouter than she promised to be when we parted, but the eye was as dark and lustrous, and the ankle as taper, as when it last had demolished a geranium. Gradually her reserve abated— old feelings removed a constrained formality—we laughed and talked—ay, and kissed, as we had done formerly; and when the old quartermaster's latch-key was heard unclosing the street-door, I found myself admitting, in confidence and a whisper, that "I would marry if I could." What reply Biddy would have returned I cannot tell, for Roger summoned me to the parlour; and as her cold prevented her from venturing down, she bade me an affectionate good-night. Of course she kissed me at parting—and it was done as ardently and innocently as if the hawthorn hedge divided us.

Roger had left his companions earlier than he usually did, in order to honour me, his guest. The new butler paraded oysters, and down we sat. When supper was removed, and each had fabricated a red-hot tumbler from the teakettle, the quartermaster stretched his long legs across the hearthrug, and with great apparent solicitude inquired into all that had befallen me since I had assumed the shoulder-knot and taken to the trade of war.

"Humph!"—he observed—"two steps in three years; not bad, considering there was neither money nor interest. D——n it! I often wish that Biddy was a boy. Never was such a time to purchase on. More regiments to be raised, and promotion will be at a discount. Sir Hugh Haughton married a stockbroker's widow with half a plum, and paid in the two thousand I had lent him. Zounds! if Biddy were a boy, and that money well applied, I would have her a regiment in a twelvemonth."

"Phew!" I thought to myself. "I see what the old fellow is driving at."

"There never would be such another opportunity," Roger continued. "An increased force will produce an increased difficulty in effecting it. Men will be worth their own weight in money—and d—n me, a fellow who could raise a few might have anything he asked for."

I remarked that, with some influence and a good round sum, recruits might still be found.

"Ay, easy enough, and not much money either, if one knew how to go about the thing. Get two or three smart chaps—let them watch fairs and patterns—mind their hits when the bumpkins got drunk, and find out when fellows were hiding from a warrant. D—n me, I would raise a hundred while you would say Jack Robison. Pay a friendly magistrate; attest the scoundrels before they were sober enough to cry off; bundle them to the regiment next morning; and if a rascal ran away after the commanding officer passed a receipt for him, why all the better, for you could re-list him when he came home again."

I listened attentively, though in all this the cloven foot appeared. The whole was the plan of a crimp; and, if Roger was not belied, trafficking in "food for powder" had realised more of his wealth than slop-shoes and short measure.

During the development of his project for promotion, the quartermaster and I had found it necessary to replenish frequently, and with the third tumbler Roger came nearer to business.

"Often thought it a pity, and often said so in the club, that a fine smashing fellow like you, Terence, had not the stuff to push you on. What the devil signifies family, and blood, and all that balderdash. There's your aunt—worthy woman—but sky-high about a dead captain. D—n me—all folly. Were I a young man, I'd get hold of some girl with the wherewithal, and I would double-distance half the highfliers for a colonelcy."

This was pretty significant—Roger had come to the scratch, and there was no mistaking him. We separated for the night. I dreamed, and in fancy was blessed with a wife, and honoured with a command, Nothing could be more entrancing than my visions; and when the quartermaster's *maître d'hôtel* roused me in the morning I was engaged in a friendly argument with my beloved Biddy, as to which of his grandfathers our heir should be called after, and whether the lovely babe should be christened Roderick or Roger.

Biddy was not at breakfast; the confounded cold still confined her to her apartment; but she hoped to meet me at dinner, and I must endure her absence until then as I best could. Having engaged to return at five; I walked out to visit my former acquaintances. From all of them I received a warm welcome, and all exhibited some surprise at hearing that I was domesticated with the quartermaster. I comprehended the cause immediately. My aunt and Roger had probably a fresh quarrel; but his delicacy had prevented him from communicating it. This certainly increased my respect for the worthy man, and made me estimate his hospitality the more highly. Still there was an evident reserve touching the Maginns; and once or twice, when dragoons were mentioned, I fancied I could detect a significant look pass between the persons with whom I was conversing.

It was late when I had finished my calls; Roger had requested me to be regular to time, and five was fast approaching. I turned my steps towards his dwelling-place, when, at a corner of a street, I suddenly encountered an old schoolfellow on horseback, and great was our mutual delight at meeting so unexpectedly. We were both hurried however, and consequently our greeting was a short one. After a few general questions and replies, we were on the point of separating, when my friend pulled up.

"But where are you hanging out?" said Frederick Maunsell. "I know your aunt is absent."

"I am at old Maginn's."

"The devil you are! Of course you heard all about Biddy and young Hastings?"

"Not a syllable. Tell it to me."

"I have not time—it's a long story; but come to breakfast, and I'll give you all the particulars in the morning. Adieu!" He struck the spurs into his horse, and cantered off singing,

"Oh! she loved a bold dragoon,
With his long sword, saddle, bridle."

I was thunderstruck. "Confound the dragoon!" thought I, "and his long sword, saddle, and bridle, into the bargain. Gad—I wish Maunsell had told me what it was. Well—what suppose I ask Biddy herself?" I had half resolved that evening to have asked her a very different question; but, faith, I determined now to make some inquiries touching Cornet Hastings of the 13th, before Miss Biddy Maginn should be invited to become Mrs O'Shaughnessy.

My host announced that dinner was quite ready, and I found Biddy in the eating-room. She was prettily dressed as an invalid should be; and notwithstanding her cold looked remarkably handsome. I would to a dead certainty have been over head and ears in love, had not Maunsell's innuendo respecting the young dragoon operated as a damper.

Dinner proceeded as dinners always do, and Roger was bent on hospitality. I fancied that Biddy regarded me with some interest, while instantly I felt an increasing tenderness that would have ended, I suppose, in a direct declaration, but for the monitory hint which I had received from my old schoolfellow. I was dying to know what Maunsell's allusion pointed at, and I casually threw out a feeler.

"And you are so dull, you say? Yes, Biddy, you must miss the dragoons sadly. By the way, there was a friend of mine here. Did you know Tom Hastings?"

I never saw an elderly gentleman and his daughter more confused. Biddy blushed like a peony, and Roger seemed desperately bothered. At last the quartermaster responded,—

"Fact is—as a military man, showed the cavalry some attention—constantly at the house—anxious to be civil—helped them to make out forage but damned wild—obliged to cut, and keep them at a distance."

"Ay, Maunsell hinted something of that."

I thought Biddy would have fainted, and Roger grew red as the footman's collar.

"Pshaw! d—d gossiping chap that Maunsell. Young Hastings— infernal hemp—used to ride with Biddy. Persuaded her to get on a horse of his—ran away—threw her—confined at an inn for a week—never admitted him to my house afterwards."

Oh! here was the whole mystery unravelled! No wonder Roger was indignant, and that Biddy would redden at the recollection. It was devilish unhandsome of Mr Hastings; and I expressed my opinion in a way that evidently pleased my host and his heiress, and showed how much I disapproved of the conduct of that *roué* the dragoon.

My fair friend rose to leave us. Her shawl caught in the chair, and I was struck with the striking change a few years had effected in my old playfellow. She was grown absolutely stout. I involuntarily noticed it.

"Lord! Biddy—how fat you are grown."

A deeper blush than even when I named that luckless dragoon flushed to her very brows at the observation, while the quartermaster rather testily exclaimed,—"Ay—she puts on her clothes as if they were tossed on with a pitchfork, since she got this cold. D—n it, Biddy, I say, tighten yourself, woman! Tighten yourself; or I won't be plased!"

Well, here was a load of anxiety removed; and Maunsell's mischievous innuendo satisfactorily explained away. Biddy was right in resenting the carelessness that exposed her to ridicule and danger; and it was a proper feeling in the old quartermaster to cut the man who would mount his heiress on a break-neck horse. Gradually we resumed the conversation of last night—there was the regiment if I chose to have it—and when Roger departed for the club, I made up my mind, while ascending the stairs, to make a splice with Biddy, and become Colonel O'Shaughnessy.

Thus determined, I need not particularise what passed upon the sofa. My wooing was short, sharp, and decisive; and no affected delicacy restrained Biddy from confessing that the flame was mutual. My fears had been moonshine; my suspicions groundless. Biddy had not valued the dragoon a brass button; and—poor soul—she hid her head upon my shoulder, and, in a soft whisper, acknowledged that she never had cared a jackstraw for anybody in the wide world but myself!

It was a moment of exquisite delight. I told her of my prospects, and mentioned the quartermaster's conversation. Biddy listened with deep attention. She blushed—strove to speak—stopped—was embarrassed. I pressed her to be courageous; and at last she deposited her head upon my breast, and bashfully hinted that Roger was old— avarice was the vice of age—he was fond of money—he was hoarding it certainly for her; but still, it would be better that my promotion should be secured. Roger had now the cash in his own possession. If we were married without delay, it would be transferred at once; whereas, something that might appear to him advantageous might offer, and induce her father to invest it. But she was really shocked at herself—such a proposition would appear so indelicate; but still a husband's interests were too dear to be sacrificed to maiden timidity.

I never estimated Biddy's worth till now. She united the foresight of a sage with the devotion of a woman. I would have been insensible, indeed, had I not testified my regard and admiration; and Biddy was still resting on my shoulder, when the quartermaster's latch-key announced his return from the club.

After supper I apprised Roger of my passion for his daughter, and modestly admitted that I had found favour in her sight. He heard my communication, and frankly confessed that I was a son-in-law he most approved of. Emboldened by the favourable reception of my suit, I ventured to hint at an early day, and pleaded "a short leave between returns," for precipitancy. The quartermaster met me like a man.

"When people wished to marry, why delay was balderdash. Matters could be quickly and quietly managed. His money was ready—no bonds or post obits—a clean thousand in hand, and another the moment an opening to purchase a step should occur. No use in mincing matters among friends. Mrs O'Finn was an excellent woman. She was a true friend, and a good Catholic; but d——n it, she had old-world notions about family, and in pride the devil was a fool to her. If she came home before the ceremony, there would be an endless fuss—and Roger concluded by suggesting that we should be married the next evening, and give my honoured aunt an agreeable surprise."

That was precisely what I wanted; and a happier man never pressed a pillow than I, after my interesting colloquy with the quartermaster. The last morning of my celibacy dawned. I met Roger only at the breakfast table; for my beloved Biddy, between cold and virgin trepidation, was *hors de combat,* and signified in a tender billet her intention to keep her chamber, until the happy hour arrived that should unite us in the silken bonds of Hymen. The quartermaster undertook to conduct the nuptial preparations; a friend of his would perform the ceremony, and the quieter the thing was done the better. After breakfast he set out to complete all matrimonial arrangements; and I strolled into the garden to ruminate on approaching happiness, and bless Heaven for the treasure I was destined to possess in Biddy Maginn.

No place could have been more appropriately selected for tender meditation. *There* was the conscious hedge, that had witnessed the first kiss of love; ay, and for aught I knew to the contrary, the identical flower-pot on which her sylphic form had reste; sylphic it was no longer, for the slender girl had ripened into a stout and comely gentlewoman; and she would be mine—mine that very evening.

"Ah! Terence," I said in an under tone, "few men at twenty-one have drawn such a prize. A thousand pounds ready cash—a regiment in perspective—a wife in hand; and such a wife—young, artless, tender, and attached. By everything matrimonial, you have the luck of thousands!"

My soliloquy was interrupted by a noise on the other side of the fence. I looked over. It was my aunt's maid; and great was our mutual astonishment! Judy blessed herself, as she ejaculated,—

"Holy Virgin! Master Terence, is that you?" I satisfied her of my identity, and learned to my unspeakable surprise that my aunt had returned unexpectedly, and that she had not the remotest suspicion that her affectionate nephew, myself, was cantoned within pistol-shot. Without consideration I hopped over the hedge, and next minute was in the presence of my honoured protectress, the relict of the departed captain.

"Blessed angels!" exclaimed Mrs O'Finn, as she took me to her arms, and favoured me with a kiss, in which there was more blackguard than ambrosia. "Arrah Terence, jewel; what the devil drove ye here? Lord pardon me for mentioning him!"

"My duty, dear aunt. I am but a week landed from Jersey and could not rest till I got leave from the colonel to run down between returns and pay you a hurried visit. Lord! how well you look!"

"Ah! then, Terence, jewel, it's hard for me to look well, considering the way I have been fretted by the tenants, and afflicted with the lumbago. Denis Clark—may the widow's curse follow wherever he goes!—bundled off to America with a neighbour's wife, and a year and a half's rent along with her, the thief! And then, since Holland tide, I have not had a day's health."

"Well, from your looks I should never have supposed it. But you were visiting at Meldrum Castle?"

"Yes, faith, and a dear visit it was. Nothing but half-crown whist, and unlimited brag. Lost seventeen points last Saturday night. It was Sunday morning, Christ pardon us for playing! But what was that to my luck yesterday evening. Bragged twice for large pools, with red nines and black knaves; and Mrs Cooney, both times, showed natural aces! If ever woman sold herself, she has. The Lord stand between us and evil! Well, Terence, you'll be expecting your quarter's allowance. We'll make it out somehow—Heigh-ho! Between bad cards and runaway tenants, I can't attend to my soul as I ought, and Holy Week coming!"

I expressed due sympathy for her losses, and regretted that her health, bodily and spiritual, was so indifferent.

"I have no good news for you, Terence," continued Mrs O'Finn. "Your brother Arthur is following your poor father's example, and ruining himself with hounds and horses. He's a weak and wilful man, and nothing can save him, I fear. Though he never treated me with proper respect, I strove to patch up a match between him and Miss Mac Teggart. Five thousand down upon the nail, and three hundred a year failing her mother. I asked her here on a visit; and though he had ridden past without calling on me, wrote him my plan, and invited him to meet her. What do you think, Terence, was his reply? Why, that Miss Mac Teggart might go to Bath, for he would have no call to my swivel-eyed customers. There was a return for my kindness! as if a woman with five thousand *down*, and three hundred a year in expectation, was required to look straight. Ah! Terence, I wish you had been here. She went to Dublin, and was picked up in a fortnight."

Egad! here was an excellent opportunity to broach my own success. There could be no harm in making the commander's widow a confidante; and, after all, she had a claim upon me as my early protectress.

"My dear aunt, I cannot be surprised at your indignation. Arthur was a fool, and lost an opportunity that never may occur again. In fact, my dear madam, I intended to have given you an agreeable surprise. I—I—I am on—the very brink of matrimony!"

"Holy Bridget!" exclaimed Mrs O'Finn, as she crossed herself devoutly.

"Yes, ma'am. I am engaged to a lady with two thousand pounds."

"Is it *ready*, Terence?" said my aunt.

"Down on the table, before the priest puts on his vestment."

"Arrah—my blessing attend ye, Terence. I knew you would come to good."

"Is she young?"

"Just twenty."

"Is she good-looking?"

"More than that; extremely pretty, innocent, and artless."

"Arrah—give me another kiss, for I am proud of ye;" and Captain O'Finn's representative clasped me in her arms.

"But the family, Terence; remember the old stock. Is she one of us?"

"She is highly respectable. An only daughter, with excellent expectations."

"What is her father, Terence?"

"A soldier, ma'am."

"Lord—quite enough. He's by profession a gentleman; and we can't expect to find everyday descendants from the kings of Connaught, like the O'Shaughnessys and the O'Finns. But when is it to take place, Terence?"

"Why, faith, ma'am, it was a bit of a secret; but I can keep nothing from you."

"And why should ye? Haven't I been to you more than a mother, Terence?"

"I am to be married this evening!"

"This evening! Holy Saint Patrick! and you're sure of the money. It's not a rent-charge—nothing of bills or bonds?"

"Nothing but bank notes; nothing but the cash down."

"Ogh! my blessing be about ye night and day. Arrah, Terence, what's her name?"

"You'll not mention it. We want the thing done quietly."

"Augh, Terence; and do you think I would let anything ye told me slip? By this cross"—and Mrs O'Finn bisected the forefinger of her left hand with the corresponding digit of the right one; "the face of day shall never be the wiser of anything ye mention!"

After this desperate adjuration there was no refusing my aunt's request.

"You know her well"—and I looked extremely cunning.

"Do I, Terence? Let me see—I have it. It's Ellen Robinson. No—though her money's safe, there's but five hundred ready."

"Guess again, aunt."

"Is it Bessie Lloyd? No—though the old miller is rich as a Jew, he would not part a guinea to save the whole human race, or make his daughter a duchess."

"Far from the mark as ever, aunt."

"Well," returned Mrs O'Finn, with a sigh, "I'm fairly puzzled."

"Whisper!" and I playfully took her hand, and put my lips close to her cheek. "It's—"

"Who?—who, for the sake of Heaven?"

"Biddy Maginn!"

"Oh, Jasus!" ejaculated the captain's relict, as she sank upon a chair. "I'm murdered! Give me my salts, there. Terence O'Shaughnessy, don't touch me. I put the cross between us"—and she made a crural flourish with her hand. "You have finished me, ye villain. Holy Virgin! what sins have I that I should be disgraced in my old age? Meat never crossed my lips of a Friday; I was regular at mass, and never missed confession; and, when the company were honest, played as fair as everybody else. I wish I was at peace with poor dear Patt O'Finn. Oh! murder! murder!"

I stared in amazement. If Roger Maginn had been a highwayman, his daughter could not have been an object of greater horror to Mrs O'Finn. At last I mustered words to attempt to reason with her, but to my desultory appeals she returned abuse fit only for a pickpocket to receive.

"Hear me, madam."

"Oh, you common fool!"

"For Heaven's sake, listen!"

"Oh! that the O'Finns and the O'Shaughnessys should be disgraced by a mean-spirited simpleton of your kind!"

"You won't hear me."

"Biddy Maginn!" she exclaimed. "Why bad as my poor brother, your father, was, and though he too married a devil that helped to ruin him, she was at all events a lady in her own right, and cousin-german to Lord Lowestoffe. But—you—you unfortunate disciple."

I began to wax warm, for my aunt complimented me with all the abuse she could muster, and there never was a cessation but when her breath failed.

"Why, what have I done? What am I about doing?" I demanded.

"Just going," returned Mrs O'Finn, "to make a Judy Fitzsimmon's mother of yourself."

"And is it," said I, "because Miss Maginn can't count her pedigree from Fin Macoul, that she should not discharge the duties of a wife?"

My aunt broke in upon me.

"There's one thing certain, that she'll discharge the duties of a mother. Heavens! if you had married a girl with only a blast, your connections might brazen it out. But a woman in such barefaced condition—as if her staying in the house these three months could blind the neighbours, and close their mouths."

"Well, in the devil's name, will you say what objection exists to Biddy Maginn making me a husband to-night?"

"And a papa in three months afterwards!" rejoined my loving aunt.

If a shell burst in the bivouac, I could not have been more electrified. Dark suspicions flashed across my mind—a host of circumstances confirmed my doubts—and I implored the widow of the defunct dragoon to tell me all she knew.

It was a simple, although, as far as I was concerned, not a flattering narrative. Biddy had commenced an equestrian novitiate under the tutelage of Lieutenant Hastings. Her progress in the art of horsemanship was no doubt very satisfactory, and the pupil and the professor frequently rode out *tête-à-tête*. Biddy, poor soul, was fearful of exhibiting any *maladdresse*, and of course, roads less frequented than the king's highway were generally chosen for her riding lessons. Gradually these excursions became more extensive; twilight, and in summer too, often fell, before the quartermaster's heiress had returned; and on one unfortunate occasion she was absent for a week. This caused a desperate commotion in the town; the dowagers and old maids sat in judgment on the case, and declared Biddy no longer visitable. In vain her absence was ascribed to accident—a horse had ran away—she was thrown—her ankle sprained—and she was detained unavoidably at a country inn until the injury was abated.

In this state of things the dragoons were ordered off; and it was whispered that there had been a desperate blow-up between the young lady's preceptor the lieutenant, and her papa the quartermaster. Once only had Biddy ventured out upon the mall; but she was cut dead by her quondam acquaintances. From that day she seldom appeared abroad; and when she did, it was always in the evening, and even then closely muffled up. No wonder scandal was rife touching the causes of her seclusion. A few charitably ascribed it to bad health—others to disappointment—but the greater proportion of the fair sex attributed her confinement to the true cause, and whispered that Miss Maginn was "as ladies wished to be who love their lords."

Here was a solution to the mystery! It was now pretty easy to comprehend why Biddy was swathed like a mummy, and Roger so ready with his cash. No wonder the *demoiselle* was anxious to abridge delay, and the old crimp so obliging in procuring a priest and preparing all requisite matters for immediate hymeneals. What was to be done? What, but denounce the frail fair one, and annihilate that villain, her father. Without a word of explanation I caught up my hat—and left the house in a hurry, and Mrs O'Finn in a state of nervousness that threatened to become hysterical.

When I reached the quartermaster's habitation, I hastened to my own apartment and got my traps together in double quick. I intended to have abdicated quietly, and favoured the intended Mrs O'Shaughnessy with an epistle communicating the reasons that induced me to decline the honour of her hand; but on the landing my worthy father-in-law cut off my retreat, and a parting *tête-à-tête* became unavoidable. He appeared in great spirits at the success of his interview with the parson.

"Well, Terence, I have done the business. The old chap made a parcel of objections; but he's poor as Lazarus—slyly slipped him ten pounds, and that quieted his scruples. He's ready at a moment's warning."

"He's a useful person," I replied dryly; "and all you want is a son-in-law."

"A what?" exclaimed the father of Miss Biddy.

"A son-in-law?"

"Why, what the devil do you mean?"

"Not a jot more or less than what I say. You have procured the priest, but I suspect the bridegroom will not be forthcoming."

"Zounds, sir! do you mean to treat my daughter with disrespect?"

"Upon consideration, it would be hardly fair to deprive my old friend Hastings of his pupil. Why, with another week's private tuition, Biddy might offer her services to Astley."

"Sir—if you mean to be impertinent"—and Roger began to bluster, while the noise brought the footman to the hall, and Miss Biddy to the banisters, 'shawled to the nose.' I began to lose temper.

"Why, you infernal old crimp!"

"You audacious young scoundrel!"

"Oh, Jasus! gentlemen! Peace for the sake of the blessed Mother!" cried the butler from below.

"Father, jewel. Terence, my only love!" screamed Miss Biddy over the staircase—"What is the matter?"

"He wants to be off;" roared the quartermaster.

"Stop, Terence, or you'll have my life to answer for."

"Lord, Biddy, how fat you are grown!"

"You shall fulfil your promise," cried Roger, "or I'll write to the Horse Guards, and memorial the commander-in-chief."

"You may memorial your best friend, the devil, you old crimp"—and I forced my way to the hall.

"Come back; you deceiver!" exclaimed Miss Maginn.

"Arrah, Biddy, go tighten yourself," said I.

"Oh! I'm fainting!" screamed Roger's heiress.

"Don't let him out!" roared her sire.

The gentleman with the beef-steak collar made a demonstration to interrupt my retreat, and in return received a box in the ear that sent him half way down the kitchen stairs.

"There," I said, "give that to the old rogue, your master, with my best compliments"—and bounding from the hall door, Biddy Maginn like Lord Ullin's daughter, "was left lamenting!"

Well, there is no describing the confusion, a blow-up like this occasioned in a country town. I was unmercifully quizzed; but the quartermaster and his heiress found it advisable to abdicate. Roger removed his household goods to the metropolis—Miss Biddy favoured him in due time with a grandson; and when I returned from South America, I learned that "this lost love of mine" had accompanied a Welsh lieutenant to the hymeneal altar, who not being "over particular" about trifles, had obtained on the same morning a wife, an heir, and an estate—with Roger's blessing into the bargain.

"Why, what a fool you were, Terence," said O'Connor: "had you but taken fortune at the flood, and made Miss Biddy Mrs O'Shaughnessy, what between cash and crimping, you might have been now commanding a brigade."

"Ay—when you know how I failed twice afterwards, you will admit that I have been an unlucky suitor."

"What! two efforts more—and still doomed to single blessedness?"

"True enough;—in our next bivouac I'll give you the particulars. 'Tis late—to roost, boys! That hill was so infernally steep, that a man might as well escalade a windmill—nobody but the devil or Dick Magennis could climb it without distress."

Wearied by the day's exertions, none of the party objected to the gallant major's proposition. Quickly their simple resting-places were arranged—and as quickly they were occupied. The light cavalry had long since detached their pickets—and every necessary precaution had been taken to guard against surprise. The hum from the distant bivouacs became fainter—the fires sparkled more brightly in the gloom—group after group betook themselves to sleep—the tattoo echoed through the hills—"while the deep war-drum's sound announced the close of day."

VII

NIGHT IN THE PYRENEES—THE MURDERED SENTINEL—AND THE GUERILLA CHIEF

From camp to camp, through the foul womb of night,
The hum of either army stilly sounds,
That the fix'd sentinels almost receive
The secret whispers of each other's watch.

King Henry V

Who's there? Stand, and unfold yourself.

Hamlet

Go—get some water,
And wash this filthy witness from your hand.

Macbeth

IT WAS A CLEAR AND starry night, the moon had not risen, but the dark masses of mountain occupied by the rival armies was visible for many a mile. An hundred thousand warriors were stretched upon the adjacent hills, and yet there were frequent intervals, when the rifle outpost was silent as a hermit's cell. Few sounds rose above the rush of the river, which swollen by the heavy rains tumbled over a ridge of rock, and deadened, in its roar of waters, noises that otherwise would have fallen upon the ear. Far off occasional sparkles from the watch-fires showed the position of the more distant brigades, while at times the sharp challenge and prompt reply rose above the stillness of the night, and indicated that the sentinels were on the alert, and the outpost officer making his "lonely round."

The bridge where Major O'Connor with three companies of his regiment was posted was a pass of considerable importance; and from the proximity of a French picket a vigilant lookout was indispensable. The severity of the weather, fatiguing duty, and privations in food and shelter, consequent on being cantoned in a mountain position, had produced a partial discontent; and as great inducements to desert were offered by French emissaries, who visited the bivouacs with provisions, scarcely a night passed but some outpost was found abandoned, and the sentry missing when the relief came round. Of course an increased vigilance on outlying services was rendered necessary; the pickets were cautioned to be alert; and the officers directed, by making frequent and uncertain visits to the advanced posts of their command, to satisfy themselves that the sentries were on the *qui vive*; thus guarding against surprise from the enemy, and making any attempt to quit the lines, without observation, almost an impossibility to a deserter.

When so much regarding general safety and prevention of crime depended on individual character and conduct, officers were strictly enjoined, when on duty at any advanced post, to place no sentry contiguous to a French picket, in whose steadiness the greatest confidence could not be reposed. Only the bridge in front of the rifle bivouac separated the troops that occupied it from the French tirailleurs; each of its extremities was held by a rival sentinel. The respective pickets were scarcely a pistol-shot asunder. It was the most advanced, the most important of the entire outposts, and none but an approved soldier was ever placed upon the bridge after beat of tattoo.

That an experienced and intelligent officer, like the command of the Rifles, should feel the great responsibility of the duty he was entrusted with, may be imagined, and at all hours of the night he visited his sentries in person. It was near morning, when silently rising from the bearskin on which he lay, he took his cloak and sabre, and left the bivouac unnoticed by his sleeping comrades, whose slumbers appeared as sound as if the enemy were beyond the Pyrenees.

He paused at the door of the hovel, and for a few moments gazed in silent admiration at the strange and stupendous objects with which he was on every side surrounded. In front, far as the eye could range, the French and English cantonments might be traced, as "fire answered fire." Behind, a scene of Alpine magnificence was displayed, grand and imposing beyond conception. In the dim starlight, pile over pile, the higher ridges of the Pyrenees rose, until they lost their summits in the clouds; while the lower pinnacles, capped with snow, seemed spread around in wild confusion, and assumed grotesque and fanciful appearances, as the uncertain light revealed or hid them. The deep repose of midnight—the immediate proximity of an enemy—the chance that the next sun would set upon a field of slaughter, and that the unearthly stillness that reigned in these solitudes now, would, in a few hours, be succeeded by the rush of battle, and roar of red artillery all weighed upon the heart, and rendered this mountain night scene, even to a careless spirit, grand, solemn, and imposing.

O'Connor found the picket duly vigilant, and learned from the subaltern in command, that the chain of sentries had been recently visited, and all were found at their posts. The night, it appeared, had passed without alarm, the French bivouacs had been unusually quiet and no movement had been observed at the outposts, except that occasioned by the ordinary reliefs along the line. O'Connor inquired who had charge of the bridge; and when the sergeant named the man, he determined to proceed thither before he returned to his humble bearskin.

The sentry, whose fidelity had excited the suspicion of his commanding officer, had more than once proved himself a daring soldier; he had volunteered two forlorn hopes, and was always foremost when skirmishing with the French light troops. But O'Connor, who carefully studied the individual character of those placed under him had seen, in the suspected man, much to dislike. In disposition he was dark, violent, and unforgiving, and even in his gallantry, there was a reckless ferocity regarding human life that made his officers detest him. His dissipated habits had barred him from promotion; and repeated breaches of discipline obliged his commander to withhold the reward that otherwise his acknowledged bravery must have won.

The connecting sentries were vigilant, and at their posts; but when O'Connor approached the bridge, no challenge was given. His suspicions were confirmed; for on reaching the spot where the sentinel was always placed, he found the post unoccupied; a rifle and appointments were lying on the ground, and it was quite evident that the late owner had gone over to the enemy.

This discovery mortified the soldier deeply. Since the British army had entered the Pyrenees, frequent as the offence had been, O'Connor had not lost a single man by desertion. The occurrence was annoying, and he blamed himself for not using greater circumspection. To prevent any recurrence of the crime, he determined for the future to double the sentries along the chain, and as the time for relief was not distant, he resolved to remain until it arrived, and watch the bridge himself.

He took up the deserter's rifle, and ascertained that it was primed and loaded. All was quiet—every sound was hushed, or so faint as not to be heard above the rushing of the waters. In the clear starlight he could perceive the French sentinel moving slowly backwards and forwards, occasionally stopping to look over the battlement of the bridge at the swollen river, as it forced its current through the narrow arch; and then resuming his measured step, humming some popular canzonet, which he had first heard under a sunny sky, and probably from lips he loved.

Ten minutes had elapsed. O'Connor kept a cautious guard, and in a short time the relief might be expected. A noise from the further side of the bridge suddenly arrested his attention. The French sentry challenged—a voice replied—and next moment a dark figure glided into the light, and closed with the tirailleur. A brief colloquy ensued, and the Frenchman appeared not quite satisfied with his visitor, as he kept his musket at the port, and remained some feet apart. Was this man the deserter?—No. If surprise were contemplated he would have been retained to guide the assailants. O'Connor strained eye and ear in the direction, but the low and hurried communication was drowned by the rushing of the river; and it was impossible to conjecture who the stranger was, or what might be his errand.

A few minutes ended this uncertainty. Suddenly the unknown sprang within the sentry's guard—a blow was struck—a loud exclamation and a deep groan succeeded, and then one figure only was visible in the starlight. That was the stranger's! and at a rapid pace he crossed the bridge, and confronted the English sentinel.

"Stand—or I'll fire!"

"Hold—for God's sake!"—replied a voice in tolerable English. "I am a Spaniard, and a friend."

But the sentinel was resolute.

"Friend or foe," he cried, "keep your distance."

"By Heaven!" rejoined the Spaniard, "I must and will cross over."

"One movement of hand or foot," returned the sentry coolly, "and you are a dead man."

"Am I not a faithful ally? What fear ye?"

"I fear nothing," replied the English soldier.

"Have I not this moment rid you of an enemy?" said the stranger.

"Then have you done a cowardly and murderous action," was the sentry's answer.

"I must pass—give way, or I'll force it."

"My finger is on the trigger," returned the soldier. "Another step—another whisper—and I'll send a bullet through your heart."

Both paused—and for half a minute neither spoke. They stood almost within arm's length; the soldier with the rifle at his shoulder, the Spaniard with a knife grasped firmly in a hand, still reeking with the blood of the slaughtered Frenchman. A noise was heard—the measured steps of an advancing party approached, and in a few moments the relief appeared upon the bridge, and by O'Connor's orders secured the formidable stranger.

The Spaniard offered no resistance. Two sentinels were left at the deserted post, and the relief, with their commandant and the prisoner, returned to the outlying picket. Once only the stranger spoke, and it was in reply to a command given to the guard to look to his safe custody.

"Think ye," he said, "that I am likely to return to the French outpost, and inform the detachment that I stabbed their comrade to the heart?"—and a loud laugh, as in derision, accompanied the observation.

The dark mantillo in which the Spaniard was enveloped had hitherto concealed his person, and in the waning starlight, nothing save a tall figure and swarthy features could be discovered; but when, stopping before the fire around which the picket were collected, the blaze revealed his face, one glance assured O'Connor that his prisoner was no ordinary man.

The stranger was scarcely thirty; and were it not for his stern and vindictive expression, his face would have been singularly handsome. The dark and brilliant eye sparkled from beneath a brow which appeared to darken at the slightest contradiction; the nose was finely formed; the teeth white and regular, while coal-black hair curling in rich profusion to his shoulders, and a high and noble forehead completed the outlines of a countenance, that none could deny was handsome, but few would wish to look upon a second time.

A trifling incident marked the character of the stranger. The officer of the picket presented a canteen to his commander, and then politely offered it to the prisoner. He bowed, and put forward his hand; but the subaltern started—for in the blaze he observed that it was discoloured to the wrist.

"Are you hurt?" he said. "There is blood upon your hand."

The Spaniard's lip curled in contempt.

"Ay, likely enough," he coolly answered. "Many a time the heart's blood of an enemy has dyed these fingers deeper; but it would be uncivil to stain a friendly flask;" and, stepping aside, he rinsed his hands in a little rivulet that trickled down a rock beside the watch-fire; then taking the canteen, he drank and returned it with a bow.

"Are you the commandant at this fort?" he inquired, as he turned to O'Connor.

"I am," was the reply.

"Your name, sir?"

The soldier gave it.

"Indeed!"—exclaimed the Spaniard. "Are you he who led the assault at Badajoz?"

The soldier bowed, as he replied in the affirmative.

"Enough—I would speak with you aside;" and followed by O'Connor, he walked some distance from the watch-fire.

"You have seen me before," said the Spaniard sharply.

"It is very possible," was the soldier's reply. "Under which of the Spanish commanders have you served?"

"Under none," replied the stranger.

"Are you not a soldier, then? Just now you hinted that more than one Frenchman had fallen by your hand."

"Yes; some have perished by my hand, and many a hundred by my order," returned the prisoner.

"Indeed? May I inquire who it is that I am addressing?"

"Willingly. Heard ye ever the name of Vicente Moreno mentioned?" asked the Spaniard.

"Moreno? Him whom the French hanged at Grenada in the presence of his wife and children—"

"And"—continued the stranger, interrupting him—"whose last words to her he loved so tenderly were spoken from the scaffold, telling her to return to her home, and teach her children to follow the example of their father; and if they could not save their country, like him to die for it."

"Yes, I recollect the occurrence well," replied O'Connor. "It was the cruel murder of a brave man, and awful was the retaliation it occasioned."

"Ay," said the Spaniard—"the martyr of liberty was well and speedily avenged. Before the second moon rose above the grave of the slaughtered soldier, seventy French captains were shot like mangy hounds, by my order, in the market-place at Marbella."

"Ha!"—exclaimed O'Connor, as he looked, keenly at the Spaniard—"am I then speaking to—"

"Moreno, the Guerilla, the younger brother of him they murdered in the square of Grenada, stands beside you."

O'Connor started! "And was the assassin of the French sentinel the far-famed chieftain of the mountain bands of Ronda? He whose exploits wore rather the semblance of romance than the colour of reality; whose career had been so successful and so sanguinary, that it was computed, from the hour he devoted himself to avenge his brother's death, that more than two thousand French had been slain by the bands he commanded!" While O'Connor recollected the ruthless character of this dreaded chief, all marvel at the scene upon the bridge ceased; for to stab an enemy who was in his way, would not be a consideration of a pin's fee to one, who in cold blood, had shot his prisoners by the dozen.

"Doubtless you are both hungry and fatigued," said the soldier, resuming his conversation with the Guerilla. "Our bivouac is hard by, and, such as it is, there we have food and shelter. Will you accept what I can offer?"

"Most willingly," replied Moreno; "both will be welcome. For thirty hours I have tasted no food, and have been hiding in the rocks all day, and travelling hard since sunset."

"You have then been engaged in some important enterprise?" said the soldier.

"I have been occupied as I have ever been, since I devoted myself to avenge my murdered brother, and my enslaved country."

"In what, may I inquire?" said O'Connor.

"Doing a deed of desperate vengeance," replied the Spaniard, in a deep voice that thrilled to the heart. "Vengeance is what I think of when awake—vengeance is what I dream of sleeping."

"Have you been harassing the enemy?"

"I have," returned the Guerilla, "been doing a deed that will carry terror to every Frenchman, and make the usurper tremble, when the name of Juan Moreno is pronounced. But I am weary; give me some food; and when I rest for a few hours, if you will walk with me up the heights, I will relate my last adventure."

"Come," said the soldier; and leading the way, he introduced the weary Spaniard to the hut, struck a light, and placed before him the best cheer a scanty larder could produce.

The Guerilla ate like one who had been for many hours fasting, finished a flask of wine, and then apologising for keeping his host from his repose, stretched himself beside the soldier's bearskin, and, as if in the full consciousness of security, dropped into a sound sleep, which remained unbroken until the *reveillée* disturbed the bivouac at day break.

One circumstance struck O'Connor as being remarkable. Wearied as the Guerilla was before he lay down on his cloak, he took a crucifix from his bosom, and repeated his prayers devoutly. A hand, red with recent murder, punctiliously let fall a bead at every *ave*; and when his orisons were ended, he replaced the emblem of salvation, which he appeared to venerate so much, within the same breast where the knife, that had just despatched two unsuspecting victims, was deposited.

VIII

THE GUERILLA BIVOUAC—
ANECDOTES OF THEIR WARFARE
AND LEADERS

Othello. O, that the slave had forty thousand lives;
One is too poor, too weak for my revenge!
SHAKESPEARE

WHEN THE DRUM BEAT, MORENO started from his humble bed, and for a moment stared wildly round at the inmates of the hovel, who were all in motion at "the loud alarum" of the reveillée. O'Connor observed that even then his matins were not forgotten, and a hurried prayer was muttered ere he rose. Beckoning the soldier to follow, the Spaniard bowed courteously to all around, and then, wrapped in his mantillo, slowly proceeded towards the upper heights.

After an hour's ascent, which to O'Connor was particularly tiresome, but to the Guerilla easy as if he journeyed on a plain, they stepped upon a plateau among the hills, which overlooked the English and French positions. To the soldier's astonishment, Moreno pointed out the stations of the enemy's corps with surprising accuracy, and named the commanders, and numerical force of each brigade. Once or twice he referred to a written document, taken from his pocket, which was evidently a French despatch. After a short halt, he rose from the rock he had been sitting on, intimating it was time to continue his route, and invited O'Connor to keep him company for another mile.

The soldier assented; and striking into a path rendered difficult by the obstruction of a fall of snow, the Guerilla led the way with the precision of one perfectly familiar with the localities of the mountains, until, in the bosom of a deep ravine, they suddenly found themselves in the centre of a band of independents.

The appearance of this formidable body was far more picturesque than military. They might have numbered one hundred, and all were armed and equipped according to individual fancy. Some were showily attired—others slovenly to a degree; and dresses of rich velvet were singularly contrasted with the coarser clothes worn by the peasantry of Andalusia. They looked more like a banditti than an organised band; but their horses were in excellent condition, and their arms of the best kind, and perfectly effective. The single phrase "my friend" obtained for the visitor a rapturous welcome; and a brief description of their rencontre on the bridge, which O'Connor overheard repeated by the Guerilla, seemed to recommend him to the troop as a fitting comrade for their bold and reckless leader.

There was in the whole system of Guerilla warfare a wild and romantic character, which, could its cruelty have been overlooked, would have rendered it both chivalrous and exciting. Men totally unfitted by previous habits and education suddenly appeared upon the stage, and developed talent and determination that made them the scourge and terror of the invaders. But theirs was a combat of extermination—none of those courtesies, which render modern warfare endurable, were granted to their opponents—the deadliest hostility was unmitigated by success—and, when vanquished, expecting no quarter from the French, they never thought of extending it to those who unfortunately became their prisoners. A sanguinary struggle was raging; and *væ victis* seemed, with "war to the knife," to be the only mottos of the Guerilla.

The strange exploits of many of these daring partisans, though true to the letter, are perfectly romantic; and the patient endurance, the deep artifice, with which their objects were effected, appear to be almost incredible. Persons whose ages and professions were best calculated to evade suspicion were invariably their chosen agents. The village priest was commonly a confederate of the neighbouring

Guerilla—the postmaster betrayed the intelligence that reached him in his office—the fairest peasant of Estremadura would tempt the thoughtless soldier with her beauty, and decoy him within range of the bullet—and even childhood was frequently and successfully employed in leading the unsuspecting victim into some pass or ambuscade, where the knife or musket closed his earthly career.

In every community, however fierce and lawless, different gradations of good and evil will be discovered, and nothing could be more opposite than the feelings and actions of some of the Guerillas and their leaders. Many of these desperate bands were actuated in every enterprise by a love of bloodshed and spoliation, and their own countrymen suffered as heavily from their rapacity as their enemies from their swords. Others took the field from nobler motives: an enthusiastic attachment to their country and religion roused them into vengeance against a tyranny which had become insufferable— every feeling but ardent patriotism was forgotten—private and dearer ties were snapped asunder—homes, and wives, and children were abandoned—privations that appear almost incredible were patiently endured, until treachery delivered them to the executioner, or in some wild attempt they were overpowered by numbers, and died resisting to the last.

Dreadful as the retaliation was which French cruelty and oppression had provoked, the Guerilla vengeance against domestic treachery was neither less certain nor less severe. To collect money or supplies for the invaders, convey any information, conceal their movements, and not betray them when opportunity occurred, was death to the offender. Sometimes the delinquent was brought with considerable difficulty and risk before a neighbouring tribunal, and executed with all the formalities of justice; but generally a more summary vengeance was exacted, and the traitor was sacrificed upon the spot. In these cases neither calling nor age was respected. If found false to his country, the sanctity of his order was no protection to the priest. The daughter of the collector of Almagro, for professing attachment to the usurper, was stabbed by Urena to the heart; and a secret correspondence, between

the wife of the alcalde of Birhueda and the French general in the
next command, having been detected by an intercepted despatch, the
wretched woman, by order of Juan Martin Diez, the Empecinado,
was dragged by a Guerilla party from her house, her hair shaven, her
denuded person tarred and feathered, and disgracefully exhibited
in the public market place—and she was then put to death amid
the execrations of her tormentors. Nor was there any security for
a traitor, even were his residence in the capital, or almost within
the camp of the enemy. One of the favourites of Joseph Bonaparte,
Don Jose Rigo, was torn from his home in the suburbs of Madrid,
while celebrating his wedding, by the Empecinado, and hanged in
the square of Cadiz. The usurper himself, on two occasions, narrowly
escaped from this desperate partisan. Dining at Almeda, some two
leagues' distance from the capital, with one of the generals of division,
their hilarity was suddenly interrupted by the unwelcome intelligence
that the Empecinado was at hand, and nothing but a hasty retreat
preserved the pseudo king from capture. On another occasion, he was
surprised upon the Guadalaxara road; and so rapid was the Guerilla
movement, so determined their pursuit, that before the French could
be succoured by the garrison of Madrid, forty of the royal escort were
sabred between Torrejon and El Molar.

A war of extermination raged, and on both sides blood flowed in
torrents. One act of cruelty was as promptly answered by another; and
a French decree, ordering that every Spaniard taken in arms should
be executed, appeared to be a signal to the Guerillas to exclude from
mercy every enemy who fell into their hands. The French had shown
the example: the Junta were denounced, their houses burned, and
their wives and children driven to the woods. If prisoners received
quarter in the field—if they fell lame upon the march, or the remotest
chance of a rescue appeared—they were shot like dogs; others were
butchered in the towns, their bodies left rotting on the highways,
and their heads exhibited on poles. That respect, which even the
most depraved of men usually pay to female honour, was shamefully
disregarded; and more than one Spaniard, like the postmaster of

Medina, was driven to the most desperate courses, by the violation of a wife and the murder of a child.

It would be sickening to describe the horrid scenes which mutual retaliation produced. Several of the Empecinado's followers, who were surprised in the mountains of Guadarama, were nailed to the trees, and left there to expire slowly by hunger and thirst. To the same trees, before a week elapsed, a similar number of French soldiers were affixed by the Guerillas. Two of the inhabitants of Madrid, who were suspected of communicating with the brigands, as the French termed the armed Spaniards, were tried by court-martial, and executed at their own door. The next morning six of the garrison were seen hanging from walls beside the high road. Some females related to Palarea, surnamed the Medico, had been abused most scandalously by the escort of a convoy, who had seized them in a wood; and in return the Guerilla leader drove into an ermida eighty Frenchmen and their officers, set fire to the thatch, and burned them to death, or shot them in their endeavours to leave the blazing chapel. Such were the dreadful enormities a system of retaliation caused.

These desperate adventurers were commanded by men of the most dissimilar professions. All were distinguished by some *sobriquet*, and these were of the most opposite descriptions. Among the leaders were friars and physicians, cooks and artisans, while some were characterised by a deformity, and others named after the form of their waistcoat or hat. Worse epithets described many of the minor chiefs—truculence and spoliation obtained them titles; and, strange as it may appear, the most ferocious band that infested Biscay was commanded by a woman named Martina. So indiscriminating and unrelenting was this female monster in her murder of friends and foes, that Mina was obliged to direct his force against her. She was surprised, with the greater portion of her banditti, and the whole were shot upon the spot.

Of all the Guerilla leaders the two Minas were the most remarkable for their daring, their talents, and their successes. The younger, Xavier, had a short career, but nothing could be more chivalrous and romantic than many of the incidents that marked it. His band amounted to a thousand, and with this force he kept Navarre, Biscay, and Aragon, in confusion; intercepted convoys, levied contributions, plundered the custom-houses, and harassed the enemy incessantly. The villages were obliged to furnish rations for his troops, and the French convoys supplied him with money and ammunition. His escapes were often marvellous. He swam flooded rivers deemed impassable, and climbed precipices hitherto untraversed by a human foot. Near Estella he was forced by numbers to take refuge on a lofty rock; the only accessible side he defended till night-fall, when lowering himself and followers by a rope, he brought his party off with scarcely the loss of a man.

This was among his last exploits; for when reconnoitring by moonlight, in the hope of capturing a valuable convoy, he fell unexpectedly into the hands of an enemy's patrol. Proscribed by the French as a bandit, it was surprising that his life was spared; but his loss to the Guerillas was regarded as a great misfortune.

While disputing as to the choice of a leader, where so many aspired to a command to which each offered an equal claim, an adventurer worthy to succeed their lost chief was happily discovered in his uncle, the elder Mina. Educated as a husbandman, and scarcely able to read or write, the new leader had lived in great retirement, until the Junta's call to arms induced him to join his nephew's band. He reluctantly acceded to the general wish to become Xavier Mina's successor, but when he assumed the command, his firm and daring character was rapidly developed. Echeverria, with a strong following, had started as a rival chief; but Mina surprised him—had three of his subordinates shot with their leader—and united the remainder of the band with his own. Although he narrowly escaped from becoming a victim to the treachery of a comrade, the prompt and severe justice with which he visited the offender effectually restrained other adventurers from making any similar attempt.

The traitor was a sergeant of his own, who, from the bad expression of his face, had received among his companions the *sobriquet* of Malcarado. Discontented with the new commander, he determined to betray him to the enemy, and concerted measures with Pannetia, whose brigade was near the village of Robres, to surprise the Guerilla chieftain in his bed. Partial success attended the treacherous attempt; but Mina defended himself desperately with the bar of the door, and kept the French at bay till Gastra, his chosen comrade, assisted him to escape. The Guerilla rallied his followers, repulsed the enemy, took Malcarado, and shot him instantly, while the village curé and three alcaldes implicated in the traitorous design, were hanged side by side upon a tree, and their houses razed to the ground.

An example of severity like this gave confidence to his own followers, and exacted submission from the peasantry. Everywhere Mina had a faithful spy—every movement of the enemy was reported—and if a village magistrate received a requisition from a French commandant, it was communicated to the Guerilla chief with due despatch, or woe to the alcalde that neglected it.

Nature had formed Mina for the service to which he had devoted himself. His constitution was equal to every privation and fatigue, and his courage was of that prompt and daring character, that no circumstance, however sudden and disheartening, could overcome. Careless as to dress or food, he depended for a change of linen on the capture of French baggage, or any accidental supply; and for days he would exist upon a few biscuits, or anything which chance threw in his road. He guarded carefully against surprise—slept with a dagger and pistols in his girdle—and such were his active habits, that he rarely took more than two hours of repose. The mountain caverns were the depositories of his ammunition and plunder; and in a mountain fastness he established a hospital for his wounded, to which they were carried in litters across the heights, and placed in perfect safety, until their cure could be completed. Gaming and plunder were prohibited, and even love forbidden, lest the Guerilla might be too communicative to the object of his affection, and any of his chieftain's secrets should transpire.

Of the minor chiefs many strange and chivalrous adventures are on record. The daring plans, often tried and generally successful, and the hair-breadth escapes of several, are almost beyond belief. No means, however repugnant to the laws of modern warfare, were unemployed;

while the ingenuity with which intelligence of a hostile movement was transmitted—the artifice with which an enemy was delayed, until he could be surrounded or surprised—appeared incredible. Of individual ferocity a few instances will be sufficient. At the execution of an alcalde and his son at Mondragon, the old man boasted that two hundred French had perished by their hands; and the Chaleco, Francis Moreno, in a record of his services, boasts of his having waited for a cavalry patrol in a ravine, and, by the discharge of a huge blunderbuss loaded nearly to the muzzle, dislocated his own shoulder, and killed or wounded nine of the French. The same chief presented to Villafranca a rich booty of plate and quicksilver, but he added to the gift a parcel of ears cut from the prisoners whom on that occasion he had slaughtered.

Profiting by the anarchy that reigned in this afflicted country, wretches, under political excuses, committed murder and devastation on a scale of frightful magnitude. One, pretending to be a functionary of the Junta, made Ladrada a scene of bloodshed. By night his victims were despatched; and to the disgrace of woman, his wife was more sanguinary than himself. Castanos at length arrested their blood-stained career; and Pedrazeula was hanged and beheaded, and Maria, his infamous confederate, garrotted.

Castile was over-run by banditti; and one gang, destroyed by a Guerilla chief named Juan Abril, had accumulated plunder, principally in specie, amounting in value to half a million reales. One of the band, when captured by the French, to save his life discovered the secret, and offered to lead a party to the place where the treasure was deposited. His proposal was accepted. An alguazil, with an escort of cavalry, proceeded to the wood of Villa Viciosa, and there booty was found worth more than the value affixed to it by the deserter. Returning in unsuspecting confidence, the party were drawn into an ambuscade by the Medico, who had been acquainted with the expedition; and of the escort and officials, with the exception of five who managed to escape, every one was butchered without mercy.

Such were the wild and relentless foes to whom the invaders were exposed—such were the Spaniards, who had made themselves remarkable for patriotism and endurance—surpassing courage and unmitigated cruelty. In those around him O'Connor looked upon men who, through the whole Peninsular struggle, had carried terror with their names, and in the leader, who was standing beside him apart from the band, he recognised a chieftain, in whose breast, if report were true, fear and compassion were equally extinguished.

IX

EL MANCO—A GUERILLA'S BREAKFAST

Second Murderer.   I'm one, my liege,
Whom the vile blows and buffets of the world
Have so incens'd, that I am reckless what
I do, to spite the world.

First Murderer.   And I another,
So weary with disasters, tugg'd with fortune,
That I would set my life on any chance,
To mend it, or be rid on't.

SHAKESPEARE

"WHAT THINK YOU OF MY band?" said the Guerilla leader to Major O'Connor as he observed the soldier's eye examining the formidable troop, who were preparing their breakfast in the valley below the rock to which Moreno and his companion had removed. "Compared with your own beautiful and efficient regiment, what a wretched rabble my wild followers must appear!"

"Far from it, my friend," replied the soldier. "Their clothing and appointments are certainly irregular, and one who looked to dresses, and not the men who wore them, might hold your band in slight estimation. Your followers appear active and determined soldiers, and some of them the finest fellows I have ever seen."

The Guerilla seemed pleased with the approbation his troop received from O'Connor.

"And yet," he said, "the youngest and the most powerful are not those who have shed most blood, or wreaked the deepest vengeance on our common enemy. The weakest arm is sometimes united to the strongest heart; and while our morning meal is in preparation, I will point out to you the most remarkable among my comrades."

"Nothing would give me greater pleasure," said the soldier. "Many of their histories must be singular indeed."

"Yes," replied the Guerilla; "there are among my followers; men who have met with strange adventures, and whose lives commenced very differently to the manner in which it is now most probable they will close. Injury and outrage forced most of them to take up arms; and had not the oppressors crossed these mountains, they would have worn their lives away in their native valleys, as peaceful vine-dressers or contented artisans. Mark you that old man leaning against a rock?"

"I do," returned the soldier. "The grey hair and diminutive person would lead one to reckon him the least formidable of your companions."

The chief smiled.

"Is there anything beside, which strikes you in him as remarkable?"

"I observe," returned the soldier, "that he is provided with a musket of unusual length."

"And," continued the Guerilla, "one arm is lame, from whence he has obtained the surname of El Manco. Many an enemy has perished by the old man's hand—many a French heart the bullets from that gun have searched."

"Indeed?"

"Yes," said the chief. "El Manco was wantonly injured, but he was as desperately avenged. There was not a more peaceable peasant in Castile. He occupied the cottage where his parents had lived and died, and laboured in the same farm which his forefathers had tilled for centuries. His home was in a sequestered valley among the hills, and its remoteness might have been expected to secure the humble owner from the insults of an invader. But nowhere is the wood or dell so retired, that it has escaped the cruelty and rapacity of the oppressors.

"Late one evening a small party of French dragoons appeared unexpectedly among the mountains; and the secluded valley where El Manco dwelt was soon discovered by these marauders. They approached the old man's cottage, were civilly received, accommodated with food and wine, their horses supplied with corn, and all that submissive peasants could do to propitiate their clemency was tried. How was El Manco's hospitality returned? He had no gold to tempt their cupidity, and in his peaceful occupation and feeble strength, there was no plea to excite apprehension or justify severity. But he was a husband and a father. His wife retained some portion of her former beauty; and his daughters, only verging upon womanhood, were singularly handsome. Morning had just dawned; the order to march was given; and the unhappy family supposing that, pleased with the civility they had experienced through the night, the marauders would take a friendly leave, came forward to say farewell. Half the party mounted, when, on a signal from their officer, a dozen ruffians seized on the peasant's daughters, and placed them before two dragoons. In vain the astonished mother clung wildly to one of her beloved ones; in vain the father rushed upon the horseman who held the other. He was maimed for life by a sword-cut, and his wife was savagely shot by the horseman, from whose ruffian grasp she had striven to extricate her child. Wounded and bewildered, El Manco leaned over the dying woman. In a few minutes she breathed her last, and her groans mingled with her daughters' shrieks, as they came at intervals from the mountain over which the ravishers were carrying them.

"For three months El Manco remained an idiot, and during that time no tidings of his children could he obtained. At length they returned to their once happy and innocent home;—one only to die, the other to exist dishonoured. The story of their wrongs seemed to rouse their wretched father—memory came back—he swore eternal, implacable revenge, and quitted his native valley forever. His only arms were the gun you see, and the knife he carries in his bosom.

Bred a hunter in his youth, he was an excellent marksman, and his intimate knowledge of the mountain district facilitated his efforts at vengeance. Placing himself in ambush beside a pass, he would wait for days and nights with patient vigilance, until some straggling enemy came within range of his musket; and an unerring pullet conveyed to the dying Frenchman the first intimation that danger was at hand. Numerous parties were constantly sent out to apprehend the dreaded brigand. Frequently they found El Manco in the forest, to all appearance peaceably employed in cutting wood; and deceived by his age, the simplicity of his answers, and his feebleness, they were contented with seeking information, to enable them to apprehend the criminal. Accident at last betrayed El Manco's secret; but before the discovery was made, more than sixty Frenchmen had fallen by the hand of that maimed and powerless being. Of course he was obliged to fly, and since that time he has attached himself to the party I command."

"It is a strange tale, certainly," said the soldier; "and to look at El Manco, none could suppose him to be capable of such desperate retaliation."

"It shows," replied the Spaniard, "that the humblest individual, when wantonly abused, has means sufficient for revenge if he has only courage to make the essay. Did you know the private histories of this band, half the number of those who fill my ranks have been forced there by injury and oppression. War drove them from more peaceful vocations, and want obliged them to adopt a course of life, for which, under other circumstances, they had neither inclination nor ability. When the noble refused to submit to the thrall of a foreign despot, and was beggared by the spoliations of the tyrant's minions, those who depended on him as retainers shared in the ruin of their protector. The hidalgo was driven from his hereditary estate, the farmer had his crops cut down, and his vineyard and olive-ground devastated. The labourer lacked his wonted occupation, and flung the implements of husbandry away, to take up knife and musket. Religious houses were suppressed—the monk was ejected from his seclusion—he entered at

manhood upon a world he was unused to—death was the penalty of
wearing his sacred habit—and the priest's cassock was exchanged for
the Guerilla cloak. Look over yonder troop, and there every calling
will be found—every gradation of rank—from the ruined noble to
the bankrupt tradesman.—But here comes breakfast. Last night, major,
you and I were like enough to prove the temper of the knife—this
morning we'll employ it for friendlier purposes."

The Guerilla's meal was a strange melange. There was broiled
mutton, an English ham, a flask of superior wine, French biscuits, rye
bread, and two or three nameless culinary preparations. Everything
was served in plate; and dish, cup, and spoon were all of massive silver.
The Spaniard smiled at O'Connor's astonishment.

"You see how we mountain soldiers live. England and France, Italy
and Spain, have furnished materials for our breakfast; and these silver
vessels, but a short time since, were ranged upon a royal sideboard. In
truth, my friend, we are indebted for them all to El Rey Jose. I picked
up a part of the baggage at Vittoria, and we have made free with
viands provided for the usurper, but which the chance of war gave to
honester men—you and me. Drink—that wine is excellent. An hour
hence we march; and if you please it, to fill up the interval, I will tell
you some adventures of my own."

X

Confessions of a Guerilla

Vengeance, deep brooding o'er the slain,
  Had locked the source of softer wo;
And burning pride, and high disdain,
  Forbade the rising tear to flow
                    Lay of the Last Minstrel

I AM THE YOUNGEST SON of an old soldier. My mother died while I was an infant; and my father, after serving in the Royal Guard for thirty years, quitted the corps from ill health—retired to his native village—and, on his pension and paternal estate, lived hospitably, until, at a good old age, he slipped away calmly from the world, respected and regretted by all who knew him.

There were twenty years between Vicente, my elder brother, and myself. At our father's death he was a man, and I but a school-boy. Although left an orphan, I had no destitution to complain of; Vicente was the best of brothers—he treated me with parental tenderness—watched over my education—directed my studies—and, when I arrived at that time of life when a profession should be selected, he procured for me an appointment in the capital, and allotted me a liberal portion of his income, to enable me to maintain myself as a gentleman, until, by the routine of office, I should obtain some more lucrative post. Never was a man less adapted by nature for a life of rapine and bloodshed than I. My disposition was quiet and contemplative—books were my chief delight—I read much—and, not contented with the literature of Spain, applied myself to learn the languages of modern Europe, and acquired a sufficient knowledge of French and English, which enabled me to speak both with tolerable fluency. Such were my earlier habits and pursuits; and at twenty-two none could have supposed it possible that, in a few brief months, the peaceful student of Madrid should become the brigand chief of Honda.

The director of the office, to which I was attached, was a man of noble descent and amiable character. He was called Don Jose Miranda. His place was very lucrative; and as he had a small estate, and was a widower with but one child, it was believed that the young Catalina would inherit, at her father's death, a very considerable fortune.

The director appeared partial to me from the beginning—took pains in teaching me the duties of the office—showed me every civility in his power—and frequently brought me to his house, a villa, pleasantly situated at about a league's distance from the city. There I passed many a happy hour—for there I first became acquainted with Catalina.

I saw and loved her. You, a soldier from boyhood, who, haply, know the passion but by name, would smile at the weakness I must confess, did I own the ardour, the devotion, with which my heart worshipped the director's daughter. Who could look on Catalina and remain unmoved? She was then scarcely sixteen, and just sprinting into womanhood, with all the charms that render beauty irresistible. Then I was different from what I now am—care had not settled on my brow—this hand was unstained with blood—this heart was not wrung by injury and insult—this bosom was not burning with revenge. Then no anxieties disturbed it; and all it throbbed for was the object of its love—the young, the peerless Catalina.

I did not sue in vain. My mistress listened to my declaration of attachment with evident pleasure—and I was accepted. The director, when a female relative who superintended his household affairs and the education of Catalina informed him of our *liaison*, expressed no dissatisfaction; on the contrary, his kindness towards me appeared increased.

Months passed over—my love became more ardent and engrossing— and, unable to endure a longer suspense, I obtained Catalina's consent to demand her hand from the director, and formally made the necessary communication. He heard me, and objected only to the want of a sufficient fortune on my part; but, at the same time, he proposed to remedy that evil. He was becoming old—the state of political affairs was more than threatening—a national convulsion was at hand—he wished to retire from official labour—and, he said, that he would signify his intention to the government, and obtain the appointment for me.

It was done. His application was favourably received—and it was duly intimated by the minister of finance that I should be Don Jose's successor. All objection to my union with Catalina was removed, and the day was named on which she was to become my wife.

The revolution broke out suddenly—events were hurried to a rapid crisis—the French occupied Madrid—and every department of the executive was thrown into confusion. In all the state offices persons suspected of attachment to their lawful king became obnoxious to the usurper: they were unceremoniously discarded, and the minions of the invader substituted in their stead. I had no fancy for political intrigues, consequently I had never been a partisan, and it might have been supposed that I should have escaped the wrath of the despot; but before I suspected danger an event occurred which overturned all my hopes, and rendered me forever a wretched and a ruined man.

Driven to madness by foreign oppression, the peasantry of Andalusia had broken into insurrection, and declared deadly hostility to the invaders. Valdenebro appeared at their head—while my brother Vicente joined the mountaineers of Honda as their leader. Before any intelligence reached me of these events, a great portion of my native province was in arms; and an enemy's detachment, which had imprudently advanced into the mountains, became entangled in a defile, and were cut off to a man, by a sudden attack made upon them by the Moreno.

I was at the director's villa, and, ignorant of this occurrence, was seated beside my beloved Catalina—my arm was around her waist, her head was resting on my bosom, and her dark and sparkling eyes turned upon mine, as, in playful raillery, she taxed me with some fanciful offence. A bust without, a tramping of feet and ringing of spurs, was heard along the paved corridor. Presently the door was thrown open, and a French officer of dragoons strode haughtily across the chamber, while his orderly remained standing in the doorway. I sprang up, placed myself between Catalina and the intruder, and demanded his name and business. He smiled ironically.

"I am called Henri de Blondville," he said, "a captain of hussars; and you, if I am not misinformed, are Don Juan Moreno."

"I am Juan Moreno," I replied.

"Then I must interrupt your *tête-à-tête,* my friend. Here, Pierre—here is your prisoner." Half a dozen hussars instantly came in. I remonstrated, but it was unavailing, and demanded to know the nature of my offence, and the authority by which I was treated like a malefactor.

"This is my warrant," replied the Frenchman, as he scornfully touched the handle of his sabre. "Secure the gentleman," he continued, addressing his myrmidons. I was instantly seized—handcuffed like a deserter torn from the house, and not permitted to await the recovery of Catalina, who had fainted on the sofa, nor allowed to bid my affianced wife farewell.

I was mounted on a dragoon horse, escorted by a troop of cavalry, and not permitted to procure a cloak or a change of linen. Transferred from troop to troop, without rest, without food, until I was completely worn down with suffering and fatigue, my journey terminated at Grenada; there, without any colourable pretext, I was thrown into a damp and solitary dungeon, where none but desperate malefactors were confined.

A long month wore heavily away. I lay pining in a loathsome cell, never seeing a human countenance except the keeper's, who visited me at midnight with a supply of coarse food, barely sufficient to sustain life. My bodily sufferings were severe enough, but what were they compared to the mental agony I endured, when my deserted bride and her helpless parent were remembered. My offences, whatever they might be, would probably be visited on them; and when I thought of the licentious character of the invaders, I shuddered to think that Catalina was so beautiful and so unprotected.

The thirtieth night of my melancholy captivity arrived, and the hour of the gaoler's visit was at hand. I heard a sudden uproar in the prison, and, even remote as my dungeon was, the shouts of men, and the sharp discharge of small arms, reached it. The affray was short as it had been sudden—the noises died away—the conflict was over, or the combatants were engaged at a greater distance from my cell. It was a strange and unusual event, and I longed for the appearance of the keeper, to ask him what had caused this midnight tumult.

At last the key grated in the dungeon lock, and my gaoler entered. He looked like a person who had been engaged in a recent affray; and to judge from his torn clothes, and head bound up in a bloody handkerchief, he had suffered in the scuffle. When I asked what had occasioned the late confusion, he regarded me with a ferocious stare—left the loaf and pitcher down—and, as he turned to the door, muttered, "I suspect, my friend, that *you* will know more about it in the morning!" and abruptly quitting the cell, left me to solitude and darkness.

Day broke, and I waited impatiently to learn the meaning of the keeper's threat, nor was I long kept in uncertainty. The footsteps of several men sounded in the vaulted passage, my dungeon was unlocked, and the keeper entered, accompanied by a military guard with drawn bayonets, and desired me to rise and follow him. I obeyed; and, mounting by a flight of stone stairs, found myself in the prison-hall where General Sebastiani, attended by a numerous staff and a few civilians, was sitting in judgment on a prisoner.

That he was one was evident enough, for I remarked that both his hands and feet were strongly fettered. His back was turned to me as he confronted his judge; but from his hat and mantillo, I guessed him to be a Spaniard. The hail was encircled by a triple file of soldiers, and a deathlike silence ensued, as the French general ceased speaking on my entrance with the guard.

"Approach, young man," he said, after a minute's pause.

I did as I was ordered, and came forward to the table where my fellow captive stood.

"Look up," continued the Frenchman, "and tell me if you know the prisoner?"

The captive remained, regarding steadily the person on whose decision his fate rested. I raised my eyes to examine his face. Great God!—it was no strange countenance that met my glance—the prisoner was my brother!

"Vicente!" I exclaimed. He started at the well-known voice, and next moment we were in each other's arms. Gently disengaging himself from my embrace, he held me at a little distance as he mournfully replied,—"And is this wreck of manhood thou, my beloved brother? Alas, Juan—thy free spirit agrees but poorly with a tyrant's thrall. I need not ask how thou hast fared; that withered cheek and sunken eye tell plainly enough how well chains and captivity can work the wrath of the oppressor. I heard but two days since of thy arrest; and I would have delivered thee, but for the treachery of yonder miscreant"—and he pointed his finger scornfully towards a man who was standing at a distance, and whom I recognised at once to be the alguazil of my native village. This explained the cause of the midnight disturbance, and the gaoler's menace. My brother had made a desperate attempt to effect my liberation. He surprised and cut down the prison guard. His success would have been certain; but a traitor had betrayed him, and his own capture and certain death resulted.

Sebastiani and his staff watched our interview with marked attention. He whispered to an aide-de-camp, who withdrew from the hall, and the general then addressed himself to me.

"Juan Moreno," he said, "attend and answer me."

I bowed, and the general proceeded.

"You are accused, that, contrary to the royal decree, condemning to death all Spaniards taken in arms, and all who abet and assist them— you have been in communication with the brigands in the mountains of Ronda, and that, through information sent from the capital by you, much of the mischief they have perpetrated has been caused. How say ye—are these charges true—and are you guilty of this treason?"

Before I could reply, my brother addressed Sebastiani.

"General," he said, "you have offered me liberty and preferment, and I have refused them, because I could only accept them with the loss of honour. Judge whether, to free another, I would do that, which, even to save myself, I have declined doing. Think not that I am reckless of life. No—there are ties which bind me to it ardently. I am a husband—and I am a father. Now by the hope of Heaven, which must enable me with firmness to go through the scene that is approaching—by the unsullied honour of a Spaniard, Juan Moreno is guiltless of the charge you have accused him of."

There was a pause—and the solemnity of my brother's declaration seemed to confirm my innocence with the greater number of those who had listened to him. An impression had evidently been made upon the French officers in my favour, when the corregidor of La Mancha, the villain Ciria, who had joined the enemy, and pursued every patriot with undying hatred, remarked that the anxiety of a brother to save his kinsman was just and natural; but, unfortunately, the testimony of an unprejudiced man had established the fact, that a treasonable correspondence existed between Vicente and me.

Moreno darted a withering look at the betrayer of his country.

"What!" he exclaimed. Mind ye the assertions of yon pale-faced traitor?—A miscreant false to his nation and his God! One who, like the arch deceiver of old, has sold for silver the blood of innocence so frequently. Would the denunciations of such a wretch be deemed worthy of belief by any man of honour? But I am wrong to permit an abject traitor to disturb any portion of the brief space of life that now remains."

"Moreno!" said Sebastiani—"you have two lives at your disposal. Save you brother's and your own. Accept my offers, or you know the alternative."

"I know it, general; and I have made my decision from the moment I became your prisoner."

"Pause," said the Frenchman. "Remember, no hope but one remains. Your hand cannot save—"

"But," said the Guerilla with a smile, "they can avenge me! I have a last request. Allow me a confessor, and a few minutes of private conversation with my brother."

"Both are granted. I have already despatched my aide-de-camp to his convent for the priest you named, and you may retire into the adjoining room with your brother until the monk arrives."

"I thank you, general, for this indulgence; nay, I feel convinced that in your own heart you loathe the duty which obliges you to visit the man who strikes for freedom with the penalties traitors only should incur."

We were conducted into a small chamber which opened off the hail, and looked out upon the market. One close-barred window gave it light; and through the open lattice we saw the scaffold erected, on which, in another hour, Vicente was to seal his loyalty with his life.

"Juan," he said, "thou knowest how tenderly I love thee; and, brief as my span of existence is, I would use it in preparing thee for death or life. If thou art to be another victim, bear thy doom manfully, and prove upon the scaffold how calmly a Spaniard can abide the tyrant's decree. If thou art spared, devote thyself to avenge thy country's wrongs—thy brother's slaughter. Now tax thy energies, for I have evil news to tell. Canst thou hear of ruined hopes?—of—"

"What!"—I exclaimed, as he hesitated.—"What of Catalina? Have they wronged her?—Have they—"

"Patience, my brother, and man thyself—none can wrong—"

He stopped again.

"Go on, Vicente. Go on. All this is torture."

"The dead"—he added solemnly.

"The dead!—Is Catalina dead?"

"She is," he returned. "Ten days after you had been torn away, while thy betrothed was lying in a fever, they seized the old man, and incarcerated him. The shock was fatal. She became delirious, and expired on the third day, without the consolation of knowing that a lover watched her couch, or a parent closed her eyes. Jose Miranda heard the tidings—he never raised his head afterwards, and in a week they laid him in the same cemetery where Catalina rests."

"God of justice!" I exclaimed, "can such villainy and oppression escape unpunished?"

"Thou mayest yet have vengeance in thy power; and the last efforts of my life shall be used to save thine. Should I succeed, remember Vicente and avenge him. Here comes the priest. Farewell, a last farewell, my Juan. The monk will visit thee when the trial of my firmness is over, and tell thee how calmly thy brother died!"

We embraced—were separated—I re-conducted to my cell, and Vicente led to execution. In the presence of his wife and children they hanged him like a dog. How his last moments passed—how nobly he submitted to his martyrdom—thou know'st already.

The fading sunbeams penetrated the grated loophole of my dungeon—and it was resolved that I should never see them set again. Moreno's firmness on the scaffold had incensed the bloodhounds who had sent him there, while the deep sympathy exhibited by the spectators alarmed and exasperated Ciria and Fernandez, his renegade confederate, and the betrayer of my brother. They urged on Sebastiani the expediency of example, and exhorted him to check this popular display of pity and admiration. The French general yielded a reluctant consent, and the warrant for my execution next morning was officially prepared.

It was an unusual hour for a visit when I heard the keeper turn his key. He came accompanied by a monk, and showed me the fatal warrant. The death of my affianced bride—the murder of my gallant brother; the total wreck of worldly happiness had rendered life so valueless, that, but for the hope of revenge, I would have parted with existence, and felt that death was a relief.

"Art thou prepared to die, my son?" said the friar, after the gaoler had read the fatal mandate.

"Better I trust, father, than they who are spillers of innocent blood."

"Art thou ready," continued the monk, "to submit to thy fate with resignation; and, like a Christian man, forgive thy enemies and persecutors?"

"I will meet my doom like a man," I replied, "and my last exhortation to those who witness my end, will be vengeance on my murderers."

"Hush! my son," replied the priest. "As thou hopest forgiveness thou must render it. Leave us, good Pedro, alone. I would hear his confessions; and for his soul's sake, persuade this youthful sinner to die in a holier mood."

The gaoler bowed—laid down his light—withdrew and, having secured the door, left me to the pious admonitions of my ghostly comforter.

Before the sound of the keeper's steps was lost in the distant passage, the monk suddenly flung back his cowl, and displayed a dark and vindictive countenance.

"Joan Moreno, it is no shaveling who speaks to thee, but a devoted comrade of thy brother. I have planned thy escape: hear and attend to what I say. At the end of the stone corridor without the door there is a window that opens on the market-place. It is, to all appearance, strongly secured with iron stanchions; but several of the bars have been sawed through; and could you but quit this cell, the rest were easy. There is but one way—it is simple and sure—when the keeper comes here at midnight stab him to the heart, and hasten to the outlet I have described. There I, with some trusty companions, will be waiting. Whistle twice, and we will know thou art at the grate. Take these, and hide them until they are wanted;" and he gave me a dagger, a pistol, some food, and a flask of wine.

"Drink," he said; "and when the time comes for action, think of Vicente Moreno; remember thy martyred brother, and strike home to the heart of one of his murderers. But I must free thee from thy fetters;" and stooping, he unlocked the chains, told me his plans again, and exhorted me to be prompt and resolute. I needed nothing to rouse my vengeance; and hiding the weapons and the wine beneath the mattress, waited the gaoler's coming, whose steps were heard advancing along the vaulted passage.

"Well," he said, "holy father, hast thou made any progress in fitting this youth for death?"

"Alas! no," replied the false monk. "For one so young, he appears desperately hardened. Wilt thou think on what I have said to thee, Juan? and by all you value, follow my advice, I conjure you."

"I will do as the brother of Vicente Moreno should do; and to the latest hour of existence, I will remember his wrongs, and imprecate curses on his enemies."

"Now, by St Jerome," exclaimed the keeper, "I will witness thy dying pangs upon the gallows with as much pleasure as I looked upon those of the rebel whom you speak of. Come, holy father, leave the young brigand to himself, and let him amuse himself with the prospect of a hempen necklace until tonight, when I will bring him the last loaf he will require at my hands."

He followed the disguised Guerilla, and I was left once more in solitude and darkness.

Had I felt one sting of compunction in robbing a human being of life so suddenly, the remarks of the truculent scoundrel, in allusion to my brother's death, would have removed it. I ate the food, drank the wine sparingly, concealed the weapons in my bosom, and coolly waited for the hour when the work of vengeance should commence.

Midnight came—the deep-toned bell of Santa Margarita told the hour, and sounded the knell of my first victim. Pedro entered the cell as he usually did; and when he had laid down the loaf and pitcher, informed me that one hour after daybreak I should be required to be ready.

"You, I presume, intend to witness the ceremony," I said carelessly.

"I would not take a doubloon, and miss the sight," he replied. "Youngster, you have already cost me a broken head"—and he pointed to his bandages. "In his mad attempt to save you, I received this blow from Vicente Moreno."

"And this from Juan"—I added—striking the dagger to the hilt in his bosom. Thrice I repeated the blow as he was falling. The gaoler gave one hollow groan, and all was over.

I took the light and hastened to the outlet, discovered it easily, and gave the appointed signal. Hands from without promptly removed the bars. I passed my body through the aperture, and found the comrade of my brother, and some trusty friends, waiting for me. By obscure streets we quitted Grenada, and evaded the French pickets; and at the hour appointed for my execution, when I was expected to exhibit on the scaffold, I was kneeling in the mountains of Honda, in the centre of a Guerilla troop, swearing upon my brother's crucifix eternal vengeance against his murderers.

But I have been tedious in my narrative, and it is time my band were moving. I shall give the word of readiness; and while my comrades are bridling their horses, I will tell you thy last adventure.

I mentioned the names of Ciria and Fernandez, as the villains who had betrayed my brother, and consigned me to the dungeons of Grenada. Before three months passed I surprised the former in Almagro, and hanged him over his own door. Fernandez, aware that the same fate awaited him, retired to France, and thus evaded for a time my vengeance. His treachery was rewarded with an appointment in the enemy's commissariat; and, as his duties lay beyond the Pyrenees, he fancied himself secure.

Four days ago I found, by an intercepted despatch, that the traitor was quartered within the French lines, and expected another villain, named Cardonna, to meet him on some secret business at the village of Espalette. A pass from General Foy was enclosed, to enable the latter to clear the outposts. There was a chance—a dangerous one no doubt— but the dead called for vengeance, and I resolved to obtain it, or perish in the attempt. I left my band in their mountain bivouacs, passed the French sentries unmolested, and at nightfall entered the village.

To find out, without exciting any inquiries, the house where Fernandez lodged, was difficult; but I tried and succeeded. His chamber was on one side of a cottage, occupied by French soldiers; and through the window I could observe him engaged with another man in overlooking military returns. Every word spoken I heard distinctly.

"You must fetch the muster-roll," said Fernandez. "Hasten back, that the business may be settled before Cardonna arrives."

"I shall be back in ten minutes," replied the other, as he rose and left the room.

I waited for half that time, then passed into the cottage unobserved, and entered the chamber boldly. Fernandez continued writing at the table—his back was to the door; and never doubting but it was his friend returning with the roll, he never raised his eyes from the returns. I marked the spot to strike, and with one blow divided the spine. The head dropped down upon the table and not a sigh escaped his lips! With the point of my bloody knife I traced upon a slip of paper the name of "Juan Moreno," and glided from the cottage unquestioned and unnoticed. Was not that, my friend, brave revenge? To immolate, in the centre of an enemy's camp, the murderer of Vicente—the destroyer of Catalina.

My subsequent escape was truly hazardous. I hid myself during the day in a hollow bank that overhung the river, and at night succeeded in reaching the bridge—the termination you know yourself.

And now you have heard from my own lips the causes which have made my name so formidable to the invaders. Had I not been driven to the mountains by oppression, I should have dreamed my life peacefully away—and Juan Moreno would have lived, and died, and been forgotten. Cruelty turned my blood to gall, and changed my very nature. At manhood this hand was stainless as a schoolboy's—at thirty the blood of fifty victims reeks upon it. Human joys and pleasures are lost upon me. For me beauty has no charms, and gold is merely dross. Yonder mule is laden with Napoleons; and, by Heaven, I would not take the burden beyond that rivulet, only that I employ it in furthering my revenge. Once I could hang over a harp, and feel its music at my heart—now the roar of cannon, the crash of battle, or, sweeter still, the death-groan of an enemy, is the only melody for me. Living, mine shall be "war to the knife!"—and when I die, whether it be on the scaffold or the field, my last breath shall be a curse upon the oppressor. Ho, Carlos! my horse. And now farewell. You and I shall probably never meet again. May you be happy; and when you hear that Juan Moreno is no more, ask how he died."

He gave the word to march—sprang lightly to the saddle—and, at the sudden turning of an alpine pass, waved a last adieu to O'Connor, and disappeared.

XI

THE FALL OF ST SEBASTIAN

The tale of war still bears a painful sound—
I see in captured towns but mangled corpses—
I hear in victory's shouts but dying groans.

M. G. LEWIS

WHEN SOULT RETREATED THROUGH THE passes of the Pyrenees by Maya, Roncesvalles, and Echalan, the British and their allies resumed the positions from which they had been forced, and re-established their headquarters at Lezaca. A period of comparative inactivity succeeded. Immediate operations could not be commenced on either side—the enemy had been too severely repulsed to permit their becoming assailants again; while, on the other hand, Wellington would not be justified in crossing the frontier and entering a hostile country, with Pamplona and St Sebastian garrisoned by the French, and in his rear.

Nothing could be more magnificent than the positions of the British brigades. For many a mile along the extended line of occupation, huts crowning the heights or studding the deep valleys below them, showed the rude dwellings of the mighty mass of human beings collected in that alpine country. At night the scene was still more picturesque. The irregular surface of the sierras sparkled with a thousand watch-fires, and the bivouacs of the allies exhibited all the varieties of light and shadow which an artist loves to copy. To the occupants themselves, the views obtained from their elevated abodes were grand and imposing. One while obscured in fog, the hum of voices alone announced that their, comrades were beside them—while at another the sun bursting forth in cloudless beauty displayed a varied scene, glorious beyond imagination. At their feet the fertile plains of France presented themselves—above, ranges of magnificent heights towered in majestic grandeur to the skies, and stretched into distance beyond the range of sight.

That portion of the Rifles with which our story chiefly lies, had resumed their old quarters at the bridge, and occupied the same bivouac, from which Soult's advance had obliged them to retire. Although no military movements were made, this inactive interval of a vigorous campaign was usefully employed by the allied commander, in organising anew the regiments that had suffered most, concentrating the divisions, replacing exhausted stores, and perfecting the whole *materiel* of the army. Those of the British near the coast, compared with the corps that were blockading Pamplona, lived comfortably in their mountain bivouacs. The task of covering the blockade was the most disagreeable that falls to the soldier's lot. Exposed to cold and rain, continually on the alert, and yet engaged in a duty devoid of enterprise and interest, nothing could be more wearying to the troops employed; and desertions, which during active service were infrequent, became numerous, and especially among the Spaniards and Irish.

It was a wet day—a thick mist hung over the valleys, and shut out distant objects from the view of the light troops cantoned on the heights of Santa Barbara. The wooden hut was but thinly tenanted—for, alas several of the brave youths who had been formerly its occupants had found a soldier's grave during the late combats in the mountains, or fallen before the shattered bastions of St Sebastian. Although not engaged in the investment of that fortress, the division had furnished a portion of the volunteers, who formed the storming party on the morning of the assault—and of that gallant band, two thirds died before the breach, or were placed *hors de combat* in the hospitals.

In the annals of modern warfare there is no conflict recorded so sanguinary and so desperate as the storming of that well-defended

breach. During the blockade every resource of military ingenuity
was tried by the French governor—and the failure of the first
assault, and the subsequent raising of the siege, emboldened the
garrison and rendered them the more confident of holding out, until
Soult could advance and succour them. The time from which the
battering guns had been withdrawn, until they were again replaced
in the works, had been assiduously employed in constructing new
defences and strengthening the old ones. But though the place
when reinvested was more formidable than before, the besiegers
appeared only the more determined to reduce it—Santa Clara, a
bluff and rocky island commanding the landing place, was carried
after an obstinate defence—a mortar battery was erected to shell the
castle from across the bay—while a storm of round and case shot
was maintained so vigorously, that in a short time the fire of the
enemy was nearly silenced.

The night before the storm was well fitted to harbinger the day of
slaughter that succeeded—a dreadful tempest of thunder, lightning,
and rain came on with darkness; and amid the uproar of elemental
fury, three mines loaded with 1500 lbs. of powder were sprung by the
besiegers, and the sea-wall blown down.

Morning broke gloomily—an intense mist obscured every object—
and the work of slaughter was for a time delayed. At nine the sea-
breeze cleared away the fog—the sun shone gloriously out—and in
two hours the forlorn hope issued from the trenches. The columns
succeeded, and every gun from the fortress that could bear opened
on them with shot and shells. The appearance of the breach was
perfectly delusive—nothing living could reach the summit—no
courage, however desperate, could overcome the difficulties—they
were alike unexpected and insurmountable. In vain the officers
rushed forward, and devotedly were they followed by their men. From
entrenched houses behind the breach, the traverses, mid the ramparts
of the curtain, a withering discharge of musketry was poured on the
assailants, while the Mirador and Prince batteries swept the approaches
with their guns. To survive this concentrated fire was impossible; the

forlorn hope were cut off to a man, and the heads of the columns annihilated. At last the debouches were choked with the dead and wounded, and a further passage to the breach rendered impracticable, from the heap of corpses that were piled upon each other.

Then, in that desperate moment, when hope might have been supposed to be over, an expedient unparalleled in the records of war was resorted to. The British batteries opened on the curtain, and the storming parties heard with surprise the roar of cannon in their rear, while, but a few feet above their heads, the iron shower hissed horribly, sweeping away the enemy and their defences. This was the moment for a fresh effort. Another brigade was moved forward; and, favoured by an accidental explosion upon the curtain, which confused the enemy while it encouraged the assailants, the *terre-plain* was mounted, and the French driven from the works. A long and obstinate resistance was continued in the streets, which were in many places barricaded, but by five in the evening opposition ceased—and the town was in the possession of the British.

A night of frightful excesses followed the capture of the city. Plunder and violence were raging through every corner of the place—the town was partially on fire—while, as if to add to the horror of the scene, the elements were convulsed, and it thundered and lightened awfully. Over the transactions of that night a veil should be drawn—for if ever men were demonised, these were the captors of St Sebastian.

What rendered the assault upon the fortress more interesting was, that, at the same time, while the operations to reduce it were being carried on, the French re-crossed the Bidassoa in great force, and attacked the Spaniards at San Marcial. In the affair that succeeded, the allies behaved most gallantly. They held the position, repulsed Soult's attempt to dislodge them, and obliged him to retire with immense loss. The number of the French killed was never correctly known, but nearly a thousand perished in forcing the bridge at Vera, which was held by a part of the light division.

An animated description of the fall of St Sebastian, by a survivor of those who volunteered from the Rifles, had occasioned some observations on the advantage of night attacks. O'Connor had been frequently appealed to upon disputed points. Gradually a deeper interest to learn the particulars of the assault on Badajoz was excited, and none could better describe that scene of blood than he who had led the storming party. The rain continued falling with unabated violence, and all the inmates of the wooden hut were collected round the rough bench which formed the table. To their unanimous request the gallant soldier yielded a good-humoured assent, and thus narrated that glorious affair, which widowed many a dame, and left many a maid "lamenting."

XII

THE STORM OF BADAJOZ

From the point of encountering blades to the hilt,
Sabres and swords with blood were gilt;
But the rampart is won, and the spoil begun,
And all but the after carnage done.

Siege of Corinth

Men, like wild beasts, when once they have tasted
blood, acquire an appetite for it.

SOUTHEY

And he had learned to love—I know not why,
    For this in such as him seems strange of mood—
The helpless leeks of blooming infancy
    Even in its earliest nature.

Childe Harold

"BADAJOZ!" EXCLAIMED O'CONNOR, WITH ENTHUSIASM, "many
a gallant deed—many a bitter recollection—are associated
with thee. Thousands of the best troops that England and France
ever sent into the field are mouldering before thy bastions—and
many a widowed wife and fatherless child will curse the name that
recalls the loss of their protectors!

"Never shall I forget the morning of the 9th of March, when the
light, third, and fourth divisions crossed the Tagus by a bridge of

boats, and, concentrating at Elvas, pushed on to Merida and Lerena. Never was an army in higher spirit—and all were anxious to come in contact with the enemy. On the 16th Badajoz was to be invested. The pontoon bridge was thrown across the Guadiana; and, though fiercely opposed by the French cavalry, the river was crossed, and we sat down before this celebrated fortress.

"Badajoz is easily described. Round one portion of the town the rivulets Calamon and Rivellas sweep, and unite with the Guadiana, which flows in the face of the works, and in front of the heights of Saint Christoval. The castle stands nearly above the union of these rivers. The fortifications are exceedingly strong—the bastions and curtains regular—while formidable outworks—the forts of Pardelaras, Picarina, and Saint Christoval—completed the exterior defences of a city that had already stood two sieges, and had since been strengthened with jealous attention and scientific skill.

"The 17th was a day of peculiar interest; and the anniversary of our patron saint was employed in reconnoitring the place, and determining the point on which our opening assault should be directed. The outwork of Picarina was selected for the first essay; and in a tempest of wind and rain, and favoured by the darkness, we broke ground within a hundred and forty paces of the fort. Three thousand men laboured throughout the night without a moment's cessation—and at dawn the garrison were astounded to see the first parallel completed.

"All the next day, under a lively cannonade from the fort and town, we laboured vigorously. At night the rain came down in torrents, but we worked on, knee-deep in water. On the 19th the trenches were advancing rapidly, and some guns were already in battery—when Phillipon, alarmed for the safety of his best outwork, determined to sally, and attempt the destruction of our labours.

"During the morning an unusual bustle was apparent in the city and fort; but the soldiers, up to the waist in water, continued pushing on the works. At noon, profiting by a dense fog, the sallyports of the fortress were thrown open, and eighteen hundred of the enemy rushed on us with fixed bayonets. A short and sanguinary struggle ensued. On the left, the French were driven back to their own gates; and though they surprised the workmen on the right, and injured a part of the trenches, the sortie was on the whole disastrous to the garrison, and cost them above four hundred killed or prisoners. We lost a number of officers and men; but the French gained nothing by the affair but a few entrenching tools. They carried off a number of spades and shovels, for which Phillipon gave a dollar each.

"The weather was dreadful; nothing but a torrent of rain. The water in the trenches, in some places, took the men above the middle, while the earth crumbled away, and prevented us from making any progress in forwarding the breaching batteries. The river rose—the flood swept off our pontoon bridge—we were cut off from our supplies—insulated from the covering force—and as badly off for food and shelter as might be. But we laboured on—the weather changed—the 24th was fine. The French attempted to check our efforts to place guns in battery and establish magazines, by an increased storm of artillery. Our men fell in dozens—engineers, who directed the works, and exposed themselves with reckless devotion, were instantly shot down—shells dropped frequently into the trenches—powder casks were repeatedly exploded while being conveyed to the magazine. Under all these discouraging circumstances, the works were completed; and, on the dawning of the 25th, two batteries were unmasked, and opened with a tremendous fire on the outwork of Picurina at the short distance of one hundred and forty paces. Of course the town and fort turned every gun within range upon ours; but so terrible and effective was the point-blank service of our two-and-thirties, that at evening a breach was declared practicable; and Lord Wellington, no admirer of the Fabian system of delay, determined, when it became dark, to carry Picurina by storm.

"Well, the storming party was selected from a part of Picton's division, and we of the light were allowed to volunteer. On we went with scaling ladders; but the ditch was so immensely deep that it was impossible to cross it. At last we broke down the gate—on rushed our fellows with the bayonet—the French grenadiers as sturdily resisted them—a regular steel affair ensued; and though a strong support moved from the town to assist the defenders of the fort, in a short time all opposition ceased—and Picurina was ours.

"I was slightly wounded in the *mêlée* within the gate, and was *hors de combat* till the morning of the 5th of April. I was then quite recovered and able to rejoin my regiment, and fortunately in good time to witness the splendid night attack, which ended in the capture of this well-defended fortress.

"On the 6th the breaches were reported practicable by the engineers, and the assault was fixed for eight o'clock that evening. The day was beautiful; and when the order was issued marking the positions the different brigades should occupy, the soldiers were in high spirits, and set merrily to work cleaning their arms and appointments, as if preparing for a dress parade. On individual officers the effect that note of preparation caused was very opposite. One, as brave a fellow as ever breathed, passed me apparently in deep abstraction. Suddenly he seemed to awake from an uneasy reverie, recognised me, and shook me by the hand.

"'God bless you, Edward,' he said. 'Farewell, old boy; before midnight I shall be in another world.' I laughed at him. 'Yes, O'Connor, it will be so. I would not own it to another; but you and I have fought side by side ere now, and you will acquit me of timidity. This, O'Connor, is my last fight! Will you oblige me in one matter? When you came up I was just thinking which of our fellows I should ask the favour of.'

"'Anything, my dear Jack, that I can do, you may command.'

"'Come aside,' he said—and we walked behind the huts. 'Here'— and he put a parcel into my hand—'when I am gone, have that little packet conveyed to England, and delivered as it is addressed; and just add a line or two, to say that it never left my bosom until I confided it to you.'

"It was a leather case, and I fancy contained a miniature and some letters. The direction was to a young lady, who, if report was to be believed, was deeply attached to my gallant friend. I took the parcel. Once more Weyland and I shook hands. We parted, never to meet again—his foreboding was verified—he perished at the head of the storming party in front of the lesser breach.

"I had scarcely deposited the case in the breast of my jacket, when Dillon, of the 2nd, encountered me—his face beaming with delight—his spirits buoyant as the school-boy's, when an unexpected holyday is announced by his master.

"'Well met, O'Connor,' he cried, as be took my hand. 'Here we are a brace of subs today, and tomorrow we shall be captains. We're both at the head of the list, and surely some of the old fellows will get a quietus before morning. Egad, tomorrow you and I will drink to our further promotion, if there be a sound bottle of Sherry in Phillipon's cellar.'

"'Yes, my dear Dillon; but you must recollect that our skins are not more impervious than those of other men to steel and lead. There's work cut out for us, take my word for it, before we'll be made free of the Frenchman's wine-bin.'

"'Pshaw!—I would not give a dollar to insure my company; and auld Clooty will never leave in the lurch a steady servant like you, Ned. Hang it, I wish it were dark, and the work begun. I intend to sup in a convent tonight.'

"'Indeed! then would it were supper time, and all were well,'—and we parted.

"Twilight came, the sun set gloriously, and many a hundred eyes looked their last upon him that evening. Soon after eight the regiments were under arms, and the roll of each called over in an under voice. A death-like silence prevailed—the division (the light) formed behind the quarry in front of Santa Maria; and after a pause of half an hour, the forlorn hope passed quietly along, supported by a storming party consisting of three hundred volunteers. I was attached to the former. We moved silently—not a man coughed or whispered—and in three minutes afterwards the division followed.

"At that moment the deep bell of the cathedral of St John struck ten—the most perfect silence reigned around, and except the softened foot-fall of the storming parties as they struck the turf with military precision, not a movement was audible. A terrible suspense—a horrible stillness—darkness—a compression of the breathing—the dull and ill-defined outline of the town—the knowledge that similar and simultaneous movements were making on other points—the certainty that two or three minutes would probably involve the forlorn hope in ruin, or make it the beacon-light to victory—all these made the heart throb quicker, and long for the bursting of the storm when wild success should crown our daring, or hope and life should end together.

"On we went; one solitary musket was discharged beside the breach, but none answered it. The light division moved forward rapidly, closing up in columns at quarter distance. We reached the ditch—the ladders were lowered—on rushed the forlorn hope—on went the storming party. The division were now on the brink of the sheer descent, when a gun boomed from the parapet. The earth trembled—a mine was fired—an explosion—an infernal hissing from lighted fuses succeeded—and, like the raising of a curtain on the stage in the hellish glare, the French lining the ramparts in crowds, the English storming parties descending the ditch, were placed as distinctly visible to each other as if the hour was noontide!

"A tremendous fire from the guns of the place, which had been laid upon the approaches to the breach, followed the explosion; but undauntedly the storming cheered, and, bravely the French answered it. A murderous scene ensued, for the breach was utterly impassable. Notwithstanding the withering fire of musketry from the parapets—light artillery brought immediately to bear upon the breach—and the grape, from every gun upon the works that could play upon the assailants or supporting columns—the British mounted. Hundreds were thrown back—and hundreds promptly succeeded them. Almost unharmed themselves, the French dealt death around; and secure within defences that even in daylight and to a force unopposed, would prove almost insurmountable, they ridiculed the mad attempt; and while they viewed from the parapets a thousand victims in the ditch, they called in derision to the broken columns, and invited them to come on.

"I, though unwounded, was hurled from the breach, and fell into the lunette, where, for a few minutes, I had some difficulty to escape suffocation. The guns of the bastions swept the place where I was lying, and the constant plash of grape upon the surface of the water was a sound anything but agreeable. The cheers had ceased—the huzzas of the enemy at our repulse had died away—and from the ramparts they amused themselves with picking off anyone they pleased. Fire-balls occasionally lighted up the ditch, and showed a mass of wretched men lying in the mud and water, mobbed together, unable to offend, and, poor wretches! at the mercy of the enemy, for retreat was impracticable. As the French continued hurling cart-wheels, planks, and portions of the masonry of the parapet, which our own battering guns had destroyed, it was pitiable to see the feeble efforts of the wounded, as they vainly strove to crawl from beneath the rampart, and avoid the murderous missiles that were instantly showered down. Now and again, the gurgling noise of some one drowning close beside was heard in the interval of the firing; while the groaning of those from whom life was ebbing—the cursing of others in their agonies—joined to the demon laugh which was frequent from the breach above, gave the passing scene an infernal colouring, that no time shall ever obliterate from the memory of him who witnessed it.

"Yet never was the indomitable courage of Britain more signally displayed than during the continuance of this murderous attempt. Although at dusk, when the English batteries ceased their fire, the breaches were sufficiently shattered to be practicable, during the three hours that intervened before the assault commenced, Phillippon had exhausted his matchless ingenuity in rendering the entrance of a storming-party by the ruined bastions utterly impossible. Harrows and planks, studded with spikes and bound firmly by iron chains, were suspended in front of the battered parapet like a curtain—a deep retrenchment cut off the breach from the interior, even had an enemy surmounted it—and a line of *chevaux-de-frise*, bristling with sword blades, protected the top. With these insurmountable obstacles before them, and death rained upon them from every side, even in handfuls the light and fourth divisions continued their desperate attempts; and many of the bravest, after struggling to the summit of the bastion, were shot down in their vain attempts to tear defences away, which no living man could clamber over.

"While the sanguinary struggle was proceeding in the bastions of Trinidad and Santa Maria, the castle was escaladed on the right, and the bastion of San Vincente afterwards, by the fifth division on the opposite quarter of the town. After a fierce contest of an hour, the third division mounted by their ladders, and driving all before them at the bayonet point, fairly carried the place by storm, and remained in possession of the castle. Nothing could surpass the daring gallantry of the escalade; and the heap of dead men and broken ladders strewn next morning before the lofty walls showed how vigorously the enemy had resisted it.

"Leith's division were unfortunately delayed from their scaling ladders, not arriving for an hour after the grand assault had been made upon the breaches. But they nobly redeemed lost time; and while the Portuguese Caçadores distracted the garrison by a false attack on Pardaleras, a brigade of the fifth overcame every opposition, and, supported by the rest of the division, drove all before them from the ramparts, and established themselves in the town.

"It is astonishing, even in the spring-tide of success, how the most trivial circumstances will damp the courage of the bravest, and check the most desperate in their career. The storming-party of the fifth had escaladed a wall of thirty feet with wretched ladders—forced an uninjured palisade—descended a deep counterscarp—and crossed the lunette behind it—and this was effected under a converging fire from the bastions, and a well sustained fusillade, while but a few of the assailants could force their way together, and form on the rampart when they got up. But the leading sections persevered until the brigade was completely lodged within the parapet; and now united, and supported by the division who followed fast, what could withstand their advance?

"They were sweeping forward with the bayonet—the French were broken and dispersed—when at this moment of brilliant success, a port-fire, which a retreating gunner had flung upon the rampart, was discovered. A vague alarm seized the leading files—they fancied some mischief was intended—and imagined the success, which their own desperate gallantry had achieved, was but a *ruse* of the enemy to lure them to destruction. 'It is a mine—and they are springing it!' shouted a soldier. Instantly the leaders of the storming-party turned. It was impossible for their officers to undeceive them. The French perceived the panic—rallied and pursued—and friends and foes came rushing back tumultuously upon a supporting regiment (the 38th), that was fortunately formed in reserve upon the ramparts. This momentary success of the besieged was dearly purchased—a volley was thrown closely in—a bayonet rush succeeded—and the French were scattered before the fresh assailants, never to form again. The fifth division poured in. Everything gave way that opposed it. The cheering was heard above the fire—the bugles sounded an advance—the enemy became distracted and disheartened—and again the light and fourth divisions, or, alas! their skeletons, assisted by Hay's brigade, advanced to the breaches. Scarcely any opposition was made. They entered—and Badajoz was our own! Philippon, finding all lost, retired across the river to Fort San Christoval, and early next day surrendered.

"During this doubtful conflict, Wellington, with his staff, occupied a commanding position in front of the *tête-de-pont* that defends the great stone bridge across the Guadiana. Those who happened to be around him describe the scene, as witnessed from the heights above San Christoval, as grand and awfully imposing. The deep silence after the divisions moved to their respective positions—the chime of the town clock—the darkness of the night—the sudden blaze of rockets and blue lights from the garrison, followed by an interval of deeper obscurity—the springing of the mine, succeeded by the roar of artillery, and bursting of shells—while musketry and grenades kept up an endless spattering—all this, added to the uncertainty of the assault, must have tried even the iron nerve of the conqueror of Napoleon's best commanders.

"Presently an officer rode up at speed, to say that the attempt to force the breaches had failed, and the result had been most disastrous. Pale, but unmoved, the English general issued calmly his orders for a fresh brigade to support the light division; and the aide-de-camp galloped off to have it executed. An interval of harrowing suspense followed. Another of the staff came up in haste. 'My Lord, General Picton is in the castle.'—'Ha! are you certain?'—'Yes, my Lord. I entered it with the 88th.'—''Tis well—let him keep it. Withdraw the divisions from the breach.' An hour after, another horseman announced the fifth division to have completely succeeded in escalading San Vincent. 'Bravely done! Badajoz is ours!'—was the cool half-muttered observation of the British commandant.

"Well—I have been tedious—but these boys seem interested in the details of occurrences which marked that fearful night, and I shall now relate the strange adventure that consigned an orphan to my charge.

"When our division entered the town all opposition was at an end; for the French, fearing that a dreadful retaliation would ensue, precipitately abandoned the city, and secured themselves in Fort Christoval, until they effected a capitulation and were permitted to retire to Elvas. In the morning I obtained a few hours' repose, notwithstanding the deafening yells of the excited soldiery, and their incessant discharge of musketry, as they went firing through the streets, or blew open the doors of the wine-houses, and indeed of all other dwellings, which were vainly closed against them. I had seen the breaches in all their horrors—I had again crossed them in daylight—and I turned my steps towards the castle and bastion of San Vincent, to view the places where my more fortunate comrades had forced their way.

"It was nearly dusk; and the few hours while I slept had made a frightful change in the condition and temper of the soldiery. In the morning they were obedient to their officers, and preserved the semblance of subordination; now they were in a state of furious intoxication—discipline was forgotten—and the splendid troops of yesterday had become a fierce and sanguinary rabble, dead to every touch of human feeling, and filled with every demoniac passion that can brutalise the man. The town was in horrible confusion, and on every side frightful tokens of military license met the eye. One street, as I approached the castle, was almost choked up with broken furniture, for the houses had been gutted from the cellar to the garret, the partitions torn down, and even the beds ripped and scattered to the winds, in the hope that gold might be found concealed. A convent at the end of the strada of Saint John was in flames; and I saw more than one wretched nun in the arms of a drunken soldier.

"Farther on the confusion seemed greater. Brandy and wine casks were rolled out before the stores; some were full, some half drunk, but more staved in mere wantonness, and the liquors running through the kennel. Many a harrowing scream saluted the ear of the passer by— many a female supplication was heard asking in vain for mercy. How could it be otherwise, when it is remembered that twenty thousand furious and licentious madmen were loosed upon an immense population, among which many of the loveliest women upon earth might be found? All within that devoted city was at the disposal of an infuriated army, over whom, for the time, control was lost, aided by an infamous collection of camp followers, who were, if possible, more sanguinary and pitiless even than those who survived the storm!

"It is useless to dwell upon a scene from which the heart revolts. I verily believe that few females in this beautiful town were saved that night from insult. The noblest and the beggar—the nun, and the wife and daughter of the artisan—youth and age—all were involved in general ruin. None were respected, and few consequently escaped. The madness of those desperate brigands was variously exhibited; some fired through doors and windows; others at the church bells; many, at the wretched inhabitants as they fled into the streets to escape the bayonets of the savages who were demolishing their property within doors; while some wretches, as if blood had not flowed in sufficient torrents already, shot from the windows their own companions as they staggered on below. What chances had the miserable inhabitants of escaping death, when more than one officer perished by the bullets and bayonets of the very men whom a few hours before he had led to the assault?

"As evening advanced, the streets became more dangerous; and after I had examined the spot from which the escalade of the castle had been effected, I determined to leave the fortress by the first sallyport, and return for the night to our half-deserted camp; for everyone who could frame an excuse had flocked into the luckless town for plunder, and the tents were in many places left without an occupant. Having been for a week quartered in the city after the last year's siege, I fancied that I could find my way to the flying bridge; but the attempt was not an easy one. A swarm of drunken rioters infested the road; and at last I resolved to leave the more frequented streets, and endeavour to free myself from this infernal scene of tumult and villainy, by a safer but more devious path.

"I turned down an unfrequented lane. I remembered that a lamp before an image of the Virgin had formerly burned at the corner, but of course it had been unattended to during the horrors of the past night. Not fifty paces from the entrance, a dead man lay upon his face. I looked at the body carelessly—life was scarcely extinct, for the blood was oozing from an immense wound in the back; and as the jacket was still smoking, the musket of the assassin had probably been touching the wretched man, when the murderer discharged it. It was the corpse of a dragoon; he, of course, had stolen into the town for plunder, and the unhappy delinquent paid a deep penalty for his crime. He held a loaded pistol in his hand. I wrenched it from his grasp with difficulty; for even in death he clutched it. I was now better armed, and I hurried down the lane in the direction of the sallyport.

"This unpretending quarter appeared to have partially escaped the ravages to which the better portion of the town had been exposed. Only a few of the outer doors were broken in, and as I proceeded, the yells and firing became more distant. Just at the bottom of the lane there was a large inn. Within all was quiet as the grave—business and bustle were over. No doubt the spoilers had been there, and, save in an upper window, not a light was to be seen. On coming up, the cause of its desolation was manifest. The outer door had been blown open, and a dozen casks, some spilt or staved, others lying untouched before the gate, showed too plainly that its remote situation had not screened it from the plunderers.

"Two lanes branched off to the right and to the left. To choose between them puzzled me, and I halted to determine which I should trust myself to. I was still undetermined when an uproar, in which several voices united, arose in the upper story of the deserted inn, and apparently in that room where I had observed the light burning. The report of a musket was followed by a shriek so loud, so horrible, so long sustained, that even yet it peals upon my ear. I forgot all personal consideration—and, as if directed by a fatality, rushed into the gate, and ascended the staircase. Cries and curses directed me onwards. The door of the chamber from which they issued was unclosed. I sprang forward, and the scene within was infinitely worse than even the outrages I had witnessed could have harbingered.

"Near the door, a Spaniard, whose dress and appearance were those of a wealthy farmer, or a small proprietor of land, was extended on the floor quite dead; and a ruffian in the uniform of one of the regiments of the third division, was standing over the body, busily engaged, as well as drunkenness would admit, in reloading his musket. Beyond the victim and his murderer a more horrible sight met the eye. The woman, whose piercing scream had attracted me to the scene of slaughter, was writhing in the last agonies of death, while a Portuguese Caçadore coolly wiped the bayonet that had been reddened in her blood. What occurred on my entrance was the transaction of a few moments. Both ruffians turned their rage on me, and I endeavoured to anticipate them by commencing hostilities. With the pistol I had taken from the dragoon I shot the Irishman—I blush to say it but he was my country-man—through the heart, and then attacked the Caçadore. In size and strength we were pretty fairly matched. He was armed with a fixed bayonet—I with a sabre, ground to the keenness of a knife; but his own crime gave me the advantage, and sealed his fate.

He was a cool and dangerous cut-throat, and collecting all his energies
for a rush, he thought to transfix me against the door. We had light
enough for a brief combat, as the drapery and curtains of the room
were in a blaze. He gathered himself for the trial—I was ready—he
made a full lunge with all his force, but his foot slipped in the blood
of her whom he had just massacred, and a slight parry averting his
push, the bayonet burst through the panel up to the socket, and the
villain was at my mercy. As he vainly strove to disengage his weapon,
I stepped back and struck him across the head. He fell forward. Thrice
I repeated the cut—for the scoundrel was full of life and I was not
contented until his skull was fractured by reiterated blows, and the
brain scattered against the wainscot. I see you shudder, Mortimer; you
have yet to learn how quickly war will brutalise us. At your years I
could not have treated a rabid dog so savagely; but that scene withered
every feeling of human pity, and I, for the time, was as truculent as the
villains I had despatched.

"The curtains blazed more fiercely, while I stood like a presiding
demon above four bleeding corpses—the murderers and their victims.
The blood of the dead Caçadore had spurted over me, and from hilt
to point my sabre was crimsoned. On the floor a quantity of gold and
silver coins were scattered, while the glare of the burning tapestry gave
a wild and infernal light that fitted well that scene of slaughter. I could
stay no longer—the woodwork was already in flames—and a few
minutes would wrap the devoted house in a sheet of fire. I stooped
and picked a cartridge from the cartouche-box of the dead Irishman,
to reload my pistol. Something beneath a chair sparkled. Was it the
eyes of a dog? I removed the antique and cumbrous piece of furniture
and there a child, some three years old, had cowered for shelter! To
leave it to perish in the flames was impossible. I caught it up—it never
cried—for terror I suppose had taken away the power of utterance,
and rushing from the room, found myself again in the street.

"I had escaped one peril only to rush upon another. Seven or eight
men were drinking from a spirit cask, which lay before the door
of the burning hostelry. They were loaded with plunder of divers

kinds—and with the little reason left, were endeavouring to secure it by leaving the sacked city and hastening to the camp. That camp they were not likely to find, for every wine-butt in their route was duty tasted as they passed along.

"My appearance was instantly observed. 'It's one of the foreigners,' said he who seemed to be the leader, as he remarked my dark uniform—'Shoot him, Jim!'

"Fortunately the command was given in Irish, and I replied promptly in the same language. In a few moments we understood each other perfectly. They wanted to secure their booty, and I volunteered to be their leader, and effect a retreat.

"To prohibit drinking for the future, under a threat of abandoning them instantly, was any first order; and it was, though reluctantly, acceded to. I next examined their arms, and ordered the muskets that had been discharged to be reloaded. The booty was next secured; and forming them into something like military order, I gave the word to march, and proceeded towards the sallyport, the leader of a banditti, whom no consideration, but an avaricious anxiety to save the produce of the night's villainy, could have induced to quit a scene of violence and blood so congenial to their brutal fancies. I brought them and the hapless orphan safely from the town; although their own pugnacity, and the appearance of the rich booty they had obtained, involved us in several skirmishes with parties who were flocking into the city, on the same vile errand as that in which my 'charge of foot' had been so success fully engaged."

"And did you discover who the murdered parents of the poor infant were?"

"Alas!—no. The orphan's parentage remains to this hour wrapped in obscurity. When, after two days and nights of violence and pillage, Lord Wellington with difficulty repressed those dreadful excesses, by marching in a Portuguese brigade, attended by the provost-marshal with the gallows and triangles, I hastened, as soon as I could venture it safely, to the place where I had witnessed the slaughter of the unfortunate strangers. The inn was burned to the ground; but I made out the proprietors, who had obtained a temporary shelter in one of the detached offices that had escaped the flames. They could give me no information, nor did they even know the names of their murdered inmates. They, poor victims! had arrived in Badajoz from a distant part of Andalusia only the day before we invested the town, and remained there during the siege. Having a large sum of money in their possession, they fancied themselves safer in the city than in attempting to remove homewards, as the roads in the vicinity were infested by Guerillas and professed banditti. They stopped accordingly, till Badajoz fell; and, in common with many hundreds of unfortunates, their lives and property paid a sad penalty for the obstinacy of Philippon's defence."

"And what became of the poor orphan, O'Connor?" asked O'Shaughnessy.

"I sent him to England, placed him at a school, and when he is old enough he shall be a soldier. Should I fall, he is not forgotten. But come—to bed—to bed. Sound be your slumbers, boys!—before the night of tomorrow, many a stirring spirit will be quiet enough—and on the sward of a battle-field, 'sleep the sleep that knows not breaking.'"

XIII

THE DEAD LIEUTENANT

Vain was ev'ry ardent vow,
Never yet did Heaven allow,
Love so warm, so wild, to last.

MOORE

THERE IS NO SADDER OFFICE imposed upon a soldier than to arrange the simple property of some departed comrade for the rude auction to which, when death occurs on service, the assets of the fallen are submitted. Everything recalls the deceased; and every article, however trifling, renews past recollections. In that jacket, haply, the tale was told which set the table in a roar; and these epaulets may have sparkled in the ball-room, or glittered on the field of battle.

In a convent adjoining the bridge of Vera, a young officer had expired shortly after the night encounter between the British light troops and the French column, which forced that passage in their retreat. Though vastly superior in force, and with darkness and a storm favouring the attack, the posts were gallantly contested; and when the Rifles were obliged to yield to numbers, they occupied the convent walls, and kept up a fire so incessant and well directed, that the narrow bridge was heaped with corpses, and the loss of the retiring enemy was computed at nearly a thousand men. The British casualties were comparatively trifling—and Frederick Selby was the only officer that fell.

Nature had never designed Selby for the trade of arms. His constitution was weak, and his appearance effeminate. He was shy and timid among strangers—wanted decision to seize on fortune if she smiled—and if she chose to frown, he had no reactive spirit to bear the rub, and trust boldly to the chances of tomorrow. From his reserved character he had no intimates—and avoided all friendly intercourse with his brother officers. On service he performed his duty as a thing of course, but never displayed the ardour of a martial spirit; and in the winter season when a campaign ceased, he seemed to dream his life away: how he employed himself in cantonments none knew, and indeed none inquired.

He was the second son of a gentleman of considerable fortune, and had, as it was generally understood, been intended for the church. He graduated accordingly at one of the universities; when circumstances occurred which changed the colour of his profession, and sent to the field one far better suited for the cloister.

Death, however, disclosed the secret, that while living he had kept closely; and in his writing-case the memorials of an unfortunate attachment were found. He had loved a female of humble parentage, and it would appear that a sentimental engagement had been formed, discovered, and dissolved. To remove him far from the object of his passion, his father had purchased a commission, and sent him upon service. The wide sea rolled between him and the forbidden fair one; but the heart remained unchanged—and he died cherishing a passion which time and absence could not subdue.

That most of the private hours of the deceased were spent in literary composition, many fragments in prose and poetry, mixed among letters from me of his family, proved. The effusions generally alluded to the unhappy attachment that had sent him from his native land; and some of them were addressed to his mistress. These were, of course, carefully destroyed. One, however, was of a different description—it seemed some legendary tale connected with the ancient house of Selby. On turning over a few pages O'Brien ascertained that there was nothing in the manuscript to render its destruction necessary; and, as the parades were over and military duties ended for the day, he amused his companions in the bivouac by reading them the legend of "Barbara Maxwell."

VOLUME III

I

BARBARA MAXWELL

He clasped her sleeping to his heart,
  And listened to each broken word;
He hears—why doth Prince Azo start,
  As if the archangel's voice he heard?
That sleeping whisper of a name,
Bespeaks her guilt, and Azo's shame!

Parasina

Imogen. False to his bed! what is it to be false?
Pisanio. Alas, good lady!
Imogen. I false?

Cymbeline

THE NIGHT WAS DARK AND stormy—the snow fell fast—and the wind howled through the leafless branches of the old oaks which encircled Selby Place. Doors shook and casements rattled, as the frequent gusts struck them heavily. All without was gloomy and inclement, while the scene of joyous revelry within formed a striking contrast. Christmas had passed, and right hospitably had that ancient festival been observed. Twelfth-night was come, and all that was noble and fair for many a mile around were assembled in the baron's halt; while in buttery and kitchen, yeomen and domestics were carousing merrily.

  The feasting was ended, and the hall cleared for the dance. The music struck up a sprightly measure; and in the silver stream that a hundred tapers shed over the polished floor, stately dames and bright-eyed damsels were led from their seats by the noblest of the youth of Britain.

It was the mirthful season of the year, venerated alike by saint and sinner, when a world's deliverance had been achieved, and why should not all be happy? Beauty was beaming from sparkling eyes, wine had cheered the heart, and glee and roundelay lightened the bosom of every lurking care. Yet in that joyous company one spirit was depressed; and he who should have been the happiest of all sighed in secret, although, with a forced smile of welcome, he did the honours of his father's hail to the distinguished guests whom the old baron had collected.

But three months had passed since George Selby had been united to a young and beauteous bride. Who had not heard of Barbara Maxwell? When the wine-cup was drained to beauty, Barbara's was the name that hallowed it. If the minstrel lacked a theme for his ballad, whose would he choose but Lord Nithsdale's daughter? The hunter left the chase to gaze upon her, if her white jennet passed him on the moor; and even the fair themselves owned that Barbara was fairer. All said she was born to be loved; while, unconscious of the charms which envy admitted to be peerless, her unassuming gentleness would win a heart that could look on loveliness like hers, and be unmoved.

Long and ardently George Selby had wooed, and long had success been doubtful. A lover's path is rarely smooth, and his had been beset with difficulties. But what will not the ardour of youthful passion overcome? George Selby's truth and constancy succeeded; and Barbara knelt with him at the altar, and became his for ever.

We have already hinted that obstacles had delayed Selby's marriage; and though he had won his love, the union, strange as it may appear, had not been one that either of their families approved. Among the flower of the northern youth, Selby was the first. He was barely touching on ripe manhood, and his face and figure were just what please woman. Gifted with natural talents, his education had been sedulously attended to—and in the manly exercises of the times he was accounted perfect. His turn had been a military one—and he had already served two campaigns in the Low Countries, and gained brilliant reputation as a rising soldier. But Barbara's charms won him from war to love, and at her feet he laid his youthful laurels. Heir to the ancient title and estates of a family coëval with the Conquest, Selby might have sought the proudest damsel at the court of his royal master; and old and powerful as the house of Maxwell might account themselves, the lineage of the bold bridegroom, in pride and antiquity, was equal even to that of the lords of Nithsdale.

And what could cloud a union of two persons thus formed for each other? Alas that which has caused many a heart to bleed, and flung thorns in the path of love—that which has caused the deepest attachment to pine away and perish! Selby and his beautiful bride were professors of different creeds, and both bigoted in their respective beliefs on matters of religion. George dissented warmly from the errors of the Italian church—while Barbara had been taught from infancy to consider that of her forefathers the true and apostolic faith, and that to the shorn priest of Rome the power alone rested to remit her sins, and point the path that would lead her to salvation.

That love—and tenderly they loved each other—should stifle any unhappy misgivings in two young breasts might have been expected, and under common circumstances such would have been undoubtedly the case. But a fierce and acrimonious temper pervaded the religionists of these uncharitable days—a dreadful discovery had just been made—and accident brought to light the foulest conspiracy that the demon spirit of bigotry had ever fabricated.

Within a few days after Selby had wedded Barbara Maxwell, the infernal plot to blow up the king and parliament was accidentally detected, and the chief of those concerned arrested, tried, and brought most justly to the scaffold. A dreadful sensation was created by the atrocity of the plan; and men, hitherto tolerant, became ruthless persecutors. The fears of the timid could not be readily allayed, and the fiercer-minded turned them to account. Determined to uproot popery from the land, all of that faith were branded as disloyal; and many, utterly ignorant of the intended murder of the king and council of the nation, were falsely implicated in a conspiracy, from which, in their very souls, they revolted, while every Romanist was obnoxious to suspicion. Barbara's elder brother, to whom she was most devotedly attached, happened at the time to be travelling abroad. The tenacity with which the Maxwells clung to their fathers' faith and resisted the attempts of the reformers, caused them, amongst others, to be suspected. The master of Nithsdale was denounced as a principal in the infernal plot; and a journey, solely undertaken for pleasure, was tortured into a political embassy to the court of Spain, to require for the conspirators countenance and assistance from abroad.

That Selby's young bride should not feel unpleasant consequences from this burst of national indignation, which the atrocious designs of the popish party so justly drew forth, would be impossible. All who surrounded her were uncompromising followers of the reformers, and were, from old prejudice and late disclosures, deeply incensed against every disciple of the church of Rome. Barbara had been taught to consider Protestant hostility to her faith as implacable; and, conscious of the enormity of the recent plot, with the sensibility of a soft and fearful nature, she fancied that she perceived an abated ardour in George Selby's love, and read distrust in looks, that were never turned upon her but in kindness. Even the homage her charms elicited from her husband's kinsmen was mistaken—and gentle attentions were, as she imagined, used only to hide concealed dislike.

Lord Nithsdale had been residing for some time in the ancient dwelling of the Maxwells—the castle of Caerlaverock and the inclemency of the season for many weeks prevented Barbara from having any communication with her father's insulated home. Nothing beyond the general rumour had reached her respecting the plot. She heard that many of those implicated had been brought to justice, and paid the penalty of their treason. In deference to his lady's faith, George Selby, with the tact of gentle breeding, seldom alluded to a subject which he knew must pain her feelings, and Barbara was perfectly unconscious that suspicion had fallen on any of her own proud name. She grieved that men professing her religion could have imagined a design so desperately wicked, and by their crimes brought obloquy and shame on the unoffending members of their own faith.

When it was asserted that Ralph Maxwell was connected with the conspiracy, George Selby behaved as a brave man should, and stoutly maintained the innocence of his absent relative. His devotion to his bride was tender and respectful, and such as her birth and beauty demanded; and though he observed with pain a striking alteration in her manner, never for a moment did he permit his own regard to appear abated.

On the Twelfth-night, according to the ancient usage of the Selbys, all that was distinguished in the north of Cumberland had assembled in the castle hall. Noble as was the feasting, and light the revelry, one circumstance clouded the general joy. She who should have been the meteor beauty for all to gaze on, had, with evident exertion, contrived to sit through the banquet: her deep dejection could not be concealed; and while all beside were waiting for the dance, Barbara had left the hall.

Where was the bride? In vain the eyes of many sought her through the spacious chamber. The ball was stayed—the lady inquired for— and her maid presently returned with an apology from her mistress, excusing, under the plea of indisposition, her temporary absence from the company. The baron knitted his dark brows in anger, and took his son aside. What passed was brief, and in a whisper. A red flash coloured young Selby's cheek, and bowing to his father he left the hall. The lord of the mansion waved his hand—the music played a merry air—and the dance commenced.

If the mission on which George Selby went had been to induce his fair lady to rejoin the company, it failed; for he returned alone. His look was agitated, and his manner unusually excited. He stopped but for a short time in the ball, beckoned a favourite kinsman to follow, and turning down a dark corridor, entered a recess at the extremity, whose remoteness from the scene of merriment permitted an unreserved conversation to pass between his cousin and himself.

"George," said the latter, "what has disturbed you thus? Believe me, others besides me have noticed it. Rouse thee, man. Our customary festival, and the noble company who have met to share our Twelfth-night revelry, demand a merrier mood than thine."

"Alas!" replied the youth, with a deep sigh, "alas! Harry, I am very wretched; and I cannot, with so sad a heart put on a smiling countenance."

"And what thus chafes you, George, and at such an ill-timed season?" inquired his kinsman. "If it be not a secret—"

"Secrets I have none from thee, Harry. Friends from infancy like us—"

"Why yes, George," returned Wyndham—"few brothers love each other better. My mother lived only to give me birth, my father was slain six months after, and I was thus left an orphan. I was nursed in the same chamber that thou wert—in boyhood the same teacher schooled us; we played at the same games; and when we grew up, and went together to the wars, one tent covered us, and on the same field we rode our first charge, side by side together. Can Harry Wyndham do aught to relieve his friend's distress?"

"Alas!—no. My sorrows are beyond thy friendly ministry."

"And yet, George, surely thou shouldst be happy if ever man was. Hast thou not won an honourable reputation? Hast thou not before thee a rich inheritance? Art thou not of noble lineage? But far beyond all these, art thou not mated to the loveliest and gentlest maid, that the Border, famed as it is for beauty, ever boasted?"

"And there lies my sorrow, Hal."

"Indeed!—'tis strange."

"Strange, Harry, it may be; but, alas! it is too true," returned young Selby with a bitter sigh.

"I am lost in wonder!" exclaimed his friend and cousin.

"Look down the corridor, and be certain there be no listener near."

Wyndham obeyed and replied,—

"We are safe from intrusion—none can approach but I shall see them. Whoever comes hither must cross yon stream of light, and it will reveal him to us. Speak, George—speak freely to your kinsman."

"Harry," returned Selby, "I know your love for me, and can I mark mine better, than by opening to you those secret sorrows that shall be hidden from all else, even my father. Alas! that I should have lived to make the sad confession. Barbara loves not! or if she does, her love is for another!"

Wyndham started as if a dagger pierced him.

"Hold, George—for God's sake—hold! Art mad, or doting? By Heaven! had any tongue but thine breathed such a thought—so damning to the reputation of my gentle kinswoman—I would have stabbed him!"

"If, Hal, thou canst feel thus, marvel not that my cheek is blanched, and my heart agonised beyond what thou or any other can imagine."

"But," exclaimed Wyndham passionately—"why these dreadful doubts? What, George, can have produced this sad and horrible suspicion? She—Barbara Maxwell! She—whose angel looks are only emblems of her purity. By my soul's hope, the thing is utterly incredible! George, my friend, my brother, banish these idle fantasies. The blessed sun is not more stainless, than the sweet and guileless beauty who sleeps upon thy bosom!"

"Oh! that I could but think so! Listen to me, Harry—listen, for I will tell thee all. Thou knowest that in creeds we differ; and ere Barbara consented to wed me, fearful she might be influenced in the exercise of her religion, she stipulated that she should be permitted to worship Heaven as she pleased. I plighted a knight's word that in this her will should be undisputed; and I have kept that promise faithfully. Lest in a household like ours, where all are ardent Protestants, anything should interrupt her in the performance of her religious duty, I fitted for her use the oratory our grandame used, before the blessed reformation turned our house from idle ceremonies to the true faith. There Barbara's devotions were sacred from intrusion—none but herself had access to that suite of chambers—she alone keeps the key—and when she would meditate or pray, no eye, save that which looks on all, watches her secret orisons."

"'Twas right, George," exclaimed Selby's kinsman. "Need I tell thee how much I hate that idolatrous communion but till it please Heaven to point out the path, and clear the film away which papal delusions have cast over Barbara's reason, as a true knight and lover, thou must protect her in the free exercise of what she thinks religious worship."

"I have done so, Harry, and so will I continue doing. But to proceed. For a time, if ever man knew happiness, I found it in Barbara's arms. She trusted to the creed in which she had been so artfully schooled; but though her views were false, there was in all she thought and did such fervid purity, that, if innocent adoration be pleasing to the Deity, hers must have been acceptable. Once, and once only, I stole unguardedly upon her privacy. She was kneeling before the altar of the Virgin Mother. I approached in silence; and, unconscious that anyone was listening, I overhead her supplication. The orison that passed her rosy lips was for my present and eternal happiness; and so innocently but ardently was the petition offered up, that I knelt beside her and united my prayer to hers. Was it wrong? What though the Virgin smiled upon us, it was not the senseless canvass on which the Florentine had poured the magic touches of his pencil that I worshipped. No it was to Him alone who had power, that I bent my knee. We rose. She flung her arms around me, and as she kissed me, murmured, 'George, though our creeds may differ, surely, lord of my love! our hearts are one!'"

"And can a doubt touching the love of such a woman cross thy mind, George?"

"Alas! my friend, what an alteration has a few weeks made. From the time that infernal conspiracy was discovered, I have remarked her become thoughtful and depressed. Fancying that she feared I should imbibe a prejudice against popery, that might even extend itself to her, I endeavoured by renewed attentions to prove that my love was unchangeable. She seemed to feel my kindness, wept upon my bosom, and thanked me for my confidence. Suddenly a change came over her. She became timid, absent, and desponding. If I entered her chamber unexpectedly, she started as if I were an object to be feared. Her devotional exercises were redoubled, and yesterday she was for several hours secluded in her oratory. To a casual observation which her long absence inadvertently elicited, she blushed and trembled liked a guilty thing. But last night damnation!"—and he struck his forehead wildly with his hand. "Even to you, loved and trusted as a brother, I can hardly mention it. Last night, uneasy thoughts had kept me waking, while Barbara was slumbering at my side. The chamber lamp beamed out with uncommon brilliancy, and I could not but regard with a husband's pride the angel form that rested on my arm. She was dreaming. I saw her face flushed with pleasure—she pressed me to her bosom—laid her lips to mine—kissed me with ardour—and murmured—'Welcome, my beloved—thrice welcome. How could you remain so long away? Come to my heart, my love'—and, O God! the name she named was not—*mine!*"

He shuddered in an agony of passion—both remained silent for some moments, until Selby recovered and continued,—

"You marked her bearing at the banquet—her sadness was apparent to every guest; and when, by my father's command, I sought her chamber, to entreat she would return to the company, her maid—the daughter of her nurse—in whom she reposes boundless confidence, told me in evident confusion that her mistress had retired to the oratory, and begged she might not be disturbed. What, Harry, can all this mean? Is it a fitting season for telling beads, when the noblest in the land have come to my father's hall for mirth and revelry? Yes, I might pardon readily this ill-timed devotion; but, oh God! how can I excuse that guilty kiss—how extenuate that damning exclamation!"

In vain for a while did Wyndham strive to calm the excited feelings of his unhappy kinsman. By degrees Selby's violence softened down, and he was composing himself to rejoin his father's guests, when Wyndham touched his arm, and pointed to a female figure which crossed the light, and hastened towards the place they had conversed in.

"It is Barbara's attendant," he whispered. "What can bring her here?"

Gillian approached; and as she drew near the recess, the kinsman heard her mutter,—

"Where can he be? They said he passed this corridor. Hist! Master of Selby!"—and she raised her voice.

"Who calls?" said George Selby, advancing. "What would you with me, Gillian?"

"You, *here*, master! and in the dark too! No wonder I have sought you vainly."

"Your business, Gillian?"

"Is to say, that my lady is desirous to return. She feels her spirits lighter, and only waits for you, Master of Selby, to conduct her to the hall."

"George," said Wyndham in a low voice, "go instantly. Notwithstanding all your doubts, I'll pawn my life upon her love. Never could evil heart inhabit a form like Barbara Maxwell's. Go, my kinsman; I'll before you, and announce that your lady's indisposition is so far abated, as to enable her to meet your father's guests again. Believe me, the tidings will be welcome."

"Ay—Gillian, say to your mistress that I shall be with her presently; and thou, Hal, excuse my absence as thou best canst."

He then hastened to his wife's apartment, while his kinsman rejoined the merry company, and intimated that the "Border flower," as Barbara was called, might be presently expected.

But where went Barbara Maxwell? When she left the hall she hastened to her own chamber, and summoned her attendant. Gillian presented her mistress with a light, placed a basket in her hand, and then took post in the passage, while her lady proceeded to the oratory. 'Twas a strange time for prayer! but it was not to pray that Barbara stole from the festive throng. Softly she unlocked the chamber of devotion; and when the door opened, what did the taper glance on? Was it the sculptured effigy of some holy martyr, or the softer features of the penitent Madonna? No.—Stretched on a sofa, a young cavalier was slumbering; and instead of rosary and missal, a rapier and pistols were laid upon the lady's table!

On tiptoe the bride of George Selby approached the sleeping knight.

"Hist, Ralph, wake 'tis I—'tis Barbara!"

The stranger sprang up, clasped the fair visitor to his heart, and kissed her again and again.

"Why hast thou left the hall?" he said. "I half repent me that I chose this place for shelter. Thou wilt be missed, my sister, and thy absence will pain thy gallant husband, and possibly occasion surprise, if not beget displeasure."

"And didst thou think, dear Ralph, that I would leave thee here in darkness, and without food, while I was gaily feasting? Oh, no—I fancied the tables would never be drawn; and my impatience, I am sure, was far too marked to pass unnoticed. Come, Ralph, let's see what Gillian has provided,"—and she lighted a lamp that hung from the ceiling, while the Master of Nithsdale quickly unclosed the basket.

"Ah! blessings on thee, Gillian. Look, Barbara, what fare the gipsy has lighted on. A pasty that would tempt a monk; and two flasks, Rhenish and Burgundy, if I judge rightly from the colour. If this be hardship, as you called it, may my visitations never be more severe. Why, in the next room, there is a pallet fit for a cardinal's repose. Well, I'll to supper, and do thou return. Do, dearest sister, thy absence will seem remarkable."

"I cannot leave thee, Ralph; for there is a mystery in this concealment that has made me truly wretched."

"Tush—I'll tell it thee tomorrow."

"Now, Ralph—be it now—if thou lovest me."

"Well, if it must be so, our supper and story shall proceed together. Draw that cork, Barbara; 'tis not the first time thou wert my Hebe, girl—*girl*—Ah! girl no longer. Pardon me, honoured *dame*—I cry thy mercy. My next visit, mayhap, will dub me uncle."

"Hush, thou malapert. Come, do not trifle with me. If you knew how miserable I am and have been, you would without delay remove my doubtings."

"Well, well, Barbara; it must be done. Sit down. Wilt thou not pledge me? Right Rhenish as ever crossed the sea. Thou must drink, Barbara; else, as you know, I may be drugged, unless I insist upon that security."

"How teasing, thou trifling boy. I'll poison thee tomorrow, if I be kept in suspense a moment longer."

"Well, girl, the tale is simple—but I would rather thou wouldst stay for it till morning."

"Not one moment, Ralph. 'Tis no light event that obliges the Master of Nithsdale to hide him in his sister's chamber, when his peers are feasting beneath the same roof-tree."

"Come, thou knowest where to pinch me, Barbara—and how to stir the hot blood of the Maxwells. 'Tis idle to conceal aught from thee now. Fill me another goblet, and I will satisfy thy questioning." He sipped the wine she gave him, and then continued:

"Residing in England, thou hast heard, no doubt, much concerning that villainous conspiracy?"

"Oh, yes—and deeply has it grieved me. Those, Ralph, who are opposed to our religion, will brand us all with the obloquy that horrible design has raised against a whole community."

"True, girl, and there lies the cause of my temporary concealment. I was, as you well know, travelling for improvement. I heard abroad a strange story of the detected plot. It was, as I then believed, a wild and exaggerated rumour. I posted homewards, and landed on the coast some sixty miles from this. Judge my astonishment, when there I saw a printed proclamation, and, among many names, a reward offered for my apprehension as one of the chief conspirators!"

Barbara Maxwell sprang from her chair.

"For *thee*, Ralph! Thy name enrolled among a gang of murderers! Didst thou tear down the lying paper, and cudgel to death the villain who had dared affix it?"

"I did neither, Barbara. The paper remains untorn; and it would have been poor vengeance for the Master of Nithsdale, to beat the beadle's brains out—if he had such."

"Go on, Ralph. What didst thou, in God's name?"

"What a Maxwell should. I despatched servants for my tried friends, Hay and Seton. They will be here the third day from this. We will ride post to London. I'll reach the presence of James—ay, though I stab

the door keeper—fling down my glove before his royal feet, and call
on the villain that defamed me to obey the challenge and fight me
to the death."

"Thou, Ralph—thou, cognisant of that murderous scheme?"

"Ay—Barbara. They had it that I was a foreign agent. By Heaven!
I nearly lose all temper, to think that such a felon charge should
have been whispered against one of the house of Nithsdale. What,
though we have held our fathers' faith, when has our loyalty been
impeachable? Look to the motto of our arms. When once, our fealty
slighted and our services forgotten, in his extremity a king sent to
our ill-used ancestor for support—when the royal cause was almost
hopeless, and others had refused to arm, or sent an evasive reply—
what was the answer of our grandsire? '*I am ready.*' But come, Barbara,
you must away. Remember, my love, that a stronger tie than sisterly
regard now binds thee!"

"Ralph—why remain here? Come among thy equals boldly, and
proclaim your innocence. I will bring my husband here. My life on
it, George Selby will maintain his brother's honour against any who
dare insinuate aught against it."

"He has already done it nobly. In a company some days since, my
name was coupled with the traitors. Boldly did thy lord assert me to
be innocent, and flung his glove upon the floor for any to take up, who
would venture to question my loyalty. Barbara, thou hast chosen well;
and Selby shall be to me a brother—ay—in love as well as law. But
thou must go—nay, not another minute. Banish that fearful look. Away,
then, in thy brightest smiles—and tell thy husband that in the court of
England's king there is no beauty can match the 'Border flower.'"

"Oh—thou wouldst coax me by gross flattery. Answer one question
more, and I will leave thee till tomorrow. Why wait the coming of
thy friends, and hide thee for another hour? Are not the houses of
Nithsdale and Selby united? Hast thou not kinsmen and supporters if
thou need'st them, almost within thy call."

"No, Barbara—the heir of Caerlaverock has been foully wronged,
and he alone shall assert his injured honour and wipe the stain away.

Did I need assistance, was not my father's hall nearer than this of Selby? Did I need allies, is there a Maxwell in the Border that would hold back to right me; ay, even were it only to be effected by the sword? Had I sought Caerlaverock, my enemies would whisper, that the power of the father had screened the offending of the son. Did I permit thy husband to know that I was returned, and his kindred espouse my quarrel, would it not be said, that the loyalty of the house of Selby had saved the Master of Nithsdale from the consequences of his treason? No—let two days pass. My trusty friends will answer my call. I will burst upon my enemies unawares; and ere they dream that I have ventured on the sea, I will knock at the palace-gate, proclaim the traitor has returned, and were the slanderer proud Buckingham himself, if hand and rapier fail not, wash off the stain upon my honour in the blood of him who coupled treason with the name of Ralph of Nithsdale."

"And must I leave thee in this solitude, and thy spirit chafed thus?"

"Oh—go, my sister. Farewell till morning"—and with a playful effort he led the fair one to the door, bade her a kind *adieu*, and next moment was the lonely occupant of the oratory, and left to his meditations for the night.

When Barbara returned to her chamber, the visit of her lord was announced. Aware how strange her absence must have appeared, she despatched Gillian to seek him. George Selby obeyed the summons promptly, and hastened to his lady's dressing-room. A heavier heart never obeyed the call of beauty—for that kiss—that sleeping exclamation—haunted his memory.

"I shall never know happiness again," he muttered, as he approached the door. "Oh, Barbara, thou hast racked my bosom sorely; and yet were it bared to thy view, there wouldst thou find nought but thine own loved image."—He knocked.

"Come in, love," responded a voice that once thrilled upon his heart like music. There stood Barbara; recent excitement had added to her charms—the flushing cheek—the sparkling eye—Oh! she had never looked so beautiful!

"George," she said, "I fear my absence has displeased thee; yet, trust me, love, I did not mean intentional offence. I have been ill and nervous. Some of these days I will confess the cause, and when known, I feel it will be pardoned. Am I forgiven, love? You once said, when lovers quarrelled, a kiss should seal their reconciliation"—and she held her rosy lips to his. "What makes you so sad, George? Have I not owned my fault; and, is it not my first offending?"

"Oh, Barbara," he replied, in a voice so melancholy, that the sunken tone almost made the bride shudder—"Would that woman's love were less maddening, but more enduring!"

"What mean you?"—and she coloured to the forehead. "Thy words imply a doubt on mine."

A deep sigh was the only response; while Barbara's eyes lightened.

"And is mine already questioned?" she said, with more than customary warmth. "What, George, was then this suit so easily won—my plight of love so lightly given—that a doubt is cast upon its permanence?"

Piqued at the insinuation her husband's words conveyed, she disengaged her hand from his, and turning her head away, tears rolled down her cheeks. To see that loved one weep—to mark the flush of indignation, that even a suspicion of her constancy elicited—was more than Selby could endure. In a moment he was kneeling at her feet, and imploring forgiveness for his infidelity. The first of love's offendings needs merely to be owned. In a moment, all but their mutual attachment was forgotten—hand in hand they re-entered the merry hall—Selby, with the buoyant air of one conscious of possessing the brilliant beauty that leaned upon his arm—and, "from having lost their light awhile," the eyes of Barbara, "the blue of heaven's own tint," beaming more brilliantly than ever!

George Selby glanced over the sparkling throng: he wished that his kinsman, who had so recently heard the confession of his uneasiness, should see now that suspicion was thrown to the winds, and that he was once more happy. But Wyndham was nowhere in the room; and on inquiry, his cousin learned that since their interview in the corridor he had not returned to the dance. Astonished at his friend's continued absence, Selby despatched a servant to seek him in his own chamber. The room was untenanted—the castle was searched in vain—but Harry Wyndham was nowhere to be found.

An hour passed—a domestic whispered something to the bridegroom. Promptly the latter left the hall—the dance proceeded—and the kinsmen remained absent.

When he parted from his unhappy cousin, Wyndham was returning to the company he had quitted, when he suddenly encountered Herbert the falconer, in the passage. To an inquiry of what brought the old man to such an unusual place, and at such a time, he replied it was to find out his young lord.

"You cannot see him, Herbert. He is particularly occupied. Are there not fitter times to speak about thy wood craft, old boy, than when thy master is engaged as he is this evening?"

"Wood craft!" exclaimed the falconer. "Dost thou think me mad, Master Wyndham, or fancy that hawk or hound would bring me to his presence now? Next to him I would speak to yourself, were we but safe from eavesdroppers."

"Is it of moment, and am I interested in what you have to say, Herbert?"

"Hear and judge, Master Hal," returned the falconer.

"Come to my room, Herbert. I know thee too well to doubt that any but some pressing errand would at this hour bring thee hither."

Wyndham procured a lamp, and Herbert followed him. They entered the youth's apartment, and closed the door carefully.

"Now for thy tidings, Herbert, and cut the story short, or my absence may be noticed by my uncle, and chafe his temper."

"I have seen a ghost," said the falconer.

"Pish—what folly, old man. My kinsman would not have thanked thee much to have called him from his guests, and given him such intelligence."

"You may smile, Master Wyndham, but I saw it plain as I see you; and afterwards observed its shadow on the wall."

"Ghosts leave no shadows, master falconer. Hast thou not been too familiar with the ale-butt? Come, Herbert, keep thy spectre for tomorrow, and to bed. I'll to the hall"—and he raised the lamp, and moved towards the door.

"Stay—for God's sake! listen but a moment. I am not drunk or doting. The tale will surprise you."

"Well, be brief, Herbert. Know ye not what discourtesy it is to leave my uncle's festival?"

"My tale shall be a short one, Master Hal. I was returning from the hazel copse, where I had harboured an outlying stag for our chase tomorrow; and my nearest path, you know, lay through the ancient pleasure-grounds. I entered the shrubbery, and when I turned the angle of the building, saw a light beaming from the window of the old oratory, which the Lady Margaret occupied some fifty years ago, and which, as I have heard, the Master's bride uses for her acts of devotion. It was marvellous, I thought, that when all were feasting in the castle, anyone should remain at prayer; and, fearing some taper had been forgotten, I waited to ascertain what had caused light in a part of the building to which so few have access. Presently the window that looks to the angle of the tower was unclosed. A man stood there for a minute, looked out upon the night, muttered something I could not hear, closed the casement, and retired."

"Pshaw, Herbert, it was only the Lady Barbara, or Gillian her maid. When was it, old man, that this occurred?"

"Not five minutes since. Had proof been wanting that my sight had not deceived me, a shadow of a man, as it were in the act of fencing, fell on the tower wall. I looked some minutes longer; the shadow disappeared, but the light, when I left the tower, continued burning steadily."

"Good Herbert, is this no coinage of the brain—no trickery of vision?"

"None, by the God of heaven! It struck me to be so strange, that I could not rest until I apprised the Master of the circumstance."

"Better, Herbert, have told it as you have to me. A man—a light; it must be looked to. Go—I will join thee at the southern tower. Keep thy counsel, Herbert."

"Fear me not, Master Wyndham. I am no tale-maker."

"Well," said the youth, "if this tale be true, I cannot fathom woman. No, no—it's impossible. The fame of Barbara Maxwell was never tainted by a breath of suspicion. 'Tis a mistake; but duty to my kinsman demands that I should clear the mystery away."

He threw a cloak round him—belted on his sword—and in a few minutes joined the falconer at the appointed place.

"The light burns steadily," said the old retainer; "and not a minute since, a form too tall for woman's crossed the casement."

"Herbert, we will soon put thy story to the test," returned Wyndham. "The casement is not high; move softly on, and I will mount upon your shoulder. I cannot intrude upon the lady's privacy, for she is in the hall ere now. Come, and step cautiously."

In silence the youth and his companion placed themselves beneath the oratory. Some minutes passed, and nothing but the moaning of the storm disturbed the stillness of their watch. Faint strains of distant music were now and again borne on the wintry blast, and their cheerless vigil formed a sad contrast to the merriment that reigned within the building.

"Herbert, thy eyes have for once deceived thee," said Wyndham to his old companion. "The lady has left her taper burning; that was the light, and herself, most likely, the form that crossed thy vision. The snow-drift blinded thee on thy return from the thicket. Keep close counsel. Trust me, old friend, none save the lady and her maid enter that lonely chamber, from which the light is glancing."

"No," returned the falconer—"no, Master Hal, I am not astray. There is not among the youngest retainers in Selby Hall an eye that tracks a slot, or drives a cross-bolt truer. Saints of heaven! is not that the shadow of a man?"

Clear and distinct a figure was traced on the lighted space, which the lamp within the casement of the lady's oratory had thrown upon the tower opposite!

"Hush and assist me to climb the fretwork of the window," said the youth, in a low whisper to his attendant; and unbelting his sword, and flinging off his cloak, Harry Wyndham mounted easily with Herbert's assistance, and placed himself before the framing of the lattice.

The sight he witnessed appeared rather the delusion of a dream than anything of reality. Holy saints! In the private chamber of the high-born dame—the place sacred even from the visit of a husband—a young and handsome cavalier was calmly seated, and the disposition of everything about told that the chamber had been his residence for some time. His cloak was flung upon the couch—his sword and pistols were laid upon the table, and his plumed hat suspended from the wall, while, with a feeling of perfect security, he read by the lamp, whose light had caught the falconer's eye and roused his suspicion. Nor had the stranger's comforts been neglected. The requisites for making a comfortable meal were still remaining on the table; and wine-flasks and a goblet showed, that in all besides he was most carefully attended to.

As the light fell directly on his face, Wyndham could mark it accurately. A nobler countenance was never painted by an artist. The profile of the unknown was strictly Grecian, while coal-black hair, a thin moustache, a high and noble forehead, eyes sparkling with intelligence and shaded by arched brows, completed a face as manly as it was handsome. Suddenly the stranger pushed away the book, and rising from his chair, strode once or twice across the chamber. His figure was tall, slight, and elegant; and his dress—in those days no trifling indication of the wearer's rank—was rich enough for any earl in Britain. After a turn or two he resumed his seat, replenished the goblet that stood before him, and then quietly resumed the book he had for the time laid aside.

Wyndham had seen enough. Softly he descended from the window, and with the falconer retired to a short distance.

"Hast thou seen aught strange, Master Hal?" inquired the retainer.

"I have seen, Herbert, that which, hadst thou sworn t, I would not have given credence to."

"Was it a living thing that haunts that deserted chamber?" inquired the old man suspiciously.

"It was a sorry sight to witness, and one that must be concealed even from thee, Herbert. Thou art faithful. Watch, as thou lovest thy young lord, that casement until I return to thee. I will not be long absent."

"Trust me, Master Wyndham, I will be vigilant. A cat shall not move, but I will mark it."

"Hush—the figure again! I must not lose a moment."

Resuming his cloak and sword, he hurried to the castle, leaving the falconer to observe the chamber that contained the unknown and unwelcome visitor.

When George Selby was called from the hall, the servant directed him to the library; and great was his astonishment when he found the room well lighted, and several of his more immediate relatives assembled at the summons of his kinsman. A gloomy and deathlike silence ensued upon his entrance; and his surprise was still more increased, when his father, in deep emotion, came into the apartment leaning on Harry Wyndham's arm. A creeping thrill of horror—an undefined feeling that some dreadful event was at hand—a terror that something calamitous would presently ensue—shook George's nerves, and seemed to chill his life-blood, while, with a convulsive effort to know the worst, he broke the fearful silence which all observed.

"Noble sir, friends and kinsmen, in God's name, what means this strange and ill-omened meeting? Speak—in mercy, speak!"

"George," replied the baron, "thou hast ever been a good and duteous son. Wilt thou for filial love, and in honour of these grey hairs, listen to thy father's counsel and promise to abide by his advice?"

"My noble father, what is it that impends over me? What misfortune has befallen? If you would not break my heart, speak out—tell me the worst. Am I not a man? Have I not nerve to bear adversity?"

"Yes, my son. Courage was never wanting to a Selby—but coolness often."

"I will be calm, father. Speak, if you would not kill me"

"George," said the baron, in a broken voice, "the will of Heaven must be obeyed, and its decree submitted to. Life is but a chequered scene—grief follows on the heels of joy—and sorrow clouds prosperity. Thou hast been fortunate, my son; and thou art about to feel what all must feel."

"Go, go—go on," exclaimed the youth impatiently.

"Man thyself." The old baron paused—the words appeared to choke him—"Barbara is false!"

"False!" cried young Selby. "What lying tongue dared couple falsehood and Barbara?"

"Calm thee, my boy. There is, alas! proof—damning proof—within these very walls!"

"Oh God! and are my worst suspicions true? and could that image of an angel be the wretched thing you call her?"

"Were the person with whom she had offended placed within your power—"

"Ha! Dost thou, my noble father, ask a Selby what vengeance he would exact from the man who had dishonoured him? Blood! father, blood!—an ocean, if it flowed within his veins, would be all too little to wash my shame away!"

A murmur of approbation filled the room.

"I cannot, will not, blame thee, George; but he that has thus injured thee, must, if noble, have fair play. Vengeance, but not murder, becomes the hand of a Selby."

"But where is the villain? Is he in the house? Is he among the company?"

"Patience, my son—patience. Think ye that I would rob thee of thy just revenge? No, George. Old as this arm is, were there none other to avenge the injury, mine should at least attempt it."

"Barbara—once idolised Barbara—a short month since had a saint taxed thee with harbouring an unholy thought, I would have said he slandered thee!" exclaimed George Selby; and, overcome with grief, the unhappy youth leaned for support upon Wyndham's shoulder, and sobbed as if his heart was bursting.

To see a brave man weep is fearful. The bosom must be heavily overloaded, when tears are forced from eyes which have, all unmoved, looked on the reddest battlefield. His father vainly attempted to soothe him, and his kinsmen evinced the tenderest sympathy.

"George, we have a duty, and a painful one, to perform—justice first, my son, and vengeance afterwards. Thou knowest the temper of the times, and that thy erring wife is of a faith opposed to our profession. If we act unadvisedly, the Romish party will not scruple to assert that we have wrongfully accused her of falsehood to thy bed, only to work her ruin—and the penalty of crime will be imputed to our hatred of her religion. Hast thou courage to witness the disclosure of her shame, and remain here, while to her own face we establish her dishonesty?"

"Yes, my father; but the exposure of her guilt must not be before any save our own kinsmen. Barbara, though thou hast withered my young heart, and humbled my pride to the very earth, I will not have thy fall exhibited to those who are even now gazing on thy beauties; and fancying thee too pure and glorious for this sinful world."

"Thou art right, my poor boy. Here her offending shall be proved—and here the painful scene shall end."

"And here," murmured the unfortunate youth, "shall I take the last look of that face which earthly beauty never equalled."

"Go Hal," said the baron—"assume a look of indifference if thou canst, and without causing observation, lead the Lady Barbara hither. Is Herbert outside?"

"He is, my lord," replied one of the Selbys.

"Let him remain till we require him here."

A period of five minutes elapsed, while the old baron endeavoured to confirm the fortitude of his son, and enable him to support the painful discovery of Barbara's unworthiness. The door was softly unclosed—George Selby turned his head away, and leaned against the mantelpiece—his kinsmen looked upon the floor—while radiant in beauty, and little dreaming of the scene that awaited her, 'the Border flower' gracefully approached the place where the baron was standing.

Struck with the appearance of the party, she hesitated, and stopped in the middle of the room.

"I crave your pardon, my lord. I have mistaken Master Wyndham— and been, without design, an intruder on these gentlemen."

"Would that it were so, lady. You have been sent for here, and I have been called on to disclose as sad a tale as ever passed a father's lips."

"My lord!"—and the blood mounted to her cheeks.

"Yes—'tis a trying visitation. I speak not of my own withered hopes, when I see the wrecked happiness of my only child, just as he had started on his earthly career, with as brilliant prospects as ever opened upon any."

"My lord—what means all this? My husband's silence—the unusual presence of these gentlemen?"

"It means, lady—that thou hast sullied thy own fair fame, and rendered him who confided in thee wretched, miserable, and dishonoured."

Pale and red by turns, Barbara Maxwell was silent for a moment; but suddenly, and as if a new impulse strengthened her, she advanced a step or two, and boldly addressed the baron.

"Never, Lord of Selby, did I fancy that the day would come when such a charge as thou hast made dare be uttered in the hearing of a husband. Go on—and let me know the crime by which Barbara Maxwell has stained her reputation?"

Those near George Selby observed a shuddering of the whole frame while his beautiful wife was speaking.

"Would, lady, that this were the indignation with which the innocent repudiate a charge of guilt. Why dwell upon the odious accusation? You have outraged the confidence of him to whom your loyalty was plighted. Start not, dame. Boldness cannot screen thy error. That place where my sainted mother prayed, now harbours the paramour of my worthless daughter."

George Selby, who had continued leaning against the mantel like a being beaten by misfortune almost to a state of apathy, bounded from the place he had reclined upon, and bursting past his kinsmen, exclaimed in a voice of thunder,—

"Ha! in the oratory. Heaven, I thank thee!"—and catching up a sword, he threw aside those who vainly attempted to restrain him. His hand was already on the door, when Barbara rushed forward and seized him by the arm.

"Off!" he cried. "Off—lest I harm thee! Bad as thou art, I would not willingly injure a hair of thine."

But fearless and undismayed, Barbara held his arm.

"Sirs—gentlemen—hear me, and only for a moment. I am strange to you all. I am a woman; and, at least by men, that plea should be admitted. Once—had any told me an appeal to another would be required, I would have said he spoke a falsehood. What wouldst thou? I own at once that there is a knight where none has been before. I have but one boon to ask—let him be brought hither—and let the guilty be confronted."

"Lady, I can refuse you nothing," replied George Selby, in a tone almost inaudible.

"Wilt thou, Master Wyndham, do me a small kindness, and summon my attendant hither?"

The youth bowed, left the chamber, and presently returned with Gillian. All seemed amazed, and marvelled what the result of this strange scene would be.

Calm as if she was merely despatching her tirewoman on some ordinary message, 'the Border flower' pulled forth a key, and drew a jewel from her finger.

"Tell the knight thou knowest, Gillian, that Barbara Maxwell requires and demands his presence. Give him this ring—he will not disobey my summons. Good gentlemen, I pray your patience. Sheath thy weapon, Master of Selby. Surely against the peril of a single rapier there need not all this preparation, and with thy kinsmen around thee too."

George Selby, as if under the influence of a spell, obeyed and sheathed his sword. The baron seemed bewildered, and the dead silence was for some minutes unbroken. A quick step was heard along the corridor—the door flew open—a tall and noble youth entered the chamber, and, advancing to the bride, demanded haughtily to know "who had dared to offer her offence?"

"Ralph!"—cried the lady of young Selby—but ere she could say more, her husband started as if an adder stung him, and half unsheathing his sword, exclaimed,—

"The very name she murmured in her sleep!"

Wyndham seized his arm, and the baron whispered,—

"Peace, my son—peace, an' thou lovest me."

The young stranger threw a bold glance round the room, and taking the lady's hand, continued,—

"Barbara—for what purpose am I required? I could only gather from your tirewoman that someone had shown you a discourtesy— what means this mystery—and why are these gentlemen collected? Doubtless thy gallant husband is not here, or a slight offered to his fair dame would not require a brother's arm to redress it?"

"Brother!" exclaimed several voices, while George Selby dropped his rapier on the floor—Barbara clung to the stranger's arm—and the baron in amazement advanced to the unknown, and inquired his name and title.

"A name," replied the youth haughtily, "I need not be ashamed to own; although some villains availed them of my absence, and branded it with treason. I am Ralph Maxwell of Caerlaverock!"

"The Master of Nithsdale!" exclaimed several voices.

"What an unfortunate mistake!"

"Unfortunate, indeed!" murmured young Selby, with a bitter sigh. "It has cost me wife and happiness, and I have lost an angel by my accursed idiocy. To doubt her purity—to fancy Barbara could err! Fool—dolt—madman"—and he smote his forehead passionately.

"Now, by mine honour, all this is to me unaccountable;" and turning to his sister, the Master of Nithsdale continued,—

"Wilt thou explain this mystery, Barbara; and is yonder gentleman your lord?"

"He was, Ralph; and, had I believed him, one who would have cut the throat of any knave who would have whispered aught against my loyalty. But circumstances have changed—my fame is sullied—and even my fidelity to his bed is more than questionable. On these grave charges am I arraigned before this noble lord and these good gentlemen. I sent for thee to witness the proofs of the delinquency, which has severed the holy bond that bound me at the altar to George Selby, and sends me back with thee, my brother, to my father's hall, a fallen star—detected, disgraced, and repudiated."

A momentary silence was broken by the unhappy husband.

"Lady—'tis but an idle attempt for me to try and deprecate your honest indignation. I have lost you. You will, no doubt, return with your noble brother, and I leave England for ever. When I am gone—when the last token comes to thee, Barbara, from my dying hand—then forgive my madness; and give a tear to the memory of him who committed one offence, and expiated his insanity by a short and suffering existence. Wilt thou not bid me farewell—one brief—one last farewell?"

The deep, the agonising melancholy of George Selby's look and voice—the emotion of the old baron, as tears ran down his furrowed cheeks—while their stout kinsmen bent their sorrowful faces on the floor, was a scene that none could view unmoved. All waited in intense suspense for the lady's answer; and when she advanced close to the spot where her hapless lord was standing, the listeners held their breath while the doom of the Master of Selby was uttered.

"You have asked me to say farewell, George; and the time was, when your slightest wish would have been to me a holy obligation. I had chosen you from a score of suitors; and strong in the faith of your love, though we sought Heaven by different creeds, I laughed at the whisperings of those who would have insinuated a doubt of our being happy. That I loved you as a wife should love, my heart best knows. I would have followed thee through weal and woe—had malice tarnished your escutcheon, I would have descended with you to obscurity, and a murmur would not have escaped my lips—had poverty be fallen us, the cottage would have been to me as welcome as the hall—had sickness stricken you, who would have found me absent from your couch? Well—let this pass. You ask me to say farewell."—A deep and painful pause succeeded, and every heart beat faster. "Lord Nithsdale's daughter has no forgiveness for a slight upon her constancy—but George Selby's wife thus punishes the doubtings of her husband—"

Ere the last words were uttered, Barbara was weeping in her lover's arms. A burst of admiration came from every lip; while, the old baron, as he wiped away a tear, caught her from his son's embrace to clasp her in his own.

"Now, by St George!" he exclaimed, "I thought myself the proudest father in Britain; but I knew not till this night thy worth, my sweet Barbara! Go, my loved children; our absence will else create surprise. Go—join the company, and I will present thy gallant brother to our kinsmen, Barbara. What—ho—wine here, knaves. Pick thee, my daughter, the fairest out, and the Master of Nithsdale shall claim his partner presently."

When Selby and his happy wife had left the baron and his unexpected guest together, the old lord filled a stoup of wine, and pledged the heir of Caerlaverock.

"Drink to me! Master Ralph, though by the mass I am half jealous of thee. Thou, than whom a welcomer never crossed the door of Selby Hall, to hide thee like art anchorite, while so many of thy noblest peers were met within these walls?"

"Why, faith, Lord Selby, I would have deemed the visit of an accused traitor a poor compliment to him who had married with my sister, until I had cleared the slander from my name."

"And in doing it," replied the old baron, "where couldst thou find any who would stand to thee more truly than my kindred and myself?" When the base lie was named, we cleared thy fame, and offered the Selby's sword to maintain the loyalty of the Master of Nithsdale."

"That, my good lord, I know; and that has bound me to my gallant brother. But, noble Selby, I will assert mine innocence where it was maligned; and from James himself demand to be confronted with my accuser."

"Tush, noble Master," said one of the Selbys. "Thou mayest spare thy journey, and spare thy horses. Before the Proclamation was two days old, the knave who gave the information had lost his ears for perjury. Thou and some others whom he denounced made his story so incredible, that the tale was sifted and found false; and to avoid the rack he mounted the pillory. So strong was men's indignation, and so harshly was the poor wretch used, that he survived his exposure barely time sufficient to make a fuller confession of his villainy."

"And was the information of such a slave deemed enough to warrant this insult to the house of Maxwell?"

"Alas! my dear boy, thou canst not even fancy the consternation which that abominable plot occasioned. Men looked on their neighbours with suspicion; scoundrels profited by the excitement, to increase the general apprehension, and turn it to account. But come—one cup more. The dance waits for us; and if there be beauty in Cumberland, I'll mate thee with a partner. Kinsmen, drink to my guest—deeper yet—drink to my son. What else can the brother of 'the Border flower' be to the father of George Selby?"

Never had a Twelfth-night ball commenced under more inauspicious circumstances, and never had the annual festival of Selby Place a more joyous termination. Long and merrily was the revelry sustained, and day broke ere the last of the guests had crossed the drawbridge.

"George," said the beautiful bride, as she sat upon her husband's knee, and twined his dark ringlets round her snow white fingers, "my heart tells me that I have been wanting in my duty to thee. When Gillian told me that my brother, after four years' absence, had arrived, I was so overjoyed to see him, that I acceded thoughtlessly to all he asked. Even his secret should not have been concealed from you. Some other wanderer may come and scare thy falconer's wits out. I need no better retirement to offer my devotions in, than that which mine own closet affords. Let then, my love, that distant oratory be locked as it was before I came to Selby Place."

What the reply was is not recorded; but ere a second Twelve-month passed away, 'the Border flower' knelt at the same altar with her husband; and Barbara Maxwell was the first of that ancient name that conformed to the tenets of the reformers, and renounced the doctrines of the church of Rome.

II
LIFE IN THE MOUNTAINS

The time I've lost in wooing,
In watching and pursuing
  The light that lies
  In woman's eyes,
Has been my heart's undoing.

MOORE

"WHY THEN, UPON MY CONSCIENCE!" ejaculated Major O'Shaughnessy, who had depressed his person to accommodate himself to the height of the door, and dropped in as the legend of the departed soldier had ended. "You are well employed in reading romances, while wiser men are settling their traps for a march. Because you have got a decent habitation of your own, I suppose you imagine we shall spend our Christmas in the Pyrenees."

"I suspect, Terence," replied O'Connor, "our tenure is nearly at an end, and our wooden dwelling-place will afford shelter, ere long, to some of the brigades in the rear."

"You may swear it," returned O'Shaughnessy. "We have been too long looking the enemy in the face, and far too neighbourly, for things to continue so. At the bridge yonder, the sentries go on and off duty with a bow, and the officers exchange snuff and compliments."

"Well, surely this is better, Terence, than the exterminatory system that our allies and the French keep up. To kill or wound a harmless sentry wantonly is barbarous, and savours more of Indian than

European warfare. But what reason have you for supposing that we shall move so soon?"

"I think," rejoined the soldier, "that I can show you a cogent one from the door," and he pointed out two long files of men and women, struggling up the face of the sierra, to a mountain cantonment that occupied the summit of the ridge. They were loaded with provisions carried in baskets on their heads, and appeared to climb the steep and rugged path with difficulty.

"Think you, friend O'Connor, that the commander will permit the snow to catch him here, when the supplies must depend upon a string of peasants like these to transport them! No, no—we shall soon advance; and it is whispered that fords across the river have been discovered by the Spanish fishermen, and that they have been sounding the bottom, while the French sentries believed they were only looking for flounders."

"Well, the sooner we're off the better," replied O'Connor. "I am anxious to find myself in 'beautiful France;' and much as our present residence has been admired, it would be rather too airy an abode when the snows come down. You dine with us, no doubt?"

"You never made a shrewder guess, Ned. The flavour exhaled from your camp-kettle, as I passed it, removed every objection. Our larder at home is not extensively provisioned; there is nothing there that I can see but a goat hung up, which seems to have died of a consumption; and from its lank look, as it dangles from a peg, I have my doubts after all that it is only a Frenchman's knapsack."

Dinner ended, and more than one bottle was emptied. A subaltern reminded O'Shaughnessy that the sequel of his amatory adventures remained untold.

"I can't venture yet. It is too early in the evening to recall these melancholy recollections."

"Well, I should have imagined," said O'Brien, "that the last pull at the canteen had sufficiently fortified you for story-telling. Surely, like myself, you are now love-proof, Terence?"

"Ay, ay, Pat. Thanks to St Patrick, the day is over when woman could touch this once too tender heart. It is now

Too cold or wise
For brilliant eyes
Again to set it glowing.

But these boys laugh, and I may as well end my confessions, I suppose. I have suffered, it is true; but I hope I have borne my disappointments like a Christian man and a stout soldier."

After some entreaty, a long deep sigh, and a longer and deeper draught from a well-filled wineskin, the gallant commander thus continued the narrative of his second disappointment in love.

III

Confessions of
a Gentleman who would have
married if he could
(Second Confession)

> There's tricks i' the world.

> O heavens! is't possible a young maid's wits
> Should be as mortal as an old man's life?
>
> *Hamlet*

> Our wooing doth not end like an old play;
> Jack hath not Jill.
>
> *Love's Labour's Lost*

YOU MAY READILY IMAGINE THAT after my recent escapade I was in no hurry to recommence a matrimonial campaign. Biddy Maginn—the devil's luck to her—had given me such a damper, that for six months I would hardly look at an only daughter over a pew, or stare in at the window of a country banker. I was so mortally afraid of women, that I am persuaded, had a priest proposed "the difference," I should have embraced him and his offer, and taken it with vows of celibacy. But it was otherwise allotted; and though men generally escape with one visitation, I was fated to undergo a couple.

I was garrisoned in Dublin. The laugh against me had nearly ceased. I was drilling regularly in the Park, a well-conditioned subaltern as need be, and as the song says,

"Minding my business, and jest as I ought to be,"

when, alas! a letter from an old crony of my mother's brought me into fresh trouble.

I need not tell you exactly what my Lady Featherstone said; but the gist of her letter was to request that I would, without delay, as I valued future fortune, repair to Bath, and trust my fate to her.

Great men are seldom their own directors; and for my part, I was in all weighty concerns aided, counselled, and assisted, by my foster-brother and servant, Ulick Flyn. Of course my Lady Featherstone's epistle was read to him—for Ulick was a marksman—and he decided at once that we should try our luck; for, as he said, "Luck's everything!" Accordingly, leave was obtained—the paymaster made an advance—and Ulick and I landed safe in Bath, determined to "take fortune at the hop."

My lady was delighted at my despatch, when next morning I presented myself at her breakfast-table. I shall never forget her. She was full five feet eight, and stiff as a drill sergeant. Thin she was—for Ulick affirmed, upon his conscience, "there was not flesh enough upon her bones to bait a rat-trap." Her maid was sent away—the door was carefully secured—and with a grave and important clearing of the voice, she thus broke the ice and entered on particulars—"Terence," says she, "it's fifteen years since I laid an eye upon you—you were then but a little boy; but as I told your poor dear mother, if the Lord spared you, you might grow up like your uncle Ulick; and Ulick was the handsomest lad in Loughrea, when I married my lamented husband, Sir Daniel. I had a steady regard for your mother; she held good cards, played a safe game, and was an excellent woman—though she died fifteen guineas in my debt, and your father never had the decency to answer my letter when I sent in my claim. Had it been a tradesman's bill, of course no gentleman should or would have attended to it; but—it was the night before she died—ten guinea points, and five on the odd rubber. Well, your father should have paid it. He's gone to his account; and God send he hasn't suffered for his neglect of me in the other world!"

"But, my dear madam, I have nothing to do with old play-debts of my mother; nor can I be answerable for my father's omissions in answering letters."

"God forbid you should, my dear boy! No, no. I have sent for you"—and she made a pause.

"For what purpose, madam?"

"To make your fortune," was the reply. "Ay, your fortune, Terence. All money in the funds, and six hundred a year secured upon the best estate in Northamptonshire."

"Then with the fortune I presume there is a lady saddled?"

"And what objection is there to one, may I ask, when she can pay for her keeping handsomely, Terence, dear?" quoth my Lady Featherstone.

"Oh, none in the world," I responded.

"Well, then," she continued, "you have no objection to a wife with ten thousand pounds *ready*, and six hundred a year?"

"The Lord forbid I should be so sinful," I replied, "as to repine at the will of Providence, if such an accident in the way of matrimony befell me."

"Now, Terence, remember I was your poor mother's bosom friend, and I am sure I may speak freely to her son."

I nodded a full affirmative, and my Lady Featherstone looked knowing as a gaoler.

"Terence, is it honour bright between us?"

I assured her, as Ollapod says in the play, that "I was full of honour as a corps of cavalry."

"It's all right," rejoined my lady, "and now for business. You most know, Terence, jewel, that I have had the worst of luck the last winter; and every year villainous tradesmen are becoming more intolerable. My rent is due—my last carriage is unpaid—my servants are clamorous for wages; and daily growing more insolent—and, to own the truth, I am afraid to look into my card account, for a mint of money would not clear it off. I must borrow two thousand pounds, or quit Bath in disgrace."

"Bad enough, madam," said I.

"Now, Terence, you must lend me the money."

"*I!* my lady. Where could *I* obtain it? I know of no way possible but by stopping the Bristol mail."

"No, no, Terence," quoth the dowager, "we need not resort to such desperate expedients. I do not require taking to the road, when we have only to go to the altar."

"Ah! I understand your Ladyship; but we talk as if success were certain. I may not like the lady, and the lady may not like me."

"Pshaw!—leave the lady to my management, I will answer for her accepting you."

"Ay, madam, but I cannot answer for myself. She may be old—ugly—disagreeable."

"She is none of these," said Lady Featherstone.

"How old is she?"

"Thirty."

"I am scarcely twenty-two," said I.

"And what signifies eight years?" demanded the dowager. "Is there not a clean thousand as a set-off against each of them, man?"

"Is she good-looking?"

"Very pleasing both in appearance and manner," replied my lady.

"Her family?—you know we are particular about that in Ireland."

"She is sister to a baronet, and of one of the oldest families in Northamptonshire. Come, I am sure I have satisfied every doubt, and you shall meet her here this evening."

"Why, yes—but there is another question I must trouble you with."

"And what may that be, my dear Terence?" replied the lady, with a most gracious style.

"In a word, Lady Featherstone, a recent mistake has made me rather particular. She has never had a blast, I hope?"

"*A blast!* what does the man mean?"

"Oh—I beg your Ladyship's pardon. I forgot you were not from Connaught, and the phrase may be strange to you. In short, my lady, no flaw in her reputation—no kick in her gallop."

"Blast—flaw—kick in her gallop!" repeated the dowager. "No wonder I can scarcely comprehend you. If you mean to ask if my friend be a person of unblemished character, I beg to assure you, sir, that I associate with none other!"

"A thousand pardons, madam; but to be candid—not six months ago I was within a point of becoming Benedict—and the lady was so provident, that before the third moon waned she would have obliged me with an heir."

"Indeed! On that score you may be quite at ease. Miss Woodhouse is propriety itself;—and now having given you all the information you demanded, will you oblige me with the loan of two thousand pounds, for which I will pass you a *post-obit* on my personal property?"

"Certainly, my dear lady; and I shall be too happy to find myself in a condition to be serviceable to you."

"Thank you, Terence; and now I will call upon Miss Woodhouse, and ask her to tea. She has one little particularity—she never goes out without her maid; and you must make yourself agreeable to the *fille-de-chambre*, for she is an immense favourite with her mistress."

"Well, madam, and which of the ladies am I to make love to first? Shall I open with *mademoiselle* or commence with the spider-brusher?"

"An excellent plan to lose both," returned the dowager. "No, Terence, urge your suit briskly with the mistress, and open your purse-strings freely for the maid. That is the sure game."

"Egad—a thought strikes me. Pray, as the *soubrette* appears to be rather an important personage, might I request you to favour me with a hasty report upon her age, looks, and inclinations?"

"'Pon my honour," exclaimed the dowager, "I hardly see the necessity; but I may briefly acquaint you that she is neither a chicken nor a beauty;—she is curious and cunning—fancies, notwithstanding there is a looking-glass in the lodgings, that men admire her still—and is ten times more solicitous to procure a husband for herself than for her mistress."

"Then I'll settle the maid in double quick!"

"Good God! sir, what do you mean?"

"Why nothing, my Lady, but that I'll run my valet, Ulick Flyn, at her."

"Ah—I understand you. Is he a person on whom we may rely?"

"He is my foster-brother, and true as steel."

"Smart—good-looking?" pursued the dowager.

"Not a handsomer light-bob in the company."

"And he will make love to a woman if you desire him?"

"That he will, madam—or if I do not. May I order him to bring my cloak here early?"

"Certainly, and I will take care that Lucy sees him."

We separated—my lady to invite the bride elect to tea, and I to acquaint my foster-brother with our plan of operations, in which it had been determined that he should take an important share.

Ulick was overjoyed at the intelligence, and quite ready to enter the field, and carry Miss Florence, as the maid was designated, by sap or storm.

At the proper hour the fosterer and I moved to the scene of action. Fortunately, a few drops of rain rendered a cloak-bearer necessary; and when we arrived at Lady Featherstone's, and I was ushered to the drawing-room, Ulick Flyn was most politely invited to the lower regions by the dowager's abigail.

I found "the making" of Mrs O'Shaughnessy already come, and was presented by the hostess as a valued and a valuable gentleman. Lady Featherstone had described my inamorata fairly enough. She was not above the age she had assigned her, and was really good-looking, with a mild expression of countenance almost approaching to melancholy. Her manners were affable and polished; and after being half an hour in her company, I came to a conclusion, that there was no cause or impediment to prevent her becoming niece to my honoured relative Mrs O'Finn.

Indeed matters seemed to progress well, and things "looked like housekeeping." I was very graciously received. The hostess was "mine trusty ally," and my aide-de-camp, Ulick, had safely established himself in the body of the place. The evening passed agreeably; and when

the hour to break up had come, Lady Featherstone proposed that as
the night was fine and Miss Woodhouse resided in the next street,
we should dispense with a coach, and walk home. No objection
was made by the lady—the servants were summoned—we bade
goodnight to the dowager, and departed.

There's nothing, my boys, like seeing a woman home, when you
want to make love to her. There you have the contact of the arm, and
at parting a tender squeeze of the hand. I had certainly the best of
fair play during the march. No one pressed my rear; for when I threw
my eye slyly back to see if the abigail was within earshot, Ulick had
her close to his side as the gizzard of a turkey, and they were in deep
conversation at the distance of half a street. As I walked off, I overheard
her say in a soft tone of entreaty, "Now, Mr Flyn, you'll be sure to
come?" to which, in a tender and insinuating voice, was responded,
"Arrah! Miss Lucy, will a duck swim?" and a salutation, loud as the
report of a pocket-pistol, was succeeded by an "O fy—how rude you
are!" and the hall-door was slammed to.

When safely housed in our inn, I inquired from my fosterer how
he had succeeded. The reply was quite satisfactory. He was to drink
tea with Miss Lucy next evening; and to use his own words, he would
put his *comether* on her. Every syllable touching fortune was correct,
and my Lady Featherstone was true as an oracle.

I went to bed. Roger and his regiment was nothing to Miss
Woodhouse, with her ten thousand (minus two), and six hundred
a year. How gloriously would I break in upon Mrs O'Finn, when I
presented her with the sister of a baronet—the scion of a stock almost
as ancient as our own!

Three days passed. Lady Featherstone played a deep game, Ulick
covered himself with glory, and on the following day, as a matter of
course, I was to propose and be accepted. The dowager had ascertained
from the lady that my suit would be received; and Ulick had so far
progressed with the ancient spider-brusher, that she admitted having
saved four hundred pounds, acknowledged he was irresistible, and
only stipulated that he should quit the army.

"And what will you do, Ulick?" I inquired. "Will you marry Miss Florence?"

"Why then, upon my soul, I won't. Of course your honour and the lady will be married first; and when you're clane off, I'll bolt by a side door and give Miss Lucy the slip. Arrah! master, sure ye wouldn't have me tie myself to an ould catabaw of her sort. Lord! she's fifty if she's an hour."

I could not remonstrate, and we retired for the night.

The day "big with the fate" of Terence O'Shaughnessy came. My worthy confederate, the dowager, made the opportunity, and I sighed and was accepted. A fortnight was, after the usual display of maiden coyness, named as the duration of my misery; and on the expiration of that painful period of celibacy and suffering, Miss Woodhouse would become Mrs O'Shaughnessy. As to Ulick, he and the *fille-de-chambre* occupied their leisure hours in arranging their future employment. There was but one difference of opinion: my fosterer preferred a farm—the *soubrette* a public-house.

Lady Featherstone was in raptures with our success, assumed a tone towards her servants and tradesmen that for months they had been unaccustomed to, and led the unhappy people to imagine there was yet a chance that they might ultimately be paid. At a card party the next night, fortune once more smiled upon her. Twice she held four honours in her hand; and whenever she cut in, the rubber was her own. As my leave of absence was limited to a month, I found it impossible to commit matrimony and arrange my wife's assets in that short period, and determined to apply to my commanding officer for an extension, and candidly apprise him of the reason of my non-appearance. I did so; and a very kind letter in reply, acceded to my request, and carried his congratulations.

Four days passed, and ten more would make me Benedict the married man. On both sides preparations for the grand event were making vigorously. Miss Woodhouse had summoned divers dressmakers to her abiding-place; and I had ordered a wedding garment for the occasion, and not omitted "new liveries" for my man.

The Lady Featherstone was the busiest of the whole. Accounts that would have lain *perdu* to the day of judgment, were examined; a card party invited for the next week; and even without permission from the coachman, she ordered her carriage for a drive, as if his wages were paid already. Everything went on swimmingly. Matrimony, after all, was the only safe path to preferment for a younger brother. In the hymeneal wheel, doubtless, there were blanks as well as prizes; but though there were Biddy Maginns—glory to the prophet—were there not also Amelia Woodhouses!

The following morning I called on my bride elect; but the lady of the bedchamber excused her mistress in not receiving me, on the plea of indisposition. I ascribed it to cold, while Ulick affirmed "the creature was naturally bothered at becoming Mrs O'Shaughnessy." My Lady Featherstone made light of the affair. Her dear Amelia was both sensitive and delicate; she feared the unusual flurry of her spirits might render some quiet necessary. In a few days her sweet friend would be quite stout, and in the meantime she suggested that it would be the more delicate proceeding on my part, to confine my attentions merely to inquiries through my servant. Of course, my Lady Featherstone was in these concerns oracular, and I confided the management of all to her and Ulick Flyn.

But the dowager was not aware that I had now with Amelia a more powerful ally than herself—to wit, the waiting-woman. Miss Florence had become deeply enamoured of Mr Flyn; and a woman of forty-five, when she loves, loves desperately. With Ulick's shrewdness, every occurrence in the lady's mansion must speedily reach me; and the admission of my man to the domicile of Miss Woodhouse was as imprudent as permitting a hostile force to establish itself in the citadel of a fortress.

The moon was at the full, and a lovelier night never fell upon the old cathedral, than when I passed it in the way to "mine inn," after losing three guineas at piquet to my Lady Featherstone. Her darling Amelia's cold was better. The truth was, she had been a little feverish; but to prevent unnecessary alarm, she had confined herself to her own room. In a day or two she would be in the drawing-room, and at the appointed time I would be blest with her hand, and of course made too happy.

This was indeed gratifying news. I sauntered homeward, communing with my own thoughts touching the disposition of a part of the eight thousand. At the corner of a street a fraction of a boy addressed me, to say that he had left my wedding-clothes at home. I gave the urchin half-a-crown; and the young tailor betook himself to an alehouse, and I to dream of approaching happiness.

With some difficulty I was admitted to my own room. Ulick closed the door carefully; and on a hasty inspection I perceived our traps were being packed, and all in preparation for an immediate move.

"Why, Ulick, what the devil's in the wind? Surely you are taking time by the forelock, in packing for our march."

With that provoking *sang froid*, which an Irishman, even in desperate cases, delights to indulge in, Ulick proceeded leisurely in folding and depositing the coat in my portmanteau, as he coolly replied,—

"Surely it's time to get the kit together when the route comes!"

"Why, what do you mean? I'm not to he married these four days?"

"No," responded the fosterer, "nor for four after that; unless you marry my Lady Featherstone. May bad fortune attend her, the dirty ould canister, night and day!"

"Speak out, man. What has happened—has Miss Woodhouse changed her mind?"

"Not that I know of," replied Mr Flyn.

"Is there a national bankruptcy?—for her money is in the funds."

"If there is, I didn't hear it."

"Is she dead?"

"Maybe she died within this half-hour."

"Come"—and I lowered my voice—"out with it, man. I guess the cause of her seclusion. Is she as ladies wish to be?"

"Arrah! Bedershin. Is it takin away the crature's character ye are?"

"D—n Ulick, you'll drive me mad. What is the matter? She's not dead—not broke—not blasted?"

"But"—and the valet made a long pause—"she's mad!"

"Mad!"

"Mad as a hatter!"

"Mad as a hatter? Go on, man!"

"Well, I must stop the packing, and tell you the story," replied Mr Flyn. "I was taking tea as usual with Miss Lucy, and, tender as she has been always, she was never half so tender as tonight. 'Ulick,' says she, for as I intended to bolt, I was, you know, civiller than ever, 'I never thought I would have loved mortal man as I do you.'—'Ah! then, Lucy,' says I, 'I think it's grammary ye have thrown over me; for if the world was sarched from Killarney to Giberalter, I'll take my book-oath the woman couldn't be found to plase me like yourself.'—'Ulick,' says she, 'you sodgers arn't loaded with money; and I don't see why you and I should not be nate and dacent at our weddin, like the captain and my mistress. There's a few trifles in the way of a present, and sure you'll not like them the worse for coming from me;'"—and Mr Flyn pointed to a huge bundle of miscellaneous garments, the gift of the enamoured *fille-de-chambre*.

"Well," continued the fosterer, "to be sure I thanked her like a gentleman. 'Agh, Ulick,' says she, 'will you ever desave me?'—'Desave you, astore!' said I. 'Arrah, who could look at that beautiful countenance of your own, and not be true as a clock, and constant as a turtle?'—'Ugh,' says she, 'I'll niver know pace till you're mine, Ulick! I wish my poor mistress may be well enough! but I'm sorely afraid we'll have to put back the weddin for a week.'—'Oh—blur-a-nouns!' says I, 'take my life at once, but don't kill me by inches. Do you tell me I must be ten days more without my charmer, and that's yourself?'—'Ah, Ulick, if you only knew the cause; but I'll tell ye everything when we're married,' says she. By Saint Patrick, I smelled a rat! 'There's a secret,' says I to myself, 'as sure as the devil's in Bannagher; and if blarney will get it out of ye, my ould girl, I'll have it before we separate.' Well, there's no use in tellin ye what I said, forby what I done, but I fairly smothered her with civility. 'Ogh,' says she, 'my darlin'—and she put her arm round my neck—her fist is as big as my own, and as yellow as a kite's claw. 'My poor lady takes quare notions in her head.'—'Does she?' says I.—'Maybe,' says Miss Flounce, 'matrimony may cure them.'—'Faith, and maybe it may. But Lucy, dear, what kind of notions do ye mane?'—'Agh, that would be tellin,' says she.—'So you wouldn't trust me, Lucy? Well, see the difference between us. I couldn't keep anything from you, even if it was the killin of a man'—and I gave her a look of reproachful tenderness that a hathen couldn't stand.—'Jewel,' says she, as she smothered me with kisses, 'I can refuse ye nothing. Well then—but it's a dead sacret—my mistress is at times a little eccentric.'—'Eccentric!' says I, 'what's that?'—'Why; says she, 'she labours under quare delusions.'—'Phew!' says I, 'she has, what we call in Connaught, rats in her garret!'—'I don't under stand you,' says she; 'but the fact is, for a few days in every month her intellects are unsettled.'—'Is it a pleasant sort of madness, Lucy? Does your mistress amuse herself with the poker—break windows—throw bottles?'—'Oh, no. Poor soul, she is quite harmless, and all she requires is a little humouring and no contradiction. One time she fancies she is dead, and then we let her lie in state, and make preparations for her funeral. At another she imagines that she has an engagement at the Opera; then we hire a fiddler, and allow her to dance off the fit. Last month she believed herself a teapot; and this one she thinks she is a canary. I suppose her approaching marriage has put the fancy in her head; for she sent for a cabinet-maker on Monday, and bespoke a breeding-cage.'—'A taypot!' said I, as I made the sign of the cross.—'Pshaw,' says she, 'it's very harmless, after all. The captain won't mind it, when he's accustomed to it.'—'Feaks! and I have doubts about that; for men don't marry to make tay, Lucy.'—'But,' says she, 'Ulick, don't let mortal know that I've told you anything, and particularly your master. He'll find it out time enough!'—and the old harridan laughed heartily. 'He little thinks, poor fellow, he is to occupy the corner of a breeding-cage.'—'Ye may say that with your own purty mouth,' says I. 'Come, Ulick, dear, I must go to the mistress and lave ye. Keep up your spirits—a week will soon pass over—and then maybe I won't be your own lawful wife.' The devil a truer word ever she said. 'Go, darlin'—and giving me this watch and a brace of kisses, I lifted my bundle, and she let me out by the back door."

I was thunderstruck. What a deep plot that of the infernal Jezebel, the dowager's, was! To obtain two thousand pounds, she would have sacrificed me to a maniac. What a pleasant time I should have had—every month, at the full of the moon, to have to send for a fiddler or a coffin-maker, after receiving the pipe of a tea pot at the hymeneal altar! What was to be done? Nothing, but what Ulick had already provided for—a retreat without sound of trumpet!

The packing was accordingly continued, and it was now no sinecure. My bridal outfit, which luckily I had money enough to pay for, made an important addition to my wardrobe; while Mr Flyn, whose personal effects had arrived in Bath very conveniently packed in a hatbox, was obliged to purchase a couple of trunks to transport "the trifles," as he termed them, which had been presented him by the lovesick spider-brusher.

To quit Bath and not convey my acknowledgments to Lady Featherstone would have been uncivil, and I favoured her with a few lines. I declined the honour she intended in uniting me to a teapot; and as confinement to a cage might not agree with me, I authorised her to provide another mate for the fair canary. I delegated to her the task of delivering my parting compliments to Miss Woodhouse; and at the request of Mr Flyn entreated, that "when her hand was in," she would bid a tender farewell to Miss Flounce, and acquaint her that he would return and claim her hand on "Tib's eve"—an Irish festival, which is stated to occur "neither before nor after Christmas." A short postscript desired her not to trouble herself in preparing the *post-obit* until she heard from me again.

Well, you may be assured that Ulick and I, notwithstanding the salubrity of the city, did not think it prudent to extend our visit. Before the reveille beat next morning, we were both perched upon the roof of a London stage-coach. I certainly had no reason to plume myself on the success of the expedition, and I returned to town, dull as a wet Sunday. The fosterer, however, was in high glee, and all the way up carolled like a nightingale. The difference was, that my attempt at the commission of matrimony had nearly been my ruin, while Ulick was "made up for life." He had been fed "like a fighting cock"—was proprietor of a silver watch—and, "tatteration to him! but he had more shirts than the sergeant-major, and more handkerchiefs than the colonel himself."

"Well, gentlemen, what think you of my second attempt to obtain a wife?"

"Bold, certainly, though not so fortunate as your merits deserved," replied O'Connor. "But, Terence, did you ever hear how the ladies bore their desertion."

"The canary-bird, I believe, with Christian resignation—but a laughing hyena was nothing to the lady of the bedchamber. The dowager, rendered desperate by my levanting, attempted to excuse herself to Miss Woodhouse, and prove that she was no participator in the flight of the false one; but she could not even obtain an audience, as Miss Flounce slammed the door in her face. Unable to hold her ground any longer, she was literally dunned out of Bath, after having instructed in the art of book-keeping half the tradesmen in the town."

"And what," said Captain Paget, "became of honest Ulick?"

Major O'Shaughnessy sighed deeply.

"He lies in a trench before the curtain of La Trinidada. In love he was a faithful counsellor, and in battle always at my side. When the light division assaulted Badajoz, I was wounded in the head and body while scrambling up the breach. A stout arm prevented me from falling—a kind voice told me to 'cheer up!' It was my poor fosterer—and the words were the last he uttered. A bullet passed through his heart, and we rolled together into the ditch. When I volunteered to lead the assault that night, Ulick joined the forlorn hope, and accompanied me. Through life we had never been a day apart—storm and sunshine fell upon us together. God rest thee, Ulick! a braver soldier never screwed a bayonet, nor a more faithful servant followed the humble fortunes of an Irish gentleman than thyself!"

The major wiped away a tear, bade us a good night, and retired to his own hut.

"Poor Terence! It is a warm-hearted animal, after all," said O'Brien. "He never speaks of his fosterer without being affected. I knew him for years, and a more attached fellow to a master never lived than Ulick. How goes time? Pshaw!—not nine o'clock. Is there any brandy in the flask? O'Shaughnessy has desperate thirst upon him while recounting those amatory mishaps, and he applied to the canteen repeatedly."

"Faith!' replied one of the subalterns, "he has made a deep inroad upon the Cognac. But, major, do you recollect the conversation we had concerning that mysterious affair at ——?"

"Yes, and I promised to tell you the particulars. Have we time for it now?"

"Oh, yes," responded several voices.

"Well, I will not delay you, but make the story as brief as I can," he said—and thus commenced.

IV

THE MAJOR'S STORY

And heedless as the dead are they
　Of aught around, above, beneath;
As if all else had passed away.
　They only for each other breathe.

Who that hath felt that passion's power,
Or paused, or feared, in such an hour?

Parasina

Yes—Leila sleeps beneath the wave.

My wrath is wreak'd—the deed is done—
And now I go—but go alone.

The Giaour

"THERE IS MORE ROMANCE," SAID Major O'Connor, "in real life, than in any fiction which the novelist can imagine, and few men have journeyed through existence long, and not encountered something touching on the marvellous. I never was a sentimental adventurer, and yet I have in my time met with strange occurrences. In the story I am about to tell, I was an inferior actor—and of the other parties, one was a lieutenant in the same company, and the lady I had seen, although I had never been acquainted with her intimately.

At the time, when the transaction occurred I was a subaltern in the 8—th. The regiment was quartered in a large garrison-town in the south of Ireland, and I had been for three months on leave. On rejoining, I was presented at dinner to an officer who had come to us from another corps, and was struck with his appearance and address. He was a remarkably handsome man—at times a little of the puppy; but when he pleased, his manners were very agreeable, and his conversation lively and amusing. As we were both in the light company, we were a good deal thrown together, and hence I became more intimate with Clinton than any officer in the regiment.

As the garrison was very full, and the barrack undergoing repairs, most of us were obliged to live out at private lodgings. Clinton and I were cantoned in the same house, and had separate apartments, with a drawing-room in common. We breakfasted, and generally had coffee together in the evening. By degrees—for my companion was in some matters exceedingly reserved—we became more intimate. Gradually he became more communicative. Much of what he was doing came under my observation; and I was soon aware, from many circumstances I noticed, that he was engaged in an intrigue.

The house we lodged in was in the suburbs of the town, remotely situated, but not very distant from our barrack. After mess we were in the habit of returning home tolerably early; for we had some desperate hard-goers in the regiment, and if a man commenced another bottle after the stipulated dinner wine was drunk, it was almost impossible to get clear of the late sitters before daylight. My companion, when at home, always left a small portion of the window unclosed—this signal was understood; for almost every night, and at a particular hour, sand was thrown against the glass, and Clinton went out to converse with an old woman wrapped closely in a grey cloak. I remarked her frequently, but never obtained a glimpse of her features, from the pains she took to conceal them from my view. She was, no doubt, an emissary of Cupid; for Clinton had generally a note or letter to peruse or answer, when he returned from his interviews with the old woman.

Sometimes, in place of a written reply, he followed the messenger directly. On these occasions he always took his sword, and muffled himself in a large blue cloak that belonged to me, which, from its size and colour, was better adapted to conceal the person than his own.

Clinton and I in age, height, and figure, were exceedingly alike. We both wore light-infantry uniforms, and at night might be readily mistaken for each other. Twice the old woman, when waiting for Clinton, addressed me by mistake; and I had repeatedly, when returning after dinner, been dogged almost to the door of my lodgings, by a man wrapped in a drab great coat such as the lower classes of the Irish wear, and which, from its loose make, renders the figure very indistinct. The frequency of the occurrence roused my curiosity—I strove to ascertain who the person was, under whose espionage I seemed placed; but I never could succeed. He always kept some distance in the rear—if I walked quickly, he mended his pace—if I loitered, he sauntered after me—if I halted, he stopped—in short, he regulated his movements by mine, and always avoided coming to close quarters. One thing struck me as being very singular—whenever I wore my own cloak, I was certain of being watched to the very door.

It was the evening before the catastrophe. The general had dined with us, and I had remained later at the mess-table than usual. It was good starlight, for there was no moon. That morning, in passing a cutler's shop, it occurred to me, from the constancy with which I was haunted by the unknown, that some outrage was intended against my person, and I thought it prudent to be prepared. I accordingly went in and had my sabre ground and pointed. On this evening I had my own cloak and sword and before I cleared the first street, observed that as usual I was closely followed. Stimulated by wine, and conscious of possessing an effective weapon, I determined to bring my pursuer to action; and halting silently beneath a garden-wall where the road made a sudden turn, I waited for the enemy to close.

A minute brought us into contact. He turned the corner of the fence, and finding me ready to receive him, sprang back two paces.

"Stand!" I shouted, as I unsheathed my sabre—"Stand! or I'll cut you down!"

"Back!" he replied, "or by Heaven I'll blow your brains out"—and I saw him present a pistol, which he had drawn from underneath his coat. We stood within a few yards of each other for some moments in a threatening attitude—I was the first to break silence, by demanding why he dared to follow me?

"To warn you to desist," returned a deep and disguised voice.

"Desist!" I exclaimed. "What am I to desist from?"

"The pursuit of one you never shall obtain!" was the reply.

"You are under some mistake."

"I am not," returned the unknown. "You have eluded my vigilance twice, and met her you best know where. Attempt it a third time— and your fate is sealed!"

"I tell you, fellow, you are in error."

"No, no—Mr Clinton, you are—"

"My name is not Clinton."

"Damnation! Have I been mistaken? May I inquire whom it is I talk to?" he replied.

"I am called O'Connor, and—"

"You lodge in the same house with—"

"Precisely so."

"Strange!" he muttered. "I would have sworn it. Height, cloak, figure—Ha! I see how they escaped me. I was on the wrong scent, and they seized that opportunity of meeting. Pray, sir, have you been ever watched home before?"

"Yes, a dozen times. If I am pursued again, I'll shoot the man that follows me."

"You had better leave that alone. It is a trade that two can work at," he replied coldly. "But you will not be incommoded again. A hunter, with the game afoot, will not turn from it to run a drag, I fancy. Fare sir. If you regard your comrade's safety, tell him to avoid the elm-tree walk in the churchyard. He has been there twice too often—he will understand you perfectly. Good night, sir."

"Stop friend. You have frequently escorted me home, I think I shall return the compliment."

"Indeed?"—he replied with a sneer. "If you are ambitious of heaven, and wish to make a vacancy in the 8—th, I would recommend a trial of that experiment. Go to your lodgings, boy. I have no wish to harm you, though I hate every man that wears your livery as I hate the devil. Go—once more, goodnight."

He turned round the angle of the wall. A momentary surprise prevented me from following for a time. When I did, he was fifty paces off, and presently appeared to vanish from my sight. I walked rapidly after; and when I reached the spot where he disappeared, found it a narrow passage between two garden walls. I looked down the opening— it was dark as midnight—I listened—his footsteps had died away—it was useless to follow—I gave up the pursuit and returned to my lodgings.

Clinton was there before me.

"You are late tonight," he said. "Have you been serenading your mistress; or, like unhappy me, waiting impatiently for the messenger of Cupid?"

"Serenading I have not been," I replied; "but I have been conversing probably with the messenger of Cupid—if the aforesaid courier wears a frieze great-coat, and delivers his commands with a cocked pistol."

"Indeed! What do you mean?"

"Why, that I have been mistaken for you—followed, until I got tired of being pursued; and when I turned on the scoundrel, found I had but caught a Tartar."

"Go on, my dear fellow," said Clinton.

"I forced him to a parley, and he proved to be better provided for battle than myself. In short, we parted as we met. In the dusk, it seemed, he mistook me; and when the error was ascertained, he gave me a pleasant message for you, with an injunction to deliver it."

Clinton eagerly demanded what its import was; I repeated, as nearly as I could remember it, the threatening language of the stranger.

"It is indeed a singular business altogether, George. I must make you my confidant, and in the morning will show you the lady, and afterwards acquaint you with a strange story. What said he about our meetings?"

"That they had occurred twice; and if you valued life, to desist from a third attempt, and avoid the elm-tree walk in the churchyard."

"Well," replied Clinton, "tomorrow you shall know more. It is late; and as we are to have a field-day, the sooner we are in bed the better."

We took our candles and separated.

The garrison review occupied the whole of the next morning; and it was scarcely over when I was obliged to go on the main guard. About two o'clock Clinton came to me, and asked me to walk out with him. I put on my cap, and we strolled arm in arm into the town.

"George," he said, "I am so thoroughly convinced of your prudence, that I am going to entrust you with my secret. I require the advice and assistance of a friend, and you are the one I would wish to confide in."

I assured him that if secrecy were necessary, he might be certain of my discretion—and he continued:

"I find myself surrounded with difficulties—I would almost say danger; but rather than abandon the affair, I would risk life freely. Would you wish to see the lady?"

"Faith! Clinton," I replied, "I have no small curiosity to see a person who has been the cause of placing me under the espionage of as truculent a gentleman as ever man conversed with in a retired lane at midnight."

"It shall be gratified," he said. "Do you observe yonder shop? It is the second from the corner of the street"

"A linen draper's?"

"Exactly so," he replied.

"Well, what next?"

"Go in—look for a handsome girl. There are several women attending in the shop; but it is impossible to mistake Agnes. Make any excuse—ask for gloves—pocket—anything that will give you an opportunity of seeing and speaking to her. You will find me waiting for you at the confectioner's."

He pointed out the place where I should find him, and I proceeded to see a fair one, who had already placed me two feet only from the muzzle of a loaded pistol.

I looked above the door, and the name inscribed upon the show-board was a Quaker's. I entered the shop—several starched and steady women were behind the counter—but none of them were of the sort whose charms could endanger the personal safety of any man. Was Clinton jesting with me? At the moment when I was deliberating whether I should not retire at once, a party of ladies came in. Immediately the shop-women were engaged in attending to them; and one, retiring to a door that opened on an inner apartment, said, in a voice that I overheard, "Agnes! thou art required here."

My eyes were instantly turned to the place whence the fair inamorata might be expected—and presently she appeared. I was almost struck dumb with astonishment. A lovelier face than hers I never looked at!

Many a year has passed away, but I shall never forget that beauteous girl. She was scarcely nineteen—tall, and notwithstanding the formality of her costume, the roundness of her arm and the symmetry of her waist and bosom could not be concealed. Her eyes were hazel, with an expression of extreme gentleness. Her hair, Madonna-like, was parted on the forehead; but the simple cap could not hide the profusion of its silken tresses. The outline of the face was strictly Grecian—the complexion pale and delicate while the "ripe red lip" formed a striking contrast in its hue, and seemed as if "some bee had stung it newly."

I was perfectly fascinated; and were anything wanted to make her irresistible, her voice was so musical, so modulated, that "the listener held his breath to hear." For a quarter of an hour I dallied under various pretexts in the shop; and when at last I could not find a fresh apology for further delay, I came away fully convinced that I had never seen an angel until now.

Clinton was at the confectioner's and we left it together.

"Have you seen Agnes?" he inquired.

"I have seen the sweetest girl in Ireland," was my reply.

"Is she not worth loving, George?" he said.

"Worth loving? For one smile I would walk barefoot to the barrack; and a kiss would more than repay a pilgrimage to Mecca."

"Faith! I half repent my having exposed you to her charms, the impression appears to have been so powerful," said Clinton, with a laugh. "But I must tell you a long tale tonight. I cannot dine at mess today; there are strangers invited, and I could not steal off in time. I have ordered something at home; and when you return from the barracks at night I shall be waiting up, and we can have a confidential *tête-à-tête*. Here come some of our fellows, and I shall be off. *Adieu*— you will be home before eleven?"

"I shall be with you as soon as I can leave the table without observation."

We parted—he on business of his own, and I to visit the guard.

The party at the mess was large, for we had an unusual number of guests at dinner. The band was in attendance—the wine circulated freely—and notwithstanding my anxiety to leave the room, it was almost twelve before I could accomplish it. I visited my guard, and then set out to keep my appointment with my friend Clinton.

The evening had been close, not a breeze moved a leaf, and there was that sullen heaviness in the atmosphere which generally precedes a change of weather. Now the night had altered—sudden gusts moaned along the trees, and doors and windows clattered. A storm was coming fast, and I hurried along to reach home before the rain began.

I had no apprehension of being followed. I looked back—no one but myself was afoot, and my old pursuer had deserted me. I passed the lane where I had met him last night. No one was there, and I reached my lodgings unmolested.

Fitzpatrick, my servant, was sitting up. I inquired for Clinton, and to my surprise was told that he had not returned since he had gone out at dusk. Had he eloped with the fair Quaker? It must be so. Well—that was easily ascertained—for he would require some clothes and his dressing-case. I took up the candles and went to his room. All there was undisturbed; his toilet as it always was, and his portmanteaus in their accustomed places. It was indeed surprising! He might have had an evening interview with Agnes—but to remain till midnight—the thing was impossible. I was lost in a confusion of suppositions, and at last rang the bell, and inquired from Fitzpatrick when Mr Clinton had been last at home?

The answer was not satisfactory. My own servant informed me that at eight o'clock, when he was engaged in folding some uniforms, my companion had entered the apartment, taken my pistols, examined the loading and primings carefully, put them in his pocket, wrapped my cloak around him, and telling Fitzpatrick to say that he would be at home at ten, left the house.

I was very uneasy—I feared something disastrous—strange misgivings flashed over my mind, and the warning of the formidable stranger was not forgotten. I could not delay longer, for I was obliged to return to the guard-room. All I could do was to leave a message for my friend, and tell him he might expect me at an early breakfast.

The rain was now falling heavily—the wind was louder and more gusty—Clinton had taken my cloak, and I put on a large coat that covered my uniform, and started for the main guard. A wilder night could scarcely have come on so rapidly; and as the clouds careered quickly across the new moon, the darkness at times was nearly impenetrable. My route to the barracks was by that remote and unfrequented lane; and as I entered it, I confess the *éclaircissement* on the preceding evening with the gentleman in the frieze coat was rather a pleasurable recollection.

I hurried along the lone and gloomy passage, and came to the corner of the garden where I had awaited and confronted the unknown. A few paces forward he and I had held our brief and threatening colloquy. I wheeled round the wall. By Heaven! there he was—the same grey-coated man—the same tall and gloomy-looking stranger!

In an instant my sabre was unsheathed, and as rapidly on his part a pistol presented.

"How now?" I exclaimed. "Why are you here tonight? Advance a step, and I'll cleave you to the chin!"

"Pish! boy—keep your threats for those who fear them. I mean you no ill; that is, if you do not draw my vengeance on you by some silly indiscretion."

"What do you want?" I replied. "You labour under no mistake tonight."

"Oh—no!" he returned coldly. "Mistakes touching the identity of your friend are ended."

"Why do you stop me then?"

"Merely to ask a question or two, and assure you that if you walk the lane till doomsday, he who confronts you now will never lay his foot upon it afterwards."

"And what is that to me? I shall come better prepared tomorrow. You have an advantage in your weapons. Put fire-arms aside—I will throw away my sword—and let the best man be the conqueror."

He laughed hoarsely.

"Foolish boy! I do not question your manhood, and I am not here to try your mettle. I came to ask a question, and bid you farewell. Did you deliver my message to your friend?"

"Now, in the devil's name!" I exclaimed, as his cool audacity irritated my temper—"What right have you to demand anything from me, or suppose that I would reply to your inquiries?"

"I have no right," replied the stranger; "nor do I ask it but as a favour. If you have no reason for refusing a reply, I beg it in mere courtesy."

"Courtesy!" I exclaimed. "Strange courtesy, when men converse with naked swords and cocked pistols."

"'Tis the last time, young man, that I shall ever cross your path. Your gay companion is doubtless revelling at his mess; or, happier yet, locked in beauty's arms."

There was a devilish expression in the latter portion of the stranger's remark, that struck me with a creeping horror I cannot describe.

"I do not understand you," I replied. "Wherever my friend is, I trust he is in safety."

"Oh—safe he is—I'll be surety for that. Will you, however, oblige me with a reply to my question? Did you deliver him the message I confided to you? Remember, I ask an answer as a compliment."

"I did."

"Humph! he was warned, then! How did he receive the warning?"

"As any brave man should treat an idle threat—with the contempt it merited."

"Indeed?"—and there was a demonic emphasis on the word as it seemed to hiss from between his lips. A strong suspicion of foul play flashed across my mind, and I felt half-assured that Clinton had been ill-used.

"I fear that you have wronged him," I said. "If so, he has friends that will assert his quarrel."

"Well, I must abide their vengeance. But wrong. He is at this moment sleeping in the arms of beauty."

"I disbelieve you. If you have wronged him—"

"Pshaw! how incredulous you are," rejoined the stranger. "Ask him the particulars tomorrow, and every word he tells you I will admit as fact. Adieu—it is the last time you and I shall ever meet!"

"Stay, you must not—shall not go."

"Pish—silly boy! I have fire-arms, you have none. Were we unarmed, I would toss you over that wall, if you were fool enough to tease me by being troublesome."

As before he wheeled suddenly round the corner—a horse was waiting for him—he jumped upon his back, waved his hand, and in a second was out of sight!

I was perfectly confounded. What was I to do? I dare not betray the secret of my friend; and yet I was desperately alarmed for his safety. Was there no middle course? I determined to confide my fears to a companion, and hurried to the guard-room to communicate as much of my apprehensions to the senior officer as I might do, without compromising Clinton's secret.

Douglas, from the confused and imperfect story that mine was, where so much of the affair was necessarily concealed, was quite unable to advise me. I sent a soldier twice to our lodgings, to inquire if my friend had returned; but he brought back intelligence of his continued absence, and at daybreak I proceeded to the house myself, to try whether I could discover any cause for his mysterious disappearance. My fears were only heightened, and his servant was now seriously alarmed for his master's safety. Again we examined his chamber—unlocked his portmanteaus—opened his drawers;—not an article was missing—everything remained in its usual place, and it was quite clear, that when he left the house on the preceding evening, he had taken nothing away save my cloak and pistols.

Three hours passed, but no tidings of the absentee. I wrote a note to the colonel, stated the strange circumstances of Clinton's disappearance, and obtained his permission to leave the guard before the relief-hour came. I hardly knew in what direction I should first proceed, or from whom I should make inquiries. I walked into the town, intending to look into the Quaker shop, and try if I could see Agnes there. I reached the street—a crowd was about the house, and there was evidently something wrong. I mixed among the throng, and learned from one of the idlers that the Quaker's beautiful shop-woman had left home the preceding evening, and as she had not returned, some thought she had met with an accident, and others said she had only run away. The last conjecture I felt persuaded was the true one. My fears for Clinton's safety vanished—the absence of both was easily accounted for—my imprudnt companion had persuaded the fair Quaker to accompany him, and an elopement was the result. It was useless to ask any questions. Before evening, it was probable that Clinton would return, or acquaint me where he was concealed; and with a load of uneasiness removed from my mind, I turned my footsteps towards the barrack, to resume my guard, and be ready for the relief.

I entered the gate, when the sentry called out, "Sergeant of the guard, here's Lieutenant O'Connor!"

The man addressed ran out—

"Lord! sir, they are looking for you in all directions. Your cloak has been found on the banks of the river. They say Mr Clinton is drowned, and all the gentlemen and half the regiment are away to look for him."

I was unexpectedly horror-stricken. The mysterious language and dark hints the stranger used, coupled with the disappearance of the Quaker girl, assured me that some dreadful calamity had befallen the unhappy lovers. I took the direction where I observed some soldiers moving; and at the distance of half a mile, a group of red coats and civilians were collected on the banks, and busily employed in dragging the river.

I ran at speed, and was quickly on the spot. Twenty voices pronounced my name, and the crowd made way for me. Colonel Hope was surrounded by a dozen officers; and a soldier beside him held a cloak that I recognised to be my own, while in the hands of another I perceived my pistols.

"O'Connor," said the colonel, "your fears for Clinton will prove too true. Are these yours?"—and he pointed to the weapons.

I replied in the affirmative, and we walked a few paces from the crowd.

"I dread that our ill-fated companion is not far from the spot where they were found."

"I am persuaded," I answered, "that his body is in the river; and God grant his be the only one! Under what circumstances were those things discovered?"

"The cloak," replied the colonel, "lay carelessly upon the bank, as if it had been thrown off for some sudden purpose. The pistols were found in the next field."

"Pray let me examine them. They were loaded when Clinton took them, and the charge a singular one. I could not find balls in the case, and my servant cut a musket-bullet into quarters, and two slugs were put into each barrel."

The weapons were brought. On examination it was clear that neither had been discharged, and the divided bullet was found exactly as I described it.

Our attention was called to the search making in the river. A cry arose among the soldiers that the drag had fastened. More hands seized the rope—something heavy came gradually up—and before it touched the surface, female garments were discernible. Next moment, the body of the beautiful Quaker was drawn out, and laid upon the bank. An exclamation of horror burst from the crowd, and all rushed forward to gaze upon a countenance that yesterday had teemed with life and loveliness, and whose beauty even death could scarcely diminish. Her dress was not in the least deranged—the simple bonnet was tied beneath the chin—the gloves were on her hands—not a riband was displaced—not a pin seemed wanting. From all appearances, our surgeon supposed that she had been twelve hours in the water. That luckless cloak of mine was thrown over the departed beauty, and we recommended a search for our missing comrade.

I recollected the sarcastic remark of the unknown, when he alluded to the absence of poor Clinton, and asserted that at that time he "might be locked in beauty's arms." Where the Quaker's body had been lying, I suspected that of my ill-starred companion would be discovered; and my conjecture was soon verified, for a few casts of the iron raised Clinton's lifeless corpse!

Like the body of the sweet victim who lay beside him, no indication of violence was visible on the soldier's. His uniform was uninjured, and not a button torn away. Death had not been inflicted by a plunderer; for a valuable ring was on the finger, and a watch and note-case in the pocket when the body was recovered. The hat alone was wanting; and on the following day it was found in a millpond, whither it had been carried by the stream.

The whole affair was involved in a deep and impenetrable mystery. There were no marks upon the bodies—no traces of a recent struggle visible on the river-bank. The night had not been so dark, that the unhappy couple could have accidentally fallen in; and if they had, Clinton was an excellent swimmer. That Agnes had any acquaintance with the drowned soldier, beyond what his calling often at the shop produced, was unknown to her friends and family. On searching her drawers no letter or note was found; and Clinton's private papers, many of them billet-doux, threw no light upon the transaction. There was one sealed packet of considerable size found in his writing-desk, with an endorsement, "To he burned when I am dead"—and in accordance with the wish expressed upon the envelope, it was immediately committed to the flames.

It was also a strange circumstance that nobody save myself had seen or encountered the man in the frieze coat, who had so frequently dogged me to my lodgings. Of course I left the house—for it would have painfully reminded me of my unfortunate companion. But though I remained for some months afterwards in the garrison, I never, from that fatal night, met any person having the slightest resemblance to the unknown.

I need not be tedious. I shall pass over the sensation poor Clinton's death occasioned among us, and the general sympathy the untimely fate of the beautiful Agnes elicited from all who had seen or known her. At the inquest nothing was elicited connected with the cause of their death and the bodies, followed by an immense concourse, were conveyed away. Clinton's, of course, was carried to the barrack, and that of the gentler sufferer was removed to the dwelling of her kindred.

By a strange accident the funerals occurred at the same time, and the processions crossed each other. One, with the unpretending simplicity of the sect she belonged to, seemed stealing quietly from the scenes of busy life, to seek that "end of all men"—the grave. The other, accompanied by all the parade that marks the interment of a soldier—the dead march pealing from the band—the firing party before the coffin—the regiment following with slow and measured step—moved to the cathedral, in whose cemetery Clinton's last resting-place had been prepared. The service of the dead was ended—thrice the volley of his own company rolled over their departed comrade—the earth rattled on the escutcheon that bore his name—the grave was filled—the music of the dead changed to a merry quick-step—and Clinton, in military parlance, was forgotten!

"And," asked a lieutenant, "was that foul and fearful deed never brought to light?"

"Never," replied O'Connor. "With the dead themselves the secret appeared to rest. Many years have since passed over, and nothing has ever transpired which could solve the mystery."

"Was a rigid inquiry instituted?"

"Yes; but all efforts failed. By degrees the wonder ceased, other local violences occurred, the interest gradually abated, and that double murder—for murder assuredly it was—is now only spoken of like those wild deeds of blood, which the Irish peasant delights on a winter night to listen to. But it is late—to bed, lads. We march by cock-crow."

In less than half an hour every sound was still, save the deep breathing of those who occupied the bivouac. It told that those it sheltered were sleeping more soundly on their truss of straw, than many a careworn head which pressed a downy pillow.

V

ENTRANCE INTO FRANCE—BATTLES OF THE BIDASSOA AND THE NIVELLE

Night closed around the conqueror's way,
　　And lightnings show'd the distant hill,
Where those who fought that dreadful day,
　　Stood few and faint, but fearless still!

Many a heart that now beats high,
In slumber cold at night shall lie.

MOORE

A T MIDNIGHT, ON THE 6TH of October, the British divisions got silently under arms. A storm was raging furiously—thunder was pealing round them—lightning in quick and vivid flashes flared across the murky sky—the elemental uproar was reverberated among the Alpine heights—and a wilder night was never chosen for a military operation. Gradually the tempest exhausted its fury—the wind fell—the rain ceased—an overwhelming heat succeeded, and when the morning broke, the leading brigades, at seven different points, plunged into the Bidassoa; while a rocket rose from the ancient steeple of Fontarabia, and the signal was answered by a combined movement from the heights, of all the divisions there drawn up in order of battle.

Perfect success crowned this daring essay. The leading columns were nearly across the river before the French fire opened. Ground difficult and broken in itself had been carefully strengthened with numerous fieldworks but all gave way before the desperate valour of the

assailants. The light division, with the Spaniards under Longa, carried
the entrenched position of Puerta-de-Vera. Redoubt and abattis were
stoutly defended; but from all, in quick succession, the enemy were
driven at the point of the bayonet. Night fell—the attack had every
where succeeded—and the victors bivouacked on the field they won,
and, for the first time, the allied forces slept upon French ground.

Here the British commander established himself, and awaited the
fall of Pamplona, which Soult's repeated defeats rendered inevitable.
The garrison still obstinately held out; and when their provisions were
nearly exhausted, it was rumoured that they intended, rather than
surrender, to blow up the works, and take their chance of escaping.
But an assurance from the Spanish commander, Don Carlos, that
should the place be destroyed, he would hang the governor and
officers, and decimate the men, prevented the attempt; and on the
30th of October the garrison yielded themselves prisoners of war,
amid the place surrendered.

Winter was now set in, and a season of unusual severity had
commenced. The allies were sadly exposed to the weather, and
increased difficulty was felt every day in procuring the necessary
supplies. Forage became so scarce, that part of the cavalry had nothing
for their horses but grass; while the cattle for the soldiers' rations,
driven sometimes from the interior of Spain, perished in immense
numbers by the way, or reached the camp so wretchedly reduced
in condition, as to be little better than carrion. Resources from the
sea could not be trusted to—the coast was scarcely approachable
in blowing weather; and even in the sheltered harbour of Passages,
the transports could hardly ride to their moorings, in consequence
of the heavy swell that tumbled in from the Atlantic. The cold
became intense—sentries were frozen at their posts—and a picket
at Roncesvalles regularly snowed up, and saved with great difficulty.
All this plainly showed that the present position of the allies was not
tenable, and that a forward movement into France was unavoidable.

But great difficulties in advancing presented themselves; and, all
things considered, success was a matter of uncertainty. Soult's army

had been powerfully reinforced by the last conscription; and for three months the French marshal had been indefatigable in fortifying the whole line of his position, and strengthening his defences, wherever the ground would admit an enemy to approach. The fieldworks extended from the sea to the river, as the right rested on St Jean-de-Luz, and the left on the Nivelle. The centre was at La Petite Rhune and the heights of Sarré. The whole position passed in a half circle through Irogne, Ascain, Sarré, Ainhone, and Espelette. Though the centre was commanded by a higher ridge, a narrow valley interposed between them. The entire front was covered with works, and the sierras defended by a chain of redoubts. The centre was particularly strong, as a regular work, ditched and palisaded, protected it.

To turn the position, by advancing Hill's corps through St Jean Pied-de-Port, was first determined on; but on consideration this plan of operations was abandoned; and strong as the centre was, Wellington resolved that on it his attack should be directed, while the heights of Ainhone, which formed its support, should, if possible, be carried simultaneously.

A commander less nerved than Wellington would have lacked resolution for this bold and masterly operation. Everything was against him—every chance favoured the enemy. The weather was dreadful—the rain fell in torrents—and while no army could move, the enemy had the advantage of the delay, to complete the defences of a position, which was already deemed to be almost as perfect as art and nature could render it. Nor did their powerful works produce in the French any false security. Aware of the man and the force which threatened them, they were always ready for an attack. Their outpost duty was rigidly attended to. Before day their corps were under arms, and the whole line of defences was fully garrisoned until night permitted the troops to be withdrawn.

At last the weather moderated. On the 7th, Ainhone was reconnoitred by Wellington in person and the plan of the attack arranged. No operation could be more plain or straightforward. The centre was to be carried by columns of divisions, and the right centre turned. To all the corps their respective points of attack were assigned; and to the light division and Longa's Spaniards, the storming of La Petite Rhune was confided. The latter were to be supported by Alten's cavalry, three brigades of British artillery, and three mountain guns.

The 8th had been named for the attack; but the roads were so dreadfully cut up, that neither the artillery nor Hill's brigades could get into position, and it was postponed for two days longer. The 10th dawned, a clear and moonlit morning. Long before day Lord Wellington and several of the generals of division and brigade, with their respective staffs, had assembled in a small wood, five hundred yards from the redoubt above the village of Sarré, which they only waited for sufficient light to commence attacking.

Nothing could exceed the courage and rapidity with which the troops rushed on and overcame every artificial and natural obstacle. The 3rd and 7th divisions advanced in front of the village. Downie's Spanish brigade attacked by the right, while the left was turned by Cole's, and the whole of the first line of defences remained in possession of the allies.

On this glorious occasion the light division was pre-eminently distinguished. By moonlight it moved from the greater La Rhune, and formed in a ravine which separates the bolder from the lesser height. This latter was occupied in force by the enemy, and covered on every assailable point with entrenchments. As morning broke, the British light troops rushed from the hollow which had concealed them. To withstand their assault was impossible—work after work was stormed—on they went with irresistible bravery, and on the summit of the hill united themselves with Cole's division, and pushed forward against the entrenched heights behind, which was the strongest part of the position. Here a momentary check arrested their progress—the supporting force (Spanish) were too slow—the ground too rugged for the horse artillery to get over it with speed. The Rifles were attacked in turn, and for a moment driven back by a mass of the enemy. But the reserve came up—again the light troop's rushed forward—the French gave way—and the whole of the lower ridge was left in possession of the assailants.

For four hours the combat had raged, and in every point the British were victorious. A more formidable position remained behind, and Wellington combined his efforts for a vigorous attack.

This mountain position extended from Mondarin to Ascain. A long valley, through which the Nivelle flows, traverses it; and as the ground is unequal, the higher points were crowned with redoubts, and the spaces of leveller surface occupied by the French in line or column, as the nature of the ground best admitted. Men inclined to fight never had a field that offered so many advantages; and there were none, save the British leader and the splendid army he commanded, who would venture to assault equal numbers, posted as the enemy were.

The dispositions were soon complete—the word was given—and in six columns, with a chain of skirmishers in front, the allies advanced to the attack.

To carry a strong work, or assail a body of infantry in close column, placed on the crest of an acclivity that requires the attacking force to halt frequently for breathing-time, requires a desperate and enduring valour which few armies can boast. Such bravery on that occasion characterised the allied divisions. Masses posted on a steep height were forced from it by the bayonet, though hand and foot were necessary to enable the assaulting party to reach them. Redoubts were carried in a run, or so rapidly turned by the light troops, that the defenders had scarcely time to escape by the rear. Nothing could resist the dash and intrepidity of the British; and over the whole extent of that formidable position, on no point did the attack fail.

In these operations the allies had 3000 killed and wounded; while the French were driven from a matchless position, with the loss of 50 pieces of cannon, 1500 prisoners, and some 3500 *hors de combat!*

Nearly at the close of the struggle, while the light division were carrying a strong redoubt with a rush; and when, with their accustomed audacity, they had pushed on against the entrenched enemy as fearlessly as if they had been formed on a plain; a stouter opposition checked them, and, for the first time, the assailants were stopped by a heavy fire from behind the abattis of the redoubt.

To pause for breath—re-attack the entrenchment—one party advancing boldly in front, while the two others in a run dashed forward right and left to turn the work—was but the business of a moment. In front they leaped over the abattis, on the flanks they jumped into the ditch, and the defenders had scarcely time to escape by the rear.

When forced back by the heavy fire from the entrenchment, O'Connor was wounded in the head, and his companions urged him to retire, and obtain surgical assistance; but he refused to quit the field, and binding a handkerchief over his bleeding temples, led on the second attack. Ever foremost, he cleared the ditch, and sword in hand sprang through the embrasure, as the last Frenchman was abandoning the redoubt. The tirailleur stopped—levelled his musket—fired—the ball passed through O'Connor's body, and stretched him on the ground.

It was a glorious moment when he fell. The cheer of victory rang in his ear; and while a dim mist gradually obscured his sight, the last objects that met the eye were French masses retiring in confusion, and red battalions advancing in double quick. He could look no longer—his head sank back—but a wild and reiterated huzza rose over the whole surface of the battle-ground, and told that Wellington was again a conqueror.

VI

SICK QUARTERS—DEPRESSION— AN UNEXPECTED LETTER

You look not well, Signor Antonio.
Merchant of Venice

No more—no more, Oh! never more on me
The freshness of the heart can fall like dew.
Don Juan

She
Grieved, but perhaps her feelings may be better
Shown in the following copy of her letter.
Ibid.

A MONTH WORE HEAVILY THROUGH, and O'Connor continued an invalid, for his wounds healed slowly. To one of his energetic disposition a state of inactivity was most disagreeable; and when every courier that arrived brought fresh details of Wellington's triumphant advance, the disabled soldier began to loathe the confinement of sick quarters and execrate the evil fortune which prevented his sharing in those proud actions that for a time closed the glorious roll of British victory—Orthez and Toulouse.

Local circumstances increased these repinings, which in disposition had engendered. The monotony of a place filled with sick men, and that, too, a wretched hamlet in the Pyrenees—dull, comfortless, and deserted—was heart-sinking to a spirit that till now had never been absent when daring deeds were doing. Every face he looked on was marked with some sad traces of disease—every one he encountered in his sombre walk seemed afflicted with premature decrepitude. If he remained within, O'Connor was obliged to witness the sufferings of his brave companions—many of whose recoveries had been pronounced hopeless, and who, conscious of the brief space of life allowed them, were slowly but surely sinking to an untimely grave. If he rambled out, the melancholy spectacle of death was frequently presented, as the corpse of some departed soldier was being conveyed to the little cemetery hard by, which now, alas! was thickly tenanted by those doomed

> "To die—to see no more,
> A much-loved country, and a native shore."

No wonder, then, that the soldier's firmness began to fail, and gloomy forebodings tormented him. While every day teemed with brave adventure, he who had been foremost in the gallant throng remained cooped in a mountain hamlet, with no occupation left but to contemplate the varied forms which human suffering can assume!

In the fever of war—in the frenzied excitement of a campaign, where battle followed close on battle—the failure of his suit to Mary Howard had been half-forgotten. He thought of her in secret; but a succession of daring operations and sparkling scenes of victory dispelled uneasy musings, and softened the painful memory of his disappointment. But now, in the silence of a sick-room, or the solitude of a lonely ramble, the image of the lost one returned with poignant vividness. Vainly he taxed his firmness—vainly he summoned resolution, and strove to "pluck from the memory" a recollection that, in his present irritable mood, stung him almost to madness. Alas the arrow was at his heart; and, sleeping or waking, Mary Howard engrossed his thoughts.

It was strange, too, that, though so long from England, no intimation of Mary's marriage had reached him. Letters, no doubt, miscarried frequently; but eight months had elapsed since the rifle detachment had marched from Ashfield; and whether his lost love had became the wife of another or still remained unwedded, was wrapped in doubt.

Still, even this uncertainty afforded at times a mournful pleasure. Though lost to him, it would have been some consolation to know that she was not the wife of his detested rival. This feeling O'Connor endeavoured to persuade himself was, on his part, totally disinterested. Were Phillips one with whom her happiness would be safe, he fancied that he could have submitted without a pang to see her consigned to the arms of another. But the soldier deceived himself. A suspicion—almost a certainty—was on his mind, that but for his rival's unfortunate intervention, Miss Howard's heart might have been his; and with a nameless feeling, from which his pride revolted, he clung to a lover's hope, and augured, from an announcement of her marriage having never reached him, that Phillips had forfeited her regard, and even yet that he and Mary should be happy.

The dulness of the Pyrenean hamlet was rendered more intolerable from a scarcity of books, or of anything besides, that could divert the tedium of a wet day. A volume of Gil Blas—two or three monkish directories—and a Racing Calendar found in the saddle-bags of a dead dragoon, formed the whole library of the cantonment. Sometimes a mutilated newspaper reached the *détenue*, and most frequently it came thither wrapping some package that had arrived from England. A trunk that had for months been following an officer, now among the wounded, found him in this miserable retirement. It contained a general refit, despatched to the sick man from his family; and O'Connor, who was present when the long-delayed supply was opened, secured a few of the wrapping papers. They were English journals; and though many were six months old, still they told what then had been passing in his fatherland. It was dark, and the soldier retired to his small apartment to peruse his newspapers, as well as a wretched substitute for a lamp would allow him.

For a time the contents of these obsolete journals were interesting. He read of *faux pas* with surprise, that in England were now forgotten. Bankers were broken, whom five minutes before he would have quoted as worth a plum; while persons who, when he saw them last, had been puzzled to procure a dinner, were now, by the bounty of the blind goddess, "men of worship," and some of them members of the senate. Some military statements and speculations were, from their gross inaccuracies and the oracular shape in which they had been delivered, exceedingly amusing; and O'Connor took up the last fragment, wondering at the interest which a torn newspaper possessed among the Pyrenees.

He would have been happier had he passed that fragment by unheeded. It was a scrap from the *Morning Post*. Ere his eye rested a second on the paper, his cheek turned pale—his brow compressed itself—and his hand trembled. There he found a paragraph, among some others containing the idle gossip of the day. Though names were not mentioned, the soldier was at no loss to understand who the parties were to whom it alluded. It stated that "the dashing Captain P—, who had recently left the Rifles for the —— Light Dragoons, and whose antipathy to the Peninsula had occupied the attention of both fashionable and military coteries, had solved the mystery last week by eloping with a village beauty. The fugitives had headed northward—and the old vicar of A—d was inconsolable."

The paper fell from O'Connor's grasp. Mary Howard was lost to him forever—Mary Howard was a wife—the wife of his rival—his hated rival! It was some time before he could collect his thoughts. He took the fragment up—the date was near six months back. She married, it would appear, immediately after he had sailed from England, and had been for months a matron, while he was nursing idle fantasies, and imagined her still free. He read the paragraph again—it was strange and incomprehensible. What necessity was there for an elopement? The old man would not oppose his daughter's happiness; for Phillips had always been a favourite. Why was he inconsolable? Was it because Mary had obtained a protector? Pshaw—that conjecture was absurd. Some mystery was attached to the transaction, and O'Connor went to bed in all the wretchedness that an ardent passion, stripped of the last hope it dared to cherish, must undergo.

Bodily wounds will heal. O'Connor recovered—but the ailment at the heart was irremediable. His spirits fled—he became reserved and dejected; and he who had been once regarded as a man who set fortune at defiance, appeared sinking beneath a fixed depression that none could account for—as none could guess the cause. *The Gazette*, issued after the battle of Orthez, reached the isolated cantonment of the wounded, and O'Connor was in the list, a lieutenant-colonel. He seemed to read his promotion with indifference, and the wonder of those about him was redoubled.

Toulouse was fought. Soult made a last and desperate essay to arrest the British general in his victorious career; but that unnecessary expenditure of human life ended in a signal defeat, and added another laurel to the conqueror's wreath. An armistice, followed by a total cessation of hostilities, immediately succeeded. The Bourbons were restored, and Napoleon abdicated the throne of France to assume the mockery of royalty in Elba.

At this period a medical officer of superior rank visited the outlying sick and wounded, who had necessarily remained at a distance from the scene of active operations, to ascertain what portion of the sufferers it would be advisable to invalid and send home. Fortunately he was an intimate friend of the dispirited soldier; and, stopping in the same hut, he had an excellent opportunity of observing the malady of his patient. He quickly perceived that the mind and not the body was diseased; and that to amuse his fancy and rouse O'Connor to exertion, would be the best means of speedily effecting a cure. Accordingly, he urged him to leave the village and repair to headquarters—there obtain a leave of absence, and ramble for a few months from place to place, wherever inclination led him. The advice was congenial to the feelings of the invalid—leave was readily granted—and as the Continent was now open to travellers, the colonel, as we must call him for the future, set out for Switzerland, *en route* to Italy.

A very short time proved that the advice of his medical director had been judicious. O'Connor's health became rapidly established, and, better still, his mental quietude was once more restored. He now had schooled his heart to submission, and learned to think of Mary Howard as of one dead to him altogether. Of her total alienation no doubt remained, and consequently idle hopes no longer obtruded themselves. O'Connor's cheerfulness returned; and, to the delight of many of his old companions whom he occasionally encountered on the road, the gallant colonel became " himself again."

He had been at this period four months a rambler, and only awaited the arrival of despatches he expected from England, to quit Rome, leave the Continent, and turn his steps towards home. The packet came—he broke the seal impatiently—it contained several letters from his agent; but what astonished him deeply was to find in the parcel one in the well-remembered handwriting of his lost Mary. He unclosed it with a trembling hand—and his surprise increased while he read the following lines:

I have seen two events noticed in the papers, which have given me pain and pleasure—your name in the return of the wounded, and afterwards in the *Gazette*, which contained the list of promotions after the battle of Toulouse. For some weeks I remained extremely wretched, until a paragraph in the *Times* relieved my anxiety by noticing you among those who were stated to be convalescent. I trust the health of my dear and valued friend is now completely re-established, and that his native air, to which the newspapers mention him as about to return, will effect a speedy cure, if such be not already completed.

At parting, you plighted me a brotherly regard, and bade me at all times freely and fearlessly confide in you. I am about to do so, O'Connor. Alas! little did I imagine then, how soon I should be obliged to remind you of that pledge, and by reposing confidence, obtain advice.

I have none other but you, O'Connor, to whom I dare apply. My father and Captain Phillips have never met since I quitted my parent's house, and consented to what, under ordinary circumstances, would have been indelicate—a hurried and irregular marriage. But a stern necessity required this sacrifice of feeling. I owed it to my husband, and I submitted.

I am not well—and to *you* I should blush to confess it—*I am not happy*. Residing among strangers—estranged from my beloved father—the absences of Phillips are become longer every time he leaves me. Military duty calls him frequently away; and, as he says, the regiment is far too dissipated to permit me to accompany him to headquarters. Yet this to me, strange as I am to worldly etiquette, appears most singular; for the colonel's wife and several ladies beside are constantly resident with their husbands.

When we meet, O'Connor, I will open my whole heart to you. I am miserable—depressed—overwhelmed with horrible forebodings—doubts which I dare scarcely think of, and which my hand could never trace on paper. Possibly my situation dispirits me, and I harass myself with vain fears. God grant that it may be so!—and I shall be too happy!

Ere you arrive in England I shall in all probability have become a mother. If life is spared in that approaching trial—come to me. I have no bosom in which to confide my fears and sorrows but one—and that is yours—my more than brother!

Farewell, dear O'Connor. I am so weak and nervous, that you will scarcely decipher what I write. Keep me in remembrance—and pity one who loves you as sisters love.

Thine, most faithfully,
MARY E. PHILLIPS.

There was a postscript, giving the necessary directions for finding her in London, and an expressed wish that their meeting might be soon.

As O'Connor read the letter over, his brow darkened and a flush came over his pale cheek. He folded it again, and placed it in his pocket-book.

"Yes, Mary, I will be with thee. Under all this mystery attendant on his marriage, Phillips has some villainy concealed. Where was the necessity for an elopement? Why not present Mary to his regiment? The scoundrel means her false; and she, poor artless dupe, at last suspects him. Let me see." He took the letter out, and examined the date and postmarks. It was written two months since, and had followed him from place to place, until it found him at Rome. The delay was most vexatious. What would Mary think? No deliverer appearing— and even her appeal for months unnoticed. O'Connor summoned his servant, and issued orders for an immediate departure.

"Mary," he said, "I may not be able to redress thy wrongs, but I can avenge them. If that false villain has abused thy confidence, his blood shall wash the stain away—ay—if I dragged him from a sanctuary."

Within three hours Colonel O'Connor had left "the eternal city," and night and day hurried by express to England.

VII

ARRIVAL IN LONDON—
A SCOUNDREL'S VILLAINY
CONFIRMED

Ophelia. I hope all will be well. We must be patient: but
I cannot choose but weep. My brother shall know of it.
Hamlet

NO ACCIDENT INTERRUPTED THE COLONEL'S journey; and in a
shorter time than could have been anticipated, he reached the
British metropolis and drove to a west-end hotel. The evening was far
advanced—he despatched a hasty dinner—and having inquired the
direction of the obscure street where his still-beloved Mary resided,
he determined to set out at once and find her without delay.

While waiting for a coach, he threw his eyes carelessly over a
morning paper; and, with considerable satisfaction, read in the list of
arrivals at a neighbouring hotel the name of his gallant countryman
O'Brien, now, and most deservedly, a major.

The address that Mary had given him in her long-delayed letter,
was to a newly-built row of houses in the vicinity of the Regent's
Park. Half an hour's driving brought him to the place; and having
discharged the coach at the end of the street, he walked slowly down
to find the number of the house.

From the appearance of the buildings and the remoteness of the
situation none of the numerous streets and terraces which environ the
Park having then been erected—O'Connor felt considerable surprise,
that this lonely and insulated outskirt should have been selected by a
man of fashion for the residence of his lady. He found the number—

opened a wicket that led to the hall-door through a small shrubbery separated from the road by a paling—and stood before the humble dwelling of her whose beauty might have adorned a palace. There was no light from any window save one in the basement storey, and after pausing for a minute to collect his thoughts, he knocked gently at the door. The candle disappeared from the room below—then beamed through the fanlight of the hall—and a woman's voice next moment inquired who he was, and what he wanted? On asking for Mrs Phillips, the door was instantly unclosed; and the owner of the house, a decent and elderly person, held the light up to examine the features of the late visitor. Accidentally, the cloak in which he had wrapped himself fell back from O'Connor's face. The woman screamed—"Can it be possible?" she exclaimed. "Good God! it is her long-expected brother!" She invited the stranger to come in—closed the hall-door—and conducted him into a clean but plainly-furnished parlour.

"Alas! colonel"—she continued—"it is no wonder I was astonished. I never expected to have seen you—nor did the dear lady herself. For many a weary week she looked daily for a letter from abroad; and when any was delivered at the door, her first inquiry was whether it bore a foreign postmark? At last, poor soul, she began to despair, and when the postman's knock was heard in the street, she would sigh heavily and murmur, "Ah! he has letters for everyone but me—and even my brother has forgotten me!"

"Damnation!" exclaimed O'Connor, passionately. "What mischief that infernal delay has caused! I know, my good woman, the letter that was expected; but the lady's only reached me ten days ago, and I have travelled night and day since I received it."

"How unfortunate!" she replied. "Had you but seen how bitterly the disappointment wounded her, you would have pitied her as I did. For hours together she would gaze upon your picture."

"My picture!"

"Ay—and it was so like you too. I knew you at the first glance, though in your picture you are dressed in green."

"But where—*where* is she?"

The woman wiped away a tear.

"Alas! it is sorry tidings for a brother. She is gone home to"—and she paused.

"Go on—go on—for God's sake."

"To die!"

"Die—Oh, no—impossible! she was in all the bloom of youth, and health was painted on her rosy cheek, when I left her but a year ago."

"Ah that year I suspect has done the mischief, sir. I fear, poor lady, health and happiness during that short period were lost."

"But when did she go?—where to?—with whom? Speak—I am in torture!"

"Her father—God pity him, poor old man!—came for her about ten days ago. They set out by easy stages for his vicarage in a carriage, and the nurse and baby, with her trunks, went by the mail. A strange dark-complexioned woman, who visited her constantly when Captain Phillips was away—and latterly he was seldom here—travelled with her as a nurse-tender!"

"A dark woman!"

"Ay—dark as a gipsy; but she was too handsome and well dressed to be one. I suppose she was some foreigner."

"Was the lady long your lodger?"

"Nearly six months. She came here a fortnight before her confinement. The captain took the lodgings."

"Her confinement? Is the child living?"

"Yes—and a lovely boy as ever eyes looked upon. He was baptized by her father, at the poor lady's request, the day before they left. It was, alas! a melancholy christening. I thought I would never weep so much, but I could not help it; for the mother, while the babe was named, sobbed as if her heart was breaking."

"What was the child called?" asked the stranger, in a broken voice.

"Edward O'Connor," replied the woman. "How pale you look, colonel! Do sit down"—and she handed him a chair.

"Tell me, and as briefly as you can" said the stranger, "all you know of my poor sister since she became your inmate."

"Willingly, colonel. I need hold nothing back from you; for it is already written to you by the lady."

"Written?"

"Ay—I have the letter looked up in my desk, and will give it to you presently."

"Well, your tale, my good friend. All that befell my sister—keep nothing from me."

"I will not indeed, colonel"—and taking a chair, the hostess thus continued:

"It was in the beginning of winter that Captain Phillips drove here in a hackney-coach, and looked at the lodgings. He inquired particularly if they were very private; and on my assuring him that they were, at once engaged them. Two days afterwards he came here with your sister; and here the dear lady continued until she left this, I fear, for the grave." The good-hearted woman burst into tears, and the soldier was deeply affected. Presently she resumed her story:

"I never saw so lovely a creature as the lady on the day she took possession of her apartments; but, alas! too soon her looks changed— her spirits fled—and I saw that she was unhappy. The captain, at first seldom remained from home a second night, but gradually he became less domestic, and latterly, and for whole weeks together, was absent from the lodgings. I saw that his letters began to pain her. Often they were thrown aside half read; and often, when I went into the room silently, I surprised the dear sufferer perusing them in tears, or gazing sorrowfully on your picture, colonel! At last the captain seldom stopped a second day at home; and during the whole period of her confinement he never visited her but once.

"The dark lady I told you of became now your sister's only companion; but it was plain that she was no favourite with Captain Phillips, for the servant had strict orders, when she was with her mistress, to apprise them of her husband's approach, if his tilbury should by chance drive up. There was, indeed, little fear of his surprising them together—for during the last six weeks that she remained here, he never was in this house but once.

"That once I shall never forget; for that dreadful visit will cause the lady's death. God forgive me if I wrong him! She had only left her room a few days—of course she was weak and nervous, and little able to support the interview that followed. The captain came; and as he did always when intending to remain, he sent his gig and servant away. They dined—he appeared unusually agreeable; and she, poor thing, happier than I had for a long time observed her. An hour afterwards a wild shriek startled me! I was sitting in the apartment underneath this one—ran up in terror—and on the stairs encountered Captain Phillips. He passed me—flung the hall door open, and ran down the street as if a robber were behind him. The shriek was again repeated—the lady's attendant called loudly for assistance—I flew to the drawing-room, and found your sister in convulsions. Her sufferings, oh God! how terrible they were! The physician was called in, and the dark lady sent for—both remained the whole night beside her; and from that moment she drooped like a withered flower, until she was conveyed from this by her heart-broken parent, to fill an untimely grave. I cannot, must not, deceive you, colonel—your sister's case is hopeless."

In deep attention O'Connor listened to the detail of Mary Howard's sufferings. That Phillips had in some way wrought her ruin and abandoned her was certain; and Ellen's prophecy was painfully recalled. As the landlady's narrative proceeded, curses escaped between his clenched teeth, and more than once he leaped in a storm of passion from the chair. The owner of the house retired for a few minutes, and brought in a packet sealed and addressed to "Colonel O'Connor." The writing was Mary's—but the characters were almost illegible, and bore painful evidence to the feebleness of the hand that traced them. Had he wanted any other proof that the packet came from his lost love, the device upon the seal would have been sufficient. It was the impression of an antique ring that he had found buried in the sands when assisting the engineers in throwing up a fieldwork in Egypt, and which, in

happier days, he had prevailed on Mary to accept. The landlady lighted
another candle and would have retired from the room to leave the
soldier to peruse his beloved one's epistle—but O'Connor hesitated to
break the envelope; and he who had led a storming party to the breach,
trembled to unclose a lady's letter.

He bade the good woman a hasty farewell—threw himself into
the coach—returned to the hotel—retired to his room—locked the
door—and there read the ruin of the most spotless victim who ever
fell a sacrifice to the machinations of a heartless profligate!

VIII

MEMOIR OF A RUINED BEAUTY

A tale so sad! a maid of noble birth
By solemn vows seduced—abandoned—left
To shame and anguish!

He was a villain!
Prayers, sighs, tears, oaths—nothing was spared to win her.
She listened and believed.

   Adelgitha. I'll meet him—
Sink at his feet—bathe them with tears—implore him
To spare a ruined wretch; and if spurns
Me and my griefs—
   Claudia. What wilt thou then?
   Adelgitha. Die!—die, Claudia, die!

                              M. G. LEWIS

M Y HAND TREMBLES—AT TIMES MY purpose fails—and I know not how to begin the sad and disgraceful disclosure. I have waited week after week for an answer to any letter. None came—and you are dead, or I deemed worthless. O'Connor, you shall never know what I felt after you had left me. That secret goes with me to the grave, and, with my imprudence, both will be there shortly forgotten.

I have a strong conviction that we shall never meet in this world, though Ellen assures me that we shall; and I cannot go to another and a better Being, without assuring you, my valued friend, that in all save worldly experience I have nothing with which to reproach myself—and that I have alas! been sinned against and not sinning.

I am weaker today. Two things alone require an explanation—my marriage, and my abandonment. While strength lasts I must make an effort, and give you a brief detail of both.

After your embarkation, Phillips visited at my father's, an acknowledged and accepted suitor. None could be more ardent— none more respectful. A distant day was named for our union; and, at his own request, the ceremony was to be performed with as little parade as could be.

As the time drew near, Phillips redoubled his attentions; and while his professions of regard were unabated, I thought I could occasionally discover a suppressed uneasiness that he appeared anxious to conceal. At last I ventured to hint my suspicions. He seemed mortified but by degrees admitted that my fears were true, and promised to repose full confidence in me on the morrow.

We strolled out next day—turned into a retired forest-walk— and there Phillips freely unbosomed himself. He had an old and singularly-tempered uncle. He was dying—the disease hopeless—a few months must bring him to the grave—and Phillips was heir to his large estates. It was the old man's fancy that his successor should form a titled alliance. Phillips had evaded matrimony hitherto, and he endeavoured to amuse the dying invalid with hopes which probably he should never live long enough to see overturned. His actions, he added, were vigilantly observed—he had grasping kinsmen jealous of the regard the old man evinced, and they would gladly seize any opportunity to ruin him with his wealthy relative. Our marriage, he feared, would afford the desired means. He cared not for himself. Of that he had already given the strongest proof, by quitting his regiment rather than leave the woman he adored, and thus exposing himself to the most offensive imputations that could be attached to a soldier's name. This he had endured without a murmur; and he was prepared now to sacrifice his brilliant prospects, and show how ardent and disinterested his love was. I listened to him with pain. I had no fortune—and Phillips's passion for me must cost him a rich inheritance. I urged him to postpone our marriage, and wait until circumstances would admit our union taking place, without the ruinous consequences which must attend it now. But he was resolved that no delay should intervene. Fame he had already sacrificed—and let fortune follow. I hinted that our marriage might possibly be kept from the knowledge of his uncle; but Phillips, with a melancholy smile, replied that there was an espionage over all he did, which would render the concealment of a public ceremony utterly impossible. Suddenly, and as if a ray of hope flashed across his mind, his eyes brightened, and he exclaimed—"Yes, Mary, there is a chance—nay, a certainty of averting the ruin which the old man's anger would entail upon us. Mary, I must prove your love. Dare you trust yourself with him who so devotedly adores you; and, waving for a month or two a public ceremonial, wed me privately?"

I started! "Oh—no, no, Phillips. I will share your poverty, if poverty is to be the price of loving; but if I consented to such a step, even you would afterwards despise me."—"Oh, Mary!" he replied, "how little do you know my heart. Were it possible that the feelings with which I regard you could he increased, that confidence would make me love you more devotedly." Why, O'Connor, weary you with the pleadings of specious artifice? I yielded a reluctant consent, and on the third night set off for Scotland with the deceiver.

We travelled rapidly for two days, and reached the frontier safely. There was no one to interrupt our journey; for my poor father was so utterly confounded when my flight was communicated to him on the next morning after I had eloped, that for many days his faculties appeared suspended, and at times his intellect seemed wandering. Late on the second evening we crossed the border, as Phillips told me; and in the private chamber of an obscure public-house, a sort of ceremony was performed by a man whose features were concealed in the twilight—a ring placed upon my finger—a scrawl, purporting to be a marriage certificate, presented to me—and I was assured that

I was duly married according to the forms required by the Scottish church. That such was the case I firmly believed. I had heard that these ceremonies were strange and hurried—no suspicion of practised deceit lurked within my breast—not a doubt disturbed me, but the consciousness that a father's feelings had been sacrificed to a husband's interest; but I had the consolation of thinking that a few months would convince my parent that I had yielded to necessity alone, and that my filial affection was unchanged and unchangeable.

We arrived in London, and the same consideration that rendered a private marriage indispensable required us to live in the strictest retirement. To every wish that Phillips expressed, I submitted without a murmur. We resided in obscure lodgings, and, excepting when we walked into the fields in the evening, or visited the theatres closely muffled up, I never left the house. This change from the life of exercise which I had previously led began to affect my health; but I kept it from my husband, and waited patiently until the necessity for all concealment should terminate.

That time came. Phillips had been away for a week, and every post brought fresh excuses for his absence. No letter came that day, and of course I expected him at night; and while I counted the hours until he should arrive, I strove to while them away by reading. An evening paper was brought in. I took it up—turned to the deaths and marriages—and in the obituary the first name recorded was that of his dreaded relative! I flung the paper down. Here, then, my trial ended—concealment was no longer necessary—mystery was over. I should be an acknowledged wife—restored to the arms of my father—and—proud and happy thought—a few months' privacy and suffering would be rewarded by a life of love; and he, whom a sacrifice of feeling had saved from disinheritance, would repay it by an enduring attachment. Oh, God! how rudely was this dream dispelled—how cruelly those hopes blasted!

I am fainter—feebler—daily. I must hasten with my sorrowful disclosure, or life will ebb away before the tale of my wrongs is told. Phillips was thunderstruck at the discovery; and, in his endeavours to elude my questioning, for the first time excited suspicions, which every day confirmed. Conscious how grossly he had wronged the being who had loved "not wisely, but too well," he became reserved, and sometimes peevish and unkind. The slightest allusion to our marriage, any expression of surprise at the continual concealment in which we lived, irritated and annoyed him; and, before my child was born, he appeared happy when any excuse offered him a plea for being absent.

I was confined—my baby saw the light—no father prayed beside his daughter's couch—no husband cheered her sinking spirits during the hour of suffering. Alas, alas! the truth was too apparent—I was no longer an object of the love of him who ruined me!

Feeble—and feebler still—my trembling fingers now hold a pen with difficulty. I am hastening to the grave; and when you return to England, O'Connor, the narrow house will be my abiding place.

I should have sank under my afflictions, or lost my reason, had not an humble, but faithful friend, watched over me as a mother tends a dying infant—that person was Ellen the gipsy. She seldom left me—when I desponded she cheered me up—and when I abandoned hope, and became nearly crazed, she placed my ill-starred baby in my arms, and asked me, would I repay his innocent smiles by robbing him of his mother? She seemed to possess a spell to rouse me in my lowest mood, and almost reconcile me to life.

Three weeks had passed—Phillips had been all that time with his regiment, if one or two of his short cold billets spoke truth—and, though Canterbury was so near, he could not obtain leave to visit his wife and child. Ellen was unusually grave. Some new misfortune was impending. What could it be? My father—was he ill—sick—dead? I asked the gipsy, but she assured me he was well, and hinted, in her own dark and mystic way, that I might see him before long. That moment the postman knocked—the maid brought up a letter—it was from my husband, and couched in much warmer terms than those in which his notes had latterly been worded—it intimated his intention of being with me that day for dinner.

Ellen read the billet over. She looked at me—perused the letter again—and muttered, "Too kind to be sincere—lady, be firm—prepare for a surprise—and it may not be one from which pleasure comes."

"I cannot be more wretched, Ellen, than I am. Let it come—I am too miserable to heed it."

The gipsy shook her head; and, as she hated Phillips, left the house immediately.

He came—I heard his step upon the stairs—my heart beat violently—but, oh! how different the feeling was from the throb of delight with which, a few months since, I listened for a lover's return! He kissed me tenderly—asked for our boy—took the child in his arms—gazed on it as a father looks upon his first-born, and—

> "Sad proof in peril, and in pain,
> How late will lover's hope remain"—

I thought some blessed influence had touched his heart, and that I should regain a husband—my boy, a father. When dinner was removed, Phillips filled a glass of wine, urged me to drink it, and exhibited a show of fondness that half-confirmed the happy change which, as I fancied, my good angel had brought about. He placed himself beside me on the sofa; and as his arm encircled me and his hand pressed mine, he said, in the soft and winning tone he could so artfully assume,—

"Mary, I have much to confess, and you have much to pardon. I have been latterly inattentive, unkind, apparently indifferent; but when all is told, you will pity and forgive me."

I burst into tears.

"Alas! Phillips, I have suffered much; but could I only reclaim that truant heart of thine, no allusion to the past should ever escape my lips, and I would think of nothing but the joyous change that had again replaced me in the affections of an alienated husband."

"Ah! Mary," he said, "I have been apparently unkind; but I, too, have been unhappy. I have destroyed myself by play, and nothing but one act can save me from perdition. You are the arbitress of my fate."

"*I!* say, what can I do? We must live humbly Phillips. Ah! I partly understand you. These lodgings are too expensive."

"Damnation!" he exclaimed. "No, no, Mary. I'll change you to a residence more fitted for beauty like yours to dwell in—a carriage— an establishment—everything which that gentle heart can long for—all shall be yours!"

I stared at him, and shuddered. I feared that misfortune had unsettled his brain. A ruined man talking as he did savoured of insanity.

"Phillips, I am contented where I am. All I ask for is your undivided love."

"And have there not been times when you would have wished yourself once more free?"

"There have," I replied. "When I thought I had outlived your affection, then I bitterly lamented the accident that made us first acquainted."

"Well, well—I have been imprudent—I stand upon the brink of ruin—and yet one step places me almost beyond the reach of fortune, and secures opulence for you, Mary, and a noble provision for your infant."

I was lost in amazement, and waited in breathless anxiety for what would follow.

"Our marriage was somewhat hurried and informal, Mary."

"Oh, yes, Phillips. Often do I repent that I wanted resolution to be unkind, and determination to refuse your suit, until we might have married without this lowering concealment."

"The world believes," he continued carelessly, "that we are not wedded."

"Oh God! how dreadful must that suspicion be to you. How insulting, Phillips, to know, that the reputation of a stainless wife, the legitimacy of a guiltless infant, are questioned from the necessity of a clandestine ceremony!"

"Mary, you have made one sacrifice—another would render me the happiest of men; for it will enable me to place you, where beauty and gentleness like yours deserve to be—in luxury and splendour."

"I cannot comprehend your meaning, Phillips."

"Hear me calmly, Mary"—and he appeared to be making a strong effort to gain courage for an embarrassing explanation. "I am, as I have told you, ruined. I have play-debts in themselves of no great amount—but to me, without any resource to meet them, destructive as if they reached above the income of a monarch. One of those dull creatures, chosen by the blind caprice of fortune to bear the weight of wealth, has fancied me as the person on whom she would lavish her riches; and no barrier stands between me and a noble independence, but our hasty and irregular engagement."

I nearly fainted; but I held up, and strove to sustain my sinking strength.

"Hasty and irregular engagement!" I replied. "Mean you our marriage by that term, Phillips?"

"Ay—if you please to call it so."

"Call it so!" I exclaimed. "What name besides should a solemn ceremony—"

"Pish!" he replied. "There was no solemnity in it."

"No, there was none indeed—but in Scotland—"

"Mary, we were never eighty miles from where you are at present."

Great God!—a sudden conviction of treachery rushed upon my mind, and I passionately exclaimed—"Who?—who performed the—"

Phillips mustered resolution to unmask the whole.

"A broken billiard-marker was the priest, my own servant the witness, and you and I, Mary, are free as air!"

I remember nothing more—a wild shriek burst from me—darkness shut every object out—I tottered, and fell upon the carpet!

I recovered my senses. Ellen plucked me from the jaws of death, and for my deserted baby's sake I strove to live. I wrote to Phillips. The letter was, I suppose, the effusion of a mind half crazed—and a cool and guarded reply was returned. It spoke of "our engagement" as "a foolish affair," and professed a readiness on the writer's part to settle a comfortable annuity on me, and a fitting provision on the infant. This insult almost brought me to the grave. Again I rallied—again I wrote to my destroyer. The appeal was to his feelings, and humbly worded, as the supplication of a wretch who begs a moment's respite from the headsman. The answer—for one was sent—told me that "our correspondence must cease"—that in another month he should be married—assured me that my father was ready to receive me with open arms, and confessed that he had intercepted the numerous letters which the heart-broken old man had written.

I wrote to my parent. Ellen guided my hand, for I was too nervous, without assistance, to scrawl the few lines I did. The kindest—the tenderest reply that ever a fond father addressed to an erring child, came to me by the following post. He would have hastened to me instantly, but wished to apprise me a day or two before his arrival, lest our meeting might be too sudden, and a surprise should injure me.

He is come. I have wept upon his bosom, and I shall set out with my heart-broken father, to die beneath the roof where years of peace and innocence glided calmly by. You will scarcely read my writing—nerves and strength at once grow weaker. Now, O'Connor, I have to prefer my last—my dying request. My boy in a few days will be motherless; and, worse than honest-born orphanage, the stain of illegitimacy will be affixed upon his guiltless name. Will you, for my sake, forget the father, and protect the child?

He is named after you, and tomorrow I set out for the vicarage. Phillips is on a visit with his bride's brother, not forty miles from Ashfield! Is not this unfeeling? They are to be married in a fortnight. Another week or two would have seen me in the grave, and surely he might have waited for that! No matter—a little longer, and my earthly trials shall have ended.

O'Connor, farewell. The last blessing of one who in death owns her love, is yours. Remember, I consign my boy to you. We shall never meet here. The flame of life is smouldering fast away. God forever bless and guard you, is the dying prayer of

MARY E. HOWARD.

London, —— 8th, 1814.

IX
THE HOUSE OF DEATH

Guiscard.   Why weep, and hide thy face?
Turn to thy Guiscard—turn to him who loves thee.
   Adelgitha.   Thou lov'st me! Oh! repeat those blessed sounds!
   Guiscard.   Canst thou doubt my love?
   Adelhitha.   *Still* lov'st me—*Still!* Pronounce that word
"Still! still!"

M. G. LEWIS

A FINE SPRING EVENING HAD set in, when a chaise and four horses were seen descending the long hill, over which the London road to Ashfield passes. The pace at which the drivers went was unusually fast, and a few minutes would bring them to the end of their journey, if the village was the intended resting-place. Suddenly the post-boys pulled up—a traveller left the carriage—and while his companion kept his seat, and proceeded towards the inn, the stranger walked forward, and turning off the common into a narrow green lane, approached "the village preacher's modest mansion."

An unbroken stillness reigned around. No busy hum—no joyous laugh told that rural labour was proceeding. The house itself had a sombre and deserted look; and the cawing of the rooks, perched upon the top branches of the sycamores that surrounded the dwelling, seemed to the traveller melancholy beyond expression.

The stranger was wrapped closely in a blue cloak; but his air and step were too soldierly to be mistaken. He stopped for a moment at the entrance of the parsonage—then raised the muffled knocker—and the door was promptly opened by a female attendant.

In a low and broken voice he made an inquiry, which was answered by a mute inclination of the head. "Is she still living?" the stranger murmured in a whisper. "Yes but her sufferings, poor lady, are nearly ended." Farther conversation was interrupted by the appearance of a stout dark woman, who touched the soldier's cloak, and, gliding into an adjoining room, beckoned him to follow.

The meeting between O'Connor and the gipsy—for these were the persons—was affectionate as it was melancholy. Ellen leaned upon his shoulder; and, while her dark eyes were moist with sorrow, she informed him that Mary Howard was in the last extremity, and that the heart which he had sought so ardently, in a few hours would cease to throb. Not a shadow of hope existed—the sufferer's strength was sinking at that moment; but, though the frame was feeble, her mental energies were unimpaired, and, in perfect consciousness of approaching dissolution, she awaited "the spirit's parting from its house of clay," with all the holy calmness of an expiring martyr.

From the commencement to the close of her illness, the gipsy mentioned that she had spoken incessantly of her rejected lover. He appeared the engrossing object of her whole thoughts; and when she wished that the span of existence might be lengthened but a little longer, it was only in the hope that she should see him, whom she valued so dearly, before the final struggle terminated. In her present exhaustion, whether a parting interview might be hazarded was doubtful—instant dissolution might ensue; and Ellen left the unhappy soldier to himself, while she went to Mary's chamber to ascertain if she might communicate by degrees the news of his unexpected return.

When left alone, the soldier cast a melancholy look round the apartment. It was the same in which his last interview with Mary had taken place. All in that chamber brought her to his recollection as she was then, bright and lovely—the rosy hue of health upon her cheek—the glow of reciprocated passion flushing in her bosom. What was she now? Oh God! that beauty had vanished like a dream, and a false love had withered that heart which then had cherished it with such tenderness.

O'Connor's meditations were speedily interrupted—a female servant whispered him to follow her. Silently he ascended the stairs— the maid opened a chamber-door—and pointing to a chair within, signed to the stranger that he should enter and sit down.

It was the apartment in which Mary Howard was dying. The light was partially obscured, and the disposition of the bed-curtains such, as to enable O'Connor, unseen himself, to look upon the faded countenance of the lost one. Her father had just risen from his knees, where he had been engaged in silent prayer; and the gipsy stood beside the bed, with her dark and brilliant eyes bent upon the sufferer, as if to watch the expected change that was to harbinger immediate dissolution. One thing struck O'Connor as remarkable; though the voice was weak and tremulous, and the delivery of what she uttered unusually slow, every syllable that passed the lips of the dying beauty was distinct and audible.

"Has the post come in yet, Ellen?" was the first question of the invalid.

"Yes, my dear."

"And no letter from abroad?"

"None, love," replied the gipsy.

"Ah Ellen, for once your prophecies have failed," said the sufferer, with a feeble smile.

"No, my sweet love, they have not. O'Connor is returning, and you will live to see him."

"Ha! Is—is his ship upon the sea, Ellen?"

"His voyage is ended—your letter only reached him a few days ago—and your adopted brother is already in England."

"Then, Heaven, I thank thee!" and she raised her still bright eyes upwards. "Ellen, thou wouldst not deceive me. When, when shall I see him?"

"Alas! love, you are too weak—too nervous. See, how the mention of his very name has brought that hectic to your cheek. You would agitate yourself."

"No, no, Ellen, I have more strength than you all suppose. I would only consign my boy to his protection, and bid him a last farewell. Where is he? Is he in the village?"

"He is near you, Mary; and only waits until you are calm enough to see him."

While this short and painful scene was passing, O'Connor's emotion became far too powerful to be suppressed. Tears stole down his sunburnt cheeks, and a stifled sob escaped involuntarily. The quick ear of the dying girl heard it.

"Hush!" she said; "that convulsive sigh came not from a woman's bosom. Art thou near me, O'Connor?"

The gipsy gave a signal that he might approach—the soldier moved softly forward, and sank down beside the bed, to prevent sudden surprise. He took the attenuated hand that lay upon the coverlet gently in his own, while the gipsy bent over the village beauty, and whispered that her long-expected brother was kneeling beside her.

"Ha! Ellen. Is the hand that holds mine his?"

"Yes, dearest. Did I not tell you he was near thee?"

"How happy then shall my last moments be!" she said with animation. "Edward, come round, that I may see you better. Fear nothing, Ellen, I will be calm—indeed I will. I am far stronger than you all believe me."

O'Connor obeyed her wish, and placed himself on a chair beside her. The old man wrung his hand in silence. At the invalid's request, the attendants left the room; her father followed them; and none remained beside the bed of death, but the soldier and the gipsy.

"Are we alone, Ellen?" the sufferer muttered.

"Yes, love; there are none here but the colonel and myself."

"Open the curtains, Ellen, and let me see that face which I prayed so fervently to look on ere I died."

She was obeyed, while O'Connor leaned over her pillow, and gently laid his lips to hers. She fixed her eyes upon him with a smile, and with her fingers parted the grizzled hair that covered his forehead, and partially concealed the sword-cut that traversed it.

"It is a fearful scar!" she murmured. "Your cheek is darker too; ay, and your hair turned grey. One year, Edward, has changed us both. And did you hasten home, as Ellen says, when you received my long-delayed letter?"

"I did, Mary. I hurried hither to avenge your wrongs, and—"

"What?" she inquired eagerly.

"Take you to this bosom for ever, and prove how imperishable my love was."

"Oh, no, no, O'Connor. Had I lived, should I have been an object for a brave man's heart to centre in? I humbled—debased—deserted. But you pitied—"

"And loved you, Mary, more tenderly than ever!"

"Then I did not forfeit your good opinion. Thank God! that consolation is left. None, save that that Omniscient Being, knows how artfully I was beset—how innocently I fell."

She paused—gained fresh strength—and thus continued—"I am dying happily. No care but one remains—my child—my child!"

"He's mine, Mary, mine from this hour. Father never attended to his offspring more faithfully than I shall watch over my adopted heir."

"Thanks—thanks! Ellen, tell the nurse to bring Edward O'Connor to his father"—and at the name a faint smile played for an instant across her pallid features. The infant came and as if in mockery of the scene of death, his rosy cheek was dimpled with a smile, as he gazed around, and looked as if those he saw were happy. The dying mother signed to the nurse to place him in the soldier's arms.

"He is yours, O'Connor. Come, let me for the last time kiss the adopted child, and him who has become the orphan's father."

The soldier stooped down—the infant's lips touched those of Mary Howard.

"Farewell, my boy—farewell, my brother!" she said, in a voice so feeble that it could scarcely be understood. Suddenly her head fell back upon the pillow. The gipsy raised it gently, and whispered, "You are weak, my love!"

No answer was returned—one long deep sigh escaped.

"Help!" exclaimed the soldier. "She is dying!"

"Hush!" returned the gipsy. "'Tis over—Mary Howard is dead!"— as she replaced her head upon the pillow, and folding her arms, gazed upon the departed beauty.

"'Tis ended!" she continued. "No mortal treachery can reach thee now. Soft be thy rest, sweet one! Even thy innocence could not escape the villainy of the world." Then turning to O'Connor, who continued gazing on the pale corpse:

"Colonel, this is no place for you. Vengeance belongs to man—to wail for the departed is a woman's office."

The soldier started.

"Ha! I understand you, Ellen! One moment of weakness—and it is the last."

He stooped down, and laid his lips to those that had once been so beautiful.

"'Tis the last time"—he murmured. "Cold—ay, cold already."

A sudden gleam of light flashed upon the pale corpse—the soldier noticed it.

"Mary, my lost one! Before that sun sets a second time, another shall be cold as thou art!"

He rushed from the room, and with rapid strides was seen hurrying from the house of death.

X

THE HOUSE OF FEASTING—
AN UNWELCOME VISITOR

Ay, seize the present hour! Ere long I'll dash
Your cup of joy with bitter.

Adelgitha

Birthless villains tread on the neck of the brave and the long-
descended.

Rob Roy

Sir, your fortune's ruined if you are not married.

SHERIDAN

THE SCENE IS CHANGED—THE house of mourning is deserted, and where our story passes to there was joy and revelry, for on the third morning the heiress of Bewley Hall was to become a bride.

Nothing was talked of for many a mile around, but the splendour and display that was to distinguish this important event. A numerous company had been invited to be present at the ceremony, and a number of the guests had already arrived at the hall.

Mr Harman, the present owner of Bewley Hall, and father to the bride elect, was one of those lucky individuals on whom fortune showers her favours. He had gone to India a needy man—and the child of humble parents, he had nothing to trust to but his own unassisted exertions. With neither money nor patronage to introduce him to the road to riches, as it frequently falls out, he contrived to find the path himself, and in his prosperous career outstripped those who had started on the same course with the adventitious aid of opulence and family connection. In five-and-thirty years he amassed an enormous fortune, returned to England, purchased the mansion of a ruined noble, accumulated property of every kind; and he who in boyhood had driven his father's bread-cart round the country mixed with the proudest in the land; and, anxious to veil in oblivion his lowly origin, he intrigued with ministers for a title, and looked forward to see his once humble name enrolled among the peers of Britain.

There are alloys generally found even in the most brilliant instances of worldly prosperity. Mr Harman was vain and ambitious. He had achieved a fortune, and he would fain have been the founder of a family; but he had no son—no male heir to continue his name. He was the father of a daughter. In early life his first worldly advancement was obtained by forming an alliance with the widow of a cotton-planter. She was the offspring of a native woman; and, unluckily, the only issue of his marriage, the heiress of Bewley Hall, exhibited in features and complexion incontestable evidence of the Indian source from which she was so immediately descended.

Still Mr Harman might have partially obtained the object he ambitioned, by forming an aristocratic alliance for his daughter. There were enough of poor and sordid titles ready to be bartered for even a portion of his wealth. But in this design he was fated to meet a disappointment. It pleased his daughter to fancy for her husband a person who had little save fashion and good looks to recommend him; and after idly attempting to combat the caprice of an obstinate girl, the old nabob yielded a reluctant consent. The day for the ceremony was named, and magnificent preparations made to give that *éclat* to the wedding, which an eastern *millionaire* so dearly delights in.

A splendid dinner had been just removed—the dessert was placed upon the table—the servants left the room—and the wine circulated freely. In honour of the joyous occasion of this merry meeting, the countenances of the guests were clothed in smiles; and the nabob, infected with the general hilarity, half forgot that he was becoming the father of an untitled son-in-law. The bride, glittering in jewels, looked with womanly pride at her handsome husband, who, in the rich and showy full dress of a hussar regiment, was seated beside her. All were happy, or at least all appeared to be so—although in secret the women envied the dusky heiress her conquest of the gay dragoon, while the men execrated their friend's good fortune, in obtaining in the hymeneal lottery a prize like the nabob's daughter.

Just then a laced and powdered functionary entered the banquet-room with noiseless step, and whispered in the bridegroom's ear that "the captain was arrived." It would appear that the newcomer was both an expected and a welcome visitor, as the dashing hussar apologised for a short absence, and hastened to the library to meet the stranger.

While passing through the lofty hall and lighted corridor, which led to the apartment where the lately arrived guest was waiting for him, Phillips glanced a look of pride and triumph on the splendour that everywhere was presented to the eye in this house of opulence. The mansion, and all it contained, would at no distant period be his own—fortune was about to heap her favours on him with an unsparing hand—long and ardently had he sighed for wealth—it was already within his grasp—the boldest flight of his ambition was achieved, and an inheritance which few nobles could aspire to was won. True, there was a wife attached—a woman without personal or intellectual accomplishments—a woman he could never love—one whom he already regarded with secret repugnance. But was there not venal beauty to be bought, and credulous and unsuspecting innocence to be betrayed? He had boundless means for effecting all he wished for placed at his disposal. What was the sacred vow exacted at the holy altar to him? No solemn oath would be regarded by the profligate; and he who could heartlessly abandon a being so pure and beautiful as her whom his falsehood had killed, would feel slight compunction in becoming faithless to a wife whom, even before marriage, he detested.

While O'Brien—for he was the unexpected visitor—waited for the footman's return, he amused himself in examining the splendid apartment to which he had been introduced. The reckless extravagance of the former owner of the Hall was evidenced in the sumptuous furniture of the library. Books of the rarest and most expensive kinds in superb bindings filled the cases and paintings, at ruinous prices, hung thickly round the walls. A large Indian screen was drawn partially across the fireplace. There O'Brien stood; and while the person to whom his untimely visit was intended remained absent, the soldier could not but moralise on the mutability of human fortune which this costly chamber betrayed.

Bewley Hall had been built by a noble earl, who after a long minority succeeded to large estates, and an immense sum of money accumulated during nonage. His youth had been consumed in travelling, and he came home delighted with everything foreign, and strongly prejudiced against his native land. The venerable mansion which for centuries had witnessed the births and dissolution of his fathers, was condemned as uninhabitable, and he commenced an edifice for himself.

The building of the hall, and embellishment of a park of immense extent, appeared the engrossing business of a life and reckless of enormous outlay, the earl pursued his object with an ardour which nothing could control. Hills were elevated and levelled—lakes sunk—bridges and aqueducts, temples and hermitages, erected from the most costly materials—trees, at their maturity, were transplanted—sprang up and disappeared, as if by magic—the whole face of nature changed; and the same plain, that ages before supplied the hospitable board of some stout old baron with venison, now floated on a silver sheet of water the dark gondola of the present lord. Day was not long enough to perfect the designs a wild imagination rapidly created. At night a fresh relay of artificers were employed; and at that silent hour, when mortal labour is supposed to terminate, the ceaseless clang of axe and trowel announced to the belated traveller that, even while he slept himself, the earl's boundless schemes were progressing.

But England did not afford sufficient scope for his extravagance. Agents in every city on the Continent were engaged in purchasing marbles and paintings, and securing the most expensive relics of antiquity. At every book sale the rarest portion of the collection fell to the earl's lot; and the very corners of the earth furnished their most curious productions to gratify the fancy of this eccentric individual.

Wealth, however great, may be exhausted; and, in a few years, the immense accumulation of a long minority was expended. But his estates yielded a ready supply; and, if possible, the earl laboured on more vigorously.

Years passed—frequent and heavy supplies had been so unsparingly procured, that at last the princely property would produce no more. The earl was a ruined man; and the hall and its appurtenances—sad memorials of his weakness—were offered for sale; but few could venture to purchase a place on which it was believed more than half a million had been expended. After a considerable delay, the sale of Bewley Hall was duly announced; and Mr Harman, "the millionaire," was stated to be the fortunate purchaser. The earl retired to end his days in comparative poverty on the Continent; and thus the best portion of the life, and the princely revenues of one of the proudest peers in Britain, had been consumed in founding a residence for the baker's boy.—*Sic transit*.

While O'Brien was pondering upon this singular freak of fortune, his reverie was broken by the opening of the library-door. The sparkling embroidery of a hussar jacket announced the coming of the person he was waiting for, while the screen partially concealed the soldier's face and figure, and, until within arm's length, Phillips did not recognise his *quondam* acquaintance. He entered the apartment in high and glowing spirits, but a few moments "changed his mood and checked his pride."

"Welcome, my dear Bouverie!" he exclaimed, as he came forward. "I feared some accident had detained you, and that I, without thy friendly counsel and support, must have faced the parson *solus* and promised to be virtuous evermore! Ha! Captain O'Brien!" and the colour deserted his cheeks—"This—is—an unexpected pleasure!" as with difficulty he stammered the words out, and held his hand forward. The visitor made no attempt to take it, but replied,—"I fear my late visit will occasion you as little pleasure as it has given me, Captain Phillips. My errand is not a friendly one. We are alone, I hope?"

"Perfectly so," was the reply, while the lip became pale and tremulous.

"Then the briefer an unpleasant communication is made," said the soldier, "the better for all. I come from Colonel O'Connor."

"From Colonel O'Connor!" and the name seemed to paralyse him. "And is Colonel O'Connor in England?"

"He is now," returned the Irishman coldly, "waiting my return at the village inn."

"And may I ask what brought him thither?"

"The same errand which recalled him post from Italy—to avenge the wrongs of Mary Howard!"

"I cannot," replied Captain Phillips, "see by what right a person totally unconnected with Mr Howard's family assumes the office of redressing a lady's wrongs who has a father to protect her."

"To moot that point is not my business; and if I might recall to Captain Phillips's recollection the last interview that took place between him and Colonel O'Connor before the latter went to Spain, my friend's determination respecting Miss Howard was clearly stated then. But we lose time. I am come to require a meeting at as early an hour tomorrow morning as Captain Phillips can make it convenient."

"A meeting! What cause of quarrel has Colonel O'Connor with me? I have done him no injury."

"Done him no injury! Captain Phillips—can you look me in the face and say so?" and O'Brien sternly fixed his eyes upon the abashed countenance of the trembling villain. "There breathed not upon earth the man who had power to wound my gallant friend save one. You, sir, were that one; and you have wrung Edward O'Connor to the soul."

"I will not affect to misunderstand you, Captain O'Brien."

"I am Major O'Brien," rejoined the Irishman haughtily.

"I beg your pardon—your promotion escaped my memory. I comprehend the nature of your errand perfectly; and it is your friend's fault if any indiscretion which I may have committed shall not be amply atoned for, and the lady and her family satisfied to the utmost extent of their wishes."

He paused—O'Brien bowed—and Phillips again continued:

"I regret most deeply the unfortunate affair that has occurred; and I am ready to offer every reparation to Miss Howard but *one*—I cannot marry her."

"Indeed! that would be impossible," said O'Brien, calmly.

"I am glad you see it in its true light," rejoined Phillips—and his face brightened. "But name any other means by which I may remedy—"

"A ruined reputation," returned O'Brien, with an expression of deep contempt. "Know you not, Captain Phillips that

'Honour, like life, once lost, is lost for ever!'"

"Well, well, as far as it can be done, I will do everything in my power to satisfy Colonel O'Connor. I will provide most amply for Mary."

"She is already provided for," returned O'Brien.

"Indeed? I cannot guess how."

"You need not. I will tell you."

Phillips's looks expressed astonishment.

"Mary Howard is beyond the reach of mortal wants. She is dead!"

"*Dead!*" repeated Phillips. "*Dead!*—it is impossible!"—and he tottered against the mantelpiece for support.

"It is too true, sir," was the cold response. "She is released from sin and suffering. Your victim is at rest. Poor girl—few and evil were the days allotted to her!"

The soldier stooped his head, for feelings unsuited to the purpose of his coming had been excited, and he wished them to be concealed. In a few seconds he turned to the pale and agitated criminal, and with an expression of stern determination, thus continued:

"Captain Phillips, nothing remains for me to do but simply deliver the message with which I am entrusted. Colonel O'Connor will expect an early meeting."

"It is utterly impossible!" exclaimed Phillips passionately. "On the second morning I am to be married; after that ceremony is ended, I shall not refuse Colonel O'Connor's message, if he chooses to repeat it."

"I must be candid, Captain Phillips. The meeting must be tomorrow, or, believe me, the ceremony you allude to will never take place. Report whispers that Mr Harman was not very desirous for the union; and there are documents in my friend's possession, connected with the betrayal of Mary Howard, which shall be exhibited to him before noon. The motives you assigned for marriage, and the feelings you express towards the lady, will not, I think, be flattering either to her father or herself."

Phillips turned ghastly pale. Another circumstance, unknown to any but himself and a chosen agent, rendered his present position so precarious, that a breath would shipwreck him, though so near the haven of his wishes. It is briefly told. When he became suitor to the nabob's daughter, Mr Harman disapproved of his addresses; and, to frustrate his designs upon his daughter, determined to provide her with a husband, and proposed an alliance between the noble earl whose property he had purchased and the heiress of Bewley Hall. Phillips accidentally discovered the purport of this secret overture; and, by bribing the courier employed on the occasion, managed to substitute another and a very different reply to that which the earl had returned. Piqued at the hauteur and coldness with which a ruined peer rejected the honour of an alliance with his heiress, Harman yielded to his daughter's solicitations, and reluctantly consented to her marrying a commoner, and a man who had neither fortune nor family to recommend him.

So far Phillips had been successful; but until the indissoluble knot was tied he remained in perilous insecurity. The earl's letter had contained a flattering acceptation of the nabob's offer; and intimated his intention of visiting England at an appointed time, which was now rapidly approximating. If he should arrive before the ceremony took place, the cheat would be discovered and the forgery exposed. Hence the delay of a few days might prove ruinous. With Phillips, therefore, all that ambitious profligacy values was at stake; and much as he dreaded a meeting with O'Connor, that desperate alternative alone was left, and he determined to accept the message.

"And is the call of Colonel O'Connor so urgent, so imperative, that a delay of three days cannot be given?" he inquired.

"Captain Phillips," replied the soldier firmly, "if my friend be not amply satisfied before breakfast tomorrow, before noon you will be exposed and degraded."

"Enough, sir. I expect Captain Bouverie, a brother officer, every moment. He came on a different errand; but if it must be, he will no doubt act for me in this affair. Where shall I send to you?"

"We are stopping for the night at the White Lion, and there I shall expect his visit."

O'Brien took his hat—Phillips rang the bell—and when a footman answered it, he conducted the unwelcome visitor to the door, and bade him a ceremonious "goodnight."

Returning to the library fire, the wretched criminal found leisure for melancholy recollections; and, strange to say, the fate of his murdered victim caused less remorse to the seducer, than dread for the consequences its discovery might occasion.

"Damnation!" he muttered through his clenched teeth. "Had these luckless letters been intercepted, this savage Irishman would have neither heard of Mary's desertion, nor come back to avenge her injuries. It must be admitted, after all, that she was cruelly betrayed; but death was produced by her own obstinacy. Had she been reasonable, I would have nobly recompensed her disappointment. But tomorrow—it is an infernal risk to run—and nothing but to meet that madman can avert my ruin. Oh! that I could remove him secretly. No, no—the thing's impossible. I must return to the company, and offer incense to that charmless half-caste, while the loveliest being I ever wooed and won is—I must not even think of it. Come, rouse thyself—fortune or ruin hang on tomorrow's chances."

The hall-bell sounded—the library-door was flung open—a stranger was announced. It was the expected guest, Captain Bouverie.

XI
THE DUEL

'Sdeath, I never was in worse humour in all my life! I could cut
my own throat, or any other person's, with the greatest pleasure
in the world!

The Rivals

Every wight has his weird, and we maun a' dee when our day
comes.

Rob Roy

WHEN O'BRIEN RETURNED TO THE village, he found his
companion writing letters in the little parlour, into which
they had been inducted on their arrival by the hostess of the inn. As
O'Connor listened to the detail which his gallant friend gave of his
mission to the Hall, a smile of stern satisfaction flashed for a moment
across his melancholy countenance, when the early opportunity a
meeting on tomorrow would afford him of avenging Mary Howard's
wrongs was announced. He folded his letters, sealed, and despatched
them, and then sat down to supper.

To one whose *hardiesse* had been so often and so desperately proved,
the hostile re-encounter now certain to ensue would be an affair of
slight consideration. That Philips would evade or decline a meeting
altogether, had been the thing he dreaded most; and the assurance
which O'Brien gave, that his enemy would not disappoint him,
removed that anxiety. While his friend had been absent, O'Connor

examined the ground in the immediate vicinity of the hamlet, and
selected a small enclosure adjoining the churchyard, whose level
sward and lofty hedges rendered it a fitting place for the decision of
a mortal quarrel. He described its situation to his friend; and soon
afterwards "the maid of the inn" announced that a gentleman had
called, and presented a card, on which "Captain Bouverie,—Hussars,"
was inscribed. The visitor was shown into another room, and Major
O'Brien joined him immediately.

After a brief conference preliminaries were settled. Fresh overtures
for a friendly accommodation having been peremptorily rejected,
Bouverie named five next morning for the hour, and acceded to the
paddock selected by O'Connor as the place of meeting. O'Brien
anticipated a stronger effort at negotiation; but secret intelligence had
reached Phillips that the earl had actually arrived at Paris *en route* to
Bewley Hall; and this determined him rather to meet the man he
dreaded, than risk a certain *exposé* which might delay his marriage
and, by delaying, mar his hopes forever.

Evening wore on, and at a late hour O'Connor and his companion
parted. How those, who were to be combatants in the morning passed
that night, may be readily conjectured. Sorrow and love—hatred and
revenge—racked the bosom of the gallant soldier; while the destroyer
of innocence, in that still hour when the torturous sting of conscience
is felt most keenly, fancied that the dead beauty in the costume of
the grave was standing before him continually, and taxed him with
her ruin. Driven by a desperate alternative to abide the challenge
of a deadly enemy, he trembled at the ordeal of tomorrow; and the
haggard expression of his pale and agitated countenance betrayed the
secret, when morning dawned, that sleep visits not the guilty.

A day of threatening inclemency wars rendered gloomier by a
drizzling rain. O'Connor's couch had been probably as restless as his
rival's; but when his friend entered his chamber, he was dressed with
customary neatness, and perfectly ready for the field. The expression of
his face was serious, almost approaching to sadness; but there was no
nervous uneasiness visible—no excited flush which would indicate that

he was about to engage in any unusual business; while the compression of the lip, and the sparkle of the eye, bespoke that calm and dangerous resolution, which renders an opponent doubly formidable.

Under the pretext of resuming their journey, the early rising of the guests was unnoticed by the inmates of the White Lion. The indifference with which breakfast was ordered in half-an-hour and post-horses directed to be in readiness to put to, removed every suspicion and although the place of meeting was within a bow-shot of the inn, no one in the house, when the soldiers strolled carelessly out, dreamed that a deadly encounter was about to happen.

The church clock was striking five, as O'Connor and O'Brien passed from the high road and crossed the stile. No peasant was astir, for the wet and gloomy morning delayed the earliest within their houses. O'Brien, beneath his military cloak, concealed the pistol-case; and, unseen and unsuspected, the soldiers reached the rendezvous, and waited the coming of their opponents.

Their stay was short—a vehicle was heard approaching—the wheels stopped suddenly and in a few minutes three men entered the enclosure. Two of them were familiar to those already there; and the third was a surgeon, whom Phillips had engaged for the occasion.

As his rival crossed the stile, the blood rushed to O'Connor's forehead, and his brows united in a deadly scowl. Instantly that cloud passed away, and an expression of stern determination succeeded the hasty ebullition his foeman's appearance had excited for a moment.

The arrangements were not effected without delay upon the part of Bouverie, as he objected to O'Brien's proposition of giving a case of pistols to each of the combatants, to use as each pleased after the firing signal had been pronounced. But in this the latter was inflexible—the weapons were duly loaded—the distance measured—the rivals placed twelve paces apart—and the signal explained distinctly.

Never did men take their ground with deadlier intent. Deep undying hatred steeled the heart of one—in his antagonist he saw the murderer of her whom he adored so devotedly, and nothing but blood could satiate the revengeful spirit that filled his bosom. With the other, the same deadly feelings existed; but they arose from a different cause. The arrangements made by his second showed clearly that O'Connor came to the field determined to destroy his rival, or fall himself; and the only chance by which his own life might be saved, was by taking that of the avenger of Mary Howard. When Bouverie presented the weapons, and Phillips observed the firm and unshaken attitude of his rival—the steady and concentrated look with which he measured him, as if selecting a spot more mortal than another on which to inflict a death-wound, the blood deserted his cheeks—his knees smote each other—and while he took the pistols in his trembling grasp, he whispered in his friend's ear,—"It is all over—I am a dead man!"

The word was given, and each arm was raised. Phillips fired instantly, and without effect; and while changing the discharged pistol for its companion, his opponent slowly brought his weapon to the present. *Three* might have been told before the trigger was drawn—a sudden shock, as if the touch of electricity, convulsed Phillips for a moment—and tottering two paces forwards, he dropped before the second or surgeon could run to his assistance.

Unmoved, as if he had only fired at a tree, the avenger of the dead beauty retained his ground, while O'Brien joined those who supported the dying man. Dying he was, for the ball had passed through the lungs, and the immense haemorrhage it caused was already choking him. Phillips heard his doom pronounced, and, with difficulty, expressed a wish that O'Connor should draw near. O'Brien beckoned to him, and the soldier came forward and stood beside his prostrate enemy. With a last effort Phillips raised and suddenly discharged the pistol he still held, before any could suspect or prevent the act. The bullet perforated the hat of his antagonist, and merely grazed the skin. Whether to curse the failure of the attempt, or express his dying hatred, he strove to speak, but the words were unintelligible. The blood rushed in torrents from his mouth, and, with a choking gurgle, he fell back in his second's arms, and expired.

Perfectly unmoved at the assassin effort of his foeman, the soldier regarded the dead man attentively. "Ellen!" he said, "thy prophecy has indeed been singularly accomplished!—Though he fell upon the field of honour, *he died a felon!* Come, O'Brien, we'll leave him to these gentlemen, and send them assistance from the inn."

While his second replaced the pistols in their case, O'Connor politely bowed to Bouverie and the doctor, assumed his cloak, and left the field leaning on his second s arm. The carriage was in waiting; and before the rustics, alarmed by the shots, could comprehend the nature of the affair, the avenger of beauty was driven from the village, as fast as four horses could expedite his escape.

THE CONCLUSION

He rushed into the field, and, foremost fighting, fell.

BYRON

The most precious tears are those with which Heaven bedews the
unburied head of a soldier.

GOLDSMITH

THE DEATH OF PHILLIPS, IT may be supposed, occasioned a powerful
sensation; and inquiries into the causes that produced his fatal
meeting with Colonel O'Connor displayed his character in its true
light, and discovered the remorseless cruelty with which poor Mary
had been sacrificed. While the memory of the dead *roué* was execrated
by all, a deep sympathy was excited for his brave and unfortunate
antagonist; and if general commiseration could soothe a wounded spirit,
O'Connor might have felt its influence and been once more happy.

But a lacerated heart commonly rejects human consolation.
O'Connor abruptly retired from the world—"peace was
proclaimed"—and the profession he once gloried in—robbed of its
danger and excitement—had now no charms for him. He left the
army, and buried himself in a deserted mansion-house which he
found upon his estate—and that estate was situated in the remotest
district of the wildest province in Ireland.

In the parsonage of Ashfield, Mr Howard passed the short and
melancholy remnant of a virtuous and "noiseless life." He bowed

with Christian humility to the visitation which deprived him of that beautiful and beloved object on whom, from infancy, all his hopes had centred. Poor Mary's boy, with the orphan of Badajoz, divided his affections—their education amused his idle hours—and leaving worldly cares for one who faithfully applied herself to the task, he calmly prepared for that great change which should unite him to his lost child in another and a better existence.

And who was she who smoothed the pillow of declining age, and watched over infant orphanage? Ellen, the gipsy—who with a devotion that might have been better expected from a *religieuse*, than one of her wild and unsettled character, abandoned her wandering tribe, and took up her residence at Mr Howard's. *There* her heart seemed fixed; and no mother cherished a first-born with more tenderness than she attended to her helpless charge. At stated times O'Connor, "a melancholy man," visited his *protégés*; and although in his intercourse with the good old vicar he assumed his accustomed serenity, at midnight when the villagers were sleeping, the soldier and the gipsy might have been found in the cemetery of Ashfield, beside the grave of her whom in life they had both loved so faithfully.

Months rolled on—Napoleon burst again upon the world—the sceptre of a mighty nation was wrenched from the feeble grasp that held it—and Europe was once more in arms. O'Connor, in his wild retirement, for a few weeks watched calmly the progress of the mighty events then transacting on the Continent. Gradually new objects interested—a new spirit was created—those feelings which circumstances had smothered for a season were animated again—one engrossing passion returned—and he left his mountain home, repaired to the metropolis, and asked and obtained a regiment.

Picton's division had marched on Quatre-Bras three hours before O'Connor, on a jaded hack, rode into the streets of Brussels. At an enormous price he purchased a fresh horse, and followed at speed the corps in which his regiment was brigaded. The road was easily made out; and long before he came in sight of the Bois de Bossu, an increasing cannonade and sharper roll of musketry told plainly that the work of death had commenced.

From stragglers he obtained information where he should find his regiment; and a wounded soldier, whom he encountered tottering to the rear, confirmed it. The colonel galloped forward—wheeled, as he had been directed, to the left—and, as his regiment were forming for cavalry, rode into the square, and announced himself their commander. He was instantly recognised, and a hearty cheer welcomed him to the battleground.

With that glorious and bloody field we have no business, save to cursorily remark that, considering the force engaged, it was not second even to "immortal Waterloo." O'Connor's was one of the regiments most pressed; but charge after charge the French cavalry were repulsed, and though sadly reduced in numbers, "few but fearless still;" it now awaited a threatened attack of infantry. It came. Steadily the diminished line, not covering half the ground it did two hours before, received the fire of their assailants. A quick and murderous volley answered it. "Charge!" cried a voice that rose loud and clear above the roar of battle. The bayonets were levelled—the rush was made—all gave way before it—but a straggling shot struck the gallant leader—and O'Connor, dropping from his saddle, "fighting foremost, fell!"

Night came. That had been the last effort of Ney. It failed—and the French retired. The British held the battleground undisputed; and at the foot of the pine-tree where he died, a grave was hastily turned up, and on the spot where he fell, O'Connor was interred by the survivors of his regiment.

Time passed. The turf was green upon the relics of the brave; and, on the anniversary of the battle, many a village maid visited the field, and many a votive wreath was hung above the graves of those who fell at Quatre-Bras.

It was on the tenth anniversary of that proud and bloody day that a female, accompanied by two handsome boys, was seen kneeling at a little mound, which indicated that a departed warrior was sleeping beneath it. The woman was sinking into the vale of years, and her hair, once of raven blackness, was thickly silvered by time and sorrow; but still the remains of beauty might be traced in features which had once been remarkable for their loveliness. The elder of the boys was apparently of Spanish lineage; and his olive complexion and dark brows formed a striking contrast to the fair skin and laughing blue eyes of his younger and handsomer companion. They remained till evening beside the grave; and, before they left the spot, hung a garland upon the branches of the pine-tree which shaded the ashes of the dead soldier.

Five years passed—the anniversary of Quatre-Bras again arrived—and two youths, now merging upon manhood, were seen kneeling at the same mound. No female accompanied them—and they were habited in deep mourning, such as children wear to denote the loss of a parent. They were the orphan *protégés* of Colonel O'Connor, and their protectress was no more. Ellen had paid the debt of nature—that wild and tameless spirit found repose where the weary rest—her own mingled with her mother's ashes—and she slept beside that gentle being whom in life she loved so well—that victim of man's perfidy—Mary Howard.